THE EXECUTIONERS THREE

AVAILABLE FROM SUSAN DENNARD AND DAPHNE PRESS

The Luminaries
The Hunting Moon
The Whispering Night

The Executioners Three

THE EXECUTIONERS THREE

SUSAN DENNARD

◆ Daphne Press

First published in the UK in 2025 by Daphne Press
www.daphnepress.com

Copyright © 2025 by Susan Dennard
Cover art © Micaela Alcaino
Map art by Jessica Khoury © Susan Dennard
Typesetting by Adrian McLaughlin

The moral right of the author has been asserted.

All rights reserved.

No part of this publication may be reproduced, stored in a retrieval system, or transmitted in any form or by any means, without the prior written permission of the publisher, nor be otherwise circulated in any form of binding or cover other than that which it is published and without a similar condition including this condition being imposed on the subsequent publisher.

All characters and events in this publication, other than those clearly in the public domain, are fictitious and any resemblance to real persons, living or dead, is purely coincidental.

A CIP catalogue record for this book is available from the British Library.

Trade paperback ISBN: 978-1-83784-090-8
eBook ISBN: 978-1-83784-095-3
Illumicrate hardback ISBN: 978-1-83784-096-0
Waterstones edition ISBN: 978-1-83784-110-3

The authorised representative in the EEA is Authorised Rep Compliance Ltd
71 Baggot Street Lower, Dublin, D02 P593, Ireland. Email: info@arccompliance.com

Printed and bound by CPI Group (UK) Ltd, Croydon CR0 4YY

*For Freddie's first readers on Wattpad and beyond:
you are Very Special Humans Indeed.*

THE EXECUTIONERS THREE

When northern wind gusts
Through trees bare of leaves,
Take heed and take watch,
For Executioners Three.

Their blood oath is summoning.

First comes the fog,
Rising from the shore.
Once rings the bell:
Cold death is in store.

The Hangsman is rising.

Next are the crows
To block out the sun.
Then twice rings the bell,
To warn everyone.

The Headsman is coming.

Third comes the ice
Wreckt upon the stones.
Thrice rings the bell.
No chance to atone.

The Disemboweler is hunting.

Last is the heat,
A sign it's too late.
No bells are rung
When the Three leave the gate.

The Oathmaster is waiting.

SUMMONING

Theo Porter had just rounded the curve by City-on-the-Berme Park—that sharp turn with all the woods and the steep slope down to the lakeshore—when *bam*! Two baby raccoons came scuttling through the fog and into his headlights.

Theo hit the brakes and yanked the steering wheel left. The two raccoons had frozen, their eyes latched onto his low beams.

A sharp squeal across the pavement. Then a thump as he left the road, crunched onto grass and underbrush, and finally crashed sharply into a witch hazel. (He recognized those red and yellow leaves from botany class—a deeply unuseful fact right about now.)

"No, no, no," he breathed to himself, heart hammering. In the dim red glow of his brake lights, he couldn't see if the raccoons had made it to the other side of the road. In the much brighter glow of his headlights, he could definitely see his Honda Civic had not.

Three summers of working had bought him this Silver Sweetheart. Now she was scratched and dented, but he prayed she was at least able to get back onto the road.

He wanted to rewind time by ten seconds. He wanted to shout at the raccoons for trying to cross the street right then—he hadn't seen them in all this fog. And he wanted to shout at himself for caring so much that he'd driven off the road to avoid them.

He could not afford a mechanic's bill right now.

"Come on," he murmured, shifting into reverse. "You can do it, Sweetheart." He eased his foot on the gas.

The Civic rolled back. Back some more. Then spun out.

Theo released the pedal. Digging the wheels in was only going to make this worse, and he absolutely could not afford a tow truck on top of everything else. He flicked on his emergency lights. There were no streetlights around, and the sun had long since dropped behind the lake. Each flash of orange revealed white fog and more white fog.

With a groan, Theo kicked open the car door. His Nokia buzzed in his jeans pocket, but he ignored it. It was probably just Davis wondering where the beer was.

Ever since the fall semester had begun, Theo had become official booze runner for the Allard Fortin Preparatory School. He'd set up a sweet deal with the dude at RaceTrac. In exchange for twenty bucks, that dude would pretend Theo's license didn't say 1982 and that the math didn't make Theo only seventeen in this year of 1999. Six cases of Natty Lite later, Theo would drive the beer to campus, sell them to his fellow Fortin Prep students at an upcharge of a dollar a can, and then pocket the difference in the envelope under his mattress. So far, he'd made almost a thousand bucks.

A thousand bucks he was now going to have to eat into if he wanted to get his car fixed.

Theo stepped around to the front of the Honda. The hood was dented, although not as badly as he'd feared. The bumper and grille were only moderately busted. So . . . yay?

He scowled at the witch hazel, which was barely scratched at all. Then he scowled in the general direction of the raccoons too, although they were long gone.

And honestly, he was glad he hadn't hit them.

Theo's breath plumed, tendrils of steam that glowed in his headlights. He was going to have to get some branches to wedge under the tires.

Fortunately, there were plenty of branches to be found. Evergreens and autumn hardwoods spanned for miles in the county park here.

As Theo scanned what little forest he could see through all that fog and shadow, he regretted not keeping a flashlight in his car. Or a jacket.

He set off into the forest. His sneakers crunched over the first downfall of autumn leaves. In seconds, the fog and trees swallowed him. The last of his Silver Sweetheart's light faded, while a rotten smell gathered around him. As if maybe some other raccoons hadn't been so lucky when they'd crossed the road.

After thirty steps or so of wading through the fog, Theo finally tripped over maple branches hefty enough to withstand his tires. He crooked down to retrieve two when something glittered at the edge of his vision.

Theo paused.

Theo turned.

A long, coiling thing lay on the ground nearby. It was reddish, speckled with dirt, and every faint flash of distant emergency lights through mist made it glisten.

It looked, Theo thought, like the pig's intestine he'd had to dissect during AP Bio last spring. Or like a rope that had been left to soak in blood.

Theo followed the length of it, his blue eyes squinting in the fog and his hand still outstretched for a branch. He had never been a paranoid guy, but this felt . . . off.

The stink was getting worse too. Licking over him on the night's cold breeze.

His phone vibrated. He flinched. And suddenly the rope thing moved, slithering backward several inches.

Nope. Theo did not like that. He swooped up two sticks and twisted toward the road in a single movement.

The branches were cold and damp in his grip with a few leaves still hanging on. They rattled with each of his steps—

faster, faster as he jogged, then practically ran toward the street. Headlights swamped over him. The trees and fog fell away.

And Theo's breath whooshed out with relief. He felt immediately safer here.

Which was silly. Really silly.

Again, his phone buzzed.

"Piss off," he muttered. "The beer will get there when it gets there."

After snapping the branch in two—a feat that required several grunts and several snarls—Theo crouched behind his left front tire to wedge the branch under rubber. It smeared dirt all over his jeans.

It also seeped cold right into his bones.

Once the second branch was also firmly in place, Theo hurried for his driver's door, dusting dirt off his hands as he moved.

That was when a bell rang.

It pealed out, echoing over bare tree branches. Riding the lakeshore wind. A sharp, clear sound, much too close to be from any of the churches in Berm's downtown.

The hair on Theo's arms pricked up. On the back of his neck too, and without thinking, his eyes snapped to the forest. Toward the general spot where he'd seen that weird, glistening intestinal thing.

Click, click went his emergency lights. Noisy, bright. *Click, click.*

The smell was stronger, and the fog—had it gotten thicker?

Theo swallowed, eyes still latched on the enshrouded trees. He almost thought he saw a person in there. A hazy, grayish figure walking this way.

"Hello?" he shouted at it. "Is someone there?"

The figure halted, and Theo was hit with an overwhelming sense that he was being scrutinized. Judged. As if every misdeed he'd ever committed was being siphoned up to the surface and weighed on some unseen scale made of dead things.

And, god, it really reeked of rotting corpses now. Theo couldn't stop imagining intestines and blood and ropes cutting into his neck . . .

In fact, every paranoid nightmare he'd ever conjured as a kid was searing through his mind. Murderers at the window. Demons in the closet. Ghosts under the bed.

Theo lifted his hands. They were shaking. "If you're, uh, not okay, let me know because I'm . . . I'm leaving now." He pivoted and bolted for the car.

"Please work," he muttered once inside. "Please work, please work." He was overreacting—he knew he was being a wuss about absolutely nothing. But that wasn't changing the fact that he could hardly breathe. That his neck felt like it was being squeezed by someone's dead fingers.

Ropes. Axes. Knives.

He revved the engine and shoved into reverse. His foot hit the gas, harder than was wise. *Spin, spin, spin.* The tires took to the branches. They crunched over maple wood. The Civic veered back onto pavement.

And Theo got the hell out of there.

The last thing he saw before he cranked into drive, his emergency lights still flashing, was a figure in the fog. Tall, broad-shouldered, and blurry around the edges, it hovered only feet from the witch hazel.

Flash. The figure stood there. *Flash.* The figure was still there. *Flash.* The figure was gone.

1

Freddie Gellar hadn't meant to get half the student body of Fortin Prep boarding school arrested. It wasn't like she'd woken up that morning and thought, *You know what? I feel like ruining lives at the rival high school today.*

Not at all. She'd simply heard shrieks coming from the woods near her house, so she'd called the cops. Like any *normal* human with a *normal* conscience would do.

Freddie stabbed her broom halfheartedly at a swarm of daddy longlegs who'd taken roost on the ladder inside the old schoolhouse. She was supposed to go into the cupola, with its broken bell, and string up fairy lights.

But so far, all she'd managed was to open the schoolhouse door, sweep around the benches that would soon get moved outside for the Lumberjack Pageant... and then cough dramatically at the gathered dust and cobwebs on the ladder.

The Fête du Bûcheron was in a little over two weeks, and that meant every inch of City-on-the-Berme Village Historique had to be ready for a shindig the locals took Very Seriously Indeed. Every year, the Village was open from Memorial Day to Labor Day. Then, the Village reopened its gates one extra day for the locals to celebrate Halloween.

Not only was it a big fundraiser for the Village, but it was also *the* event of the year for a town that was as insular as it was festive.

Which meant it was Freddie's mom's most important event of the year.

Freddie and a handful of volunteers had already spent the last two weeks helping Mom deck everything in jack-o'-lanterns, scarecrows, and an unseemly number of hay bales. La Maison Authentique du Bûcheron (the Authentic Lumberjack Homestead, which was neither authentic nor a homestead) was now a haunted house, complete with skeletons, mirrors, and hiding places for her stepdad, Steve, in ghost makeup.

La Taverne now housed all the necessary accoutrements to sell heaps of hot apple cider and Mrs. Ferris's famous jams, while La Marché d'Été (the summer market) was all ready for the jack-o'-lantern contest (whoever won that got to put a banner on their house for the entire year).

Lastly, two portable toilets had been tucked behind the tavern that didn't actually sell alcohol. No French placards for those. (*Port-A-Potty,* it would seem, was not worth translating.)

Freddie sighed toward her best friend, Divya, who leaned at the school's red clapboard entrance with all the cool poise of a runway model. The fall wind had picked up outside, lifting leaves and adding a lovely autumn glow to Divya's amber skin. It also made Divya shiver while she frantically played Snake on her Nokia.

"It just seems," Divya said now without looking up, "like a really hard mistake to make, Fred. I mean, surely you know what a bunch of rich kids drinking sounds like."

"Not really," Freddie admitted. "It's not like *I've* ever been to a party. Have you?"

Divya flashed a laser glare—and a sound like digital snake death beeped out. "You know I haven't. Unless you count our book club meet-ups with Abby and Tom. Those can get pretty rowdy sometimes."

Freddie didn't count those at all. A drunken teenage party was not the same thing as a spirited discussion of whatever novel Divya had insisted they read. (This month's selection had been *The Notebook,* which Freddie had found a little too light on murder for her tastes.)

Freddie stabbed more forcefully at this nest of longlegs (or was it a *swarm*?) blocking her from the schoolhouse bell twelve feet above. She really couldn't go up there until these were gone. With hair as wild and dark as hers, all those arachnids would get lost in a heartbeat.

Divya, meanwhile, slunk into the shadows of the school and notably *didn't* offer to help Freddie as she eased onto a bench. After all, it wasn't *her* mom who was head of the City-on-the-Berme Historical Society. And no matter how many times Freddie pointed out to Mom that it was illegal to force her daughter to prepare for the fête every year, Mom just laughed and said, "Great. In that case, you can find somewhere else to live."

Although, for all Freddie's vocal complaints (she was very, *very* vocal), she secretly loved volunteering here. City-on-the-Berme was her favorite place in the whole world. Part tourist attraction, with its only moderately accurate French logging settlement, and part outdoor center, with the county park trails winding through the forest next door—you couldn't get more autumn creeptastic than this place.

Which was likely why the fête was always the biggest event of the year for locals.

And also why Mom always put so much pressure on Freddie to help.

Last night, however, things had gone awry. After Freddie had finished helping Mom with the hay bales, she'd left her scarf behind. And seeing as it was her favorite scarf (and therefore crucial for the completion of any fall outfit), she'd set out for the City-on-the-Berme Village Historique on Steve's rickety bike after dinner.

Freddie never made it to the Village—or found her scarf, for that matter. The trail had been dangerously foggy, her headlamp bouncing beams everywhere, and there'd been an awful stench like dead animals in the air. So strong, so overwhelming, that Freddie had actually thought she might gag.

It had forced her to stop her bike just so she could cover her mouth and try to breathe. The fog definitely hadn't helped. Freddie'd had the horrifying sense it was alive and trying to climb inside her.

Then a bell had tolled from somewhere in the trees, even though there was only the one bell in City-on-the-Berme (currently over Freddie's head) and it had no clapper so it *couldn't* ring.

Freddie had not liked that sound. Nor the way she'd suddenly felt the fog tighten as if solid around her throat.

So the instant she had heard frantic shrieking from the woods nearby, she'd needed no urging whatsoever to turn around and pedal straight home again.

She had seen enough *X-Files* and read enough *Goosebumps*, thank you very much, to know how this sort of story would end.

Once home, she'd called the cops. Unfortunately, instead of finding a Person in Distress Being Slowly Dismembered in the old logging forests of City-on-the-Berme, Sheriff Bowman had found an unauthorized bonfire and a lot of underage drinking.

Divya kicked her legs onto the bench in front of her. "Look, Fred, I'll *grudgingly* accept that neither of us knows much about parties or partying or anything associated with the verb 'to party,' but surely you can tell the difference between someone screaming bloody murder and someone screaming for more beer."

"Can I, though?" Freddie asked. "Because it sounded like bloody murder to me. I mean, glass containers aren't even allowed in City-on-the-Berme, Div."

"Pretty sure the Fortin kids don't care about that part. They're also under twenty-one." Divya gave a low whistle. "Oh boy, I hope they don't know that it was you who called the cops on them."

Freddie's stomach flipped. She hadn't thought of that. "How could they possibly know?"

Divya shrugged. "Dunno. But it's a small town. People talk."

Freddie winced. That phrase—*It's a small town, people talk*—might as well have been the town motto for Berm, population 1,321. There were more deer here than people, and if the deer could talk, they probably would too.

Freddie's only possible saving grace was that almost all of the students at Fortin Prep were from out of town, and the one thing Bermians hated more than a disruption to their beloved fête was out-of-towners. They even said it that way—*out-of-towners*—like it was a dirty word, and tourists were only accepted as long as they didn't stay for more than a long weekend during the summer.

When at last the daddy longlegs were vanquished from the ladder, Freddie retrieved the necessary fairy lights from a box by Divya's bench. "Thanks for the help," Freddie said with as much sarcasm as she could muster.

"Any time," Divya murmured, once more playing Snake. "Can we go to the archives now?"

"No." Freddie sniffed. "The agreement was that you'd help me clean up the old schoolhouse, and *then* I would take you to the archives."

"But my paper is due Monday, Fred." Divya finally shoved her phone into her pocket. "I can't wait any longer."

"Well, maybe you should have thought of that before you spent the last ten minutes playing Snake." Freddie notched her chin high and sashayed away from Divya, a trail of lights dragging over the wooden planks behind her.

"I'll help now." Divya chased after.

"Too late." Freddie reached the ladder, and with one handful of lights, she lumbered up.

"Please, Fred." Divya hugged at the ladder below and shot dramatic puppy eyes upward. "Just tell me what to do. Pwetty pwease?" She fluttered her lashes. "I can plug in the lights . . . or . . . sweep?"

"I already swept." Really, had her bestie been paying any attention? "You're going to have to get more creative, Madame

Srivastava. Think *firstborn child* or *family inheritance*. Then I might reconsider."

Freddie reached the top of the ladder. Cold air billowed against her—and the Village Historique spanned beyond. Beautiful, vibe-y, and always right on the edge of falling apart because there never seemed to be enough funding.

Straight ahead was the Village Square, soon to be filled with the Lumberjack Pageant stage but currently only filled with hay bales and scarecrows, one of which appeared to be waving, thanks to the wind.

"New idea," Divya called from below. "What if I lend you Lance?"

Oh, now we're talking. "Two weeks," Freddie replied as she unknotted fairy lights. "I want him two weeks."

"One."

"Two or I climb down and leave you stranded."

"Ugh, *fine*. You can have him for two weeks."

Huzzah. Freddie grinned at the bronze bell before her, with its green outer patina. *I am so getting the better end of this bargain.*

Creak, creak, the bell agreed, since it had no clapper—meaning when a wind tumbled through the cupola or Freddie wrapped lights around it, the poor thing could only give a sad squeal upon its hinge.

Still, that didn't mean it couldn't be the bell she'd heard last night . . . And there was only one way to find out. Freddie grabbed the bell now and shook it.

Creak, creak, creak, it said in reply.

She gave it one more heave, just to be sure . . .

Creak, creak, creak.

Yep, okay. Freddie could now say with absolute certainty that this was *not* the bell she'd heard, and if this thing had ever tolled with any dignity, those days were long past.

Which was fine. It didn't need to ring. It was just a replica of the bronze bell over at the Allard Fortin mausoleum anyway.

Although, to be honest, the replica was looking pretty rough this year—like maybe the guy Mom had hired to make it hadn't done a very good job. Once she'd covered the bell in lights like a sad Christmas tree, Freddie scuttled down. She was absolutely freezing now, and truly mourning the loss of her scarf. "I'll take Lance, please." She thrust her hand at Divya.

Who scowled. Then also obeyed and withdrew the sacred keychain from her pocket. A heartbeat later, the face of Lance Bass gleamed up at Freddie.

And Freddie sighed a melty sigh as she accepted Lance's flawless face. He fit so perfectly in her palm, a tiny slice of boy band magic. Whenever Divya (or Freddie) had it with her, good things happened. *Magical* things, like finding fifty-dollar bills in the road or repeated Good Hair Days.

Freddie blew Lance a kiss, then slipped him into her puffer vest. "Alright," she declared, chin rising in triumph, "follow me, Madame Srivastava. I shall lead you to the archives!"

She marched them out of the schoolhouse. If she twisted slightly, she could see Le Moulin à Eau (the water mill) through a copse of coppery maples. Currently, no paddles spun.

South of that was Le Forgeron (the blacksmith), which technically had a working forge . . . but also *technically* lacked a working blacksmith to use it. It had been modeled on a smithy that had been in the original City-on-the-Berme in the 1600s—and it was thanks to the blacksmith at the time keeping meticulous journals that Mom had been able to make the replica bell that now lived in the schoolhouse without its clapper.

It was toward this storied blacksmith's hut that Freddie and Divya now aimed. They reached the stream that fed its forge, glittering, burbly, and dark with cold. The sign in front that read *Le Forgeron* had a fresh streak of bird poop on it. So now it just read *Le Forger*(splat).

Freddie scowled at the poop. She should probably clean it before the fête.

She and Divya were just rounding the building so they could embark into the woods when footsteps stomped out. A figure barreled into view. "Hey," he said.

And Freddie's heart lurched into her throat. Luis Mendez, star athlete and fellow senior at Berm High, had just spoken to her. Even more bizarre, he wasn't done speaking *and* he was smiling. "Gellar," he panted. "Nice to see you."

Then he was past Freddie in a gust of sweaty air.

"Um..." Divya wiggled a pinkie in her ear. "Did Luis Mendez just say your name?"

"I think so." Freddie was as fully stunned as Divya. Every day, the Berm High cross-country team ran the park's paths. Sometimes they nodded her way, but 99.9999 percent of the time, they ignored her existence.

"Gellar!" cried a new voice. Then another and another, and suddenly an entire swarm (or was it a *nest*?) of boys was charging past. Zach Gilroy and Darius Baker even slung out their hands for high fives.

Freddie complied, although she wasn't entirely sure how. Her brain had basically disconnected from her body, and she could feel her jaw dangling low. In seconds, the entirety of the boys' team had jogged past. Which meant that any second now, the girls would—

"Freddie!" shrieked Carly Zhang as she bounded by. "Nice job!"

"Nice job on what?" Freddie tried to ask, but Carly was already gone, and now cheers were rising up as a second stampede of bodies rushed closer.

"We have officially entered *The X-Files*," Divya said as feet and ponytails thundered past, and Freddie could only nod in agreement. Even the blacksmith's hut seemed faintly astonished, its wooden exterior creaking on the wind.

Then, as fast as the Berm High cross-country teams had appeared, they vanished again. Which wasn't terribly surprising, given there were only seventeen runners across both teams.

Last, because he was always last (except in the jack-o'-lantern contest of '95), came poor Todd Raskin, ever determined to dominate his asthma through sheer perserverance.

"Do you need your inhaler?" Freddie asked as he heaved past.

"Nah," he wheezed. "Thanks, Gellar. And good job!"

"I think," Divya said, slipping her arm back through Freddie's as they watched Todd tromp away, "that you're *popular* now, Freddie. This is . . . well, monumental, certainly."

"Or just weird." Despite Freddie's greatest belief in her own fortitude, her knees were quaking inside her jeans. "Why would everyone like me all of a sudden? I don't think Carly has talked to me since seventh grade."

"Erm." Divya's face scrunched into something almost pained. "I think this means they all know you got the Fortin kids arrested. Which means . . ." She paused to bite her lip. "Well, the Fortin Prep kids probably know too. After all, Fred, it's a small town."

Freddie sighed. "And people talk."

Leaves rattled beneath Freddie's boots as she trekked down one of the many sloping hills in the park that spread beyond the Village. Beneath the leaf litter, mud squicked, and every few steps, water had the audacity to splatter. Good thing Freddie always wore her duck boots in the fall.

Divya was not as well prepared. "Are you sure this path is a shortcut?" she asked, ten paces behind Freddie and lagging farther each second. Her feet, clad only in formerly-beige-but-now-mucky-brown Birkenstock clogs, were not faring well—and Divya had made sure to point this out almost every step of the way.

"Of course it's a shortcut." Freddie laughed as if to say Divya was ridiculous for suspecting otherwise. She did not mention that *this path* was really just an ephemeral stream that tended to fill with mosquitos in the summer.

"We've been out here five minutes—"

"Oh my god, *five minutes*." Freddie made a *Home Alone* face. "Div, you're the toughest gal I know. You can handle this trek—I promise. And if your shoes get too muddy, I'll carry you."

"Oh yeah?" Divya snorted a laugh. Her face was now as rosy as the cross-country team's. "You mean like that time you carried me to my room after I twisted my ankle? I remember how that ended."

Freddie flipped her hair. "I *meant* to fall down the stairs, Divya. It's called *comedy*."

"And this place is called *horror*." Divya shivered. "I mean, we could die out here and no one would know! I don't have cell service, which is always how slasher movies start—"

She broke off as wind burst through the trees. It carried leaves and dust. Freddie's hair sprayed into her face.

Then the wind settled. One breath, two, before a loud creaking split the trees.

It was like groaning wood, but subtler. Higher pitched.

And cold trickled down Freddie's neck. She gulped. "Did you hear that, Div?"

"The wind?" Divya shivered. "How could I miss it? I should've worn my winter coat."

"That's not it." Freddie turned toward the sound. It had come from farther down the hill.

The creak repeated, shuddering deep into her ear. She knew that sound, and yet she couldn't pinpoint how.

Divya scampered in close, worry pinching her forehead. "What do you hear, Fred?"

"Something isn't right." As soon as Freddie said that, she knew it was true. Deeply, terrifyingly true.

Divya tensed beside her. "Is it your gut?" Like everyone else, she knew that Freddie's gut was foolproof. Freddie had sensed three tornadoes *and* a kitchen fire before they'd happened. Plus, she'd known Divya's cat was dying before anyone else had even sensed Rasputin was acting sluggish.

She threw a hard look at Divya. Her best friend's flush was gone; her lips were pale. "Div," she said softly, "I think you should go back to the Village, okay? And call the sheriff. She needs to be here."

Somehow, Divya's face went even whiter. "What about you?"

"I've got experience with this kind of stuff."

"What kind of stuff? Creepy forests? I'm pretty sure a few weeks riding last summer with Sheriff Bowman does not mean you can waltz through here looking for trouble."

Freddie wasn't just waltzing. She'd done two summer internships with her hero, Sheriff Rita Bowman, and even though they'd never encountered anything truly horrific, she *had* learned what to do at a crime scene. "Please, Div. Just go."

"Absolutely not." Divya took Freddie's hand in hers.

And Freddie swallowed. She did feel safer having Divya there, and she supposed every sheriff needed a deputy. "Come on, then."

They resumed their march, hands held and eyes watering against the wind. The trees blurred. Freddie's boots kicked up mud and decomposing leaves. She barely noticed. The creaking sound was getting louder. It grated against her skin.

Then the forest opened up, and the girls skittered to a stop.

Freddie released Divya's hand. She knew what the sound was now: the groaning of a rope. The gritting of fibers against each other as if a body was being towed downward and swung on the wind.

She spun and spun, but there was nothing there. Nothing but raging wind and spraying leaves—

A crow cawed. High and just beyond the clearing.

Freddie's gaze lurched up, to a sycamore. To a branch so high, no human could have possibly reached it.

Yet someone had.

"Divya." Freddie clutched her stomach. "Cover your eyes. We're leaving."

2

Freddie's mom had never been one to fuss. Now, though, it was all she seemed able to do. Ever since Sheriff Bowman had called and told her to pick up Freddie from the Village Historique the evening before, Mom had been nonstop fuss-fuss-*fuss*.

Freddie wanted to throttle her.

Especially because Freddie hadn't even seen the body (which apparently belonged to a middle-aged man). All she'd seen were a pair of dangling Nikes, blue with orange accents. Mud on the tread.

And *yes,* it was true that those shoes were imprinted on Freddie's brain for all of time now, but cups of tea and Snickers bars weren't exactly helping. Nor was tucking Freddie into bed, stroking her hair every ten seconds, or surprising her with a "real breakfast" of bacon and eggs.

By the time Freddie was supposed to meet Divya to walk to school the next morning, she was desperate to get away. She didn't care that it was raining. She didn't care that her usual Friday outfit of cute tights and a festive fall skirt was missing an accent scarf and now getting wet. Nor did she care that, in her race to leave the house, she'd forgotten to trade her glasses for contacts.

Why, Freddie didn't even care that she couldn't roll her bike by the handlebars *and* fit under Divya's umbrella either. She was free, and it tasted so good. Drizzle-frizzed hair or eighth-grade glasses couldn't ruin it.

Divya, it would seem, felt the same. She and Freddie had just stepped off Freddie's leaf-strewn lawn onto the street when Divya tipped back her umbrella and said, "My mom wants me to see a counselor."

"Mine too." Freddie's nostrils flared, and she pushed the bike faster. "Parents don't know anything."

"Old people don't know anything." Divya stomped her feet. "I mean, I didn't even see the body!"

"And I only saw his shoes!"

"So we definitely aren't traumatized." Divya flipped her braid over her shoulder.

"Definitely not." Freddie mimicked the movement with her rapidly expanding curls. "It takes more than a little murder to scare the likes of us."

"Exactly. No, wait." Divya skidded to a halt. "*Murder?* What are you talking about? It was a suicide."

Freddie squeezed her bike brakes. "That was not a suicide, Div."

"Uh, Sheriff Bowman herself said it was a suicide."

"The body was hanging twenty feet off the ground." Freddie rolled the bike backward, then ducked under Divya's umbrella. At least far enough to protect her hair.

"So? Maybe the man wanted a climb before he died."

"A climb on what ladder? And on what branches? There wasn't a single thing he could've used to get up there."

"So what are you trying to say?" Divya launched back into a march. Rain sprayed Freddie once more. "Are you saying you know better than Sheriff Bowman?"

"Maybe?" Freddie pushed her bike after Divya. "You didn't hear the screams on Wednesday night."

"You mean the screams of drunk prep schoolers?"

"But what if that wasn't what I heard, Div? What if I *did* hear screams for help?"

"Sheriff Bowman was in those woods arresting people. Surely if there'd been a murder underway, she would've heard those screams too."

"Okay, but how do you account for the dead guy's clothes? He was wearing jogging shoes. Who dresses up like that to go kill themselves?"

"I don't know." Divya shook the umbrella. Rain splattered. "But I do know you're not a detective. Just because you solved one shoplifting case when you were riding with Bowman does not qualify you as a pie."

"A pie?" Freddie cocked her head. "You mean a . . . PI?"

"It can be pronounced both ways."

"It definitely cannot."

"That's not the point!" Divya shook the umbrella again, and this time, rain splattered Freddie's face. "The point is that you aren't a *Pee Eye,* and while I get that your gut is doing its spidey-sense tingling, maybe you should leave it to the actual professionals."

Freddie's fingers instinctively tightened on the brakes. The bike gave a skittering skip. She knew Divya was thinking about Sheriff Bowman right now, since Bowman was the current "professional" in charge of such things.

But Freddie couldn't help but think of her dad instead. He had been local sheriff before Bowman—meaning he *would* have been the "professional" that Freddie would leave this murder to . . . if he hadn't died when Freddie was five.

Sometimes she wondered if it was mere coincidence she wanted to follow him on the same career path. Her mom had divorced Frank when Freddie had been only two, so she'd barely known the man, and she'd learned young to never ask about him.

The consequences just weren't worth the curiosity. Mom always clammed up and got stony—sometimes for days at a time—while Freddie's stepdad, Steve, just looked heartbreakingly sad.

Freddie hated it. And she hated how even thinking of Dad made her own insides get stony. Made her feel guilty, like she'd broken some rule that no one had ever actually told her was in effect.

She squeezed again at the brakes. They squeaked a sympathetic reply.

"I know I'm not a professional," Freddie finally admitted, pushing past the sudden rocks in her abdomen. "Not yet anyway. But you know I'm the Answer Finder, Divya. Everyone at school asks me to find them sources in the archives. Like all the time."

This earned one of Divya's *you sweet, innocent child* faces. "Oh my Honey Bunches of Oats. You're just being used."

"You mean *you're* using me."

"Never." Scowl. "Second of all, having access to the archives via your *mom* doesn't qualify you to investigate murders."

"Ha!" Freddie cried. "So you *do* think it was a murder!"

"Silence." Divya's eyes narrowed in a way that spoke of bodily harm in Freddie's future.

Fortunately Freddie was saved the indignity of not getting in the last word by an explosion of flapping wings. Then a shadow stretched over Freddie and Divya. They lurched their faces upward, to where . . .

Freddie gasped.

Birds. Hundreds of them, maybe even thousands, covered the sky like a thundercloud. Freddie huddled toward Divya, who huddled toward her, and they both took shelter beneath the umbrella.

At least until muddy water sprayed upward in a geyser, drenching Freddie's entire body. She shrieked, Divya yelped. Then the crows were past and a black Jeep Cherokee was skidding to a stop on the road.

"Jerk!" Divya bellowed, launching herself at the Jeep. *"Giant jerkity jerk!"*

A door slammed and a voice called out, "Are you okay?" A boy scrambled around the back of the Jeep. "Crap, I am so sorry! My bad, my bad, are you okay?"

"No," Divya snarled. "You almost killed us."

Freddie grabbed for her best friend. "That's Kyle Friedman," she hissed.

"I'm aware." Divya lifted her voice again. "You should watch the freaking road. My friend here is soaked—" She broke off with a yelp as Freddie stabbed Divya's wrist with her nails.

Kyle Friedman was the coolest guy in school, and he had been ever since sixth grade when he'd shown up at school with the words *Surf's Up* monogrammed onto his L.L. Bean backpack. He progressed to the *hottest* guy at school two years later, when he hit puberty and his jawline came in.

"I'm so sorry," Kyle said again, and Freddie couldn't help but notice how well the slightly panicked and disheveled look worked for him. His white button-up was turning dark with the rain, and his brown curls looked shower fresh, while pink flagged on his summer-tanned cheeks. "I didn't mean to splash you like that."

"It's fine," Freddie said, surprised by the strange syrup layer on her voice.

"No, it isn't." Divya gaped at Freddie. "These jeans are new, and your sweater is drenched."

Kyle flinched. "I really am sorry." Then his eyebrows drew together. "Wait . . . you're Freddie Gellar."

Freddie nodded mutely. Kyle Friedman had said her name. She didn't think he had ever said her name despite three plus years in the same homeroom.

It was glorious.

Then it became even more glorious when he added, "Awesome! I was looking for you."

I was looking for you too, she thought. *All my life.* She sent a silent thank-you to Lance Bass in her pocket.

"Laina told me you lived on this street, but I didn't know which house."

"Laina?" Divya repeated, anger giving way to shock. "As in Laina Steward?"

Kyle beamed. "Exactly. I'm supposed to pick you up."

"Pick who up?" This was Divya again because Freddie had lost all ability to speak. Kyle was just *so* pretty with his green eyes, golden tan, and floppy dark hair. Part surfer, part prep, part athlete, and *all* perfection.

"I'm supposed to pick up Freddie," he said. "And take her to the Quick-Bis." He paused and wet his lips, as if realizing this sounded very strange. "I mean, you don't have to come ... Or you both could come, if you wanted." He glanced between them.

"We will definitely come," Freddie breathed at the same instant Divya barked, "*Divya*. My name is Divya."

"And his name is Kyle." Freddie grabbed Divya's bicep in a death grip. "Can we please get in the car now?"

Divya glared. "What about your bike?"

"We can fit it in the trunk," Kyle offered, and Freddie only nodded. Then her heart ramped up to light speed because suddenly Kyle was touching her. He was resting one of his perfect hands on her muddy shoulder and guiding her toward his car.

She could die a self-actualized person now.

While he shoved the bike into the back, Freddie hunkered into the passenger seat and started cleaning mud splatter off her glasses. Her shoulder felt seared by his fingertips.

In a good way. *Swoon*.

Divya, meanwhile, climbed into the back and pushed through the front seats. "Um, where are your survival instincts, Miss PI? The most popular guy in school shows up to find you—at the command of the most popular *girl* in school—and you don't think that's weird?"

"Yes," Freddie whispered, glancing at Kyle back by the trunk. "I do think it's weird, but he's just so handsome."

"If you're drunk."

"As if you know anything about being drunk. Besides, you *know* I've had a crush on him since sixth grade."

"A crush that ended in seventh grade!"

"But has now resumed with heart-stopping force."

Divya emitted a half groan and flopped backward right as Kyle hopped into the driver's seat. "Are you sure you're not hurt?"

He shot Freddie a nervous glance while he cranked the car into gear.

"I'm . . . fine?" She was struggling to summon coherent words. It would seem her entire brain had been invaded by white noise. "I . . . I was just surprised," she finally squeezed out. "It was a lot of water."

Divya snorted from the back seat.

And Kyle cringed. It made his forehead pucker in the most adorable way. "Did you guys see all the crows? There must've been thousands of 'em. They'd totally blocked out the sky." He motioned vaguely to where the sun was just beginning to peek over the red and gold hills of Berm. No birds flew there now.

"We saw them," Divya said.

"I thought it was an eclipse at first." Kyle flicked the turn signal at the only stoplight in Berm. To their left, the Fortin Park lawn was covered in a fresh smattering of fiery maple leaves. "But then the darkness kept on moving, and I realized it was birds. And then . . ." He glanced at Freddie. "I splashed you. And I'm really sorry about that."

Freddie felt her cheeks erupt with pink. "It's okay."

"No, it isn't." Divya inhaled, clearly about to launch into a tirade that would likely hurt poor Kyle's sensitive feelings.

So Freddie jumped in first: "How did you know they were crows? Did you see them up close or something?"

Kyle's cheeks bunched upward—and Freddie thought her heart would melt. He just oozed with an I-don't-ever-know-what's-going-on sort of handsome. "Naw. I just assumed it was like in that poem, you know?"

Freddie and Divya exchanged a glance. "Er," Freddie said. "Poem?"

"Yeah. Something about bells tolling and crows blocking the sun."

Freddie's brows pinched together. There *was* something vaguely familiar about that, although nothing obvious was churning up in her memory banks.

And beautiful Kyle was still talking: "I don't really know. I just remember it was in an old book my mom had in the garage, and it gave me nightmares. So she threw it away."

"Understandable." Freddie nodded solemnly. "That sounds deeply traumatizing, Kyle."

Divya rolled her eyes. "Not as traumatizing as Kyle's driving."

Freddie and Kyle both ignored this comment as they rolled into the tiny downtown—even more festive than the Village Historique with its twinkling fairy lights strung around tree trunks, with its jack-o'-lanterns and autumnal wreaths, with its fallen leaves that brightened the sidewalks like new pennies.

At a four-way stop, Kyle flashed Freddie a shy smile.

And Freddie wilted. Like, literally *wilted*.

Sure, she had almost been run over, her sweater was possibly ruined, and her best friend clearly thought her selection in boys was lacking, but as far as Freddie was concerned, none of that really mattered. She was a self-actualized human now, and really: What more could a gal ask for in life?

Thank you, Lance Bass. Oh, thank you, indeed.

The Quick-Bis was the closest thing to fast food in Berm. As such, it was always crowded. No matter that it only served a handful of items, nor that it was perpetually greasy and imparted all entrants with a scent like *eau de biscuit*. The cuisine was cheap, and as the name implied: it was quick.

It was also 100 percent *verboten*. Freddie's mom never let her eat there—not even when the book club sometimes met there instead of the library.

More like Heart-Attack-Bis, Mom would say coldly whenever they drove by—and as much as Freddie always wanted to point out that one biscuit wouldn't kill her, Freddie's dad *had* died of a heart attack. So a general fury toward all things high-cholesterol seemed to be one of Mom's coping mechanisms.

Which meant in the end, it was just easier to never ask for biscuits than to risk triggering some onslaught of Dad-shaped feelings that Freddie didn't want her or her mom to have to deal with.

Originally, the Quick-Bis had been called the *BisQuick*. Until the actual Bisquick company had quickly swooped in for trademark violation. So Mr. Bromwell, the owner, had simply rearranged the sign outside, and voilà. Problem solved. Quick-Bis it was. He even plopped a cement pilgrim out front with a sign that read *Even First Settler Allard Fortin Gets His Biscuits Here*.

Freddie's mom hated that pilgrim even more than she hated the cholesterol. *Allard Fortin wasn't a pilgrim,* Mom would always rant, *and he wasn't the first settler in the region— those were the Native Americans who lived fifty miles to the north.* When the Fake Fortin (Mom's name for him) became a frequent target for drive-by tippings by out-of-towners, she cheered. When Mr. Bromwell then chained Fake Fortin in place and changed the sign to *Even the Ghost of Allard Fortin Gets His Biscuits Here,* her scowls and rants resumed.

Freddie liked Fake (Ghost) Fortin. He was kind of cute, even if one nostril had broken in the last tipping.

As the Jeep pulled past him into the crowded parking lot, the rain was really dumping down. It forced Freddie, Divya, and Kyle to bolt at top speed into the buttery building of blue and yellow decor. Not that Freddie noticed the downpour. She was floating too high on Kyle's smile.

Murder in the woods? Pshaw. Sweater that smelled like a barnyard? Eh. Kyle's hair looked *so good* all wet from the rain.

It wasn't until she reached a booth by the window that Freddie's euphoria finally cracked. Because sitting before her were the most popular kids from Berm High.

And every one of them was smiling at her.

Luis Mendez, his red letterman jacket almost as bright and gleaming as his smile, sat against the window. He had one arm slung casually around his girlfriend, Cat Nguyen, whose warmer brown skin contrasted with his paler skin. Cat's mustard turtleneck, umber sweater vest, and perfectly matching plaid skirt looked exactly how Freddie wanted to dress (yet could never actually manage).

Across from Cat and Luis sat the crowning queen of them all: Laina Steward, a Black girl with dark, cool-toned skin and long braids. She wore fishnets and combat boots no matter the weather, carried nunchucks in her backpack (and knew how to use them), was a competition cheerleader *and* class president, and *also* listened to punk rock and regularly debated Mr. Grant on the merits of socialism in a democratic state.

Laina was not only the coolest girl at Berm High School, but the coolest girl who had *ever lived*. This was a widely known fact, and no one who had ever met her could argue otherwise.

"I found them!" Kyle beamed at his fellow nobility and snagged two free chairs from a nearby table.

"Them?" Cat's smile faltered at the sight of Divya tucked behind Freddie. "It was supposed to be just Gellar."

"Who else did you bring?" Laina asked. Then her eyes slid past Freddie and her grin widened. "Divya, right?"

Divya choked softly, and Freddie turned, alarmed—only to find her best friend flushing furiously and looking as lost as Freddie had felt with Kyle.

"Yes, Madame Class President," Freddie inserted. "This is Divya Srivastava."

"Eep," Divya agreed.

"That means hello, Madame Class President."

Laina's smile widened. "You don't have to call me that—though I do think it's funny."

"President Steward, then." Freddie smiled back. "Someone with your title deserves at least a little recognition."

This earned her a full bark of laughter. Laina motioned to the empty booth seat beside her. "Sit, you guys."

Freddie moved to obey; Divya, however, did not. Which left Freddie with no choice but to grab her best friend's forearm and shove her into the booth. Then Freddie chose a newly added chair at the end.

Instead of sitting beside her, though, Kyle looked down and asked, "Want a biscuit? I'm gonna grab one."

Now it was Freddie's turn to *eep* and Divya's turn to take action. "She does. And I do too, thanks."

With a nod, Kyle ambled off—and Freddie thanked Lance in her pocket. He was really on a roll today.

"Welcome," Laina said, bracing her elbows on the table. "I'm sure you can guess why you're here. After all, your record speaks for itself."

My record? Freddie almost asked—but then it hit her. Of course. *It's a small town, people talk.* "You mean the arrests?"

"Hear, hear!" Laina drumrolled the table.

"A stroke of genius," Luis declared.

And even Cat thawed enough to say, "You knocked out two-thirds of their football team."

"About that." Freddie pushed her glasses up her nose. "There seems to have been a misunderstanding—*oof.*" Freddie's shin erupted with pain, and when she glanced Divya's way, the laser-beam stare was at maximum power.

"A misunderstanding?" Laina's drumrolling paused.

Another kick. A harder glare, and Freddie was left with no choice but to say, "Erm, yes. You see . . . it wasn't my idea alone, but Divya's too."

"Heyyyy." Luis grinned Divya's way, and Cat finally thawed completely—even offering Divya an approving once-over.

Laina just nodded like she'd known this all along. Divya blushed prettily.

"Should we wait for Kyle?" Cat tugged her purse over and unbuckled the clasp.

"Naw." Luis waved her on. "Kyle can catch up."

So Cat withdrew a worn, blue-bound book. In faded script on the spine, it read *Official Log.*

And in perfect synchrony, everyone dipped in low across the table. Even Freddie and Divya. There was a reverence in the way Cat held the book—and in the way she, Luis, and Laina gazed at its canvas cover.

"This," Cat said dramatically, "is a log of every prank ever pulled by the Berm High seniors."

Freddie and Divya both gasped in unison. Everyone in Berm knew about the prank war with Fortin Prep—because of course they did. There was no missing the spray-painted lawns or disrupted football games or dyed marching band uniforms or *insert any other obvious prank here* that happened each fall.

Yet for all that locals saw the effects of the prank war, no one ever knew who was behind them. It was like the secretest of secret societies.

"It all started when the bell went missing from the Allard Fortin mausoleum in 1975." Cat creaked back the cover on the log. "The Fortin students blamed us—even though we obviously didn't do it, since the bell was found years later."

Freddie nodded emphatically at this. She might not have known about the school prank war origins, but she *did* know heaps about the missing bell. After all, it had been her mom who'd first worked to get a replica made for the mausoleum. And then it had been *her* mom who'd found the original bell hiding in plain sight in the schoolhouse years later.

"Fortin Prep retaliated against Berm," Cat continued, "by putting underwear on the school's flagpoles." She tapped the logbook, where sure enough the first line read, *October 27, 1975: Fortin Prep stole BHS flags and put up lingerie.*

"We of course had to respond." This came from Laina, whose voice was suitably grave for discussions of such weight. "So we stole their mascot. A woodchuck named Bubba. Then they painted our football field, so we covered theirs in cat litter."

"It has gone back and forth like that ever since." Cat flipped pages. "And this journal contains twenty-four years' worth of those pranks. Now we"—she stopped two-thirds of the way in—"are right here." She tapped at the bottom of the page, where it now read, *October 13, 1999: Freddie Gellar got half of Fortin Prep arrested.*

"Oh," Freddie exhaled, heart pattering ever so slightly. Her act of terrified conscience had landed her in the Official Log. She felt Very Exalted Indeed. In fact, for the first time since Wednesday night, she felt like she might have done a *good* thing.

"And when we graduate," Luis inserted, "we'll pass this log on to a few chosen juniors, just as the class of '98 passed it on to us. So you see? This book right here is sacred, and now you have to swear to never tell a soul about it."

Again, Freddie and Divya reacted in unison, each nodding. Each offering a rapturous "We swear."

Yet before Freddie could ask if the Prank Squad was sure they wanted to include a lowlife like *her* in their ranks, a figure moved into Freddie's periphery.

Kyle, she assumed, and instantly her body flooded with heady flames.

Until she realized no one was smiling. In fact, Cat was suddenly closing the Official Log, Laina's teeth were baring, and Luis was puffing his shoulders to twice their size. Divya blinked Freddie's way, so Freddie blinked her neighbor's way.

To find that he was not, in fact, Kyle Friedman. This boy was a head taller than Kyle. Lankier too, and where Kyle's hair was a dark chocolate shade, this boy's was a dishwater blond combed into side-swept perfection. He also lacked Kyle's tan, his skin instead a perfect match for Tom Cruise's in *Interview with the Vampire.*

And the biggest difference of all: this guy wore a Fortin Prep uniform. A navy blazer with the school's initials, a scarlet tie, and fitted khakis—all of it impeccably tailored and ironed.

He looked like he'd stepped right out of the TV. Not in a hot way, like Kyle, but in the *I am a stereotypical bully* way.

Freddie instantly disliked him. Especially because he was looking at her with recognition when she had no idea who he was. "Gellar, I presume?" He plunked into the seat beside Freddie and offered a hand. "Theo Porter."

She didn't shake his hand. She didn't move at all except to mold her face into a glare. Clearly he was the enemy.

"Nice to meet you too." He grinned a devastating grin, hand lowering as his other hand whipped up a soda cup. He took a long drag; it rattled. "No need to stop what you were doing on my account, friends. Continue, continue!"

Laina was the first to speak. "Why are you here, Porter?"

He batted his eyelashes—thick, pale, and framing blue eyes. "I just wanted to see the new prankster. *She*"—he motioned toward Freddie with his cup—"got a lot of us into trouble on Wednesday night. Myself included."

He smiled again, and this time, there was a layer of respect to mingle with the mocking. "But listen." He bent conspiratorially toward them. "If you're going to escalate things over at Berm High, then we will gladly escalate things on our end. Just be warned: we don't pull our punches."

"Bring it," Luis snarled while Laina intoned, "We. Will. Crush you."

"You sure about that?" Theo's eyebrows bounced high. "There's still time to say you're sorry . . ." His eyes flicked to Freddie's.

And this time, she was smart enough *not* to blurt out *It was all a misunderstanding!*

Divya clawed a warning on her thigh anyway. Or maybe that was a claw of solidarity. Either way, Freddie didn't need it. Theo Porter made her lungs expand with heat, and there was an odd rumbling happening in her gut. Part fury, part . . . part something she didn't recognize.

Something that prompted her to declare in her primmest, most unfazed voice: "I hope you know, Mr. Porter, that soda is not a balanced breakfast. You might consider orange juice. I'm told they sell it here."

To her surprise—and seemingly to his—he laughed. Just a punch of air, but a laugh all the same. He pushed to his feet. "Great." He knocked the table. "So glad we had this talk."

Then without another word, Theo Porter shoved into the crowd and disappeared.

For several long seconds, no one at the table spoke. Then everyone erupted at once. *Did he see the log? How does he know we're the Prank Squad? Well, now we know* he *is on the Fortin squad. What a jerk. I hate his guts. I hate his face.*

"Sorry it took so long." Kyle popped out beside the table, a full tray of biscuits in hand. "There were a ton of Fortin Prep kids in front of me . . ." Kyle's precious face bunched up. "Why is everyone so pissed?"

As Cat explained what had happened, the crew slid out from the booth. It was time to get to school; Divya and Freddie would have to eat their biscuits in the car.

Unfortunately, Quick-Bis was *really* crowded now, and Freddie lost Divya on her way to the exit. She arrived there with Cat instead, and while Freddie held open the door, she gazed covetously down at Cat's shoes (knee-high riding boots that would never fit over Freddie's calves). Freddie was fighting so hard to keep the envy off her face that she didn't notice the giggles coming from above as she let the door swing shut. It wasn't until someone barked, *"NOW!"* that she finally looked up.

And straight into a bucket of water.

She screamed. Cat screamed. The water connected. Both girls were silenced by cold, cold, *cold,* and wet, wet, *wet.* It was a veritable dunking booth and made the drizzle from grumpy clouds seem a mere annoyance.

As if that wasn't already bad—and wet—enough, Fortin Prep students erupted from cars with water guns.

Luis launched from the Quick-Bis, bellowing like a bull. He was completely unconcerned by the water—and Laina, who followed a split second behind, also didn't care. Even better: she had her nunchucks.

That sent the Fortin students dispersing.

Except now Divya was shouting a warning, and when Freddie spun around, it was just in time to see Theo darting away from Cat. He had a blue book gripped in his hands.

"I got it!" he crowed, and before anyone could chase him, the Fortin Prep kids doubled down on their attack.

This time, it was water guns *and* water balloons. And this time, two trucks squealed out of the parking lot before anyone could fight back. Soon enough, all of Fortin Prep was gone, leaving Freddie and the Prank Squad shivering from the cold.

And also from an unquenchable, bone-deep rage.

Laina was right, Freddie decided while she crawled miserably into Kyle's front seat. *We will* crush *those Fortin Prep kids.*

43

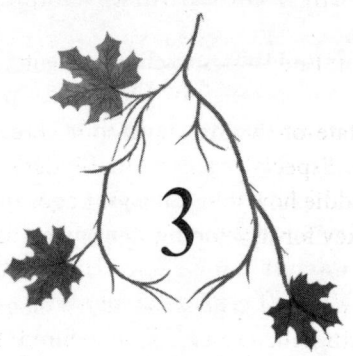

3

Freddie was devastated. Defeated. *Destroyed*.

The entire ride to school was a melancholic affair of soaking clothes and soaking biscuits. No one had said anything. All the fun from before had vanished, and as far as Freddie was concerned, Lance Bass's magic must have ended.

The keychain had betrayed her. Theo Porter was the actual devil. A pox on him and a pox on Allard Fortin Preparatory School.

At least Freddie wasn't wearing Xena today—her Nikon F100 camera that she'd saved up all year to buy. Usually Xena lived around her neck, but Freddie had loaned it to her mom the day before for some promo photographs of the Village Historique.

Now here Freddie was, staring dejectedly into her locker. Her wool sweater stank in that manure way that only wool could, and she didn't have anything else to wear.

She moaned and banged her head against the metal frame. Hadn't she been through enough on Wednesday night with the screams and the arrests and her *lost scarf*?! Then yesterday's suicide that wasn't a suicide, and now today's almost perfect morning had been ruined by a villainous out-of-towner stealing the most *sacred* object of the Berm High senior class.

The thought of going to first-period chorus and singing cheerful show tunes sounded truly torturous—and that made Freddie angry too! Normally, she loved Mr. Binder. Not only was he the chorus and drama teacher, but he also ran three local shops: West End Wines, Pottery-a-Plenty, and finally, the Frame & Foto.

With its state-of-the-art darkroom, Freddie *loved* the Frame & Foto. Especially since Mr. Binder's partner, Greg, had taught Freddie how to use it a year ago, and now she had her very own key for developing Xena's photos whenever she wanted.

Doodle-loo, doodle-loo doo, doodle-loo doo, doo!

The Nokia ringtone sounded from behind the locker door. Freddie slammed it shut, expecting to find Divya staring at a surprise phone call. Instead, she found Kyle staring at one.

"I don't know this number." His brow pinched up adorably. In his right hand was a letterman jacket. In his left was the Nokia.

Doodle-loo, doodle-loo doo, doodle-loo doo, doo!

"Should I answer?" he asked Freddie.

"Um." Freddie had no idea what to say. She was already reeling from the fact that he was standing *right* next to her.

Fortunately, Kyle came to a decision on his own. "I probably shouldn't answer at school." He hit a button and shoved the device into his pocket. Then he lobbed his green eyes onto Freddie. "Hello." He beamed. "I brought this for you to wear, since I think your sweater might be . . ." His nose curled as he offered her the jacket.

She flushed.

"You don't have to wear it, though," he added. "I just thought you might want—"

"*Yes.*" Freddie snatched the letterman from him with far too much enthusiasm. Then laughed, high-pitched and twittery. "Thank you. I . . . I'll return it after school."

"Sounds good." He shifted his weight. Glanced once at his toes. Then at Freddie's locker. Then finally he blurted, "What are you doing tonight?"

Freddie's breath caught. "Uh . . . nothing, I guess."

"Nothing? On a Friday?" His green eyes widened.

"Er..." Freddie wasn't about to admit that she and Divya usually spent Fridays at Divya's house watching TGIF on channel 9.

Kyle angled in closer, and Freddie prayed her breath didn't stink of biscuits. He was so close—close enough that she could smell him. A soft, manly soap smell that made her want to produce guttural noises in the back of her throat.

"Wanna hang out?" he asked.

She nodded. "Wh-where?"

The bell rang. She jumped. Kyle jumped. Then he laughed. "I'll come find you after school." He flashed another flawless smile, and she couldn't help but notice as he sauntered down the hall that his white shirt was still damp from the water balloons—and therefore deliciously clingy.

She watched until he was long gone. Until every person in the hall had filed away and Principal Tamura snapped at Freddie to get to class. Then Freddie frantically peeled off her sweater and slipped Kyle's jacket over her undershirt.

It smelled *divine*.

She raced down the mustard halls, carried on a cloud of wonderment. Kyle Friedman had asked her out. He had asked her to meet *at a place, for some time*. And as she coasted blissfully through chorus, then trig, then history, she once again decided Fridays were the most perfect day of the week. Theo Porter hadn't ruined it—he'd made it amazing. Theo Porter and a Lance Bass keychain.

And that was only a fraction of Freddie's amazing day. Because it wasn't merely the cross-country team or the Prank Squad who smiled at her (and at Divya too). The *entirety of Berm High* had something nice to say. She got high fives from four teachers, three lunch servers, and Coach Lenox, who said, "Way to knock out the Woodchucks for a whole season!"

Freddie had basically become a superhero overnight, and all of this small town talking, she decided, was *the best*.

Of course, when the final bell rang and Freddie scrambled

out of seventh-period Spanish to bolt for her locker, she nearly collided headfirst with Principal Tamura.

"Simmer down," said Tamura, grabbing Freddie's shoulders. A dejected Divya stood three feet away.

"What's going on?" Freddie asked Tamura, who was—as usual—dressed way too well for Berm High in her tailored pinstripe suit and fire-engine-red lipstick.

"Follow me," Tamura responded. "Both of you. You'll be meeting with a counselor in my office right now."

"Right now?" Freddie squawked.

"That is literally what I just said."

"But . . . I can't." Freddie flung a wild look at Divya. "I'm meeting Kyle Friedman at my locker."

"Oh, I'm so sorry," Tamura said. "You're meeting a boy? Why, that changes everything."

"Really?" Freddie's lips began to quirk.

"Of course not." Tamura thrust a pointed finger down the hall. "Walk, Gellar. Now. The nice gentleman is waiting."

"But we don't need counseling," Divya moaned, as Freddie fell into shambling steps beside her bestie. "I didn't even *see* the dead body."

"And I only saw his shoes." Freddie gazed, grief-stricken, behind her. Students flooded the hallway, but she couldn't see Kyle. She hugged his letterman jacket more tightly to her. It smelled like manly man soap, but how long would that last?

"Your parents both think you'd benefit from talking to someone." Tamura strode ahead, and upon reaching her office door, she shoved it wide. "Now go on in and be good, okay? Show the nice man what our Lumberjack spirit is all about."

The girls shuffled in. Freddie glowered at Divya and Divya glowered right back until they were in the office and facing a handsome man with gray hair and dark brown eyes. Like an older, less goofy Ross from *Friends*—but with a silver beard added.

"Hello, girls," he said with a smile. "I'm Dr. Born."

"Hi," they mumbled in unison.

"Thank you, Principal." He nodded toward Tamura at the door. "We won't be more than an hour."

"An hour?" Freddie turned to Divya with horror.

"Kill me now." Divya buried her face in her hands.

"I can hear you, you know." Dr. Born circled behind Tamura's desk while the door clicked shut and cut off sounds of free students who weren't trapped in purgatory. *They* got to meet their crushes at their lockers. *They* got to live happily ever after.

Dr. Born sat at Tamura's desk and waved for the girls to sit too. So Freddie and Divya complied, dropping stiffly onto matching black armchairs. Tamura's office was as sleek as she was. Freddie had no idea where she'd gotten the modern-style furniture, but it definitely wasn't from anywhere in Berm. And it definitely didn't match the rest of the ancient school.

"So," Freddie began at the same time Dr. Born said, "I want to begin . . ." He trailed off, smiling once more. "Go ahead, Freddie."

"Thank you." She sat taller. "Who hired you? My parents or Divya's?"

"Both."

This surprised Freddie. For years now, she'd heard Steve nudging Mom to go into therapy and finally reckon with her grief over Frank Carter's death. Now Mom was essentially forcing her own daughter to do what she wouldn't?

Pot, meet kettle.

Also, pot, meet stubborn daughter who wasn't about to take this lying down.

"And who found you?" Freddie continued. "You're obviously not local, or we'd know you."

"I live an hour away, but I practice here once a week."

"Is this normal?" Divya inserted, donning her sharpest glare. "Interrogating two people at once?"

"Well, we don't call it 'interrogating,' but yes. Sometimes when people have witnessed something traumatizing together, it's helpful to work through it together as well."

"I didn't even see the dead body," Divya repeated.

"And I only saw his shoes," Freddie chimed.

"Tell me about that, Freddie." Dr. Born lifted a fancy pen off the desk. The kind of pen that Freddie thought people only gave as gifts but never actually used. "I want to know what you saw, and more importantly, what you felt seeing it."

"Well, here's what *I* want to know, Dr. Born." Freddie folded her hands on her lap. "Why is it that our parents hired *you* when there are counselors right here in Berm?"

"Freddie." A hint of warning in the man's voice now.

"And how much do you charge? Is it by the hour? Or is there some kind of two-for-one special?"

"Freddie." No hinting now. He was annoyed. "I see what you're trying to do, and you won't succeed at it. The fact that you're even trying to deflect this session suggests you do need counseling."

"She does." Divya nodded and stood. "But *I* do not. And thank you so much for understanding—"

"Sit back down, Divya. Please." Now Dr. Born was really annoyed—although it was also clear he was trying to hide it. "Your dad is the one who reached out to me, Divya, so please consider that *he* is worried about you."

Divya plunked back into her armchair. "*Fine*. Interrogate us."

"Still not an interrogation." He tipped down his chin so he could stare from the tops of his eyes. A classic adult look of condescension. "And what about you, Freddie? Will you cooperate?"

She hesitated, knowing she really had no choice. But knowing she also really didn't want Dr. Born to win this easily, she counted One Lance Bass. Two Lance Bass. Three Lance Bass.

"Alright," she declared, pulling back her shoulders. "I will cooperate."

Dr. Born's posture relaxed. His kindly smile returned. "Thank you. Now, as I said before: I want you to walk me through what you saw, paying particular attention to how it made you feel."

Two hours after counseling had ended, Freddie found herself slumping into her family's living room where her stepdad, Steve, scanned the *TV Guide*. He'd lately taken to shaving his balding scalp, and Freddie thought it looked Much Better Indeed. His pale skin was very healthy beneath that disappearing hair! Freddie's mom, meanwhile, sorted through a heap of muslin on the couch. Like Freddie, her dark brown curls were wild and no amount of product or scrunchies could control them.

"No TGIF tonight?" Mom asked distractedly.

"I'm not feeling it," Freddie muttered. Having missed her special time with Kyle, she didn't feel up to anything beyond moping, moaning, and occasionally wallowing.

"In *that* case," Mom declared, "you get to help me mend these gowns for the pageant."

Freddie sighed. "I'd rather not."

"I'd rather you did."

"I'm a terrible seamstress."

"And no one will notice a crooked hem from the stage."

"*I'm* helping," Steve said.

Freddie stuck out her tongue. But then did end up plopping onto the carpet and holding out her hand. "Hand it over, Ma."

Her mother did exactly that, passing off a 1600s-style gown in a deeply unflattering brown. Every year, when the Historical Society put on the Fête du Bûcheron, they capped off the day with the Lumberjack Pageant.

(It had briefly been known as the Reconstitution Historique des Bûcherons when Mom had first joined the society in 1979 and tried to organize the chaotic group, but the original members had quickly revolted against that title. There was *historical accuracy* and then there was *what the locals could actually pronounce, Patty.*)

Every year, Mr. Binder directed the play, Mom handled the costumes, and Freddie was forced to perform. *This* year, though, Mom had sworn Freddie wouldn't have to participate. Sure, Freddie would help assemble the sets, and yes, she'd help take tickets and donations at the entrance . . .

But! She would absolutely not have to go on the stage. No way, no how. Last year, Freddie had played a lumberjack, and the fake beard had stuck on a little too well. So rather than shame herself with a five-o'clock shadow at the post-pageant party, she'd fled for home.

She was pretty sure she still had little hairs stuck to her chin.

"Who's playing our esteemed founder Allard Fortin this year in the pageant?" Freddie asked as she frowned at the gown now draped across her lap. It had a nice little tear at the bodice. Perfect for those old paintings in which a woman's single boob always seemed to be falling out.

"No one yet," Mom admitted, a nervousness to her voice that made both Steve and Freddie look up. She forced a laugh. "Oh, we're just a little late getting enough volunteers is all. But they'll come. They always come. It's not like locals don't know it's happening."

That was true. Everyone knew about the fête—and usually, everyone volunteered to be in the pageant. In fact, there was a competition every year for *Most Outrageous French Accent,* and the winner last year had been Greg.

Boy, had he earned it too. *WELCUMMMM TO ZEE VILLAJJJ EE-STORRRR-EEECK!*

"I can make sure we get volunteers," Steve suggested. "It's a small town. People talk. There's probably just a mix-up with the dates—"

"No, no," Mom cut in. She stabbed the gown on her own lap with a needle. "I can handle it."

If *It's a small town; people talk* was the motto of Berm, then *I can handle it* was Patricia Gellar's. She'd been a rare transplant from outside Berm, back in 1979, a few years before Freddie had been born. And although Mom had tried to blend in with the locals, she'd also been a little too hung up on *historical accuracy* at the Village. It had rubbed Bermians wrong. Couldn't she just *blend in like the old head of the Historical Society had done? Did she really have to make everything so French?*

The answer had been yes, it did need to be more French. And no, Patty couldn't just blend in. While Mom had agreed she wouldn't go all in by renaming the park *La Ville Sur La Berme Village Historique,* she had insisted they at *least* tweak a few things.

City-on-the-Berme Village Historique had become the compromise.

It had taken the first half of Freddie's life for Mom to finally prove that having an accurate park was, in fact, better for tourism—but it was no wonder she was nervous. Bermians loved to boycott things when they were mad. (No one in the entire town had bought a box of Bisquick since the Incident with the Trademark.)

Steve, whom Freddie knew secretly smoothed things over for Mom, just shrugged at Mom as if to say, *Suit yourself!* Which totally meant he'd be whispering in ears tomorrow.

"It'll be fine," Mom insisted. "People always want to commemorate *les bûcherons.*"

"More like," Freddie countered, "they want any excuse to drink spiked cider and whine about biased judges in the jack-o'-lantern contest."

"It's not *whining.*" Steve tipped up his chin. "Judge Raskin absolutely played favorites with his son in '95 . . . Oh, look!" He snapped up the *TV Guide.* "Reruns of *The X-Files* are on channel seven. Wanna watch?"

"Duh," Freddie replied, and seconds later, the familiar voices of Agents Dana Scully and Fox Mulder filled the living room. (Mulder was *almost* as hot as Lance Bass.) An hour later, after many poked thumbs and a crudely repaired bodice, the phone rang.

"It's Divya," Steve said after glancing at the caller ID. He passed the cordless receiver Freddie's way. She scrabbled to her feet and marched from the room.

"What's up, Div?"

"You have five minutes to get dressed in something black before Kyle gets there to pick you up."

Freddie stopped dead in her tracks. "Say what now?"

"You heard me. Kyle Friedman, who makes you all *woo-woo*, is going to be at your house in five minutes. We're going to Fortin Prep for . . . Well, I don't actually know that part. Retribution, I assume."

"How do you know any of this? Did Kyle call you?" Freddie shoved into her bedroom and dove for the closet. Black, black—what did she have in black that also made her look like the Most Appealing Girl Who'd Ever Lived?

"Laina called me."

Freddie choked. "Um, excuse me? How does she have your number?"

"I gave it to her." Divya's voice went breathy. "In AP Econ, she asked me for it."

Freddie gasped. "You minx! You didn't even tell me."

"I was distracted by Dr. Born."

"There was time before that! Or after!"

"Oh, shut up and get dressed, will you? You're down to four minutes now."

Before Freddie could squawk any further indignation, the line went dead—and she was left with only four minutes to make herself beautiful.

She failed. Miserably. She just didn't own enough black, which left her wearing dress pants with sneakers. And although she had a decent black turtleneck, the black sweatshirt she pulled on for warmth was . . . Well, she had been much smaller when she'd gotten it from the Lumberjack Pageant six years ago, and the lumberjack axe had started to flake off.

Freddie traded her glasses for contacts, and finally, last but never least, she slipped into Kyle's letterman jacket. No doubt he would want it back, but she would savor it while she had it.

Mmmm. Manly man soap smell.

"Hey Mom!" Freddie roared, swinging out of her room—only to barrel straight into Mom and Steve standing right there. They looked sheepish.

"Were you just listening to my call?"

Mom gave an appalled gasp that Freddie didn't believe for one second. Then, in a deft change of subject, Mom reached out and pinched Freddie's collar. "Where did you get this jacket?"

Freddie couldn't keep from smiling. "Kyle Friedman lent it to me. And now he's on his way here. To pick me up."

"Kyle Friedman?" Steve asked. "Wasn't he the kid who tried to start a local surf team?"

Mom, meanwhile, grew hearts in her eyes. "He offered you a Fruit Roll-Up in fifth grade, didn't he? When we had to pick up a box of old documents at his house. What a charmer."

"Yes," Freddie said, surprised her mom recalled that. Then again, it had been a Very Exciting Day for Mom—reclaiming forgotten documents in the old Historical Society members' garages. It had also been a Very Exciting Day for Freddie, since Fruit Roll-Ups were also *verboten.*

"Me and Divya are going out with him and his friends."

"Did you hear that?" Mom threw Steve an exultant smile. "She has friends!"

Freddie scowled. "I've always had friends."

"More like friend, singular," Steve countered.

Once more, Freddie stuck out her tongue. Then she turned to her mother. "You have Xena?"

"Oh, yes!" Mom scooted for the kitchen. "Thank you so much for letting me use her."

Freddie followed on her heels. "Did you replace the film?"

"Of course." Mom snagged the Nikon F100 off the counter and handed it to Freddie.

Who instantly hugged the camera close. "Did you miss me,

little warrior princess? I know, I know. I missed you too, my sugar wookums."

Steve cleared his throat. "Get a room, you two."

Freddie side-eyed him. "Don't listen to the mean man, Xena."

"When will you be back?" Mom pushed in. She was bouncing on her toes. "Late? Teenagers should stay out late."

"I don't know, Mom. You're the adult here."

Mom blinked. "Okay. Then just be back in time for Y2K. No one knows what's going to happen. It could get dangerous."

"That's two and a half months away."

"Yes, it is."

"Be serious, Mom. My ride is probably here by now!"

"Her ride, Steve. Did you hear that? She has a *ride*."

"Mom!"

"Okay, okay. Does one A.M. seem fair? Maybe two is better." She tapped her chin.

Freddie's eyes widened. "Only if you want me to get arrested. The city has a curfew of midnight for anyone under eighteen."

"Well, then midnight it is!" Mom slapped her hands onto Freddie's shoulders and twirled her toward the front door. "Although," she whispered as she pushed her daughter forward, "I won't tell Sheriff Bowman if you're a bit late."

"Your parenting skills are questionable, Mother."

"As are your teenager skills, Daughter."

"You're cruel."

"And you love me. See you at midnight—or later!"

Freddie opened her mouth to say goodbye, but the words never came. Kyle's Jeep gleamed on the street below, and instantly her heart lurched into her eye sockets. *The world is such a magical place,* she thought as she floated toward him.

And it could only get more magical as long as Lance Bass remained in her pocket.

4

Freddie thought her lungs might punch through her esophagus. In a good way. Because where she'd expected Divya and Laina to be in the Jeep, it turned out to be only Kyle.

Freddie was pretty sure that qualified this moment as a date.

"Thanks for the jacket," she said as she clambered into shotgun. She slipped it off, and a great wash of cool air and sadness wafted across her. At least she had Xena back, though, and safely around her neck.

"You're welcome." Kyle grinned. "Did it work?"

"Erm." Freddie wasn't sure how to answer that question. After all, it was a jacket, not a power tool. "Yes?"

He grinned even wider.

"So where are Laina and Divya?" Freddie asked as he shifted into drive.

"Laina's got her mom's car tonight, so she's driving them. And Cat is driving her and Luis, so we're all meeting at the cul-de-sac."

"The . . . cul-de-sac?" Kyle acted as if Freddie should know the place. "Um, what is this cul-de-sac?" Freddie asked when it became clear Kyle hadn't understood that her previous repetition was actually a question.

"You know, Mrs. Elliot's unfinished subdivision." Devastating grin. "If you cut through the woods, you end up right next to

Fortin Prep's landscaping shed. There's a gate there, and no one ever locks it."

As the Jeep turned off of Freddie's road, Kyle's swoony green eyes latched onto her. "Sorry I didn't come to your locker after school. I forgot I had detention."

"Oh." Freddie blinked. "And here I thought I'd missed *you* because I had . . ." She trailed off. There was nothing at all she could say that wouldn't lead to questions or strange looks about the hanging—and neither questions nor strange looks were what Freddie was going for tonight.

"I . . . stayed late after class. To tutor Divya." *She is going to kill me.* "Why were you in detention?"

"I skipped school." He winced adorably.

And Freddie really didn't think he could get any cuter. She'd always found Bad Boys appealing—particularly if they wore tight pants and sang about summer nights and greased lightning. "Do you perhaps have a leather jacket?" she asked hopefully. "Or a motorcycle?"

"No."

"Alas." She sighed.

"I think someone left one at my family's dry cleaners, though." He smiled. "A leather jacket. Not a motorcycle." This made him laugh and, in turn, made Freddie laugh too.

"Do clothes often get left at the dry cleaners?"

"All the time. We've got, like, a bajillion Quick-Bis uniforms. Oh, and a *ton* of Fortin Prep uniforms too. It's my job to track down their owners, but if I don't find them"—he shrugged—"then the stuff gets donated. Or just thrown away."

"What a dutiful son," Freddie breathed. Hard-working *and* charitable.

Two more turns, and Kyle steered them onto the curvy road beside the lake. The sun was almost gone, leaving the road dark and the lake hidden behind trees and shadow.

"Hey," Kyle said, thumbs tapping on the steering wheel to a melody only he could hear. "Can I get your phone number?

That would make it a lot easier next time I want to hang out with you."

Next time. He'd said *next time*.

Freddie nodded frantically, incapable of doing much else. A *real* boy was showing interest in her! And he was getting her phone number. She never wanted to return the Lance Bass keychain. *Ever*.

Of course, moments later when Kyle attempted to type Freddie's house number into his Nokia while he was still driving, some of the magic dissolved. Freddie snatched the mobile—perhaps a bit roughly—from his hands.

Which was when the moment *really* spiraled from her control because once she'd added her home number and explained how her mom wouldn't let her have a cell phone, she caught sight of the road ahead—a road that Kyle was not watching.

A road upon which a figure stood.

"Look out!" Freddie braced herself. Kyle's brakes shrieked. The car swerved toward the woods . . . Trees zoomed in fast.

The Jeep squealed to a stop.

And with her pulse roaring in her ears, Freddie gaped at Kyle. "Are you okay?"

He didn't answer. He was angling back to see who stood in the road. "Oh no," he moaned. "It's the sheriff. I almost hit the *sheriff*."

"Well, you clearly have a talent for something," Freddie consoled.

Sheriff Rita Bowman's heart-shaped face appeared at the window. She rapped her knuckles against the glass, to which Kyle emitted another groan.

"Jesus, Friedman." Bowman glowered at him once the window was down. "I ought to write you a ticket. Are you stoned again?"

Kyle grimaced. "N-no, ma'am."

"Gellar?" Bowman asked, her blue eyes sliding to Freddie. "What the hell are you doing with this knucklehead?"

Freddie gulped. Bowman's eyes were such a pale, crystal blue. Like ice on the lake during winter. They were terrifying, really, and they made Freddie want to offer up every illegal (or even slightly immoral) thing she'd ever done.

For that reason alone, she just adored Rita Bowman. One day, she was going to be just like her. The summers she'd spent riding with Bowman throughout the Berm area had been the best summers of her life. She'd felt so at home in the squad car.

And while sure, Freddie had also been unable to escape the inevitable thoughts of her dad—like wondering if he'd ever sat in the same seat where she'd sat at the station's front desk or if he'd ever also complained that the coffeemaker was utter crap—she'd used the opportunities as training.

Tamp down thoughts. Tamp down feelings. Focus only on the task at hand.

Which was what Freddie did right now as she tried desperately *not* to offer up all her secrets to Sheriff Bowman.

"Why aren't the both of you at the football game?" Bowman asked.

"I find the sport barbaric," Freddie answered at the same moment Kyle offered, "I was there. The Lumberjacks were winning."

"So why'd you leave?" She frowned at Kyle. Then at Freddie. "And where are you two going right now?"

"Fortin Pr—"

"Kyle's house," Freddie interrupted.

And somehow, Bowman's expression soured even more. "God, Friedman. I'm gonna pretend I didn't hear you." She pointed at Freddie. "And I'm gonna pretend I believe you. Now move along—"

"Wait!" Freddie lurched her seat-belted body at the sheriff. "What are *you* doing out here?"

"And what's that smell?" Kyle's nose wrinkled.

Freddie blinked. Then sniffed. Sure enough, there was a decidedly dead odor in the air.

Her skin crawled. She'd smelled this exactly on Wednesday night in the fog.

"I'm cleaning up roadkill," the sheriff muttered, obviously displeased by this activity. "And I'm checking the roads for... *unsavory* critters." At Freddie's and Kyle's blank looks, she added, "I keep getting complaints of animals—mostly raccoons and turkeys—crossing the road in huge numbers. So I'm looking into it."

"But that's not your job."

"Nope," Bowman admitted with a shrug, "but my family has a saying: *On n'est jamais si bien servi que par soi-même.*"

Kyle cocked his head to the side. "Huh?"

"It wasn't English," Freddie murmured.

"Oh."

Bowman just glared. "It means one is never better served than by oneself. In other words, if I want this done right, *I* need to do it. It's less hassle for me to look into these roaming animals than it is to deal with County Animal Control."

"Have you found anything?" Freddie asked, curiosity building in her belly. "Like, why are they all roaming? *That* seems weird."

"Eh." Bowman shrugged with just the perfect amount of Agent Dana Scully skepticism. "Or maybe it's just a natural migration cycle, Freddie. Either way, you two be careful, okay? Especially you, Gellar." She leveled a cool stare onto Freddie. "You've had enough excitement lately. And it's not just turkeys that are on the move. I've had reports of coyotes and wolves too."

"Cool." Kyle perked up.

Bowman sneered. "Not cool, kid. Wolves can rip you to shreds. Coyotes too, so just stay out of the park and be smart." She backed up a step and then, almost as an afterthought, added, "And watch the damned road, Friedman. Or next time I'll arrest you."

The cul-de-sac was exactly as Kyle had described, a gravel spot set at the end of a long, unfinished road that Mrs. Elliot had thought would be a great spot for vacation rentals. She'd been an *out-of-towner*, so the Bermians had already disliked her on principle. Add in the fact that she'd wanted to bring in more out-of-towners, and she had become public enemy number one.

To absolutely no one's surprise except perhaps her own, Mrs. Elliot's permit requests had been denied. Eventually, she'd gone back whence she came with only this road to linger—a warning that Berm did not take kindly to tourists who overstayed their welcome.

Laina's mom's Volvo was already at the abandoned cul-de-sac when Kyle pulled up, and Cat's old Taurus joined them three seconds later. Everyone convened at Kyle's trunk, where he opened the door with much fanfare.

And revealed ten industrial jugs of corn syrup.

"*This* is your plan?" Freddie chewed her lip. All this time, they'd been driving with sugary contraband in the trunk, and she'd had no idea. Thank goodness Sheriff Bowman hadn't seen this. There would have been no plausible explanation that Freddie could have conjured for possessing so much corn syrup, and knowing Kyle, he would have just blurted out the truth anyway.

"It was one of the ideas in the Official Log," Cat explained. She leaned into the trunk, looking enviously stylish and totally Bond-worthy in her pleather pants, black boots, and fitted turtleneck. She lugged out the nearest jug.

Kyle hauled out a second and third. "We'll pour it all over their bleachers. Just in time for the big soccer match with Elmore." He offered Freddie a green-eyed wink. "Sticky asses for the rich pricks!"

Freddie's heart fluttered.

"What do you think of the plan, Gellar?" Laina had moved to Freddie's left side while Divya had moved to her right. Laina wasn't dressed too differently from earlier, except for the addition of a black leather jacket. Divya, meanwhile, had traded in her jeans for black cords and a black hoodie that Freddie didn't recognize.

She hoped that meant Divya had borrowed it from Laina.

"Yeah, got a better idea, Prank Wizard?" This was from Luis, who was hauling out the next two jugs of syrup.

Prank Wizard. Freddie bit back a smile. *See?* she wanted to demand of Divya. *I am the Answer Finder, and now the Prank Wizard too.*

"We need to take Fortin Prep *down*," Luis went on. "They hit us hard this morning, so we can't be gentle here."

Freddie's smile fell away—because the disappointing reality was that this *did* feel pretty low caliber. After all, it was just sugar on the bleachers. A hose could wash it away in five minutes.

But she also had no better ideas. Not when the nearness of Kyle was making her brain melt, so she simply shrugged and said, "Let's do this!"

"Excellent." Luis clapped his hands. "Boys can each carry two jugs, and girls can snag one—"

"I can snag two, thanks." Laina bowed into the trunk and plucked up two. She made it look so easy that Freddie was shocked when she grabbed one and, *oh my god,* it was so heavy. She had never considered herself weak, but she suddenly felt Deeply Inadequate Indeed.

"One jug leftover, I guess." Kyle slammed the trunk shut, locked the doors with a *key fob* (how fancy!), and then turned to face everyone. "Ready?"

"Not without these." Cat held out six black masks. They were just cheap paper and really did nothing to hide anyone's faces. Not to mention, once everyone had slipped them on, they looked vaguely like the Hamburglar (which made Freddie's stomach rumble).

Still, she couldn't help but grin at Divya, who grinned right back. And when Divya slipped her fingers around Freddie's forearm and *squeezed,* Freddie recognized it for the physical-touch version of *Wheeeeeeeeeee!*

Freddie agreed.

"Everyone grab your syrup," Laina ordered, and without waiting to see if people complied (of course they did—no one would dare disobey President Steward), she set off into the trees.

Where it was slow going. With the moon hidden behind clouds, there was almost no light to see by. And sure, Freddie understood why, from a stealth perspective, they hadn't brought flashlights with them, but she wished they had at least brought *one.*

The night's breeze clattered through dead leaves. Cold and damp, as if winter were already on the way.

And for some reason, it made Freddie's gut churn—not in a hamburger-hunger way, either. This was the clenching she'd felt on Wednesday night when she'd heard those screams. It was the boiling she'd felt yesterday in the woods before they'd discovered the body.

The others seemed to sense it too. No one spoke, but everyone kept checking over their shoulders. Again and again, sideways glances into the evergreens and maples. Except the only thing Freddie saw was darkness; the only thing she heard was their footsteps stamping over autumn leaves.

Until a screech ripped through the night.

Freddie jumped; Divya dropped her jug.

Then a thousand screeches laid claim to the forest, and the darkness around them *moved.* A great upward explosion of shadows.

Birds, Freddie realized. Countless birds erupting from the branches and taking to the sky—and all of them cawing in a grating, mind-searing pitch. *Crows,* she amended, because it was definitely crows this time. And so much more intense than that morning had been, since she and the others were right in the middle of it.

Freddie had never seen anything like it, never heard anything like it. It took several minutes for all the squawking to fade . . .

Which in turn revealed a new sound: moaning.

Laina clutched at her face. "My head."

Divya reached her first. "What's wrong? What's wrong, Laina?"

Then Cat was to her other side. "She gets really bad migraines. Laina, are you okay?"

But still, Laina only moaned: "My head, my head."

"What do we do?" Kyle's eyes bulged white in the darkness. "Should I call nine-one-one?"

"I will," Luis said. He yanked out his Nokia. But before he could dial any numbers, Laina's moans became a single long scream.

It shattered the forest, worse somehow than the crows. Like a single, targeted scalpel compared to a hundred loosed arrows.

Then Laina fell silent, and for several long seconds, no one spoke. Freddie's heart bumped against her ribs. Her gut positively *roiled,* a volcano about to shoot free. Until at last, Cat whispered, "Luis, call nine-one-one, please."

"No, no." This was Laina. Her voice was a hoarse whisper. "No, I'm fine, guys. I'm fine now."

A great exhale left everyone's lungs. Luis shoved close to her face. "What's my name?"

Laina recoiled. "Luis Mendez."

"And how many fingers am I holding up?"

"Three, you ass. I'm *fine*." Laina shook off Cat's and Divya's arms. "Stop looking at me like that. You know I get migraines."

"Um, not ones that make you scream," Cat pointed out. "I thought you were having a stroke or something."

"It was just . . . the crows." Laina rubbed at her temples, frowning. "Sometimes . . . noises trigger me." For half a moment, her glower was replaced by confusion. The tiniest of frowns that passed in an instant—but Freddie noticed it.

And Freddie *noted* it.

"Let's keep going, please," Laina insisted. "I feel fine now, okay?"

No one argued, and Laina gave them no chance to anyway. She stomped off at top speed, forcing the Prank Squad to scamper after. Except Freddie, who hung back. And while part of her knew she was being silly . . .

Another, distinctly abdominal part of her said: *Hey, wait just one second, please.* So she did, and with squinting eyes, she searched the trees. Maples. Oaks. Ash and pine.

She wasn't a superstitious person as a rule. Definitely a scientific Dana Scully versus an insta-believer like Fox Mulder. But even Freddie had to admit that crows and a screaming Laina had been freaky. *Super* freaky.

The question was, though, what logical explanation could have caused the crows to take off? Maybe a sudden barometric pressure change—that could cause migraines too, Freddie thought. Or . . . didn't birds sense magnetic changes in the earth? Maybe that had gotten them going.

Freddie gnawed her bottom lip, scanning the trees. There was something fuzzy and pale about two hundred paces away. Human in shape, but so blended into the forest, she couldn't get her gaze to actually land on it. Her eyes kept pinging away. She thought again of magnets.

Then the smell hit her, like a rotting carcass. Like screams on a foggy night—

A hand landed on her arm.

Freddie flinched so hard, she released her jug. *Glump!*

"You okay?" Divya whispered.

"Yeah," Freddie lied while her heart inexplicably thundered *No!* "I just thought . . . I saw something, but it's probably just trees." *And I've probably been watching too much* X-Files.

"What does your gut say?"

"Nothing," Freddie lied again. After hefting up her syrup, she kicked into a not-so-quiet jog along with Divya.

Freddie did throw a final look back, though, toward whatever it was she thought she might've seen. But there was nothing to look at now. Just darkness and leaves and a whispering wind unseen.

5

Despite what people often assumed, Allard Fortin Preparatory School wasn't named for the local founder, José Allard Fortin. Instead, it was named for his descendant: Roberta.

After her older sister was disowned (rumor was she fell in *lurrrve* with a Very Unsuitable Boy) and then both her parents passed away, Roberta decided to just ditch the whole Allard Fortin legacy. And also ditch Berm while she was at it.

She and her older sister actually became the first of the Allard Fortin bloodline to ever move out of town. Then, rather than let the family's estate go to waste with no Allard Fortins to fill it, Roberta—as the heir—turned it into a scholarship school.

It was a great idea in theory. Like, kudos to Roberta for trying. But it was not so great in practice. Turns out schools are expensive to run, and the Allard Fortin fortunes were about as depleted as their bloodline. So, one year after the school's opening, the mission changed.

Bye-bye, charitable outreach of 1973. Hello, wealthy alum of 1974.

And wowzas, was it a fancy school now. Like, if Freddie's loyalty to Berm High weren't so profound, she'd be jealous of all the fountains and gardens and the two gourmet cafeterias. Also, there was a fancy library *and* a Maximum Drama mausoleum right in the middle of campus, where Allard Fortin 1.0 was buried.

The estate might no longer be bound to the dead bloodline of Allard Fortins, but the school did at least keep his crypt spotless.

As Kyle had promised, the gate to the school grounds was indeed unlocked—and even propped open by two enormous bags of birdseed. A welcoming glow flickered from lamps that had *actual* wicks and *actual* flames. A ridiculous expense . . .

That also looked pretty cool, honestly.

"Come on," Laina hissed. Since the Strange Incident with the Crows, she had remained a drill sergeant hell-bent on proving she was fine.

Which was maybe why Laina was the first to scoot through the gate, while everyone else crept more cautiously behind. Freddie and Divya brought up the rear, their corn syrup jugs glooping with each step. And for the first time since abandoning the cars, Freddie's sixth sense reared back enough for her BFF awareness to wiggle in.

"Hey," she whispered, "where did you get that sweatshirt?"

Divya smiled slyly, and the frown that had folded across her brow since the crows smoothed away. "Laina lent it to me."

Freddie's grin stretched almost to her ears. "*Eeeee.* You two have moved very quickly, haven't you?"

The smile faded. "I . . . don't know." Now it was back to the frown. "I'm not sure she . . . you know. Likes girls. She did date that guy from Elmore High last year."

"Maybe she likes girls *and* boys."

"I hope so," Divya said, and the look on her face—the earnest hope . . . It made Freddie's heart tighten.

The gate squeaked as Freddie nudged it a bit wider to slip through, and a split second later, she stepped onto the grounds of Allard Fortin Preparatory School. Freddie had seen it all before, of course—she'd come to a few soccer matches. Plus, there'd been that summer when Mom had been hired to restore the mausoleum after time, weather, and occasional vandalism had taken their toll. Freddie (only eight at the time) had been forced to tag along every day for an entire summer.

But for each of those visits, Freddie had been *allowed* on campus. Right now, she was 100 percent trespassing. And it turned out breaking the rules was exhilarating.

In fact, it was making Freddie reconsider *everything she had ever known*. Like maybe it was time for a new ten-year plan. No more law enforcement; a life of crime was summoning instead.

With Laina at the lead, the Prank Squad tiptoed over maple- and oak-lined paths (where nary an acorn or fallen leaf dared to disrupt the view). "The Fortin cross-country team runs here," Luis whispered, pointing to trails that snaked into darkness. "But," he added with a toothy grin, "they're mostly flat. Which is why they always lose, and I always win."

"And always will, babe." Cat offered a boyfriend-indulging smile.

A few more bends in the path and a new light filtered their way. Laina made a SWAT-team motion toward the trees, so they all ducked off the paths.

"It's the field lights," Kyle said, frowning his ever-confused frown as they gathered beside a barren willow. "But why are they on? There's no game."

"Yeah." Cat nodded, wearing a more intelligent frown. "It's an away game tonight. The students should be gone."

Except, Freddie thought, *I did get them arrested.* It was possible a lot of them were bound to campus now.

"Well, shnikies," Laina swore at the same moment Luis dropped his corn syrup to the ground. They both ripped off their masks.

"What the hell are we gonna do?" he asked. "We have all this syrup, and we *have* to retaliate somehow. This morning can't go unanswered."

He sounded Very Shakespearean, and Freddie approved. Baz Luhrmann's *Romeo + Juliet* was her favorite movie. Except, of course, this wasn't Verona Beach, and tragically, Leonardo DiCaprio wasn't here.

While everyone debated the best course of action, Freddie spun in a slow circle, searching for inspiration. Trusting her gut to guide her . . .

Her eyes landed on a different set of lights through the trees. It was the ever-spotless Allard Fortin mausoleum. *Oh yes.* She grinned a criminal grin. *That will do nicely.*

"President Steward?" Freddie dropped her jug to the ground. "How do we feel about changing our target? The Fortin crypt is right over there."

"Ooooh," Kyle said. "We could pour the syrup on his skeleton!"

"No!" Freddie flung up her hands. "No, no, *no.*" She would never deface a piece of history. Her mom would literally kill her. "No touching the three-hundred-year-old mausoleum, please. My mom worked really hard at the restoration, okay? However, feel free to sully the gardens and benches all you want."

"Oh, nice." Luis made an approving nod. "I've heard those gardens are a popular make-out spot. It sure would suck to find it covered in corn syrup."

"Especially if"—Freddie pointed to a nearby trash can, her eyelashes batting innocently—"there's trash all over the syrup."

"Oh, and *birdseed,*" Divya said. "There were bags of it back at the gate."

"Gnarly." Laina punched the air. "They'll have raccoons and birds crawling all over by morning."

Kyle whooped (albeit softly) and everyone else gave gleeful nods.

"Boys." Laina stood taller. "Go fetch that birdseed. Cat, Divya, Freddie?" She slid her mask into place. "Let's dump some corn syrup."

During Freddie's summer with her mom on campus, Freddie had learned that the Fortin mausoleum looked way cooler on the outside than it did on the inside. The interior was tiny, dusty, and contained nothing more than a boring stone coffin.

As such—unsurprisingly—Mom's restoration efforts had mostly focused on the crypt's exterior: on the four Allard Fortin busts (that honestly looked just like Fake Fortin at the Quick-Bis); on the marble sign that read, *Le pouvoir réside dans le service* (Power resides in service); and on the columns and domed roof and broken weather vane.

Above all, though, Mom had focused on the bell.

She'd felt a deep attachment to it, having worked so hard to make a replica as her first order of business upon taking over the Historical Society. And her attachment had only grown when the missing bell had mysteriously turned up in the schoolhouse in 1987. She'd known it was the Real Deal right away because apparently the grayish verdigris (that blue-green patina that forms on copper) had revealed a distinctive ratio of tin and copper that was no longer in use—not even for the replica. It was too easy to crack, particularly in cold weather.

With painstaking care, Mom had removed the original bell from the schoolhouse cupola and returned it to its rightful spot in the mausoleum belfry. How the bell had gotten dumped in the Village in the first place was a question Mom never did get an answer to. Nor did she ever figure out what had happened to the original clapper.

So the replica clapper had gone into the original bell, while the replica bell had gone clapperless into the schoolhouse, where Freddie could get daddy longlegs stuck in her hair each year when she put up fairy lights. And Mom had used that summer to write at length about why José Allard Fortin might have requested a bell in his mausoleum in the first place.

It had been nine years since Freddie had last stood this close to the mausoleum. It looked exactly as she remembered. There was the domed white building; there was the original bell with its gray-green verdigris; there were the four busts and the sign and the knee-high fence Mom had insisted on adding because, in her words, *Rambunctious teens cannot be in close proximity to history.*

Fair point, Patty. And your own daughter was living proof of that right now.

There were other new additions too, such as two fountains, some rosebushes, and then the yew hedges that probably *would* make really great kissing corners.

In fact, Freddie hesitated at one such corner because what if Kyle were to decide he wanted to make out? Shouldn't Freddie leave at least one corner clean for such a possibility?

In the end, she didn't. It was just too much fun pouring out corn syrup and then flinging birdseed like rice at a wedding.

Emptying trash bags also filled her with Deeply Criminal surges that she enjoyed way too much. Plastic wrappers, cigarette butts, crushed pop cans—who knew what scandalous chaos she might engage in next?

In fact, Freddie was so proud of the mess she created that she tugged Xena from her puffer vest and captured her masterpiece for all of time.

Snap. Flash! Snap. Flash!

To make the night even better, Kyle called Freddie *Prank Wizard* on three separate occasions.

Perhaps because she was positively effervescent on adrenaline and Kyle's smiles, she decided to take the night one step further.

"I'm going to the dorms," she told Divya. "So if I'm not at the gate when you leave, then wait for me at the cars."

"What?" Divya closed her garbage bag and shimmied toward Freddie. The stench of trash curled into Freddie's nose. "Why do you want to go to the dorms?"

"Because if I can figure out which room Theo Porter is in, then maybe I can get the prank book back."

"By *breaking in*? We've already committed enough crimes here to permanently smear our college applications, thanks."

"I know what I'm doing."

"How?"

"Instincts, Div. Instincts." Freddie reached over a hedge of sunflower seeds and Quick-Bis wrappers to pat Divya's shoulder. "It won't take long, I promise."

"Okay, but what if it does take long? Are you gonna walk through those creepy woods by yourself? You do remember the crows? And then how Laina had her migraine?"

"Yeah, about that." Freddie chewed her lip. "You think she's alright now? Ever since we left the forest, she's been a bit . . ."

"Intense?"

Freddie had been thinking *possessed,* but Divya's word was probably better. "Yeah," she murmured. "Keep an eye on her while I'm gone, okay?"

Then before Divya could stop her, Freddie spun away.

"This is why you always find dead bodies!" Divya hissed at her back. "You have *no common sense.*"

Freddie didn't respond, although she did think this comment was unfair. After all, she'd only ever found one dead body, and it had only been his shoes. Besides, what kind of future sheriff would she be if she was afraid of an old campus filled with rich kids?

After a quick skip along more perfect pathways, Freddie found the dormitories. They were spread out over the original stables, carriage house, and servants' quarters. All three buildings were within sight of the main estate, with its excess of gables and arches and towers . . .

Freddie cut in close to the former stables, creeping toward the first lit room. Xena was once again tucked *inside* her vest because Freddie didn't need to look like a Peeping Tom, thanks. Especially since almost no one seemed to have their blinds closed.

Like, come on, people. Just from a safety perspective, that was silly. And from a Rival-Student-Looking-for-a-Stolen-Logbook perspective, it was *very* silly.

Freddie was almost to the end of the stables with nary a Theo Porter found, when she heard music drifting into the cold night.

I never want to hear you sa-a-ay
I want it tha-at way!

Freddie's expression soured. Ugh, Backstreet Boys. NSYNC was so much better. Everyone knew that, and Freddie had half a mind to throw rocks at the offending room, just so they'd turn off Nick Carter's yowling.

Except that was when Freddie reached the source of the music... and saw who was in the room next door.

Theo Porter.

Dancing.

And not just any dance, either, but the *actual* choreography from the *actual* Backstreet Boys' music video.

A laugh burst from Freddie's lungs. She had to clap a hand to her mouth to hold it in. Xena dropped an inch inside her jacket. *Oh my god, oh my god.* This couldn't be happening. Mr. Perfectly Polished was a BSB fan—and not just a low-grade one, either.

She crept as close to the window as she could get without stepping right into the light pouring from his room. She craned onto her toes, peered cautiously within... But Theo's eyes were closed, and he was totally lost in the song.

You are, my fire! My one, desire!

Loath as Freddie was to admit it, Theo wasn't half bad. Possibly swoony, in fact, with his uniform tie gone and the jacket flung on the bed. (If you could look past the devil horns and forked tongue.)

Prank log, she reminded herself. *Find the prank log*. It took every ounce of self-control that she possessed to tear her eyes away from Theo Porter and not yank out Xena for some blackmail-worthy photos. She searched what little she could glimpse of his room.

Fortunately, he was tidy. Almost too tidy. There were no knickknacks on his desk. No photos or posters on the wall. Just a lofted bed and a desk with a computer and a stack of textbooks...

And at the bottom of the books was a familiar blue canvas spine.

"Bingo," Freddie murmured, a grin splitting her face. She had no idea how she'd get in there, but now she at least knew where the sacred logbook was.

Freddie was all set to turn and bolt for the gate, when the music cut off. Theo paused mid-croon. His eyes opened. He looked at the window.

He looked at Freddie.

For a split second, she simply stood there, gawping uselessly while he gawped uselessly at her. Then he was moving while she was still trapped in place. It was a real slow-motion, life-flashing-before-her-eyes kind of moment.

Even when Theo shoved open the pane, Freddie simply stared. He squinted down at her.

"Gellar?" he sputtered. Fury hardened the lines of his face. "What the hell are you doing here?"

At the sound of Theo's voice, Freddie finally snapped out of her Shutdown Mode. "Mr. Porter," she cried, opening her arms. "Fancy meeting you here!"

"What's going on?" Theo's gaze darted up, down, sideways—clearly estimating if he needed to climb out of the window.

"Do you really want to know why I'm here?" Freddie smiled her boldest smile, and with all the melodrama she could squeeze into her body, she mimicked Theo's dance moves. *"You are, my fire! My one, desire!"* Freddie flung her arms to the sky. *"I want it tha-at way!"*

He looked like he was going to murder her. He lifted a foot onto the windowsill.

But she was already spinning.

Theo's shouts chased after her. Something about "This isn't over!" and yada yada yada. Empty threats, really, since the Prank Squad had already worked their magic.

By the time Freddie reached her friends at the gate (how cool that she could actually call them her *friends,* plural), she was gasping, sweating, and pretty sure Xena's bouncing had left a bruise on her boobs. "I saw the logbook!" she squealed. "I know where it is!"

"Yesssss!" Laina thrust a fist into the air and whisper-shouted, "Lumberjacks, *ho*!" just like the ThunderCats.

The boys chest-bumped, Cat did an impromptu handspring, and Freddie and Divya danced the Macarena. Then, because there was still that pesky risk of getting caught, they pushed through the gate and hurried into the woods.

Where the excitement died.

It was worse than when they'd been doused with cold water at the Quick-Bis. One moment, everyone was as rowdy as a pack of five-year-olds trick-or-treating. The next moment, they were silent and stiff, glancing over their shoulders every few steps.

Laina still took the lead, marching at a speed that left everyone half-jogging to keep up. Not that Freddie minded. Her gut was waking up, and she wanted *out of here*. It felt like cold fingers tickling inside her belly. Like the fog was back and stroking against her neck.

Only once, halfway through the forest, did anyone speak. "Stop looking at me," Laina snapped at Cat.

"I'm not looking at you," Cat insisted, but even Freddie could hear the lie. Because *everyone* was looking at Laina—whenever they weren't wincing into the terrifying trees.

"Bull," Laina muttered. "You're looking at me like I'm gonna wig out again. I mean, not that I wigged out before. You guys know I get those headaches."

"Of course," Cat murmured, and they all fell into silence.

Once back at the cul-de-sac, Kyle asked: "Meet at my place?"

"Sounds good," Luis answered before shutting himself into Cat's car. Laina gave a thumbs-up, and in seconds, only Kyle and Freddie were left behind.

"I just want to make sure the leftover corn syrup is secure," Kyle explained with an angelic grin next to his Jeep.

"Why don't *I* do it?" Freddie suggested. It wasn't that she didn't trust Kyle . . . but, well, she also didn't trust Kyle. "Go ahead and get the car's heater going for me?"

His grin expanded, and while Freddie adjusted a bungee cord in his trunk, the Jeep purred to life. The radio clicked on; "Livin' la Vida Loca" soon blasted out; and Kyle started dancing so wholeheartedly the entire SUV bounced with him.

Confident the jug was secure, Freddie shut the trunk and dusted off her hands. She was just stalking to the passenger door when a sound pealed out.

It cut through the hum of the engine and the muted crooning of Ricky Martin. Distant yet unmistakable: the tolling of a bell.

It was exactly like the bell she'd heard on Wednesday night.

Freddie's skin crawled. A great rip of goose bumps that erupted across her neck and arms. Because that sound had *not* come from the direction of Fortin Prep with its mausoleum bell and presumably bells for class too. Nor had it come from the direction of Berm's downtown where there were two churches.

Instead, it had come from the west, from the forest of the county park, where the only bell even close to the trees was—as recently confirmed—a very, very *not* functional replica bell inside the schoolhouse.

Maybe the clanging is a trick of the wind, she thought as she leaped for the car. *Maybe there's someplace that the wind funnels through that . . . sounds . . . like . . . a bell.*

Yeah, that logic wasn't strong. But that didn't mean there wasn't a rational explanation somewhere to be found. Freddie had heard what sounded like a bell on two different nights now, so all she had to do was pinpoint from *where* it was ringing.

And that, she decided, would be a good task for her Answer Finder self tomorrow.

6

The next day, Freddie scoured the entire Village Historique for any "secret bells" hiding in the buildings while the other volunteers helped Mom assemble the pageant stage. But alas, there were no hidden bells or cymbals or gongs or anything at all that might produce a reverberating *clang!* to fill the forest.

What Freddie did find, however, was that all the fairy lights in the schoolhouse had fallen down. Which was Vastly Annoying, and Freddie blamed Divya for the mess. After all, if Divya had only *helped* Freddie on Thursday afternoon, then Freddie might have done a better job and the wind would not have obliterated her handiwork.

Freddie made sure to point this out to Divya when the girl arrived after lunch so they could finally venture to the archives.

"It is *not* my fault," Divya declared as she marched beside Freddie through the forest. (Yes, this time, they took the proper trail instead of a shortcut.) "And besides, I've already given you Lance for a whopping *two weeks,* so we are more than even."

"Harumph," Freddie replied.

"Harumph," Divya agreed, and for a time they stomped along in grumpy best friend silence. Freddie had her bike and pushed it by the handlebars. Divya had her Birkenstocks, which remained totally improper for the terrain.

Eventually, the silence was too much for Freddie. "Hey, did you see today's paper? The *Sentinel* released the dead guy's name."

Divya made a pained grunt. "Yeah, I saw. It was Dr. Fontana. He took care of my hamster once, you know."

"Oh." Freddie's stomach sank. "I'm sorry. I did *not* know."

"It's alright," Divya said, even though Freddie could tell it wasn't. And she understood why: it was one thing to find a faceless dead guy. It was quite another to find out you knew him. But before Freddie could pull a Dr. Born and ask how it made Divya feel, they reached the archives.

"Oh thank goodness," Divya cried. "I'm freezing. It's heated, right?"

"You betcha," Freddie said in her brightest voice, pushing aside all thoughts of helpful counselor tactics or dead veterinarians. "Gotta keep all those documents at a balmy sixty-five degrees." Mom was very particular about this. Meanwhile, the Bermians had been very particular that these archives *not interfere with the aesthetic of City-on-the-Berme*, so it looked like a woodsman cottage set off from the Village by half a mile.

Although, it was also not a historically accurate woodsman cottage. The lone window beside the narrow front door was framed in bright red paint, making it the sort of place one expected Keebler elves to topple out of rather than historians with advanced degrees.

Mom really liked to complain about that red paint.

Freddie tromped up to the wooden hut. A sign at the side read *Les Archives* and its roof was only a few inches above Freddie's head. This building was—anachronistic or not—her mother's pièce de résistance: a collection of all primary documents regarding Berm's history.

When Patricia Gellar had first taken over as director, it hadn't just been the Village that was a mess with its dilapidated buildings and overgrown paths. There'd also been boxes upon boxes of journals and ledgers and letters just stashed in random garages around town. Including, apparently, Kyle Friedman's garage—although Freddie had forgotten this fact until her mom had reminded her yesterday.

And Freddie had remembered that trip to gather forgotten documents even more vividly when she'd wound up at Kyle's house last night. After leaving the cul-de-sac, the Prank Squad had convened in his family's basement to watch a bootlegged version of *Austin Powers: The Spy Who Shagged Me*. (Bootlegged! Wow, Kyle really *was* such a Bad Boy.)

Laina had finally relaxed into her usual self by then, and she'd even managed to crack a few self-deprecating jokes when Will Ferrell's character had fallen down the hill and been "very badly injured."

"That's what I should have said in the woods," she'd joked. *"Perhaps you could toss me a Band-Aid or some antibacterial cream!"*

Everyone had laughed, Divya loudest of all.

Once Freddie had gotten home again, though, she hadn't been able to stop thinking about the tolling bell. Or of the crows. Or of Laina's scream. Or, most disturbing of all, of the dead guy she'd found in the trees who'd apparently been a vet from Elmore, Dr. Bob Fontana.

The paper that morning had said he ran marathons and had left behind no surviving family members to mourn him. Which meant he also had no one left behind to think, *Hey, that's weird. Why would Bob kill himself the night before he had a long run planned? Maybe I should look into that.*

There was only Freddie to look into it, and although Divya might tease her, Freddie *was* the Answer Finder and she *was* going to get to the bottom of this.

Freddie wriggled her keys from her hoodie pocket, and in moments, the door groaned open to reveal an empty room with an open hatch in the middle of the floor. A ladder slunk down into darkness.

"Wait-wait-wait-wait." Divya's hands shot up. "The archives are underground?"

Freddie's eyebrows bounced high. "What did you think?"

"That this was it." Divya motioned to the interior of the hut. "And that there just weren't very many things inside."

Freddie laughed, head shaking. "There's *tons* of stuff inside! Aisle after aisle . . . And it's all down there." She pointed into the hatch. "As is forced-air heating. So come on. This place gets spooky after sunset."

"Because it's not spooky now?" Divya watched with open skepticism as Freddie hunkered through the hatch. "I mean, I'm sorry, Fred, but this is like something out of a—"

"*Goosebumps*?" Freddie offered. She hit the flagstone floor and fumbled along the nearby wall for the light switch. *Flip.* A series of fluorescent bulbs hummed to life, revealing a long, bunker-like tunnel filled with twenty-one rows of documents.

The only disruption in the curved ceiling and shelves was a central support beam where a legally required emergency phone, first aid kit, and fire extinguisher were fastened.

"No, not *Goosebumps*." Divya's clogs clanked on the ladder rungs.

"*X-Files*?"

"No."

"*Scooby-Doo*?" Freddie was really reaching now.

"No," Divya intoned. Her feet hit the floor. "I was *going* to say *Northanger Abbey*."

"I don't know what that is."

"Freddie! It was my book club pick last October. Did you not read it?"

"Right! *North Hanger Abbey*!" Freddie had *not* read it.

"Northanger." Divya glared as she strutted past. "You're a great disappointment to me."

Freddie cringed. That was fair.

She towed Divya toward the left wall, to where a desk held piles of books and loose papers. "So this is everything my mom could find on nineteenth-century shipping in the area. She came this morning before we set up the stage. And while you study those, I'm going to dig up stuff on . . . well . . . stuff."

"Oh lord," Divya groaned. "I know that face."

"What face?"

"Your *Pee Eye* face. But what you'll find about a murder that wasn't a murder in here, I don't know."

Freddie batted her lashes. "I'll be four rows down, Madame Srivastava, if you need anything. And remember." She shook a finger in Divya's face. "Don't steal records. No documents can leave the archives."

"As if." Divya gave another shudder.

While Divya got to work examining the old tomes, Freddie went straight for the PC near the middle of the room. It took a while to boot up because the beast was almost a decade old and ran on MS-DOS, meaning it had only a super-primitive archival program and no mouse. But Freddie didn't need a mouse to get answers.

She typed in what she needed, exactly as her mom had taught her, first opening the main directory and then the archival software her mom used.

Soon, a blue screen was blinking at her with a menu. Freddie hit *1* on the keyboard, bringing her to a keyword search. Then she typed in *bell* and watched as the computer spat out a list of relevant documents.

It was a lot, and most had nothing to do with the Village Historique but instead referred to bells on various shipping vessels and lighthouses all along the lake's coast. In other words: not useful.

So Freddie narrowed her search to *bell + Berme*.

This was a much shorter list, but perhaps unsurprisingly, almost all of the documents were recent additions to the archives—as in, written and added by Mom since 1980 when she'd commissioned the replica bell for the mausoleum.

There were, however, four journals from the famed blacksmith who'd kept detailed recollections of his bellfounding for José Allard Fortin. After scribbling down their locations, Freddie set off down the aisles. All four were in the same location. All four were *also* in French. However, to Freddie's surprise, tucked next to the diaries was a book titled *The Curse of Allard Fortin:*

How Murder Shaped His Legacy. She'd never heard of it, and with a title like that, it was only natural she'd slide it off the shelf and take a peek.

It was a simple hardcover with a worn black jacket and a faded title in yellow sans serif font. The author's name was listed as *Edgar Fabre,* and when Freddie creaked open the book, she found it had been published in 1949.

After that was a short table of contents.

And after that, a poem.

"Aha!" Freddie thrust up a pointed finger. "Eureka! And gesundheit!"

"That's not what *gesundheit* means," Divya called from several rows over.

Freddie ignored her, hunching forward to study the poem—which she would bet a lifetime's supply of Quick-Bis biscuits was the one Kyle had seen as a kid. Meaning this book must have been one of the many documents once living inside his garage.

And no wonder poor Kyle had been traumatized. The title alone made Freddie's blood run cold.

THE EXECUTIONERS THREE

When northern wind gusts
Through trees bare of leaves,
Take heed and take watch,
For Executioners Three.

Their blood oath is summoning.

First comes the fog,
Rising from the shore.
Once rings the bell:
Cold death is in store.

The Hangsman is rising.

Next are the crows
To block out the sun.
Then twice rings the bell,
To warn everyone.

The Headsman is coming.

Third comes the ice
Wreckt upon the stones.
Thrice rings the bell.
No chance to atone.

The Disemboweler is hunting.

Last is the heat,
A sign it's too late.
No bells are rung
When the Three leave the gate.

The Oathmaster is waiting.

Freddie read the poem three times, her eyes lingering on the parts about bells ringing and crows blocking out the sun . . .

And of course, the part about a hangsman.

With cool detachment she would later be proud of, Freddie set the book on the shelf. "Hey, Div?" She dipped her head out of the aisle. "Can I borrow some paper?"

"Uh, sure." Divya frowned but did tear a sheet of notebook paper from her binder. "Did you find something about the murder?"

"Maybe." Freddie hurried toward her.

"For real?"

"Maybe," Freddie repeated. She obviously didn't think anything in this poem was *real*, but she couldn't deny the similarities between what she'd just read and what had been happening in recent days.

She wanted to ask Kyle if this was the poem he'd seen as a boy.

And she wanted to ask her mom if she knew that this book and its poem were in here. After all, Mom had been the driving force behind the archives. She had built the keyword system that had led Freddie to this poem. So surely that meant Mom at least knew something about this book and where it had come from.

Yet as Freddie twisted to return to the poem so she could copy it down, Divya said, "Hey, do you smell that? It's like the school dumpster after Taco Tuesday."

The hairs on Freddie's neck stood tall. She inhaled, deep and full. Nothing. Nothing.

Then the scent hit her nose. An awful, revolting scent like rotten meat left for days in the sun. And *exactly* like she'd smelled in recent days.

Before Freddie could reply that oh yes, she smelled it, the lights flickered and snapped off.

Divya yelped. Freddie fumbled over to her friend in the dark. She found Divya right as Divya found her.

"Oh god, oh god," Divya whispered. "What's going on?"

"It'll be okay," Freddie whispered back, unsure why she felt the sudden need to be quiet. "Mom was just complaining about the electrical wiring the other day."

"But what if the lights don't turn back on, Fred? How will we get out?" Divya was breathing faster now.

"There's a window at the back. And light *does* come in there. Our eyes will adjust soon enough." Even as Freddie said this with total calm, her gut was kicking into Full Rebellion. A vicious curdling that made her knees weak and the hairs stand so tall on her neck and arms and legs it actually hurt.

Like, *hurt*.

And oh god, now there was that sense of something at her throat. She grappled at her neck with the hand that wasn't holding Divya, half expecting she'd find blood there. That a gaping hole would be spurting arterial heat onto her fingers . . .

But there was nothing wet. And no ripped flesh either.

The lights flipped back on.

Both girls winced at the onslaught. "I'm leaving," Divya rasped, her face ashen.

"Yeah," Freddie agreed. Her heart felt anchored to her intestines. The sense of blood at her neck was fading fast, but not the stink. And not the certainty in her gut that she and Divya should *not* be here. "Grab the books."

"What about the rules?"

"Screw the rules." Freddie started shoving the volumes into Divya's backpack. "We're basically hoodlums now anyway."

Divya nodded. Together, they gathered all the texts Divya needed, before slinging back four rows to grab *The Curse of Allard Fortin*.

Then the girls fled for the ladder, and they did not look back.

"I think that's the fastest I've ever pedaled," Freddie declared as she propped Steve's old bike against a spruce. "Good thing you fit on my handlebars."

Divya winced and rubbed her butt. "I don't know about that. I can feel my tush bruising as we speak. Although, better that than facing whatever was back there."

"Which was what, exactly?" Freddie raised an eyebrow. Now that they were well removed from the archives and the stench, she felt *deeply* foolish. This was not how future sheriffs behaved.

"Ghosts, probably," Divya answered. "Or maybe aliens."

"And I thought *I* watched too much Mulder and Scully."

Freddie swung the backpack of stolen goods off her back, and after carefully removing Xena from her neck, she tore off her hoodie and flannel, leaving only a white T-shirt with her jeans. She was so hot from pedaling. The last hill out of the forest was brutal, but at least the street was now visible through the trees.

"Alright, Madame Srivastava," Freddie said once all was rearranged. "Back on the handlebars you go. Unless you want to walk?" she tried hopefully.

"No." Divya shuddered. "This place is wiggins central, and I want to go home. I can't *believe* you rode your bike here on Wednesday night."

Freddie couldn't believe it either, honestly. And as ashamed as she was for freaking out in the archives, she was also glad she wasn't alone right now. City-on-the-Berme might be her favorite place in the world, but it had lately veered away from fantastic fall vibes toward major murder vibes.

Channel Sheriff Bowman, she told herself. *Channel Dana Scully. You are a skeptic! You are not afraid!*

While Divya grunted and shoved back into the narrow space between the upright bars, Freddie flung a final glance into the forest below.

No such thing as ghosts. No such thing as aliens. No such thing as creepy Executioners from a creepy poem . . .

Her thought didn't finish. Not before her eyes caught on a blip of red. She almost fell over—and Divya *did* fall with a screech.

"Sorry," Freddie called, scrabbling off the bike and half leaping toward the patch of red.

It was a red sports bottle tucked beside a witch hazel.

Freddie slowed to a stop before it. The cross-country team often left water along their routes before their long runs. Other local runners did too, and this was a particularly popular spot because it was the three-mile mark from the Village.

Without touching the bottle, Freddie crouched down so she could study it, her attention homing in on a strip of masking tape attached to the bottle's side.

Wed. run, lap 2, it read in handwritten marker. Then below that and written on the bottle directly was faded black marker that read: *Fontana.*

Dr. Fontana had put this bottle here for his Wednesday run.

Wind burst through the trees, shaking leaves around the bottle—and sloshing the water within. Because it was completely full. Completely untapped. Meaning Dr. Fontana never made it to lap two.

Freddie's muscles moved yet again with cold detachment, this time aiming her hand for Xena's lens cap. Her gut was screaming anew, except now with the familiar burn of her Answer Finder self. She was almost certain she was staring at proof that Bob Fontana's suicide definitely hadn't been a suicide.

Freddie started snapping pictures.

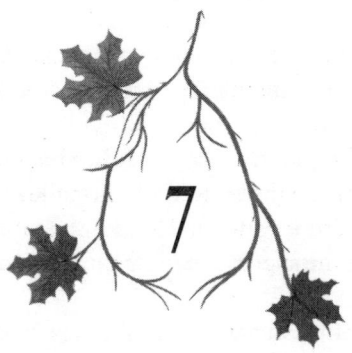

7

After dropping off Divya at her family's brick two-story on Maple Street (and forcing Divya to a blood pact of secrecy regarding the stolen archives material), Freddie shoved herself back onto the bike and pedaled home. Everything in her body ached, but she was *so close*. And there was still one more thing she needed to finish before she could collapse on her bed: her civic duty.

Yes, a life of crime might call to her with its siren's song (that sounded a lot like Lance Bass), but at the end of the day, Freddie was an Upright Citizen and liked being one.

She spotted Bowman's house as soon as she turned onto the street. Bowman lived across from Freddie. Not directly, but two houses over in a white stucco with ivy that covered everything in green—or, at this time of year, in coppery red.

It glowed like the jack-o'-lanterns on everyone's front porches, and when Freddie coasted to a stop in front, she caught sight of a dented Honda Civic in the driveway. Its taillights were still on, and as Freddie rolled up behind it, the car cut off and the driver's door swung wide.

A jean-clad leg slid out along with a pair of black Vans. Then a pale head and navy-striped rugby tee followed. Suddenly Theo Porter was standing in Sheriff Bowman's driveway.

Freddie squeezed her brakes so hard she almost tumbled off. Only a lucky angle let her regain balance—which, thank *god*. She did not need to crash her bike in front of Theo Porter.

He blinked at Freddie. She blinked at him. It was weird to see him without his Fortin Prep uniform. Plus, his hair wasn't so perfectly combed right now, and Freddie had to admit it looked better that way. He had very full, very touchable hair—and *ugh*, why was she even thinking that about the enemy?

"What are you doing here?" He shut the car door.

"I need to see the sheriff." Freddie slung off her bike. "What are *you* doing here?"

"Uh, the sheriff is my aunt." He shrugged like this was the most obvious thing in the world.

And with a swoop in her gut, Freddie supposed it was. *Wow*, what a terrible detective she was. She'd known Bowman's maiden name was Porter, and she'd known that Bowman had a nephew in high school. Except . . . she thought he lived in Chicago.

"How come I've never seen you in town before?" Her grip tightened on her handlebars. He was walking toward her. Not threatening, but still the enemy. Montagues versus Capulets, basically, on fair Verona Beach.

He paused three paces away. "I hadn't been arrested before now, that's why." He folded his arms over his chest, and his thumb tapped his bicep. "Now, however, I am required to eat dinner with my aunt and uncle every night until I graduate. Thank you for that."

"You're welcome," Freddie said cheerily.

Theo's thumb tapped faster.

"The research *does* suggest that eating together as a family leads to better life choices, Mr. Porter."

His lips twisted—although with amusement or annoyance, she couldn't say. And now his thumb was really tapping. "My aunt is a terrible cook, Gellar. Like, I'd rather eat glass shards."

"Good thing for you," said Sheriff Bowman, walking up behind her nephew, "that tonight we won't be having either. We're going to the Quick-Bis."

Theo's hand fell to his side, and for half a second, his eyes squeezed shut. Freddie could practically hear him thinking, *Crap, crap, crap.* But when his eyelids lifted again, it was with the slightest smile. "Well played, Gellar. Well played." Then he angled toward his aunt and added, "You have Spider-Man stealth, Aunt Rita."

Bowman grinned. "I do. And Freddie here has a great poker face." She moved next to Theo. He was half a head taller, but side by side, the family resemblance was unmistakable.

Freddie really couldn't believe she'd missed it. After all, small town. Talky people.

"Hi, Gellar," Bowman drawled. "What can I do for ya?"

Freddie toed out her kickstand, and after making sure the bike wouldn't suddenly topple sideways, she said, "I was hoping to talk to you. *Alone.*"

"Sure. Go wash your hands, Theo."

"I'm seventeen. Not seven."

"I also said, *'Go wash your hands.'*" Bowman's glower, which wasn't even aimed at Freddie, still made her digestive system invert on itself.

Theo seemed to feel the same because he instantly chirruped, "Yes, ma'am," and turned to go.

Although, before his long legs could carry him completely out of sight, he did glance back at Freddie and offer a head-cock that might have been a goodbye.

Bowman folded her arms over her chest—a literal carbon copy of her nephew from two minutes before. It was almost uncanny. The only difference was that Sheriff Bowman was the toughest person Freddie knew, and yet again, Freddie wanted to offer up every slightly naughty act she'd ever committed.

Which was perhaps why what came out next was a complete jumble of disorganized mayhem. Yes, she managed to describe what she and Divya had found in the woods, as well as how they'd found it. And where they'd been too. But she repeated the *why* of it all twice—and she definitely repeated the *where* at least six times.

She also might have mentioned the corn syrup prank.

By the end, Freddie had flung off the backpack full of stolen goods and was all ready to confess to her theft too. Bowman didn't interrupt. She just listened, her face devoid of all emotion and her thumb tap-tap-tapping as Theo's had.

"So let me see if I got this right, Gellar: you and Divya were working at the archives and you took the shortcut home. Then on your way home, you found a water bottle that belonged to Dr. Fontana, and you think he left it there for Wednesday."

"I *know* he did! It literally said, 'Wednesday run, lap two.'"

"Was there a date on it?"

"Well . . ." Freddie's lips screwed sideways. "No, but it had to have been from the same Wednesday. Why would he have left it there otherwise?"

"I have no idea, and I also don't make assumptions." Bowman gave Freddie a thorough, spine-tingling once-over. Then fixed her gaze on Xena. "I see you have your camera."

"Erm . . ." *Squirm, squirm.*

"Did you take pictures of the bottle, Gellar?"

"Uh . . ." *Squirm, squirm.*

"Photographing a crime scene is illegal. I know I've taught you that."

"But it isn't a crime scene. Not yet."

Bowman thrust out a flat hand. "Give me the camera, Gellar."

"But . . ." Freddie frowned down at Xena. She'd only just gotten her sugar wookums back. *And* she'd taken three pictures of Kyle last night, while they'd hung out in the basement. She'd planned to develop the photos tomorrow in Greg's darkroom and then place them on her NSYNC shrine. After all, without photographic evidence of last night, how could Freddie know it had really happened? Had Kyle *really* put his arm around her and said "cheese"?

This must be what an existential crisis felt like.

"Fine," she grumbled at last, and she unhooked the strap

from her neck. But when she shifted to offer it to Bowman, she found the sheriff's eyes had gone out of focus. Like she was staring at something far, far away. Even her lips were parted.

Freddie glanced behind her, expecting to find someone there... But nope. There was no one and nothing beyond the usual autumn street lined with too many jack-o'-lanterns. And when Freddie looked again at Bowman, the sheriff was rubbing her eyes.

"Sorry," Bowman murmured. "It's been a long few days since you found Dr. Fontana. Now, the camera, please? I'll take the film out and return it to you tomorrow. And I'll go after dinner to find this bottle, okay?"

"After dinner?" Freddie's eyes bulged as she handed over Xena. "You can't wait that long! What if it rains and the bottle gets washed away?"

"It's not going to rain." Bowman heaved a sigh. "Listen, Gellar: if that sports bottle is what you say it is, then we've got a real game changer on our hands. But I gave my deputies the night off, *and* I promised Jason I wouldn't ruin dinner unless it was an absolute emergency."

Freddie's spine deflated—and it only deflated further as Bowman proceeded to list twenty-three different reasons that Freddie should not have done what she'd done. "... obstruction of justice, a complete lack of experience, just plain *stupidity,* and oh yeah, you're not a cop. You're just pretending to be one. Want me to keep listing?"

"Please don't," Freddie mumbled. "Besides, I'm not pretending anything, Sheriff."

"And I'm Miss America."

"You could be," Freddie offered. "With cheekbones like those."

"Enough." Bowman's nostrils flared. "You're too much like your dad, Gellar."

Freddie's stomach sank. The stones took hold. Because Bowman never spoke of Frank Carter—even though the man had been her former boss and trained her. Yet Freddie had never known if Bowman's blatant omission was because she knew about the Gellar family unspoken rule—*Thou shalt not discuss Frank Carter*—or if she, like Mom, just had a lot of baggage she didn't want to deal with.

Freddie swallowed. "Is being like my dad . . . a bad thing?"

Bowman's cheeks twitched. She noticeably didn't reply. "Thank you for stopping by, Gellar. I'll return your camera tomorrow. Now, *go home*."

Freddie winced. She wished she hadn't asked about her dad. Shame was bubbling up now, and she hated this feeling. *Hated* it.

Tamp down thoughts, she reminded herself. *Tamp down feelings. Focus on the task at hand.* Did Dana Scully let weird, amorphous emotions get in her way? Absolutely not.

Nor did Sheriff Bowman right before her, who was once more fixing those blue, wiggle-inducing eyes onto Freddie. "One more thing, Gellar: for the love of god, please don't get tangled up in this school rivalry, okay?" She jerked her head toward the house. "I don't need two of you geniuses out there causing trouble."

Freddie sighed. She was flattered Bowman had called her a genius. She was not flattered to be compared to Theo.

"I already knew it was you who'd pranked the prep school— even if you hadn't just confessed."

"Oh."

"And I *told* you, it's dangerous in those woods. Also, Mrs. Elliot's cul-de-sac is private property. Now, go home."

"Yes, ma'am." Freddie watched Bowman leave, disappointment oozing down her spine.

She didn't want to quit the pranks. Not on top of everything else. Although, the more Freddie considered it as she toed in her kickstand and rolled the bike toward the street, the more she decided that if anyone was to blame here, it was Sheriff Bowman herself. After all, *she* had stopped Freddie and Kyle on the lakeshore, and then *she* had let them go.

Yes. This was sound logic. Nary a post hoc fallacy in sight.

Freddie was halfway to the street when a voice called, "Hey, Gellar! Wait."

She glanced back and found Theo jogging toward her. His eyes were wide, and his hair was especially mussed now. Like maybe he'd been running his hands through it for the past five minutes.

She wished it didn't look so good that way.

"I wanted to tell you . . ." He slowed to a stop on the other side of her bike. "Nice job with the birdseed and the trash. It took me and the other weekend students four hours to clean up the mausoleum gardens. It was . . ." He squinted into the distance. "*Inspired.*"

Freddie's lips twitched. "I don't think you're supposed to compliment the enemy." She also didn't think the enemy was supposed to be delighted by such compliments either.

"What can I say?" He bounced a single shoulder. "I expected the BHS kids to completely implode without their prank book. They can't come up with any ideas without that thing. Then you show up and ruin my plans."

This felt like another compliment, and Freddie really wished her heart would stop thumping so much at the prospect.

He is the enemy, she scolded inwardly. *The Mercutio to your Tybalt!* Except, now that Freddie considered it, he looked more like Leonardo DiCaprio than John Leguizamo.

"So you, uh . . . You came out here just to compliment me?"

"Uh . . ." Theo scrubbed nervously at his hair. There was a restless energy to him; he couldn't seem to stand still. "I mean, it was either come find an excuse to talk to you, or spend the next five minutes on the couch waiting for my uncle to come home. And trust me: five minutes is more than enough time for my aunt to list all my faults. In detail. Again."

"You do seem to have a lot of them."

"Hey now." He shoved his hands into his pockets. His knee juddered. "You don't know anything about me."

"I know you drink beer on school nights and drink soda for breakfast. And that *doth* not a wholesome human make."

He gave a weak laugh at her joke, but it was forced. Distracted. There was definitely something else he wanted to say—something that was the *actual* reason he'd come out here.

So Freddie took a page from Sheriff Bowman's book and preserved her silence. Sure enough, after three Lance Basses of quiet, Theo cleared his throat. "So, uh . . . do you really think that Fontana guy was murdered?"

This was not what Freddie had been expecting. "Were you eavesdropping just now?"

"Oh, absolutely."

"Ugh." Freddie shook her head, genuine annoyance unfurling in her chest. "That's one more thing that makes you a Very Bad Human Indeed. And in case you can't tell, I am saying that phrase as a proper noun. So you know it's serious."

Theo's eyes crinkled, and this time the smile was real. So real that Freddie felt her own lips lifting in return.

But she instantly fought off the reaction. Theo Porter was *not* worthy of her smiles; Fortin Prep students were all terrible Montagues—enemy, enemy, *enemy.*

Then again, Theo was also not worthy of her *time,* yet here she was filling it for him. She supposed she might as well exact a teensy bit of revenge.

"So tell me, Mr. Porter." Freddie stretched one leg over her bike. "What does the song 'I Want It That Way' actually mean?"

Red fanned up his neck and face. "I was, uh . . . wondering if you would mention that."

"How could I not? Your performance was . . ." She squinted into the distance. *"Inspired."*

"Huh." Now he was really fidgeting. Hands in the pockets. Hands out. Fingers through his hair. Thumb tapping at his thigh.

"You were almost as good as the NSYNC concert I attended last June."

He scoffed, and somehow the color on his cheeks flared brighter. "Justin Timberlake," he said, "has *nothing* on Nick Carter."

"Well, my favorite is Lance anyway."

"Not an improvement."

"Wrong. Plus, at least all of NSYNC's lyrics make sense."

"No way." Theo's eyes narrowed. "I mean, explain to me what 'Tearin' Up My Heart' is actually about. He's upset when he's with her *and* when they're apart?"

Freddie didn't know whether to be impressed that Theo knew the lyrics or horrified that he could misunderstand them so badly. "He's so in love with her that it rips him apart when he's with her *and* when they're apart—how is that hard to comprehend?"

"Because it's illogical."

"Or you have a heart made of iron."

There it was again—the surprised laugh—and for several heartbeats, Freddie found herself grinning full wattage right back.

Maybe Theo Porter isn't so bad, she thought. Then half a heartbeat later, *NO, WAIT. HE IS THE ENEMY. HE KILLED TYBALT. RED ALERT. RED ALERT. STOP SMILING.*

Fortunately, Freddie was saved from having to get her face under control by a blue Explorer. Mr. Bowman was home. Freddie waved to him. "It would seem you don't require my presence any longer, Mr. Porter."

"Thanks for helping out." Theo ran his tongue over his teeth. "Although, it *is* the least you could do after getting me arrested."

She rolled her eyes. Mr. Bowman was pulling into the driveway now. It really was time to move, yet for some reason, instead of pedaling away, she found herself pinning Theo with her haughtiest stare and saying, "I'm going to get that prank book back, Mr. Porter. Just you wait—you and the rest of your filthy Montague clan won't even know what hit you."

"I have no idea what you're talking about," Theo said. "But if you actually manage to get it back, Gellar, then I will be very impressed."

"Oh, come on now." Freddie pushed into a slow ascent. "You're already impressed by me. You said as much earlier. But don't you worry!"

She pedaled past Mr. Bowman, who waved from the driver's seat. Then once at the road, she released the handlebars and shouted back, "It's only natural to think I'm amazing! *I have that effect on everyone!*"

8

Freddie stayed up too late watching *I Love Lucy* and *The Munsters* with Mom and Steve. She felt *so* guilty about stealing from the archives that she was too ashamed to skulk off to her room early. Which meant Freddie didn't get to explore *The Curse of Allard Fortin* until well after midnight.

But by then, she was so tired all she managed to do was open the book to chapter one and read the title ("My Family's History as the Allard Fortin Blacksmith"). After that, her eyes simply would not stay open any longer.

Alas, her sleep wasn't restful. Instead, her dreams were filled with crows and foggy shapes in the woods. With bells pealing and teenagers screaming.

The final dream she had was of the Hangsman from the poem. Made entirely of shadows, he stalked her through a starlit forest. She ran and ran but never gained ground. The world was a blur of black and white, until at last she reached the Village Historique and ran into the old schoolhouse.

There, she had no choice but to stop. She had no choice but to turn and face the Hangsman. Her dream-heart thundered; her mind was white with panic. Each step he stalked closer—a pulsing mass of darkness—the more she also spotted flames flickering within.

He reached her. His hands stretched out. And suddenly the shadows around him sucked inward, like a tornado forming, but in reverse. Then he was not an ancient executioner at all.

Instead, he was Theo Porter, frowning, restless, and offering her something. Freddie looked down. He held a heart made of iron. "*On n'est jamais si bien servi que par soi-même,*" he said. "This is for you, and only you can break it."

He was wrong, though. Freddie had no idea how to break it. But she took it all the same, cold and beating and glinting in the darkness.

Then she awoke, sweaty. Confused by the morning sunlight flickering through her blinds. Perhaps most startling of all, though, was that she had "I Want It That Way" stuck on repeat inside her brain.

"My profoundest apologies," she croaked to the NSYNC shrine in her corner. Then she dragged herself from bed, turned on her CD player, and hit Play. It wasn't until she heard JC Chasez and Justin Timberlake (backed up by beautiful Lance, of course) that she finally felt safe again.

That dream had felt too real.

When she eventually felt like herself again (it took three full listens of "I Want You Back"), Freddie wandered into the kitchen to turn on the Mr. Coffee—only to find Mom and Steve already sitting at the table. They were both fully dressed, and Mom had even brushed her hair.

"Uh . . ." Freddie said, rubbing her eyes. "Is this a mirage? Am I still asleep? It's not even ten A.M. Why are you two awake?" Mom and Steve were *not* early risers on weekends.

"We thought we'd go to the Quick-Bis for breakfast." Mom smiled with a degree of perkiness that suggested she'd already been up for at least an hour.

Steve matched that smile, and all Freddie could think was *The mind, it reels.* "But you don't like the Quick-Bis," she said to her mom.

"I . . . do . . . *sometimes.*"

Freddie wasn't a fool. She knew when she was about to be manipulated. She also knew when her stepdad was salivating—and that moment was right now.

"Shall we go?" Mom asked, still suspiciously perky.

Grumble, Freddie's stomach replied. Then Freddie's vocal cords answered: "*Fine. To the Quick-Bis we go.*"

This earned a giddy clap from Mom and a soft "Mmmm, biscuits," from Steve.

"Just let me put on real clothes." Freddie shambled back to her room. One pair of tan corduroys, her favorite white peasant top, and an olive-green cardigan later, she headed into the bathroom to put in contacts and brush out her hair (just in case she ran into Kyle).

Five minutes after that, Freddie found herself climbing into Steve's truck, and another fifteen later, they were all sinking into the same booth Freddie had shared with the Prank Squad only two days before.

It was weird.

It was *extra* weird watching her mom eat a biscuit. Steve did so with gusto—actually, he ate three biscuits with gusto—but Mom kept grimacing and muttering about arteries.

Of course, after two bites, she shut up and just wolfed the whole thing down. And when Steve suggested ordering another, she nodded sheepishly. "Please?"

As soon as Steve was out of sight, Mom rested her hands on the table. "I have a proposal," she said, expression Very Serious Indeed.

"Okaaaay." Freddie braced herself.

"I would like you to be in the Lumberjack Pageant."

"Mom, *no*! You promised me I wouldn't have to do it my senior year."

"I'm aware."

"And it's already bad enough you're making me do those *counseling* sessions with Dr. Born. How much more torture can you inflict upon me?"

"Okay, okay, *but*," Mom said, slipping into her terrible *Godfather* voice, "I'm gonna make you an offer you can't refuse." To prove this point, she withdrew a box from her purse. On it were the words *Nokia 3210*.

Freddie gasped. "A phone? I get a *phone*?" She grabbed for the box.

And her mom yanked it back.

"First you have to promise to do the pageant."

Freddie hesitated, arms extended. "Why do you need me so badly?" Her eyes thinned. "I've been begging you for a phone for a year."

Now it was her mom's turn to hesitate. Then she sighed, shoulders deflating. "We still have no volunteers for the actual pageant, Fred, and when I went around this week to make sure the flyers were where I'd put them"—she motioned toward a tiny board of local bulletins and business cards near the soda machines—"I found them all missing. So then I put out more, but look! They're gone again."

Freddie's brows pinched tight. That *was* weird. Had Steve not fulfilled his sneaky Bermian insider duties and spread the word? "But that doesn't mean no one *will* volunteer, Ma. People always enjoy being in the show. People that aren't me, anyways."

"Freddie." Mom placed the Nokia box back onto the table. "Do you want the phone or not? This is a one-time offer."

Freddie's eyes held Mom's for three seconds, gauging if the threat was real. Would Mom really take the phone back if Freddie refused?

Mom made a slow blink that said, *Don't you test me, kid.*

"Alrighty, then." Freddie accepted the box. "You have a deal, Patricia Gellar. One performance in exchange for one phone."

"Great." Mom deflated in her seat. "Pleasure doin' business with you, Frederica."

By the time Steve made it back to the table, Freddie had fully unwrapped the Nokia and turned it on. "What are you going to name it?" he asked as he set down a fresh tray of biscuits and orange juice. "Dana Scully? Buffy?"

"Sabrina."

"Oh, that's a good one." Mom chomped into her biscuit with T-Rex ferocity. "Now can I get a fank-you, pwease?"

"Only if you give me one first." Freddie grinned. Then she turned to the phone, opened up Snake, and embraced the future of video games.

Four hours later, after inputting Divya's number with great ceremony into Sabrina and then, with great whining, helping her mom mend costumes, Freddie found herself at City-on-the-Berme for the first rehearsal of the Lumberjack Pageant.

The Village looked just as it had when she'd been here yesterday to help with stage assembly—except now the schoolhouse benches had been moved before the stage as well.

The sets were also fully assembled, complete with four fake pine trees, a painted lumberjack hut, and a crooked pole right in the middle that would get "chopped down" as part of the performance.

"Oh dear," Mom murmured as they walked into the square to find it completely empty. "This is worse than I feared."

"We're ten minutes early," Freddie offered. "People will come."

"Yeah. Maybe." Mom didn't sound too hopeful. And even the trees surrounding the Village looked worried. Last night's wind had torn down a lot of leaves, leaving patches of the forest barren.

"At least I have you," Mom said meekly. "I suppose we can always make it a one-woman show."

"Frederica Gellar." Freddie splayed her fingers like a marquis sign. "In three acts. See her as a lumberjack with an *outrageous* French accent! *LA BÛCHERONNE!*"

This earned her a grin as she followed Mom toward the stage.

Wind rattled through the old buildings, pulling hay loose from the bales and clattering tools in the blacksmith's hut. All that was missing were some tumbleweeds to really top off that "ghost town" vibe.

Freddie also noticed the fairy lights had fallen off the schoolhouse bell. *Again*. What the actual heck? At this point, she was genuinely starting to think someone might be pranking her.

Before she could stomp off to fix them (*again*), a low voice called: "Patty! Freddie!"

Freddie and Mom whirled about to find Mr. Binder power-walking their way. He wore an orange puffer jacket and pleated khakis. His pale brown skin, flushed red with cold, was the only hint of warmth around.

Once at the stage, he pulled Freddie into a side-hug and gave Mom a peck on the cheek. "Greg printed the scripts for us."

Mr. Binder pulled away and motioned for Freddie and Mom to follow him toward the steps. "He wasn't going to perform in the pageant this year, but . . ." Mr. Binder opened his arms to the benches. "This does not bode well for us. We may need him. I don't suppose you have any friends you could call, Freddie?"

"*No*," Freddie grumbled, hoping he didn't press any harder. The truth was she'd rather swim in the lake during winter than invite her new Prank Squad friends to this.

"Alright, then. The show must go on." With a little shake, he changed from the guy who was a family friend into the guy who always told Freddie her jazz hands weren't good enough. *Sparklier, Freddie! Make them sparklier!*

After hopping the stage steps, Mr. Binder pulled a rolled-up stack of paper from his vest. "I tweaked the script a little this year, if you want to have a look."

"I'm sure it's fine, Jim." Mom didn't even glance at the pages he handed her. She was chewing her lip and staring at the empty Village. Outdoor heaters stood sentry at the end of each bench. They looked defeated with no one at all to keep warm.

"I just don't understand," Mom murmured. "I put up flyers in all the usual places. And it's a small town! People talk!"

"There's still five minutes." Freddie patted her mom's shoulder. "People will come—I'm *sure* they'll come."

People did not come. Literally no one showed up, and five minutes later, after ascending the clattery stairs onto the stage, Freddie found herself standing all alone at the center and staring mournfully down at her mom and Mr. Binder. Her fingers were cold, so she shoved them into her peacoat pockets.

And she couldn't stop dreaming of her lost scarf. It would be so welcome right about now.

"You're such a good sport," Mr. Binder called from the front row. "I'll get Greg and Principal Tamura to come to our next practice, but for now, why don't you go ahead and get . . ." He trailed off. "Wait, Patty—do you hear that? I think people are coming!"

Sure enough, Freddie heard it too: car engines. Lots of car engines.

At first, Freddie thought, *OH MY GOD, THANK YOU, JESUS.* Until the engines cut and voices followed. Voices that—weirdly—sounded like teenagers. Moments later, she could see the people reaching the gate, and although they were very clearly her own age, she didn't know any of them.

Except for the figure at the fore—a lanky, sauntering person with his hands in his pockets and a smirk that bordered on evil.

Freddie darted for the stage steps. "No, no, no." She leaped down two at a time. Gone were any thoughts of missing scarves or torturous pageants. Instead, she suddenly understood exactly how Tybalt had felt when he'd learned Romeo had crashed his party. She flew over the dirt and reached Theo Porter before her mom could.

He grinned at Freddie like she imagined the Big Bad Wolf might: hungry and *very* pleased with himself.

"*What,*" she spat, "are you doing here?"

"What does it look like?" He bobbed his shoulders innocently. "We're volunteering."

"No you're not—"

"Freddie!" Mom cried. "Stop that!" She shoved in close and thrust out a hand. Her eyes glowed with excitement; her cheeks glowed with cold. "I'm Patricia Gellar. Thank you so much for coming. And so many of you, too!"

Theo—curse him—bared a smile that oozed Romeo charm. The effect was only enhanced by his perfectly combed hair, his fitted gray sweater, and his flattering navy fleece jacket.

Boys didn't dress that nicely outside of catalogs. And *oh* how Freddie wanted to destroy him.

"You must be Freddie's mom." Theo shook her hand. "I'm Theo Porter, ma'am. And can I just say how much we *love* your daughter over at Fortin Prep?"

"You do?" Mom's eyebrows popped high. "I mean, of course you do!" She giggled before twisting to Freddie and whispering, "You are officially the best daughter ever. What a surprise!"

Freddie held her tongue. Because what else could she do? She was *not* the best daughter ever, and Theo was obviously up to no good.

Well, over her dead body would he ruin this pageant.

"Oh, Freddie, this means you won't have to play all the roles!"

"Yay," Freddie said flatly, her focus never leaving Theo. To think that only yesterday she'd thought he might be an okay guy.

"And Greg won't have to perform either!" Mom's elated gaze swept over the benches—which now had more than enough bodies to fill the pageant.

Freddie hoped they all got beard hairs stuck to their chins.

"Yay," Freddie repeated. Theo was staring back at her, but instead of murder in his eyes, there was only delight.

"Well, get back up on stage, Traveler Number One!" Mom poked Freddie's shoulder. "You're up first, remember? And"—she lifted her voice, waving a script high—"we need a Traveler Number Two to join her—"

"I'll do it." Without breaking eye contact, Theo grabbed the script. "Lead the way, Gellar."

Freddie spun on her heel and stalked back onstage. There was nothing she could do. Absolutely nothing. Since the Fortin Prep students were volunteers, she couldn't tell them to just bugger off.

God, where was a fire alarm to pull when she needed one? Because obviously all these people weren't here to simply *help*. Theo Porter had something else up his nefarious sleeve, and no doubt it would be very bad for Mom's pageant.

It was, Freddie had to admit, *inspired,* and if she weren't so angry with Theo, she might have been a little impressed.

She skipped up two steps at a time, then strode for the center of the stage beside the not-yet-sawed fake tree. Theo joined her a heartbeat later. He was really smiling now, as were all the other Fortin Prep students, lounging on the benches and looking like they owned the Village.

"Quiet, everyone!" Mr. Binder bellowed. He, at least, looked as discombobulated as Freddie felt. *He,* at least, seemed to understand these out-of-towners were likely up to no good. But he didn't send them away. Instead, he moved onto the stage and proceeded to introduce the pageant, laying out how parts would be assigned (to whomever raised their hand first) and what the goal of the project was (to raise money for City-on-the-Berme upkeep).

Freddie took the opportunity to step in close to Theo.

"Why are you here?" she whispered. Frosty wind pushed against them. It ruffled his hair and made his cheeks and nose pink. Which looked . . . good. Unfortunately.

"I told you." He batted those long, pale lashes of his. "We're just here to volunteer. You see, Gellar, I don't know if you heard"—he bent down conspiratorially—"but we all got arrested last week, so now we have to do community service to atone for our collective sins."

As he was saying this, a thought occurred to Freddie. One that only added to the murder on her mind. "Did you take down all of my mom's flyers?"

"I don't know what you're talking about." He uttered this in a way that suggested he knew exactly what she was talking about.

"Listen to me, Mr. Porter." She closed the space between them. His blue eyes glittered in the afternoon light. This was not the Theo Porter from her weird dreams, offering her a heart of iron. This was a creature of darkness and evil and rich-boy terror.

"If you in *any* way mess with this pageant," Freddie whisper-hissed, "I will destroy you. Do you understand? This event is the most important fundraiser of the year for my mom."

"Understood." He flashed another innocent smile. "But you don't need to worry, Gellar. I told you: we're only here to volunteer."

"And I'm Miss America."

"You could be, with cheekbones like those."

Freddie made a guttural scoff. Theo had stolen that line from her, and now she really, *really* didn't understand how she'd ever smiled at him yesterday.

"Alrighty," Mr. Binder said with a flourish of his script. He turned to Freddie and Theo. "Let's get started, shall we? Today, we will read our lines while I take you through the basic stage directions. Does that sound good?"

"Absolutely," Theo declared while Freddie simply mumbled, "Yep."

"Great. So Travelers Number One and Number Two are a young couple—"

"What?" Freddie recoiled.

"—who have just found City-on-the-Berme after months of hard travel. I want to see relief and adoration on your faces. Can you do that?"

"Absolutely," Theo declared again while Freddie simply chomped down on her tongue. She was doing this for Mom. *For Mom, for Mom.*

Okay, and a little bit for Sabrina too.

"Fantastic." Mr. Binder strode to the edge of the stage. "Begin."

Freddie sucked in a long breath and lifted her script. She could do this. "Thank goodness we have finally arrived—"

"Louder!"

"—FOR 'TIS COLD HERE IN AUTUMN." She was practically yelling now. She lifted her gaze to Theo.

"It's alright," he read. Then he splayed a hand to his chest. "*I* am here to keep you warm, my love."

Oh god. Freddie gritted her teeth. *For Mom, for Mom.* "Look, there's a light through yonder—"

Mr. Binder coughed. "You skipped a part, Freddie! Read it again. *All* of it."

"Just shoot me now, please." She inhaled through her nose. Exhaled through her mouth. Then she read the line again—properly and *loud*. "LOOK, *MY LOVE*, THROUGH YONDER TREES. Maybe 'tis a logging camp. I have heard of a generous man named Allard Fortin here. Perhaps 'tis he?"

Theo's nostrils flared, like he was trying to hold back laughter. "I think you are—"

"Louder!"

"I THINK YOU ARE RIGHT, MY LOVE. LET US APPROACH AND SEE."

"Good." Mr. Binder clapped lightly. "Now you kiss and walk off stage holding hands."

"Wait, *what*?" Freddie rounded toward Mr. Binder. "There's no kiss in here." She rattled the pages at him.

"There most certainly is." He lifted his own copy. "Page two, Freddie."

No, no, no. She tore back the first page . . .

And yes, yes, *yes*. There it was in very simple words: Traveler Number One and Traveler Number Two kiss affectionately.

"But it's just a rehearsal," Mr. Binder said, "so I won't make you do it now—though you *will* have to in the performance."

"Over my dead body." Freddie twisted toward Theo, thinking *surely* he was as horrified by all of this as she was. But he was simply grinning his wolfish grin.

Then, as if all of that weren't bad enough, the crowd of Fortin Prep students seemed to have figured out what was going on. "Kiss her!" one guy hollered from beside a heater. "Right on the lips!" a girl sang from the third row. "Kiss, kiss, kiss!" chanted another, and in seconds, they were all shouting it.

Freddie was definitely going to murder Theo Porter.

Except that as she watched him, his cocky grin stripped away. In fact, he looked uncomfortable, one hand on the back of his neck and the other tapping at his thigh. "I'm sorry," he said after several seconds of this. "Just ignore them and let's walk off stage."

Kiss, kiss, kiss.

Somehow, the fact that Theo was trying to be nice only made Freddie hate him more. Like, he couldn't just flip from being a Bad Human to a Good One in the space of ten seconds. That was not how this worked. Plus, if Freddie walked off stage right now—as Theo was currently twisting around to do—then that would be letting all of the jerks in the audience win.

Kiss, kiss, kiss.

No. *Freddie* was the Prank Wizard here. This was *her* Village Historique, *her* pageant, and those Fortin kids had messed with *her* mom.

"Wait."

Theo was halfway across the stage now. He didn't hear Freddie above all the shouting.

Kiss, kiss, kiss.

So Freddie said it louder: "WAIT."

This time he heard. This time he paused and glanced back. And before Freddie could really consider what she was doing or that her mom was watching or that she might *seriously* regret this once it was done, she kicked into a jog.

Five bouncing steps brought her to him. His forehead creased. "What is it?" he asked. Then he seemed to realize what she was doing—why she was rolling onto her toes and bringing her face to his.

She gave him a split second to pull away. A chance to escape if this wasn't what he wanted. But Theo didn't pull away. Instead he leaned in, and Freddie's lips reached his.

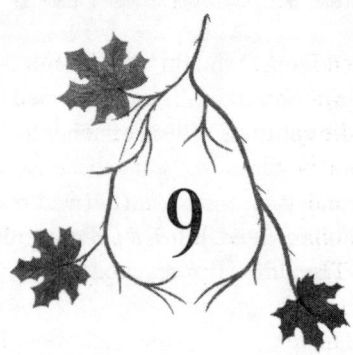

9

The extent of Freddie's love life could fill twelve journal pages. She knew this because she'd done it. Eight pages had gone to boyfriend number one, and four pages had gone to boyfriend number two.

Boyfriend number one (of the whopping eight pages) had been Freddie's next-door neighbor throughout grade school. His name was Andy, and one day, when he had been twelve and Freddie eleven, he had asked her if she would be his girlfriend. She had flushed and said, *Yes,* and for the next six weeks, they had been Very Serious Indeed. Sometimes they'd held hands. Sometimes he had come over for dinner, and twice, they had kissed.

Okay, so the first kiss had only been on the cheek, because Freddie had panicked at the last minute and turned sideways. The other, though, she had faced with determination. It had started as a peck, then quickly escalated into something slobbery that Freddie hadn't liked at all.

However, she'd assumed her distaste for kissing had stemmed from her own inexperience (after all, Andy was allowed to watch PG-13s, and she was not). Plus, she and Andy were fated in the stars—she was sure of it. One day, they would progress to further bases and maybe even get married. That was how love worked.

Until Andy's family moved away, and as devastated as Freddie had been, she'd forgotten about him three weeks later when a girl named Divya Srivastava had walked up to her and asked her if she wanted to join her book club. Who needed boys when Freddie could have a best friend?

Freddie's second boyfriend, who had been awarded only four pages in her journal, was named Carl. It had really only been a summer fling, *almost* worthy of a *Grease* musical number, except that John Travolta was much more interesting than Carl could ever hope to be.

Carl had been fifteen; Freddie too. And when he hadn't been wearing his Fortin Prep Math Camp polo, he'd worn T-shirts that said things like *Never Trust an Atom, They Make Up Everything* or *This Shirt Is Blue If You Run Fast Enough*.

He'd also worn a hoodie that said *The Truth Is Out There* on the back, and that was what had first caught Freddie's eye. A funny guy who *also* liked *The X-Files*.

With Carl, Freddie had had her first real kiss (many of them, actually). Including the kind with tongue. She had seen PG-13s at this point, and unfortunately, she'd learned that the movies made kissing look *way* more exciting than it actually was. When the summer had eventually come to a close and Carl had been getting ready to leave, he'd asked Freddie if she would still be his girlfriend when he went away. She had answered with a polite "No, thank you." (This had not gone over well, as one might imagine.)

After that summer, Freddie had decided that kissing wasn't very interesting—and certainly wasn't for her. Clearly other people enjoyed it, and that was great for them, but she had better things to do with her time. And for two years, she had stuck by this assessment.

Until today.

Until *right now*, when she was kissing Theo Porter.

Of course, she hadn't gone into this kiss planning to Kiss Him for Real. It was just going to be a pop kiss on the lips—a way to show Fortin Prep that she, Freddie Gellar, was in charge.

Except that wasn't what was happening at all.

When Freddie had stretched onto her toes and brought her face to Theo's, he had stiffened. Surprised, certainly, which she would have expected. But when he had leaned in, and when his lips had brushed against hers...

Well, *that* she hadn't expected.

She also hadn't expected her own body to react like it was—as if time were standing still and she'd forgotten how to breathe.

For several long seconds, they just stood there. Her cold lips on his warmer ones, their eyes wide open.

Then Theo gave the softest sigh, and Freddie felt her entire stomach explode. Like a thousand sparklers going off. And when Theo closed his eyes and deepened the kiss, she found herself doing the same. She didn't hear the audience cheering. She didn't hear Mr. Binder shouting at them or her mom squealing.

It was just Theo. And her.

And god, he *knew* where to put his tongue. And his teeth. Why, it turned out the PG-13s hadn't lied to Freddie at all, and if this was what kissing was supposed to be like, then she'd been missing out for two years.

It wasn't until something smacked Freddie's arm that she finally pulled away. She blinked, completely dazed, and found Mr. Binder standing there with a rolled-up script.

Behind him, the Fortin Prep kids were going wild. Standing ovations, wild applause, and a few cheers of "Woodchucks, Woodchucks!"

"That is *quite* enough." Mr. Binder flung a pointed finger to the backstage area. "Get off my stage, and please for the love of god, don't kiss like that in the show."

Heat erupted on Freddie's face. Her chest too. And neck. Basically every organ inside her was awash with shame. Yet just because the kiss hadn't gone according to plan (and just because her whole body was trembling and her lips were, for some inexplicable reason, craving more) didn't mean she couldn't salvage the situation.

She stepped away from Theo, resolutely avoiding his gaze, and with the cheekiest grin she could muster, she swooped a bow.

The Fortin students loved it. Oh, she might have gotten them arrested, but it would seem history could be forgotten in favor of some good old-fashioned hormones.

Her performance complete, Freddie fled the stage. Her mom was waiting for her beside the schoolhouse. "Who *are* you?" Mom asked, eyes bulging with delight. "And what did you do with my daughter?"

"Not now, Mom." Freddie threw up a hand and marched toward a patch of maples, beyond which was the water mill. She needed silence. She needed solitude. She needed *not* to think about Theo Porter and the way he'd tasted.

Which had been like honey, and that made no sense at all. How could a boy possibly taste like honey? The PG-13s hadn't said anything about that.

Freddie groaned, stomping past three scarecrows who all seemed to be laughing at her. She would *not* think about Theo. She would *not* think about that little sound he had made before deepening the kiss. She would not think about the sounds that *she* now wanted to make remembering it all.

Freddie reached the stream that fed both the forge and the mill. It was even colder here than on stage, with burbling water to add a bone-deep chill. She scarcely noticed. She was boiling inside her skin.

Freddie reached the mill's sign. But rather than veer toward the entrance of *Le Moulin à Eau,* she circled around to the back. To where the paddles would spin when the sluice gate was lifted.

It was calm here, the little tributary a mere trickle and the wind more like a gentle breeze. Partially stripped trees towered before her, their fallen leaves now a carpet of amber and gold, while the remaining leaves made a fluttering array of jazz hands Mr. Binder would appreciate.

Freddie's heart thundered in her ears. Her lungs couldn't seem to fill up, no matter how deeply she inhaled.

What the hell had just happened? What had Theo Porter done to her? Surely this wasn't a normal reaction to kissing. Surely having one's fingers grip white-knuckled to one's pants legs wasn't *normal*.

Theo Porter was the enemy. Period. She had kissed him to prove a point. Now the point had been made, and she could stop thinking about him. After all, their gangs were *sworn enemies* of Verona Beach.

She heard footsteps crunch on gravel. She didn't have to turn to guess who was coming.

"Freddie," he said. "I'm sorry."

She didn't know why he was apologizing. He hadn't done anything wrong. *She* had been the one to kiss him.

"It wasn't right for them to egg you on . . . egg *us* on. I should have stopped them."

Slowly, Freddie twisted to face him. Except this was a mistake because her common sense shut down at the sight of him. He was talking to her. His lips were moving, and there were words coming out, but he might as well have been speaking in Klingon for all she understood.

And in that moment, she realized that this was why she had avoided meeting Theo's eyes on stage: it had been simple self-preservation. As if her body had known that if she looked at him directly, Very Bad Choices would ensue.

Theo Porter was absolutely, undeniably gorgeous.

With his hair all wild—and made wild by her fingers. With his face flushed from cold and kissing, with his lips red and his jacket askew, with his slightly panicked expression and restless, weight-shifting energy . . .

In two long steps, Freddie reached Theo. He shut up, his breath catching in a way that made Freddie's gut tighten. Then, in a voice she was certain could not belong to *her*—it was so composed, so matter-of-fact!—she said, "I would very much like to kiss you again. Do you think that would be okay?"

"God, yes," he replied.

And that was all it took. Then his mouth was back on hers, and the sparklers were going off again.

This time, though, Freddie was the one who made the sound. A soft moan that just slid out from her chest and that she couldn't seem to stop. But Theo must have liked it because he made one to match it, and now he was digging his fingers into her back and pulling her more tightly to him.

It wasn't tightly enough, though, so she gripped him too. And the next thing she knew, she was walking backward. She couldn't tell if he was pushing her or if she was pulling him or if maybe it was a mixture of both.

Her back hit the mill. His mouth left her lips. Cold air washed in, and for half a second, she thought he must have come to his senses. He was going to leave now, and this moment between them—whatever it was—would end.

But then his lips moved to her neck, and she realized in a hot, skittering flash of thought that he was *not* leaving. And also, she realized she had *not*, in fact, reached self-actualization on Friday morning.

Now, however, she could most definitely say she had.

Her whole body was covered in chill bumps. She gripped Theo's head again—god, his hair was so soft—and tugged his face back to hers. His lips were swollen. His pupils completely dilated.

But before their mouths could resume what they'd begun, a shout sliced through the air: *"Porter? You over here, man? I got it!"*

Freddie gulped in a breath, trying to process what those words might mean. They had come from the other side of the mill, near the stream.

"Porter?" he called again. *"Come on, man. I've got the key."*

"It would seem," Freddie said, her voice shockingly rough, "that someone needs you."

Theo nodded. He wasn't looking toward the Village, though. Just at Freddie. From her lips to her eyes. Then back to her lips.

It made her want to kiss him all over again.

"You're here for a prank," she forced out. A reminder to herself that they were enemies. Alike in dignity perhaps, but *enemies* all the same. She hated him, and ten minutes ago (or maybe it had been longer—really, where had the sun gone?) she had wanted to murder him.

Again, Theo nodded. "We aren't pranking the pageant." His voice was even rougher than hers. "We just needed . . . something of Mr. Binder's."

"A key?"

"Yeah, a school key. But we aren't damaging anything with it. I promise."

She swallowed. "You . . . probably shouldn't share all of your prank secrets. I'm the enemy after all."

"I know. I just . . ." He wet his lips. "I just don't want you to think I'm a Very Bad Human Indeed. Proper nouns and all."

Ah, it was too much. Having him quote her—having him care. Freddie kissed him again. He growled and pressed into it. Deepened it immediately, kissing her so hard. A clash of tongue and teeth.

But then he was pulling away. *Backing* away three steps, and freezing, miserable air rushed between them. Even the wood of the mill seemed to creak in frustration.

"You're dangerous." Theo ran a hand through his hair. A tiny frown knit his brow. "So dangerous, Freddie Gellar."

She wasn't sure why, but she liked that he called her that. And she liked the way he looked at her too, hungry and helpless at the same time.

Freddie leaned against the mill. "You need to go."

"I know." Theo didn't move.

"If they found out we were . . ." She couldn't bring herself to say *kissing*. She wasn't sure why. It just felt so . . . personal.

Instead, she waved between them and finished, "That probably wouldn't be good."

"No." He swung his gaze toward the Village Square, and he finally, *finally* seemed to collect himself. He stood taller. Smoothed at his sweater and jacket. Brushed at his hair. And then pinned Freddie with a final blue-eyed stare. "Enemies, yeah?"

"Enemies." She nodded decisively. "In fair Verona, where we lay our scene."

"Sure." He smiled, a crooked thing.

"I still have to get that prank book back," she reminded him. Or maybe she was reminding herself. Everything had gone so muddy behind her eyeballs.

"Not a chance in hell, Gellar." Theo stuffed his hands into his jacket pockets. "See you later?"

"Yeah," she murmured, watching him leave. "See you later."

10

Freddie did not go back into the Village Square. She couldn't stand the thought of her mom's squealing or the Fortin students leering. Besides, she was in desperate need of legitimate psychoanalysis, and there was only one person on the entire planet she trusted for that.

Also, she needed to get rid of Lance Bass.

"Take him back." Freddie's eyes screwed shut and she held out the keychain like a toxic dead thing. "I don't want him, Divya. His magic is broken, and now he feeds off only darkness."

"Huh" was all Divya replied. She bent out of her family's front door and examined the short space between porch and street. "Where's your bike? Wait—did you just walk here?"

"From City-on-the-Berme, yeah." Freddie shuffled inside, Lance's dangling face kept as far as possible from her person. "It's only three miles on the park path."

"Yeah, but . . ." Divya frowned at the sky before shutting the door. "It's, like, super dark outside and there might be a murderer on the loose."

"I have bigger concerns, Div." Freddie rubbed the side of her face. "Please just reclaim Lance. I am in great distress."

Divya's eyebrows shot high, and for the first time since Freddie's arrival she took a long, hard look at her best friend. Then her eyes locked onto Freddie's neck, and her jaw slung low.

"Oh. My. God." She grabbed Freddie's chin and tipped it up. "Is that a *hickey*?"

Heat ignited on Freddie's face. She nodded miserably. "Probably."

"Oh, my dear Honey-Baked Ham, let's go to my room." Divya laced her fingers into Freddie's and towed her out of the foyer, up the carpeted stairs, and into her bedroom, where sounds of Nirvana drifted through the wall from her brother's room.

"Take Lance. Please, I beg of you."

"Fine." Divya snatched him back and pushed him into her own pocket. "Though it's your loss, Fred."

Once the door was shut, Divya flung herself onto her bed and Freddie flung herself onto the floor. Face down. Nose into the carpet. "I've made a huge mistaaaaake, Divya."

"How?" Bed springs creaked as if Divya were shifting positions. "I thought you were madly in love with Kyle. Surely making out with him is what you want."

Freddie moaned and covered the back of her head with her hands. "It wasn't Kyle I made out with."

"Wait, *what*?" A thump shook the house. Suddenly Divya was on the floor beside Freddie and trying to peel back Freddie's hands. "Who the heck did you make out with?"

Freddie groaned into the carpet.

"You don't *know* anyone, Frederica Gellar." Divya tugged and tugged. "Tell me right this instant who you made out with!"

Freddie curled into a sideways ball. "It's the enemy," she whispered to her knees. "The Leonardo DiCaprio to my Claire Danes."

"The . . . Leonardo?" Divya's voice pitched upward in confusion. "I don't understand—"

"*Theo Porter*, Divya. I made out with Theo Freaking Porter."

Divya gasped—a great burst of air that was the loudest gasp Freddie had ever heard. Enough so that she thought Divya's lungs might have seized and CPR was necessary.

Freddie stretched out, all ready to use her best *Baywatch* lifesaving techniques . . . only to find Divya was not in need of assistance. Oh no, Divya was lunging in close, grabbing Freddie's wrists, and now pinning them to the sides of her head.

"*Please,*" Divya said, "tell me this is a joke."

Freddie cringed and shook her head.

"So you actually kissed Theo Porter? *The* Theo Porter from Allard Fortin Preparatory School? *The* guy who dumped water all over us on Friday?"

All Freddie could do was nod. And nod some more while Divya continued to list all the reasons Theo Porter was a Very Bad Human Indeed.

"*The* Theo Porter you got arrested last Wednesday? *The* Theo Porter that's the sheriff's nephew—"

"Wait, you knew about that?"

"Everyone knows about that."

"I didn't."

"Because you're a terrible pie."

"PI."

"Whatever." Divya released Freddie's wrists, and pushed back onto her haunches. "You can't tell anyone about this, Fred. We *just* made some actual friends outside of the book club, and if they find out what you've done, they'll ditch us."

"I know."

"And I really like Laina, okay?"

"I *know.*" Shame coiled in Freddie's lungs. "And I don't want to screw it up for you and President Steward."

"Good. Thanks. That means you haven't told anyone about this, right?"

"Um . . ." Freddie gnawed her lip. "Actually, a whole swarm . . . or is it a nest? Doesn't matter. A bunch of Fortin Prep students saw us and—"

"Nooooo, Freddie. Say it isn't so."

"—but, they didn't see *all* of it." Pushing Divya back, Freddie hauled herself into a sitting position. The room spun. "All they saw was the part that looked like a prank. By *me.*"

Divya wagged her head. "Just tell me everything that happened, please."

Freddie's head lolled back. She stared at Divya's ceiling, covered in glow-in-the-dark stars. "So my mom is making me do the Lumberjack Pageant, right? And today was the first rehearsal..."

It was fully night by the time Freddie left Divya's. She called her mom (on Sabrina!) to tell her where she was, and then she set out for the brisk walk home. It led her through downtown Berm, where people hurried by, shivering on the sidewalks. A marquis sign on the Fortin Theater advertised a screening of *Scream* for Halloween. Lights flickered inside the tens of jack-o'-lanterns, and a smell like cinnamon filled the night.

Normally Freddie loved this walk. Right now, she was too focused on her own internal miseries to really notice. Why had kissing Theo Porter seemed like such a good idea at the time? Where had her logical detective brain gone?

Freddie hurried past Fortin Park with its brass statue of the second Allard Fortin (André) and a new scattering of fallen maple leaves. Then past Mr. Binder's shops: Pottery-a-Plenty (closed), the Frame & Foto (also closed), and West End Wine (open and crowded). A block after that, and Freddie left downtown behind. She had just reached the intersecting road that would lead to her house when she spotted a figure farther on, hunched and hustling.

Freddie instantly knew who it was: Mrs. Ferris—who also happened to be Sheriff Bowman's mother and lived a few doors down from her.

And actually, now that Freddie was considering it, that also made Mrs. Ferris Theo's grandmother.

Wow, she *really* should have made all these connections sooner. For such a small town, people really weren't talking enough.

Every day, Mrs. Ferris power-walked around the neighborhood. *You don't stay healthy at age eighty-seven otherwise,* she liked to say. Then she'd ask if Freddie had a boyfriend—or a partner of any gender because she was Very Progressive Indeed—and when Freddie would inevitably say no, Mrs. Ferris would laugh and say, "Good. Stay away from love. I went through three husbands after my Mr. Porter died, and not a one was worth the hassle. Plus, my son gave up everything for love, and look where that landed him."

Freddie had never actually known where that landed him, since Mrs. Ferris's son (and presumably Theo's father) had never lived in Berm. But now, Freddie had many questions—although they would all have to wait, since this wasn't Mrs. Ferris's usual strolling time and she was moving at three times her usual pace.

In a heartbeat, Freddie's gut started growling. She kicked into a jog. "Mrs. Ferris!" she called. But the wind gusted Freddie's words away.

So she just dropped her head and pumped her legs harder until at last she'd caught up to the ancient lady farther uphill (and well past Freddie's own house now). "Mrs. . . . Ferris," she panted, slowing to a walk. "Are you . . . all . . . right?"

Mrs. Ferris didn't even glance at her. "Frederica, you should get home."

"So should you." Freddie dragged a sleeve over her forehead and wiped away sweat—though the wind was doing a serviceable job of drying it. "It's after nine. Way too dark for a walk."

The old lady didn't respond to this. Instead she asked, "Is the old path to City-on-the-Berme still there? The one that cuts through at the end of this street?"

Freddie's face scrunched up. "Yes, but it's not lit. And it's also not safe."

"Doesn't matter, doesn't matter. I'm already too late."

"Late for what? Mrs. Ferris, please." Freddie grabbed for the old lady's arm. "Stop walking." Freddie's fingers closed around

Mrs. Ferris's jacket, the down compressing until she reached a feeble elbow.

And the woman finally paused. She turned her wrinkled face toward Freddie. "I *can't* stop, don't you see?"

Freddie definitely didn't see. "Mrs. Ferris, that path is completely dark at night."

"Yes, yes. I brought a flashlight." Her eyes homed in on Freddie's face again. "But you need to go on home now, Freddie. It's not safe out right now." With far more strength than Freddie would have thought possible, Mrs. Ferris yanked her elbow free and set off up the street once more.

"Wait!" Freddie cried, desperate now. She launched after Mrs. Ferris. "I know it's not safe. That's why *you* should go home too."

Mrs. Ferris's face folded inward. "No, Freddie. You just have to trust me. Now go on home before it's too late."

"Let me give you a ride," Freddie begged. Yet Mrs. Ferris didn't slow, and Freddie hadn't really expected her to.

With a gulp, Freddie spun around and aimed once more for home. She needed help. Her stomach felt like it had tentacles, and they were squeezing the life from her lungs. She would never be able to convince Mrs. Ferris on her own, and she couldn't justify tackling an old woman.

In seconds, Freddie skidded to a stop before Sheriff Bowman's house. But the lights were off and no cars filled the driveway. So, she shoved once more into a sprint, and moments later, she slung through her own front door and shouted, *"Mom! Steve!"*

Steve's head popped out from the kitchen. "What is it, Fred?"

"I need to take . . . your . . . truck." She was gasping for air—partly from exertion, but partly from fear. "It's Mrs. Ferris. She's walking up toward the park trail, and she's being really weird. Can I please take your truck?"

Instantly, Steve abandoned whatever he'd been doing and strode toward her. "Let's go."

Freddie had never loved her stepdad more.

By the time they'd backed out of the driveway in his Silverado, Freddie had managed to offer a slightly coherent explanation of Mrs. Ferris's behavior—and Steve had also started to panic along with her. "She's always been kooky, but this could get her killed. The trail entrance is almost a mile away, and people drive really fast on that road."

Freddie nodded. She wanted to puke. Her gut was screaming at her to hurry. That she was probably already too late.

She couldn't stop thinking of her dreams from the night before. And while sure, she knew dreams were not reality (because life was not *The X-Files*), dreams *were* manifestations of real-life fears rooted in real-life problems.

A problem such as Mrs. Ferris heading toward a forest where someone had been murdered.

In a squeal of tires and a cough of exhaust, Steve veered onto the main road. Freddie strained to see ahead, but all the blips of light beneath the streetlamps were empty. There was no one on the road, and soon enough the truck had zoomed the full mile to where the trail began.

But still Mrs. Ferris was nowhere to be seen. Steve yanked up his parking brake, and the truck sputtered into silence before the trail's shadowy entrance. "She probably went down there." He kicked open his door and hopped out. He had to yell over the wind. "I'm going to look for her, and I want you to call Rita!"

Freddie nodded. "Be careful!" she shouted, already plugging in the number to the police station—and cursing herself for not having done so sooner. She wasn't used to having Sabrina.

"Pick up, pick up, pick up," Freddie murmured, her knees bouncing like crazy. "Pick *up*!" No one did. She got the station answering machine.

Which left her calling 911.

Yet before she could hit Send on that call, her phone screen lit up.

Steve.

"Yeah?" she said after hitting the answer button.

"I found her, Fred." Wind roared into the phone. "She's unconscious, just beyond the tree line. Someone . . . or some*thing* attacked her."

Freddie's breath choked off. "I'll call nine-one-one right away."

"Do it. And let's hope we're not too late."

RISING

Theo Porter wasn't in the mood to watch his fellow students get drunk again. Yet here he was on the lakeshore, sitting on a piece of driftwood, freezing off his ass, and wishing he hadn't come.

Every one of these people—Davis, Kelly, Mark, Tiana, and all the rest—had gotten arrested last week. Yet not a one of them seemed to care, because their rich parents could wipe their records clean with a bit of cash.

Theo didn't have cash. In fact, the school was currently reviewing his scholarship, and any day now, he was going to find himself back in Chicago. Back in his dad's crappy apartment with the weight of the mysterious favors his dad had called in to get Theo a full ride at Allard Fortin.

It would all have been for nothing.

And that was just one more crappy thing: if Theo moved back home, then it would be the final proof that he was a screwup. Ever since Mom had died, he and Dad had both been stuck on this one-way train to ever-expanding failure. This would be that final shred of proof.

Because no way in hell was Theo going to get a full ride to the Northwestern journalism program now—not with this arrest record to haunt him.

Madison joined Theo on the log. The wind off the lake pulled at her thick corkscrew curls. Her skin, almost as dark as the sky overhead, gleamed beneath the moon. She had the tolerance of someone twice her size, and the one bottle of grain alcohol that Garrett had brought was, apparently, not doing the trick. She looked as pissed as Theo was about being here.

"Cigarette?" she offered, holding out a box of cloves.

"Sure." Theo didn't like smoking, but sometimes, you just needed something that killed you a little.

She lit it for him, and together, they sucked their lives away. It burned Theo's throat. Clove-flavored death.

"Not drinking tonight?" Madison asked, eying the ruckus twenty feet away. Davis had insisted on a small bonfire, even though Theo had told him it was a mistake.

"No." Smoke twined between his teeth as he spoke. "Not tonight."

"Not feeling it?"

"No," he said, even if that wasn't true. He'd worked hard to cultivate an image. He was one of them; he belonged here; he too lived a life free from consequence.

Madison flicked ash onto the beach. "I heard you made out with that Berm High chick." She grinned sideways. "Trying to break her heart?"

Theo didn't answer that question. He just drew in another long drag and held it there. Smoke poisoning his lungs and shredding his tonsils.

The truth was, he had no idea what had happened between him and Freddie Gellar on that stage. And he had no idea what had happened between him and Freddie Gellar at the water mill either. He knew absolutely nothing about her, yet he'd barely thought of anything else for the past three hours.

Which wasn't right. She was the enemy. She had gotten him arrested. She was the reason his entire future had dried up in a single night.

He was supposed to hate her for that. It made no sense to him that he didn't.

Theo exhaled, a haze to hide the dark waves and darker sky. Beside him, Madison fell into silence. He appreciated that, and they reached the ends of their cigarettes without conversation.

"Give me your cig," Madison said, after rubbing hers out in the cold sand.

"Why?" Theo snuffed his out. "What're you going to do with it?"

"There's a trash can by the cars." She smiled slightly. "Don't wanna litter and all that."

"I'll take it, then." Theo plucked her cigarette from her hand and pushed to his feet. "I want a walk anyway."

"Thanks," she called after him. He didn't respond. Tonight, words just weren't worth the effort.

Theo aimed for the dark trail that led to a nearby abandoned logging road. Here, the park's trees hugged close to the shore, and soon pines crossed over him.

He didn't know how Davis had found this particular spot. He also didn't know how Garrett had gotten the grain alcohol. Two months ago, when he'd still been new here, Theo would have panicked at that. He couldn't stay on top if the popular kids found other sources for their booze. But now . . .

Now, none of it mattered.

Theo tromped over pine needles. The full moon leeched the woods of color and depth, but he had no trouble seeing the way. He wondered what Freddie was doing right now.

Theo reached the logging road and the cars, his own dented Silver Sweetheart (still running, but not worth fixing) and Tyson's brand-new Wrangler. Beyond them, Theo found the trash can. It stank like death. Like someone had left a carcass in there to slowly decompose.

Except when he actually lifted the lid to drop in the butts, he found the metal canister was empty.

Cold snaked down Theo's spine. He thought back to Wednesday night. To the baby raccoons and the figure he'd seen by the road.

There were noises in these woods now too. Hard to distinguish against the ceaseless wind, but there all the same. Rhythmic. Steady. Someone was walking this way.

A scream split the forest. Theo jerked toward the sound—it was so loud, so bloodcurdling and close. A woman's vocal cords stretched to their ends. And deep, *deep* in the back of Theo's brain, a single word unfurled: *Come.* So without thought, Theo went.

He strode into the forest, moving toward the scream. Moving toward the strange word that had fired from neurons at the base of his skull. It coiled around his muscles and commanded them.

His feet thrashed over unseen roots and saplings. His ankles rolled. Branches sliced at his cheeks, and the screams grew louder with each step. Until finally he ran into Felicia, sprinting through the pine trees toward him. At the sight of Theo, she screamed again.

"Body!" she shrieked. *"There's a body in the woods!"*

"No head," Tyson stammered, stumbling up behind her. His enormous eyes gawped at Theo. "He's got *no fucking head.*"

Of course not, said the voice in Theo's mind. "Go," Theo told the others. "Go back to the car."

Felicia and Tyson needed no urging, and though the front of Theo's brain told him he ought to chase after them, the *back* of Theo's brain thought otherwise. Those neurons would not let his body comply, and his feet just kept on carrying him into the trees. Over more unseen roots and saplings, through more razor-sharp branches.

Until at last, Theo stumbled from the trees and into a moonlit clearing, where a massacre met his eyes. Blood everywhere, sprayed on tree trunks, splattered across the fallen leaves. And at the center: a rigid body leaning against a fallen pine.

A body without a head and a bloodied axe several feet away.

Just like that, Theo's cool detachment fled. The impulse that had commanded him released, and the reality of what waited right there rammed in.

He staggered backward, unable to control his stomach. His vision blurred. He shouldn't have come—why had he come? And now other people were running this way. He could hear them approaching. They shouldn't see this. *No* one should see this.

"Stay where you are!" His voice cracked. He tried again, louder. As forceful as he could make it. *"Don't come this way! Go back to the cars."*

Then he saw Madison through the trees, and beside her was Davis—a hulking linebacker whose pale face glowed like the moon.

"Go back!" Theo shouted again, and this time he hurried toward them. "It's not safe!" He reached Madison, who was asking, "What is it? What happened, Theo?"

Theo shook his head, pulling his phone from his pocket. He should have done this from the start. He never should have followed those screams.

"Nine-one-one. What's your emergency?"

"There's a body," Theo said, and Madison clapped a hand to her mouth. "It's by the lakeshore in the county park—"

Theo didn't get to finish. Davis slammed into him, so hard Theo crashed to the ground. The phone went flying through the woods.

"What are you doing?" Davis roared. He climbed onto Theo, drunk and wild-eyed. "You can't call the cops!"

"There's a body in the woods!" Theo tried to shove off Davis, but Davis was twice his size. He just buried his knee in Theo's chest.

"We're out here drinking!" Davis shoved harder. "D'you wanna get us all arrested again?"

Of course Theo didn't want to get arrested again. But there was a *body in the woods*. Before he could bellow this at Davis, red brake lights flooded the forest.

Which meant Tyson must be fleeing.

Theo used the moment—the brief surprise on Davis's face—to swing. A hard hook to the jaw, then a bucking of his hips. Davis tipped sideways, enough for Theo to flip him onto his back.

"Call nine-one-one," he told Madison in the brief moment he had before Davis swung. Before Davis's fist connected with Theo's nose, and suddenly Theo was punching back too.

He and Davis rolled. They writhed. They clawed and wailed and Theo lost all concept of how many hits he landed—or how many hits he took. It wasn't until a shrieking Madison shoved between him and Davis, and then Garrett thundered in too, that Theo finally managed to break free.

He dragged himself away, limping and panting. Everything was on fire. His face, his ribs, and above all, his brain.

There was a body in the woods. A hundred yards behind them—a fucking body with no fucking head. And something still sparkled at the nape of Theo's neck.

"The cops are coming." Madison pitched her voice over Davis's swears. "*I* called them," she added, "and we need to leave before they get here. But your car is the only one left, Theo. Are you good to drive?"

"Yeah," he muttered, even though he wanted to leave Davis here. Even though he *wanted* to see that rich asshole get arrested all over again and deal with some fucking consequences for once in his life.

But Theo knew that would only make his own life hell, so after wiping blood off his face and knuckles, Theo shambled to his beat-up Civic and drove everyone—including Davis—back to campus.

Not directly, though, because he was terrified someone might notice them. Or worse, someone might follow.

Someone willing to use an axe on another person. Someone who maybe had seen that Theo and the others had been there.

Only when Theo knew there were no cars behind them, no cars ahead, no cars *anywhere,* did he drive everyone to Allard Fortin Preparatory School.

He didn't sleep that night.

11

Freddie dreamed of the Hangsman from the poem again, but this time, he was not alone. This time, he hunted with a companion. Through woods of darkness and starlight, the Hangsman held a rope of flames—and his partner held an axe gleaming with fire.

The Headsman was now hunting too.

Heat pulsed against Freddie. No matter how far ahead she seemed to run, she couldn't escape it. Worse, she was also not alone. Mrs. Ferris stumbled alongside Freddie, and though Freddie tried to get the old woman to run, Mrs. Ferris would never move faster than a sluggish crawl.

"Please," Freddie begged, over and over again, towing at the old woman's bony elbow. "I didn't mean to leave you behind, Mrs. Ferris. I didn't know you would get hurt. *Please,* if you would just move faster, then we can get away."

But Mrs. Ferris wouldn't speed up.

Not that it mattered in the end. Neither the Hangsman nor the Headsman caught up until Freddie and Mrs. Ferris were at the old schoolhouse, and like the night before, when Freddie turned to face them, the shadows peeled away.

Then the two figures converged into one: Theo.

He held out his hand, upon which gleamed the heart. *"On n'est jamais si bien servi que par soi-même,"* he told Freddie. "This is for you, and only you can break it."

"Break what?" Freddie glanced sideways. "Your grandmother

told me . . ." Freddie's voice died.

Mrs. Ferris was no longer there. The schoolhouse was empty. The night sky shone outside.

"You, Freddie," Theo said. "Only you can break it."

"Oh." She angled back to him, frowning, and as she'd done the previous night, she cautiously accepted the heart of iron.

It beat against her fingertips.

This time, though, she realized she *did* know how to break it. Still holding the heart, she stretched onto her toes and she kissed Theo. Like she had at the old mill. So hard it left Freddie's dream-heart hammering and her dream-lips raw. And *this* time, when Freddie awoke drenched in sweat, it was for a completely different reason than the night before.

Her mouth tasted of honey.

It took Freddie twice as long to get ready that morning. To shower. To pick out clothes (four trial outfits before she finally settled on jeans, a pistachio turtleneck to hide the hickey, and her winter coat because it was getting cold outside). She needed three tries to get her left contact onto its respective eye, and she hadn't even started to dry her hair when Divya showed up to walk to school together.

"Just go without me," Freddie said wearily, and Divya—who had never been tardy in her entire life and was determined to graduate with an untarnished record—complied. There was still something Freddie needed to do before school, while the house was empty.

Because Freddie had finally remembered where she'd seen "The Executioners Three" before: in the darkest corner of the family basement, where a secret box of files hid.

A secret box that Freddie's mom didn't know Freddie knew about, and that Freddie had only ever looked at once, when she was nine years old.

She'd been pretending to be Nancy Drew—specifically Nancy Drew in *The Secret in the Old Attic*, except that her house didn't have an attic, so to the basement she'd gone. There, she'd scoured and examined and searched for clues about deceased soldiers and missing musical scores.

What she'd found instead was a cardboard box labeled *Frank Carter, Desk*. Freddie had of course recognized her dad's name, and in an instant, all thoughts of Nancy Drew had fled. Because right here were answers. Right here was her chance to maybe learn something without opening leaky tear ducts or clogging up throats.

With nine-year-old enthusiasm—and definitely a spike of guilt she had to punt aside—Freddie had torn back the box's flaps, ignoring all the dust and swatting away the nest (or was it a swarm?) of tiny spiders that had taken up roost within.

She'd found legal pads, a set of keys, a Rolodex, a stack of newspaper articles and printouts, and a bunch of pens that didn't write anymore. She'd also found her dad's badge, gleaming and cold. She would have pocketed it right away if she hadn't been afraid her mom might one day discover it missing. Although, while Freddie had sat there exploring the box, she *had* fastened it to the pocket on her T-shirt.

She'd liked the weight of it, and she still remembered how it had felt hanging there.

At the bottom of the box, underneath all the files and pads, Freddie had found the biggest surprise of all: a faded photograph of Dad holding her on the day she'd been born. He'd had a beard then, and he'd been grinning like the happiest man who'd ever lived.

For the next twenty minutes, Freddie had simply stared at that picture, trying to conjure memories of his face. She'd had a handful of her own photos with Dad in them, but he was never smiling—at least not like he'd been here. In all of *her* photos, he'd looked vaguely haunted. Vaguely lost.

Which was the way he lived in Freddie's memory too. She couldn't summon him—not precisely—but she could summon the way it felt to be around him: like he was quiet, withdrawn, and with his mind focused anywhere *but* on the people right beside him.

Freddie hadn't liked how the photo had made her feel. The cavernous shame. The hardening of her intestines like concrete had been poured in. Some heated anger too, because this guy in the photo wasn't her dad. Her real dad in all the ways that mattered—that was Steve, and it felt . . .

Well, disloyal to even wonder about the guy who hadn't stayed when she had two amazing parents who had.

And it felt even more disloyal to break the unspoken family rule regarding Frank Carter.

So Freddie had decided this was one area where she didn't want to be the Answer Finder any longer. Where she didn't *want* to open Pandora's box. So she'd closed the literal box, and she'd never gone back into that corner of the basement again.

Tamp down thoughts. Tamp down feelings.

If not for Sheriff Bowman's comment about her dad on Saturday, Freddie might never have come to this box again. But the comment plus the poem at the archives—they had finally collided in her brain in a great *Aha! Eureka and gesundheit!* moment.

Nine-year-old Freddie hadn't cared about all the weird documents; only the picture of Dad and his badge had held her attention. But seventeen-year-old Freddie knew it was the other stuff that might actually be important to her.

So she focused on the task at hand.

She dumped the box's contents onto the cold concrete floor. Newspaper clippings, Xeroxed articles, and dot-matrix printouts with the edges still on stared up at her.

And there it was: the poem from *The Curse of Allard Fortin*—exactly as it had looked in the book, because this was a Xeroxed copy. It was old, yellowed, and folded to the point of being crumpled, but it was definitely a copy of what Freddie currently had hidden in her bedroom.

Freddie's hand started to shake—just a slight tremble—as she flipped the paper over. On the back of the sheet, her dad's tiny, slanted handwriting stared up at her.

Dreams came again, it read. *Always the same. The Village Historique. Ghosts hunting.* Then below that: *Edgar didn't die?*

Freddie sucked in sharply. She'd been having dreams too, which, in and of itself, didn't mean much. After all, the poem had strong imagery, so it was totally natural for those images to crop up during a REM sleep cycle . . .

But the name Edgar? *That* was worth digging into, since it was the same name as the author of *The Curse of Allard Fortin*.

Freddie set aside the poem and turned to the next documents. They were newspapers, all dated October 1987, the year and month during which Frank Carter had died.

In fact, the anniversary of his death was only eight days from today. October 26. A day that always coincided with final preparations for the fête—meaning a day when Mom would always throw all her focus on the task at hand.

Like mother, like daughter.

Freddie stared at the headlines of Dad's collected articles. They were all toe-curlingly familiar: "Wild Animals Abandoning Local Forests" read one. And another: "Thick Fog Leads to Three Car Accidents."

One headline, though, was especially gruesome and familiar: "Suicide by Hanging in County Park." It described an unidentified corpse discovered near the beach. Other than reporting the victim's sex (female) and approximating her age (thirty-four), there were no leads as to who the person might have been. Police were, on that day in 1987, asking for people to report any missing persons.

Please call Sheriff Frank Carter, it said at the bottom, *with any leads. Anonymous tips accepted.*

The Xeroxed articles and printouts Freddie studied next had similar headlines—except that they weren't from 1987. They were all dated October 1975. Freddie's breaths shallowed out as she skimmed each one. At some point, her mouth went dry too. She kept swallowing.

First 1975, then 1987, and now in present day, there had been intense fog, lots of roadkill . . .

And hangings.

BODY FOUND IN COUNTY PARK

Newly elected sheriff Frank Carter was called to his first crime scene this weekend after a jogger discovered a body. Carter has released no details except to say the deceased was not local and appears to have died by self-inflicted wounds. Foul play is not suspected.

An interview with the person who discovered the body (and who has asked to remain anonymous) indicates the victim hung themself.

Three people had died by hanging since 1975. That felt way too big to be coincidence.

The house vibrated. A squeal split the basement, and Freddie's heart lurched. The garage door was opening, which meant Mom or Steve was home. She could *not* be caught down here.

With frantic speed, she shoved the papers back into the box and shoved the box back into its shadowy corner. She raced upstairs and slipped out the front door without ever seeing who was home and without ever being seen.

Freddie had more work to do.

By the time Freddie finally reached school, her hair was a mess from the frantic ride. Worse, her stomach was deeply displeased from skipped cereal.

She sheepishly signed in at the front desk—this wasn't the first time she'd been late (mornings were hard, okay?)—and slunk into second period right as the bell finished ringing. She felt slightly guilty about missing Mr. Binder's class . . .

But only slightly. She wasn't entirely sure she wanted to face him after what had happened on the pageant stage.

Sigh. What had Freddie been thinking? Oh yeah. She hadn't been.

Freddie joined Divya at their usual spots in the back row of trig, and Divya gazed at Freddie with unmasked horror. Two minutes later, when Mr. Gonzalez started talking about cosigns and tangents, a note landed on Freddie's desk. Though it lacked Divya's usual pencil hearts and sunshines, it was still expertly folded with a little pull-tab on one side. After a quick check that Mr. Gonzalez wasn't looking (he wasn't), Freddie tugged. The note unfolded.

> You look like death. Is Theo a vampire? Was that a hickey or a bite wound?

Freddie hastily scribbled back, Ha ha. Very funny. And NO. There was an incident last night with Mrs. Ferris. She got hurt, and we had to call 911.

> OMG. Is she okay? Are you okay?

I'm fine. Mrs. Ferris is in the hospital. In quick, broad details, Freddie relayed what had happened. What she did *not* relay were the Very Strange things Mrs. Ferris had said right before she'd been attacked.

Nor did Freddie relay the guilt that was eating her alive. Maybe if she'd stayed—if she'd just *tackled* Mrs. Ferris and forced her to go back home . . . Maybe the old woman would be safe right now.

And while *yes,* Mrs. Ferris had survived whatever had

attacked her, that was entirely thanks to modern medicine. Not Freddie. Even dream-Freddie had been more interested in making out with Theo than saving his grandmother.

Freddie knew, deep in her rumbling, roiling gut, that what had happened was *her* fault. Modern medicine could only do so much for an eighty-seven-year-old woman, and if Mrs. Ferris died...

No. Freddie would make this right. Somehow. She would get answers. She would figure out why deadly things kept happening in the City-on-the-Berme county park.

The truth was out there.

Halfway through class (after neither Freddie nor Divya had taken any notes), Zach Gilroy raised his hand and asked, "Does anyone else smell that?"

At once, everyone's noses lifted. And yes, Freddie *did* smell something like rotting fish. She and Divya shared a glance. Divya looked frightened; Freddie felt sick.

"That smells like the archives," Divya whispered.

"Yeah," Freddie agreed, and she couldn't help but glance at the fluorescent lights, expecting them to snap off at any moment. She swallowed, waiting. Waiting.

"I think it's getting worse!" This came from Todd Raskin, who was now popping the cap off his inhaler.

"It is *definitely* getting worse," Carly Zhang replied.

Divya huddled close to Freddie. "What does your gut say?"

"Nothing," Freddie admitted, her gaze still target-locked on the lights. And while Divya relaxed at this news, Freddie did not. Not because she didn't trust her own gut...

But because why did she keep encountering this awful stench? Bowman had mentioned roadkill, and that would certainly explain the rotting death stink from the forest. And maybe from the archives too.

It would not, however, explain the stench right now in trigonometry.

The heat began to rise. Not just a low-key warming either, but a frogs-in-boiling-water kind of elevation.

"Stay here," Mr. Gonzalez wheezed before ducking into the hall.

No one stayed. It stank *so badly* and the room was *so hot*. After five minutes, everyone had stripped down to their lowest possible clothing items. Then Zack started vomiting into the trash bin, and everyone got up and bolted. Including Freddie and Divya.

They found the hallway outside already packed—and also *just* as hot and *just* as foul. Which was why all the students and teachers were charging for the exits. A vast parade of bodies trying very hard not to retch.

Right as Freddie and Divya toppled outside and blessedly fresh air poured over them, the intercom crackled to life.

"Attention Berm High," Principal Tamura intoned. "There has been an issue with the furnace, and . . . it would seem . . ." Her voice choked, like she was trying to contain a gag reflex. "It would seem dead fish have been stuffed into the air ducts. Please note, school is now canceled for the remainder of the day. *Go home.*"

"Dead fish," Divya hissed at the blue sky. Then again at Freddie: "Thank god. It was just dead fish. Maybe that was what we smelled at the archives too?"

"I don't think so," Freddie murmured. Clearly dead fish in the furnace was why Theo Porter had needed Mr. Binder's key to the school. And clearly they had succeeded with their wicked plot.

"Well, if this is what Fortin Prep considers a prank," Divya declared, giving a happy hip shimmy, "then they are terrible at it."

Or ingenious, Freddie thought as she counted six separate students hurling onto the grass—and four teachers too.

Divya's phone rang, and while she answered it, Freddie examined her own phone: *10:03*, the screen read—which meant she had *hours* during which to accomplish her rapidly expanding to-do list. Now that she'd sucked it up and combed through her dad's stash in the basement, she wanted to go to the library to dig up more newspaper articles.

And *also,* while she was out, Freddie really wanted to hit up the hospital and check on Mrs. Ferris. Then there was still the fact that Sheriff Bowman hadn't returned Xena as promised—a truly unforgivable travesty.

Yeah, school getting canceled was actually a huge gift, and Freddie wondered if she might get a chance to thank Theo for it . . . She wondered *how* she might thank him for it . . .

As Divya finished her call, she glanced at Freddie. Then *behind* Freddie. "Dr. Born. Ten o'clock." She grabbed hold of Freddie's wrist.

"My ten o'clock or your ten o'clock?" Freddie flung her gaze around . . . Until sure enough, there he was with his gray head, gray beard, and keen brown eyes.

He was looking right at Freddie, his lips parting as if to call her over.

Nope, nope, nope! No *way* was she giving up her newfound freedom to that stuffy counselor from out of town.

"Run," she hissed, and Divya needed no more urging. As one, they sprinted for the back of the school. Once around the corner, they dove behind a dumpster.

A mostly empty dumpster—thank god. Freddie couldn't handle much more rot in one day. "How long should we hide?" Freddie whispered, pulling out Sabrina.

"I don't think we need to whisper," Divya replied.

"Of course we do," Freddie said, still whispering. "This is like *GoldenEye.*"

"Yeah." Divya made a face. "Which you also don't have to whisper for. It's a freaking N64 game—"

"Hello," Kyle said, suddenly appearing beside them.

Freddie flinched; Divya yelped.

He smiled, dropping to a graceful squat. "What are you two doing back here?"

"Uh," Divya answered while Freddie offered a meek shrug.

"You know," Freddie began in a whisper. Then, because she realized it *did* sound foolish, she coughed and said normally, "We're just, uh, hanging out. Behind a dumpster. As people do."

"Right." Kyle nodded as if people did do that, and Freddie found herself wondering how he could be so pretty yet so empty inside.

Then again, she supposed it was really just evolutionary fairness. If he'd gotten all the good looks *and* the smarts, the Matrix would probably glitch forever, leading to the end of all life as they knew it.

"We're going to the Quick-Bis," Kyle said, still smiling that winning smile. "Do you wanna come?"

Part of Freddie did want to go. Of course she did. She liked the Prank Squad. And she liked Kyle Friedman. (She did, she did!)

"I . . . can't," she said eventually. "I have Very Important Things I need to do."

"Oh." A flicker of disappointment. But then he rallied. "Well, do you want company? I could join you."

Freddie gulped. Kyle *had* known about the Executioners Three poem, even if he hadn't remembered specifics. Maybe he could help Freddie in other ways . . .

She should say yes. Particularly since Lance Bass wasn't around anymore, so it wasn't the keychain's magic making Kyle interested.

Yet for some reason, when Freddie looked at Kyle's face, she found herself thinking of Theo instead. Of how he'd looked in her dream, with his hands outstretched and an iron heart resting upon his palms. Kyle was beautiful and a troublemaker.

But Theo was beautiful and tortured. And for some reason, that was a lot more appealing.

Except no, no, *no*. Freddie had promised Divya she wouldn't think about Theo ever again. He was a Montague, and the risk was simply too great.

Freddie had a crush on Kyle; she *liked* him, and now she was going to tell him yes.

"I'm fine by myself," she said. "I think I'll get done faster on my own." Inwardly, she karate-chopped herself.

"Oh." There was that disappointment on Kyle's flawless face again, and Freddie hated herself for it. She was probably breaking some kind of law right now—the fifth law of thermodynamics or the eleventh commandment or something. *Thou shalt not hurt the King of Berm High School's feelings.*

"You should go to the Quick-Bis, Div." Freddie turned to her best friend (who was watching this entire scene with a very disapproving stare).

"Yes," Kyle agreed, now flashing his winning smile onto Divya. "Laina was going to call you, but I could just give you a ride instead."

"Um," Divya hesitated.

"*Or* you could go with Laina," Freddie nudged. "Didn't she already call you?"

"Yeah." Divya blushed furiously and eased out her own Nokia. "She did. So thanks anyway, Kyle."

"No problem." He pushed to his feet. "I'll see you at the Quick-Bis. And"—his green gaze shot to Freddie—"maybe you'll join us later?"

"Oh, absolutely." Freddie nodded her most emphatic, King-worthy nod. "I will most definitely join you." In seconds, Kyle had vanished back around the dumpster.

Divya crawled in close to Freddie—and now, she was the one whispering. Actually, it was less a whisper and more of a vicious snarl. "You'd better not be going to meet Theo Porter right now."

Freddie recoiled. "Of course I'm not. I'm going to get Xena back. Then I want to check on Mrs. Ferris. Oh, and I want to go to the library too."

Divya didn't look like she believed Freddie one bit. Not even when Freddie promised, "I'll call you in a few hours, okay? And I'll be able to do it from *anywhere* in Berm. You know why?" She shook Sabrina at Divya. "Because I have a cell phone now."

"And a Snake addiction like mine, I've noticed."

"I do." Freddie nodded gravely. "I now fully understand the allure of chasing dots and avoiding one's tail. It's a rich commentary on the futility of life."

"That's right, Fred." Divya patted her shoulder. "But we'll get through it together. Maybe Dr. Born can help."

Freddie choked. Then cackled. And with that imagery to warm her blood, she slunk off toward the bike racks, ready to once more brave the autumn cold in her righteous pursuit of answers.

The police station at the edge of Berm's tiny downtown was nothing more than a brick cubicle with a coffeepot at one end and a long desk at the other. A single door in the back led to a few holding cells for the occasional rowdy drunkard and to a locked cellar where "sensitive" items were kept. (Freddie had gotten to explore it when she'd interned for Bowman; it hadn't been nearly as exciting as she'd hoped. Just a bunch of shelves with a few items in Ziplocs.)

Other than Sheriff Bowman and the two deputies who usually cruised the streets in their patrol cars, Berm didn't have much need for a proper police force. If there was anything too big to handle, they called in backup from the county seat fifteen miles away.

When Freddie arrived at the station, she found Deputy Ibrahim Abadi manning the front desk. She flushed as soon as she saw him. He *always* had that effect on her. Partly because he was just so gosh darn nice (and always let her call him by his first name). And partly because he was twenty-five years old, making him only eight years Freddie's senior.

Mostly Freddie flushed because Ibrahim was Very Beautiful Indeed, with his glowing brown skin and thick, dark lashes. He smiled at Freddie (swoon) when she shuffled in. "Hey, Fred. Come for Xena?"

"Yep." She flushed even harder now. He'd remembered her camera's name. What a dreamboat.

"I'll be right back," he called before disappearing through the single door. Freddie occupied herself with Snake while she waited. Futility of life and all that. Humans were just snakes trying to outrun their own tails.

A few minutes later, Ibrahim returned with Xena in a Ziploc. "Just sign for it here." He slid a clipboard across the desk.

As Freddie scribbled down her signature, she asked in her most casual voice, "So, uh, did Sheriff Bowman end up finding that water bottle?"

Ibrahim shifted his weight, expression apologetic. "Unfortunately, no."

"No?" It took Freddie a full three seconds to process what that word meant.

Once she *did* process it, she dropped the signing pen. It clattered to the floor. "What do you mean 'no'?" she squawked. "I told her exactly where it was."

"And there was no bottle there." Ibrahim reclaimed the clipboard and glanced meaningfully at the fallen pen.

Freddie yanked it from the industrial carpet.

"Me and Knowles searched with Sheriff Bowman," Ibrahim elaborated. "But we didn't turn up anything, Fred."

"Impossible." Freddie slammed down the pen and snatched Xena off the desk. "It was *right there*, Ibrahim! I saw it with my own eyes." She tore open the Ziploc and tugged Xena free. "I *told* Bowman not to wait to look for it. Someone must've moved it!"

"Or it rolled away."

"Rolled away so far you couldn't find it?"

"We're still searching, Freddie. Plus, Sheriff says you took pictures, right?" He waved to Xena. "We'll get those developed soon, and then we'll have a better idea of what we're looking for."

"It's not hard to get a good idea. Red water bottle. About yea high." Freddie slotted her hands a foot apart. "Says *Fontana* on the side."

"I am aware, Fred." Ibrahim's voice had taken on a familiar weariness that Freddie remembered from last summer. He was a great cop, but he had little patience for Freddie's pestering. Then again, no one really had patience for her, and he was at least nicer about it than Knowles was, who always just rolled her eyes and said, "Can it, kid."

Bowman, meanwhile, had a tendency to straight up ignore Freddie entirely.

"Are you *really* aware, Ibrahim?" Freddie tugged Xena's strap over her neck. "You don't seem very alarmed by this. There was a water bottle; now there isn't. That seems like a good cause for general freakout."

"Freddie," Ibrahim warned. He leaned over the desk. "I know that look in your eyes. Don't even think about going to search for it. Understand?"

Freddie sniffed. "Why do you think I would do that?"

"Because I know you." He shook his head. "But those woods aren't safe right now, yeah? First Mrs. Ferris got mauled by some wild animal, and now we've got another body—" He broke off, eyes widening. "I mean . . . Forget you heard that."

Freddie would do no such thing. "Another body? Where? Who?" She planted both hands on the desk. *"Tell me."*

Ibrahim only scoffed. "No way. I'm not allowed to talk about it, Fred, and let's just say it's bad. Like, really bad, okay? Bowman has even called in the feds."

Freddie's eyebrows leaped high. Feds *never* came to Berm.

"The entire county park is now off-limits to the public, so promise me you'll follow the rules. Can you do that?"

"I always follow the rules."

Ibrahim's eyes narrowed. "I mean it, Freddie. Danger aside, Bowman is not in a mood you want to cross right now."

Freddie tensed. *That* warning did give her pause. Not because she was afraid of Sheriff Bowman (although she was) but because Mrs. Ferris was Bowman's mom, and having your mom unconscious in the hospital was a genuinely terrible thing for anyone to have to go through.

"Is Bowman here right now, actually? Maybe I can talk to her personally. About all of this."

Ibrahim's frown shifted from Freddie to the parking lot outside. "No, she's not here. She was supposed to come a few hours ago, but she hasn't turned up yet. Want me to leave her a message?"

"No." Freddie smiled sweetly.

"In that case, follow the rules," Ibrahim repeated. "Okay, Fred?"

"The truth is out there." She turned to go.

"Wait," Ibrahim called after her. "Don't think I didn't notice that!"

"Notice what?"

"You just quoted *The X-Files* at me instead of agreeing to follow the rules."

"Oopsies!" She shimmied backward through the front door, baring her toothiest grin. She was so innocent a halo was probably floating over her head. "See you later, Ibrahim!"

"Freddie!"

She didn't hear what else he had to say before she was outside and scampering for her bike.

12

Freddie had only ever entered the tiny Berm hospital twice in her life. Once on the day of her birth. And second, on the day her father had died.

She'd been five years old when Frank had passed away, but the beige linoleum floors and smell of rubbing alcohol had been forever branded into her brain. She remembered her mother's swollen eyes, and how Mom had hugged Freddie so tightly that Freddie had thought her ribs might break. She remembered Steve's pinched lips, and how he'd let Freddie have an entire Milky Way all to herself.

Above all, Freddie remembered the way the door into her father's room had loomed before her. Room 27 with the silver knob at Freddie's eye level. It had opened only twice the entire time she was there. She had never been allowed through.

She never got to say goodbye to Frank Carter.

They told her it was because it was too awful for a five-year-old to see, and she hadn't argued. The blanched faces on the doctors, the way they had rushed in and out with scrubs and scowls and blood all over . . .

She'd been scared of what she might find within. Then at 12:46 (Freddie had known because there'd been a clock on the vending machine), her mom had come out and told her that her dad had passed away. The heart attack had been too strong; Frank hadn't been able to overcome it.

Freddie had *tried* to feel sad about this. It was what people had seemed to expect from her. But she hadn't been sad. In the hospital or at the funeral a few days later. How could she be sad when she'd barely known the man?

Grief, she discovered, did come eventually. Less sharp and wild than in the movies, more textured and heavy. A sensation only elevated by the unspoken rule that had settled over her house like a shroud. Freddie hadn't known her dad; now she never would. She would forever be the girl whose dad had died.

In the twelve years since Freddie had come to the hospital, the linoleum had been updated to a cool gray, and they'd added fake plants that did give the space slightly nicer appeal. The alcohol smell was the same, though. And the autumn bite outside—she remembered that being the same too.

Freddie went straight to the front desk and asked to see Mrs. Ferris. The nice man told her to head to the third floor, so after an elevator ride and two hallways, Freddie found herself walking into a tiny waiting area.

It looked identical to the one from twelve years ago. So much so that her throat closed up, and her feet stopped working midstride. Over there was the vending machine. Beside it was the muted TV with closed captioning. Even the mauve seating looked exactly as she remembered.

But no. This *wasn't* that waiting area. This wasn't even the same floor. And now someone else was sauntering into the room from the opposite hallway—someone with tawny hair and a navy blazer.

He caught sight of Freddie right as she caught sight of him, and just as Freddie had done three seconds before, Theo Porter drew up short.

Freddie gasped. Theo looked *awful*. His left eye was swollen and purple, his jaw was worse, and even from across the room, she thought she could make out individual finger marks around his neck.

Without thinking—and completely forgetting what she'd

told Divya less than an hour ago—Freddie crossed the room. Theo didn't move. He just watched her approach, expression inscrutable. And the closer Freddie got, the worse he looked. Stitches cinched across his eyebrow. A gash marring his right cheek, and the top of his lip busted too.

She halted before him and stared up. She itched to reach for him, to touch him. But her mind was smarter than her muscles. She balled her hands at her sides. "You look terrible," she said instead.

He huffed a laugh. "Thanks?"

"What happened?"

His chin tipped so he could assess her from the bottom of his eyes. "I made the mistake of trying to do a good thing."

"Oh." It was all Freddie could say. Especially since she could relate to that sentiment. She'd only wanted the same when she'd called the cops on a bunch of drunk kids in the trees.

But at least that had only earned her the enmity of an entire school. *Not* a pummeled face.

Theo cut past Freddie, aiming toward a nearby chair. After knocking a backpack to the floor, he sank onto the seat. Freddie eased into the chair beside him. "Does it hurt?"

"I mean, it doesn't feel great." He picked at a loose thread on his blazer. "I see you got your camera back?"

Freddie blinked, startled by the subject change—but also willing to play along. "Yes, I did." She held out the Nikon. "Xena, meet Theo. Theo, meet Xena." She pitched her voice high. *"Hi, Theo! Don't get too close or me and Gabrielle will getcha!"*

Theo did not laugh. In fact, he didn't react at all.

And Freddie sighed. "No snooty retort for me, Mr. Porter?"

"Not today, Gellar." His tongue flicked over his upper lip. He winced. Then shifted forward to brace his elbows on his knees.

Which left Freddie staring at his hunched profile, broken and defeated. It was so strange to see him that way. This was not the perfectly composed Theo of the Quick-Bis, nor the arrogant Theo from pageant practice. Nor even the restless Theo—the one she'd seen outside of Sheriff Bowman's house and beside the water mill too.

This was sad Theo, and even if he was her enemy, Freddie didn't like to see him this way. "Is . . . is your grandmother really bad?" It was the only explanation she could conjure.

But he shook his head. "Actually, she's doing okay. The doctors were able to stitch up the cuts on her back, and they don't think the knock on her head will leave any permanent damage. Though . . ." He shrugged one shoulder. "It's hard to know for sure until she wakes up."

Freddie frowned at her hands, guilt unspooling in her belly. "So she hasn't woken up yet?"

"No." Theo glanced her way. His expression softened. "She'll be alright, though. Thanks to you. You *are* the one who found her, right?"

"Yeah," Freddie tried to say, but it came out tight. "The thing is, though . . . I just . . ." She wet her lips. Fidgeted with Xena.

"You just?" Theo nudged.

"It's just . . . Well, it's basically my fault she's here at all." Freddie covered her face with her hands. Then in a torrent of words, she told Theo all the terrible things she hadn't had the guts to admit to Divya. About how she *should* have stopped Mrs. Ferris. About how she should never have gone back to get Steve. About how if she had just been stronger or smarter or remembered she had a phone now, Mrs. Ferris wouldn't be in the hospital at all.

Freddie didn't know why she told Theo all of this. Maybe it was because she didn't feel like she deserved his gratitude, or maybe because the guilt was finally boiling over.

Or maybe it was just because he looked like a wreck and she *felt* like one. There was something comforting in that. Either way, she reached the end of her story and, face still in her hands, she mumbled, "So you see? If I had just been more forceful, then maybe she would never have gone down that trail and whatever attacked her—"

A hand landed on Freddie's shoulder. She broke off.

"You know everything you just said is really stupid, right?" Theo bent over and tried to meet her eyes.

"Uh..."

He smiled—the first smile since Freddie had walked in here. It was nice. "Most people would've gone by and ignored her, Gellar. In fact..." He straightened, pulling Freddie upright with him. "I bet people *did* go by and ignore her. But you didn't. You saved her life and I'm grateful." He shrugged. "I don't have much family left."

"Huh," Freddie replied. Not her most clever retort, but it was hard to think straight when Theo was looking at her like he was right now. He had a very intense stare (clearly, that ran in the family).

Plus, his fingers were still on her shoulder. They were warm.

"Do the police know what happened to her? Or the doctors?" Freddie was relieved she sounded like a normal human. She didn't *feel* like a normal human with his hand touching her like that.

"They're saying it was a wild animal. Maybe a wolf."

"That was not a wolf." The words slipped out before Freddie could stop them. But Theo didn't contradict her. If anything, he seemed to agree.

His hand was still resting on her shoulder.

"Whatever it was," he said slowly, "I'm not sure we'll know for certain until Grandma wakes up. My aunt is kinda preoccupied with something else right now."

Not just your aunt, Freddie thought. Something was bothering Theo too—something more than his injured grandmother. Something that explained the shiner swelling around his left eye.

"What happened to you?" she asked softly.

Theo's lips parted, as if he might answer. As if he wanted to. But a heartbeat later, he only wagged his head. His hand fell away.

For some reason, Freddie wished it hadn't. "Hey, Theo," she said before he could retreat within himself. "Can I ask a favor?"

"Maybe." A smile flitted over his lips. "Although my favors don't come cheap."

"Is that so?" Now Freddie was the one smiling. "Well, how much would this cost: I need you to call me when your grandmother wakes up."

"Ah." His smile dissolved. "*That* I will do for free."

"Oh." Freddie swallowed.

"Here." He crooked over and yanked a spiral-bound notebook from his backpack. After flipping to the last page and slipping a pen from his blazer pocket, he offered both to Freddie. "Write down your phone number."

"Oh," she repeated—although it came out a bit squeakier this time. This was the second instance in one week that she had given her number to a boy. And sure, Theo only wanted it because she had just asked him to call, but something about the way he was looking at her made it feel different.

Remember your vow to Divya! STAY STRONG.

Freddie was extremely careful not to brush Theo's fingers as she took the paper and pen. Then, after scrawling down Sabrina's number, she glanced up. "What's *your* phone number?"

"No number," he murmured, watching Freddie and not the paper. "I lost my phone last night."

"Does that have anything to do with the black eye?"

"Maybe."

"Okay." Freddie ripped her gaze away from his. Heat was gathering in her belly, and she liked it a little too much. "Well, here's my ICQ name, just in case."

"ICQ?" He laughed. "Who the hell uses ICQ?"

"What do *you* use to message people?"

"AIM, like a normal person."

"Pshaw." Freddie rolled her eyes. "But fine, you don't have ICQ, so here's my email too—though I swear to god, Mr. Porter, if you use this information for anything nefarious, I will destroy you."

"First of all, you couldn't destroy me if you tried." He bent toward her. His blond hair flopped over his eyes. "Second of all, I won't misuse your info. I *told* you I'm not a Very Bad Human Indeed."

Freddie bit her lip. She had no worthy retort for this, and like yesterday, his declaration was making her whole chest ignite with sparklers. She very much wanted to lean in and—

NO.

She jerked up taller.

BAD. BAD. BAD. She'd sworn a sacred vow, so what was she doing acting like this? Smiling and . . . and *flirting*? Divya would literally kill her, and it would be completely appropriate if she did.

"Listen," Freddie said, her voice strained. "About the, um . . ." She swallowed. She couldn't bring herself to say the word *kiss,* and now she was blushing like a summer peach. "About what happened yesterday."

"Yes." Theo was staring at her very, *very* hard. "About that."

"I didn't mean . . . That is to say . . ." Oh god, why was this so difficult? Freddie had made a promise; now she had to draw up boundaries. "We're enemies, yeah?"

"We are." His eyes narrowed.

"So yesterday was just . . ." *Spit it out, Gellar. SPIT IT OUT.* "It was, um, just a one-off. Right?"

Theo tensed. An almost imperceptible movement. Then his thumb started tapping. "Obviously." He shifted in his seat. *Tap, tap, tap.* "I mean, what is it you said on Saturday? You have that effect on everyone."

Freddie's mouth went dry. She had no idea how to respond to a statement like that. Once more, it felt like he was complimenting her—and once more, it left her heart fluttering out of control.

It didn't help that he was looking at her again with a face that had gone very still.

"Thank you for understanding," she forced out.

"Yep," he replied, and finally—*finally*—he looked away.

Freddie handed the notebook back to him. "I hope I hear good news about your grandmother soon."

"Yep," he repeated, completely withdrawn now. A statue over a gravestone.

They were enemies. This was what Freddie had wanted. Capulets and Montagues. Still, though—even though she knew it shouldn't—her heart sank when she left the waiting area, trilling a goodbye...

And only stony silence followed behind.

Freddie tried very hard not to think about Theo Porter while she cycled away from the hospital. All the way through downtown Berm. Into the drugstore to buy new film. Then while she huffed past Fortin Park, lined with piles of raked leaves. And finally to the old church-turned-library that always flooded during storms.

She even sang "Tearin' Up My Heart" in time to her pedaling. Not that it helped. NSYNC and Lance Bass could not scrub Theo Porter from her brain.

When she reached the library, Freddie tried *even harder* not to think about Theo—while she chained her bike. While she looked for newspapers. While she tried (and failed) to figure out the microfiche reader and then went searching for Miss Gupta in order to figure out said machine.

Even while Miss Gupta showed her how to insert the microfiche into the lenses, switch on the proper lamps, and print the resulting pages, Theo was *still* stuck in Freddie's head.

The way he'd looked, all broken and beautiful, with his black eye and stitches. And the way his whole face had gone still when he'd said she had that effect on everyone...

"No," Freddie groaned at the microfiche screen. *Berm Sentinel* headlines from October 1987 glared back at her. "No, no, no—"

"Is everything alright?" Miss Gupta asked from a few aisles away. Her tone, as always, was cheery and helpful.

Freddie tried to mimic it as she called back, "I'm fine! Just fine, Miss Gupta!" Because of course she was fine. Theo's gorgeous, beat-up face might've taken over her common sense, but she had come here on a mission. And when Freddie Gellar was on a mission, she did not rest until it was complete.

She was, after all, her mother's daughter. *I can handle it.*

Today, Freddie's mission was to look at newspaper articles from 1975 and 1987. Anything that her father might've missed. She might not know why he had gathered those documents—and the poem too—but there had been a reason. Something Freddie was certain connected to the current chaos.

She started with the *Berm Sentinel,* also grabbing newspapers from the neighboring towns. Alas, there wasn't much to find. Her dad had been thorough, and she only came across the same articles he'd uncovered.

Which . . . was . . . well, *strange.* Looking at the exact same article and knowing her dad had looked at it too . . . It made Freddie's joints stiffen and her stomach roil like she had heartburn. *Tamp it down,* she told herself. *Focus, Gellar.*

After three swallows, Freddie succeeded. Or at least, she succeeded enough to work through all of the *Berm Sentinel* and move on to the *County Weekly,* where she found a few wild animal reports that corroborated what Frank had found. An account of icebergs forming close to the shore, too, which made gooseflesh trickle down her arms and her gut sit up and take notice.

There was also a report of a missing person in 1975, but the guy had come from Elmore, twenty miles away. She decided it wasn't important and moved on.

After thirty minutes of scouring articles, Freddie had all but given up on finding anything from 1975 or 1987 to add to her dad's stash. Until suddenly she came across a copy of the *Elmore Gazette* (a paper that didn't even exist anymore) dated the first week of November 1975.

"City-on-the-Berme Lumberjack Pageant Leaves Historical Village," the headline read, and right away, Freddie's gut set to squishing. She knew the pageant had been moved to the high school for almost ten years before going back to the Village with Mom's help. Freddie had always assumed it was because the stage had needed replacing or something...

But nope. *Big* nope. Apparently the performance in 1975 had been disrupted by a teenager—drunk off his ass and screaming of monsters in the woods. He had been partying with his friend in the county park when the friend had wandered off by himself. The first guy had gone looking for his buddy, and found the body...

Without a head.

Like, the guy had been full-on *decapitated*. No skull attached to a spinal column. Guillotined without a guillotine.

And to make it even more wild, the police decided *that* was an accident. There had still been some logging in those days; an axe had fallen off a platform, and *kersplat*.

Who the victim had been, though, the article never named. Nor who the traumatized drunk guy had been.

Freddie needed more. Her gut needed more, because as far as she was concerned, this many deaths in a single location didn't point to bad luck so much as murder. The question remaining, however, was whether it had been a series of copycat murderers—each death echoing elements of "The Executioners Three" poem—or whether they were all committed by the same killer over the last twenty-four years.

A *serial* killer.

After printing out the article, Freddie dove back into the microfiche filing cabinets. Except when she searched for papers from October 22, 1975 (the day after this event had supposedly happened), there were none. Absolutely *none*. In fact, no papers from any town or county for the day of October 22 were anywhere inside the library.

"Uh, Miss Gupta?" Freddie called. Her gut wasn't just

awake now; it was hyped up like a Chihuahua barking at the neighbors.

"Yes, Freddie?" Miss Gupta popped up beside her.

"There seems to be a day missing." Freddie pointed at the gap in articles. "Could the papers have been misplaced? Or maybe loaned out to another library?"

Miss Gupta's forehead pinched. As she flipped through all of the yellow microfiche folders, her frown deepened. "How strange. There's no reason these articles from 1975 *shouldn't* be here. Look." She tapped a series of barcodes along the tops of the folders. "If these had been loaned out, the entire folder would be gone. But they aren't."

"Maybe . . . they got damaged and were removed?"

"Maybe," Miss Gupta murmured, though she didn't sound convinced.

And Freddie *definitely* wasn't convinced. Those articles were important to her fact-finding mission—and really, what were the odds that they had all vanished on their own? "Is there somewhere else I could go, to read articles from that date?"

"You could go to all the newspapers' offices," Miss Gupta suggested, slipping the empty folders from the cabinet. She was frowning in a very un-Miss-Gupta way now. "They should all have archives—well, the ones that are still in business. Or," she added, finally looking at Freddie. "Fortin Prep keeps an extensive collection of periodicals."

Of course they did. Freakin' rich kids.

"It isn't open to the public," Miss Gupta went on, "but they offer special research passes for people who want access. It only takes about a week to get one."

A week? Freddie's nostrils flared. She didn't have a week. There was a suicide that wasn't a suicide, an injured Mrs. Ferris, a recurring theme of hangings at the park, a freaking *decapitation* from twenty-four years ago, and now *another* dead body.

"Do the students at Fortin Prep have access to the collection?"

"I presume so." Miss Gupta's smile returned. "The school is famous for its journalism program. Didn't you know that?"

Of course Freddie knew that. Just as she knew Roberta Allard Fortin had been a total badass and famous for her investigative reporting. Freddie had just never considered that all the money going into the school might also mean they'd have a massive collection of periodicals for their students to use.

Once more, Freddie was left rolling her eyes at freakin' rich kids. They had no idea how lucky they were. Then again, right now wasn't the moment for jealousy. Not when she needed one of those wealthy chosen to trickle down some of his good fortune. Noblesse oblige and all that.

"Is there anything else I can help you with, Freddie?"

"Yeah, actually. Do you know anything about this poem?" Freddie withdrew a handwritten copy of "The Executioners Three."

But when Miss Gupta read the title, all Freddie earned was a wrinkled brow. Then a headshake. "Who wrote it?"

"I don't know. It was in a book called *The Curse of Allard Fortin* by Edgar..." Oh gosh, what was the guy's last name? "Fabre! Edgar Fabre."

"I can go look if we have that. Do you need the book?"

"No, no. I... *they* have it at the Village Historique. But maybe you could search the poem's title? And the guy's name?"

"You bet. I'll see what our database turns up." Off the librarian went, and Freddie returned her focus to the microfiche. But after Freddie had printed off a few more articles, Miss Gupta returned with her frown etched even deeper and a single book in hand. "Freddie, I couldn't find any record of that book you named. Or the author. Are you sure you have it right?"

"Um." Freddie was *mostly* sure. But she was also suddenly doubting herself. After all, the reason she owned Xena was because she *didn't* have a photographic memory like so many sleuths in so many of the books she liked to read.

"You said this was at the Village's archives?" Miss Gupta

now asked. "There are a lot of books in there that are too old to have made it into our databases. When was this published?"

"The 1940s, I think."

"Oh, not that old." The librarian flashed an apologetic smile. "I'm sorry, then. I don't think I can offer much more help. I did at least find a different book for you, though. It mentions a number of people named Fabre."

Freddie glanced at the title. *A History of Bellfounding in America*. Bells again—always bells. "Sure," Freddie said. "I might as well try it. Thanks, Miss Gupta."

After checking out the book, Freddie hurried once more into the overcast cold of midday. A few minutes later, and Divya's dulcet tones were filtering through Sabrina.

"There you are, Fred! I've been waiting *so long*."

"It's only been two hours since we left the school."

"Exactly. *So long*."

"Where are you?" Freddie asked while she unlocked Steve's bike. "Are you still with the Prank Squad?"

"Yeah. We just came up with our plan for tomorrow."

"Oh?" Freddie paused, one leg swung over the bike. "What did you decide?"

"Crickets," came Laina, her voice in President Steward mode. "We'll release them in the school."

"All that noise will drive everyone bananas," Kyle chimed.

"And," Divya picked back up, "we've already sent Cat and Luis out to every pet store and bait shop in a twenty-mile radius. By tomorrow we should have a *lot* of crickets."

Freddie had to admit: this was actually quite clever. No, it was not on par with dead fish in the air ducts and a hell-blasting furnace, but that was what the Prank Wizard was for. Freddie could work with this baseline—*and* she could shape it into her own research needs.

"We're just stuck," Laina said, "because we don't know how to get into the school. A nighttime sneak attack won't work a second time."

"And no one wants to go back through that forest again anyway," Kyle muttered.

No one argued with this.

"So you got any ideas?" Divya asked.

Freddie summoned her loudest, most belly-fueled laugh. "Do I have any ideas? Oh, Divya, never doubt the Answer Finder, also known as your Esteemed Prank Wizard."

"I wasn't."

"Great. Then let's all meet at the Friedmans' dry cleaners in ten minutes. Does that work?"

"Sure thing. See you in ten." The call went dead (oh, the wonders of technology!) and after slipping Sabrina into her pocket and checking that Xena was safely attached, Freddie set off once more into the autumn morning.

13

It was seven o'clock, and Freddie's eyes were crossing. She'd come home after prepping for tomorrow's prank with her friends, and since then, she'd done nothing but read *The Curse of Allard Fortin: How Murder Shaped His Legacy*. In other words, she hadn't opened her English or APUSH homework.

Unfortunately, she doubted her teachers would accept "saving Berm from a potential murderer" as an excuse for not turning in essays.

In *The Curse of Allard Fortin*, Edgar Fabre (yes, Freddie had, in fact, remembered the name correctly) described a diary from his blacksmith ancestor—the *same* blacksmith ancestor whose journals on bellfounding had allowed Mom to re-create the Allard Fortin mausoleum bell. Fabre claimed there'd been one more diary, and this one described a dark curse that José Allard Fortin had cast over three of his servants. And it was through this curse that he had murdered his way into being the most powerful man in the region.

Real penny-dreadful-worthy stuff. Definitely good source material for an *X-Files* episode, complete with blood oaths and unkillable Executioners to boot.

Unfortunately, also impossible, since—ya know—spirits and blood oaths and curses weren't real.

All the same, that didn't mean someone very real couldn't be inspired by such tales. And Freddie was really starting to think that she might have found the key connective tissue for her killer here.

The sound of a car door slamming drew Freddie out of her frowning thoughts. She blinked. Rubbed her eyes. Then scrabbled from bed toward her window, where, like a total creep, she peeled back her blinds and squinted at Sheriff Bowman's house.

Theo Porter was standing outside his car. He wasn't walking toward his aunt's front door, but he was instead staring at Freddie's house. Even from here, Freddie could see the bruises marring his Romeo face.

A scrub of his hair. A shift of his weight. A glance toward Bowman's door. A glance toward Freddie's house. Then *finally*, he slid his hands into his pockets and loped toward the front porch.

Freddie's lungs loosened. Distantly, she noticed her room had gotten hot.

"What are we looking at?" Mom whispered.

Freddie jumped halfway to the ceiling. "Oh my *god*, where did you come from?"

"Oh, I see," Mom said, pressing in close to the window. "We're looking at the sheriff's nephew."

Jeez, did *everyone* know Theo was related to Bowman? Freddie's heart thundered in her ears. She glanced at her bed, where her archives contraband sat in plain view.

"You should go see him," Mom murmured, still gazing out the window.

"Huh?" Freddie laughed a bit too forcefully. "Why would I do that?"

"Because you like him."

"I like Kyle Friedman."

"Really?" Mom snorted. "So you just made out with Theo onstage because . . . ?"

"To prove a point!" Freddie's hands flew to her burning cheeks.

"Wow." Mom shot her a flat-eyed stare. "If that's how you kiss to prove a point, I can't wait to see how you kiss someone you like."

"Can we please stop talking about this?" Freddie grabbed her mom's elbow, hoping to lead her from the room. "I like Kyle Friedman, and that's the end of the story. He's nice, he's beautiful, he's popular—"

"And maybe if you say it enough, you'll start believing it."

Freddie glared. Mom grinned.

But then she caught sight of the archives book on Freddie's bed. "*The Curse of Allard Fortin*," she read. Then she flipped free from Freddie's grasp and hurried to the bed. "Where did you get this? I thought all copies of this book had been pulped."

Freddie blinked. This was *not* what she'd expected Mom to say. And if Mom didn't realize it had come from the archives . . . then there was no reason for Freddie to implicate herself now.

"The library," Freddie half squeaked. "I got it from . . . the library. What do you mean it was pulped?"

"Oh, the Allard Fortin family was *not* happy when that book was printed in the 1940s."

"Printed," Freddie said, noticing that word. "Not . . . published?"

"Yeah, no publisher would print that. So Fabre here invested all his own money to print copies of a book he swore would transform the Allard Fortin legacy. And the Allard Fortins in turn sued the guy for libel. They won too. It ruined him, and he went bankrupt."

"Whoa." Freddie shuffled to the bed, a thousand ideas now colliding inside her brain. "I mean, I guess I understand why they would sue? It says on page one that José Allard Fortin was a murderer."

Mom chuckled. "Yeah, it does say that."

"Have you read it?"

"No. Technically no one should have, either, since the books got pulped. In fact, I'm shocked any copy survived, and I don't understand how it wound up in the local library."

"Haha, right." Freddie twittered nervously. "But then, how do you know what the book is about if you haven't read it?"

"Because you know Berm! The locals were as angry as the Allard Fortin family about that book and Fabre's claims. Sure, thirty years had passed when I moved to town, but a few people still remembered what happened."

"Was . . . Dad one of those people who remembered?"

Instantly, Mom's body locked up. Her grip on *The Curse of Allard Fortin* turned white-knuckled.

And Freddie felt it as her own body did the same. *You're breaking the rule! Thou shalt not discuss Frank Carter!*

Yet Freddie knew she had to be a good Answer Finder. She *had* to figure out how Dad had possessed the poem from a book that supposedly no longer existed. (A book that had been in the archives unbeknownst to Mom, and that must have—at some point—been tucked away in Kyle Friedman's garage.)

"Um," Mom began, still holding the book for dear life. "Yes. I suppose . . . Frank probably mentioned it."

Freddie bit her lip. *Tamp it down.* Then shrugged as casually as she could. "Did he ever talk about a poem from the book? About executioners?"

Mom flinched.

"Huh." In a detached movement, Mom sat stiffly on the edge of the bed. Seconds slid past as, millimeter by millimeter, she softened her hold on the book, placing it on her thighs.

Then she patted the space beside her, and Freddie complied.

"Frank did, now that you mention it." The words slid out, hollow, while Mom stared into the middle distance. "Shortly before his death, he mentioned Edgar Fabre in passing. He said the guy had written a poem, and did I know about it. I . . ." She swallowed. "I didn't, though. And unfortunately . . ." She trailed off.

Freddie feared that was the end of the story. That she would get nothing more. That she'd opened Pandora's box for no reason, and now feelings would crush out the task at hand.

But then, to her shock, Mom actually did resume. "Unfortunately," she said in a voice so soft it was almost a whisper, "I never learned why Frank wanted to know about that poem. And I . . . well, I hate that he probably never got an answer before he died."

"Oh," Freddie breathed. Her throat was suddenly very tight. Very dry.

"Oh," Mom agreed. Her face had a choked-up look. The tense, nostril-flared lines of someone trying not to cry. "He was like you, Fred, you know that? He had the same incredible instincts as you, and if there was ever a problem, then Frank had to solve it. I just . . . well, I never learned what problem sent him searching for answers about Edgar Fabre and that poem."

Freddie rocked back on her butt. She felt like she'd just been hit with a monsoon. A double whammy of monsoons, actually, because there was *so much information* revealed in this one conversation. The fact that Dad had investigated Edgar Fabre—who, if Dad's note was correct, hadn't died like people believed. The fact that Dad had been convinced that there was some important lead inside "The Executioners Three."

But above all—by a lot—was the fact that Mom was saying Freddie was like her dad. That they *both* had these magical guts—and that they *both* were Answer Finders. Deep down, Freddie had always known that. Why else would she be following in his footsteps? But she—and Mom too—had been so effective at tamping all that down. To have Mom break the rule so suddenly . . .

Freddie made herself swallow. Made herself keep pushing while she still had the chance.

"Sheriff Bowman said I was like Dad too. On Saturday. But she made it sound like . . . like it was a bad thing."

Mom heaved a sigh so heavy the bed bounced. "Yeah. I'm

not surprised. Frank wasn't easy to work with." Mom met Freddie's eyes, and hers were a different color from Freddie's because Freddie had inherited her own from this father she'd never known.

"The problem with your dad, Fred, was that he couldn't let things go. If he thought he was onto something, it consumed his whole life. And while sure, that made him a great sheriff..."

"It made him a terrible husband," Freddie filled in. *And a terrible boss. And a terrible dad.*

Mom didn't respond, but Freddie didn't need her to. Freddie knew it was true. She had grown up knowing it, even if those words had never fallen so directly from her mother's or Steve's mouth.

Frank Carter was a guy in some photos who occasionally remembered birthday cards and came by on Christmas mornings. But that had been the entire extent of his presence in Freddie's life—and she'd always known it wasn't because he *couldn't* be there, but because he hadn't wanted to.

Before Freddie could say anything else (not that she really knew what to say anyway), her mom lifted *The Curse of Allard Fortin*. "So, um, why are you reading this?"

"Oh, right." Freddie frowned. *Focus on the task at hand.* "I, uh, have a school project on ... bellfounding," she lied. "And with the fête coming up, I didn't want to bother you."

"I could literally talk about bellfounding in my sleep, Fred."

"That would be funny to watch." Freddie closed her eyes and feigned sleeping. "The ratio of tin ... to ... copper ... changes ..."

"The ... color," Mom picked up with a snore, "of ... the ... verdigris ... and strength ... of the bell."

Together they laughed, and it was like a hose to a flame: any grief or tension that had just suffused the room was now snuffed out. Both Gellars could pretend it hadn't happened, that Frank Carter had never been discussed between them and no rule had ever been broken.

"Ahem," Steve declared, poking his head into the bedroom. "Dinner is served. Tonight's menu is spaghetti Bolognese, and I hope it pleases you, m'ladies."

"So what does *The Curse of Allard Fortin* say?" Mom asked as they all sat at the table. "Oh, can you pass the pepper, Steve?"

"Um, it's pretty nuts," Freddie said honestly. "Like, full-on delusional. Fabre claims that José Allard Fortin had these three servants bound to him by blood that he brought over from France. And they basically killed people for him. Including all the competition of neighboring logging settlements. A rival suitor for his lover's hand. A British flank of soldiers. And pretty much anyone else in his way."

"Ooooh," Steve crooned, handing the pepper to Mom. "Are we talking about a certain book that pissed off everyone in town?"

"You know the book?" Freddie asked. "By Edgar Fabre?"

"Of course. Well, sort of. That whole affair was before I was born, but my dad was still angry about it right up until the day he died. *That ugly Fabre spewing his lies about our founder! I hope he rots!* They ran the guy and his family out of town, you know."

"Wait, what?" Freddie gaped. "That guy lived here? Edgar Fabre? Is he, by chance, still alive?"

"No, no." Steve pulled a pained face. "He died pretty young, I think. In the 1960s, maybe? It was unsurprising, given that the book he wrote ruined his entire life. He used all of his family's money to print it, then the Allard Fortins sued him into oblivion. Then *all* of the town where he'd grown up turned on him. That kind of stress does not lead to a long, fulfilled life."

Or maybe, Freddie thought, imagining her dad's handwriting, *Edgar didn't die.*

Except, *The Curse of Allard Fortin* was also printed fifty years ago . . . which would make Edgar pretty darn old at this point.

"Why are we talking about this?" Steve asked, pouring way too much salt on his spaghetti—and earning a glare from Mom.

"Because Freddie found what might be the last remaining copy of *The Curse of Allard Fortin.*"

"Oooh, don't let the Allard Fortins see," Steve said with a grin. "They can be quite litigious."

"From the grave?" Mom glared.

"Well," Freddie said with a grin like Steve's, "if Fabre's book was accurate, then they *could* use their cursed Executioners to kill me. Supposedly, they never die."

"Executioners?" Steve said with wide-eyed glee. "This story gets better and better. So where are these supposed undead now?"

"Yeah." Freddie waggled her eyebrows. "That's one of the many holes in Fabre's story. Supposedly the spirits of Allard Fortin's Executioners can't die. A hangsman, a headsman, and a disemboweler."

"A *disembowler*?" Steve squawked. "Oh my goodness, we should try to republish this, Patty. I mean, this is some great material. We could probably sell the rights to Hollywood. Can you imagine disemboweling on the big screen? Wait—you do know what disemboweling is, right?"

"I'm a historian, Steve, and fully insulted by this question."

"Well, *I* don't know what it is," Freddie inserted. "Isn't it just removing someone's organs?"

"Oh no." Steve's eyes lit up. "It's so much more horrifying." He leaned onto his elbows, voice dropping to a delighted whisper. "Disemboweling is where they slice open your abdomen and pull out the end of your large intestine. Then they nail it to a tree and make you *walk* yourself around the tree."

To display this, Steve stabbed his fork into the spaghetti and slowly twirled. "It's slow, brutal, and one of the most gruesome ways to die."

Freddie swallowed.

And Mom sighed a tired Historical Director sigh as she

stabbed her own fork into her noodles. "No wonder the Allard Fortins were so annoyed. Blood oaths and spirits aside, José Allard Fortin simply didn't need an executioner—much less *three* of them."

"Does that mean . . ." Freddie poked at a chunk of sauce. "That you *don't* want to read *The Curse of Allard Fortin* when I'm done? I mean, if it's all so implausible, I can just burn it."

Steve choked a laugh. Mom's glare turned deadly.

And Freddie grinned—although it was, admittedly, a forced thing. Because as fun as this conversation was, her brain was still roiling from the double monsoons, which had only gotten bigger with this new information from Steve.

Edgar Fabre had been ruined and run out of town. If that wasn't motive for murder, then Freddie didn't know what was— and Freddie's instincts knew when they were onto something. Now she just had to figure out where that guy was. Had he died or hadn't he?

The truth *was* out there.

"You feeling okay?" Mom asked after several minutes of Freddie staring into nothing.

Freddie shook herself. "Oh yeah, sorry." She blinked. "I just really need to get my homework done. Do you mind if I eat later?"

"Sure." Mom bit her lip. There was spaghetti sauce on her nose.

And with another forced smile, Freddie bolted for her room.

It was almost ten o'clock by the time Freddie finished reading all of *The Curse of Allard Fortin*. It wasn't a long book, and most of it was just a translation of what the original Fabre had written in his diary.

Which was fully unhinged.

Like, Freddie kind of understood why the Allard Fortins had sued Edgar for printing this—and she had to wonder, honestly, if Original Fabre hadn't maybe been working with a little too much lead at his forge. Because how else could one explain such delusion?

For example, the diary said that not only did the servants go around killing any enemy of José Allard Fortin, but their blood oath meant their spirits would stay alive for all of eternity—and those spirits could, in turn, be controlled for all of eternity too.

Ropey, Hacky, and Stabby. That was what Freddie had started calling the Executioners in her head, since there were no actual names for these supposedly cursed souls in Fabre's diary.

There was at least one piece of the book, though, that might be relevant to Freddie's search for answers, and it came at the very end: allegedly, Allard Fortin's bell—which he used to summon his Executioners—had broken. Its clapper was too big and the winters here colder than those back in France. So he'd hired Original Fabre to make a new bell according to very specific, very strange specifications that had included a tin-to-copper ratio that Original Fabre hadn't thought was wise.

His thoughts hadn't mattered, though, since that was what Allard Fortin had wanted.

Fabre's desire to be paid hadn't mattered either, since—according to him—once the bell was complete, there was nothing to stop Fortin from commanding his Executioners to kill him.

Obviously, none of this was even remotely real, except for perhaps the commissioning of a new bell in the 1670s and a disgruntled blacksmith who'd wanted his money. People said all sorts of awful things when there were unpaid bills involved.

But whether or not the history was accurate didn't actually matter. What mattered was that someone in the *present day* was obviously pulling inspiration from these stories.

So to the internet Freddie turned, hunkering down at her family's computer in the den.

Edgar Fabre, she typed into Ask Jeeves.

Unfortunately, Jeeves had nothing to offer. So then she tried *The Curse of Allard Fortin,* which yielded only a message board about how bad parking was at the City-on-the-Berme Village Historique.

Touché.

Freddie was just sticking out her tongue at the monitor when a familiar *uh-oh* dinged from her ICQ.

Her heart rocketed through her forehead. She frantically clicked open the messenger service.

And right there, before her eyes, was a window claiming the user *verybadhumanindeed82* wanted to add her as a contact. *Do you accept?*

Freddie slammed down the Enter key, and without waiting for Theo to initiate a conversation—and not even caring if she seemed wildly overeager—Freddie typed out:

LanceInMyHeart2000
Did you get ICQ just to talk to me?

A short pause. Then:

verybadhumanindeed82
obviously

Freddie's throat clenched up.

But then she shook her head like a wet dog—because she wasn't supposed to care if Theo wanted to talk to her. He was the enemy.

Solemn vow. Solemn vow.

Besides, there was a perfectly logical explanation for his ICQ debut—and it had nothing to do with Theo *wanting* to talk to her, but everything to do with their earlier agreement.

LanceInMyHeart2000
Did your grandmother wake up?

verybadhumanindeed82
not yet

Freddie's throat clenched up all over again.

LanceInMyHeart2000
So why are you talking to me?
verybadhumanindeed82
u ask a lot of questions
LanceInMyHeart2000
And that is not an answer.

Freddie's fingers hovered over the keyboard. What could she say that wouldn't show how excited she was to be talking to him? And that also wouldn't scare him away?

No, wait—*no*. She *wasn't* excited. These sparklers in her veins were not from him. *SOLEMN VOW, GELLAR. SOLEMN VOW.* She just needed to stay on task. An opportunity had come her way; she couldn't squander that.

LanceInMyHeart2000
I need another favor, Mr. Porter.
verybadhumanindeed82
wow. ok. bold, gellar. bold.
LanceInMyHeart2000
What does that mean?
verybadhumanindeed82
u just came right out & said it
LanceInMyHeart2000
Is there some other way I should
   approach my request? Do you have
   a secretary that handles your
   schedule for you?
verybadhumanindeed82
i think they're called admins now

Freddie couldn't quite tell if this was a flirtatious retort or not. Either way, the whole conversation was making her gut swirl.

> **LanceInMyHeart2000**
> What would it cost me to get a key card to your school library?

For several *agonizing* seconds, Theo didn't respond. And for those *agonizing* seconds, Freddie's heart wound itself into tangled misery like an intestine around a tree.

Until she finally snapped and typed:

> **LanceInMyHeart2000**
> Are you still there?
> **verybadhumanindeed82**
> yeah, i'm thinking

Oh, thank goodness.

> **verybadhumanindeed82**
> when do u need the library?
> **LanceInMyHeart2000**
> Tomorrow morning.
> I can meet you outside before school starts.
> **verybadhumanindeed82**
> **very** bold
> i presume this is for a prank?
> **LanceInMyHeart2000**
> Maybe.
> **verybadhumanindeed82**
> then maybe u shouldn't have told me about it
> i mean, what's to keep me from interfering?

LanceInMyHeart2000
Quid pro quo.
I didn't interfere when you
   were stealing the key
   to *my* school.
verybadhumanindeed82
bc i distracted u

Freddie's eyes widened at those words: *Because I distracted you.* And he thought *she* was the bold one. She wet her lips and wrote back:

LanceInMyHeart2000
PUH-LEASE, Mr. Porter.
We both know I'm the one who
   distracted you.

Another agonizing pause, until at last he responded:

verybadhumanindeed82
doesn't really matter who distracted
   whom

Freddie disagreed. But she greatly appreciated his proper use of "whom."

verybadhumanindeed82
this is different from what happened
   on Sunday
that was refraining from
   interference; this would be
   straight up helping u

Ungh. And he knew how to use a semicolon! This was really too much for Freddie's little heart.

verybadhumanindeed82
  in case u've forgotten, we're
  enemies remember?

Right. Dammit. They *were* enemies. Right, right, right.

LanceInMyHeart2000
  Well, the library isn't actually part
  of the prank.
  So you wouldn't be aiding and abetting.
  Like, the prank squad will be there
  for mayhem.
  I just *also* need to find something
  in your library—and I can't get in
  without a key card.
verybadhumanindeed82
  what do u need to find?
LanceInMyHeart2000
  If you get me a card, I'll explain.

There was that pause again. And there went Freddie's heart again, knotting up. Until she finally cracked.

LanceInMyHeart2000
  Are you still there?
verybadhumanindeed82
  u r so impatient
  let a guy think
LanceInMyHeart2000
  Think *faster*
verybadhumanindeed82
  FINE
  i will give u access to the library

Freddie cheered.

> **verybadhumanindeed82**
> but in exchange, i want a 2 pg paper on the russian revolution.
> single spaced. none of that big font bs

Sure. Freddie could do that. Theo hadn't said it had to be a *good* paper.

> **LanceInMyHeart2000**
> When do you need it by?
> **verybadhumanindeed82**
> friday
> **LanceInMyHeart2000**
> Okay. I'll give it to you at rehearsal on Wednesday.
> **verybadhumanindeed82**
> deal.

Freddie sucked in sharply.
Deal.
That meant he would be at the next rehearsal. That meant, maybe... maybe they would have to kiss again, and *yes*, she knew this made *her* the Very Bad Human Indeed—and *YES*, her conscience was shrieking at her about best friend betrayals and backstabbing...

"Yarrrgggh," she groaned at the screen.

"That sounds very serious," Steve replied.

Freddie lurched around, almost toppling out of the desk chair. *How* did her parents move so quietly? "Erm, hey, Steve. *Whasssupppp?*"

Her stepdad arched an eyebrow. "I have never heard you speak that way. Nor look so guilty." His lips pursed. "Are you looking at porn?"

Freddie's whole face turned molten. *"STEVE."* She clapped her hands to her cheeks. "Of course I'm not—yuck! *Gross!*"

"Well, in that case"—Steve grinned—"you won't mind getting off the computer. I need to make a phone call, and you're hogging the line."

"Fine," Freddie muttered, twisting back to the keyboard.

> **LanceInMyHeart2000**
> I have to go. My stepdad needs the phone.
> What time can you meet?
> **verybadhumanindeed82**
> 7:15
> by the fortin crypt u ruined

Freddie choked. She had *not* ruined it—NEVER—and now there was no time to properly reply.

> **LanceInMyHeart2000**
> Okay. Cya then.
> **verybadhumanindeed82**
> that u will, gellar
> looking forward to it

14

Looking forward to it. How was a gal supposed to sleep after a comment like that? Needless to say, Freddie didn't. On the one hand, this meant she didn't have any disturbing dreams . . . or kissing dreams either.

On the other hand, it meant she began her day feeling like the Crypt Keeper. And frankly looking like him too. To make her feel *that much better about herself,* the Fortin Prep uniform acquired from the Friedmans' dry cleaners yesterday didn't fit.

It was intended for the proportions of a teenage boy, which left it too tight in Freddie's hips and boobs, and too loose everywhere else. But with half-shuttered eyes and a yawn, Freddie managed to squeeze into it. Then she snuck out of her room, ready to meet Kyle and Cat promptly at seven A.M.

Well, *they* were prompt. Freddie was two minutes late because halfway through the kitchen, a button on the shirt decided today was the day it wanted freedom. It went *sproing!*, hit the Mr. Coffee, and suddenly Freddie found herself giving those one-boobed paintings a real run for their money.

One safety pin later—the heavy-duty kind—she was finally out the front door and into the still-dark morning. Where she promptly heard "Dreams" by the Cranberries blasting from Kyle's Jeep. The volume doubled as soon as she opened the back door and clambered in. "Hey!" Kyle shouted over *Oh, my life is changin' every day.* "Looking good!"

This was quite an overstatement, but Freddie blushed anyway. Kyle's uniform—despite also being the forgotten leftover of a former student—fit his shapely body to a T. And although Cat (seated in shotgun) didn't look quite as flawless as Kyle, at least her uniform was intended for someone with breasts.

"Here," Cat said once Freddie was buckled in. She also had to pitch her voice over the music. "Put this on your hair! They all know what you look like over there."

The *this* in question was a plain red baseball cap, under which Freddie did not think her hair would actually fit. But it was at least *sort* of a disguise, because Cat was right: the kids at Fortin definitely knew what Freddie looked like. Especially after the Incident with the Kiss.

Laina, Luis, and Divya were not joining for this prank. Laina and Divya had perfect attendance records (who were these people?) while Luis never missed his morning run (ugh). Cat, Kyle, and Freddie meanwhile had nothing to lose—and Freddie had quite a lot to gain.

Kyle of course drove with his usual reckless abandon, which almost became wreck-ful abandon when an entire herd (or was it a *clan*?) of deer went sprinting across the road. He only hit the brakes in time to miss them because Cat and Freddie both screamed. *Loudly.*

Really, this could have been added to Kyle's résumé at this point: *Extracurricular activities: near-miss car accidents.*

His Jeep careened to a stop right in front of the county park's trail entrance. *The* entrance Freddie had chased Mrs. Ferris to. There was police tape across it now. *Those woods aren't safe right now,* Ibrahim had said. *First Mrs. Ferris got mauled . . . and now we've got another body.*

But there'd been no mention of a body in today's paper. Freddie had checked. No mention of feds coming to town either, or any clue as to what Ibrahim might've been referring to.

Five minutes later, the stone pillars and sign that marked the entrance to Allard Fortin Preparatory School came into view, and Kyle finally slowed his Mario Kart speeds so he could pull in.

"F-U, Fortin Prep," Kyle said at the sign—followed by a delighted, "Hey, they're the same letters! *F-U, F-P!* Say it with me, guys!"

No one said it with him.

The drive curved and crooked upward, forcing Kyle to a slogging twenty-five miles per hour. Every few seconds, Freddie would glimpse a rooftop or window or balcony from the main estate. The sun hadn't risen yet, but there was at least a grayish haze to brighten the lawns and outbuildings. Students shambled on paths and sidewalks as Kyle drove them ever uphill, and at an intersection leading either toward the main estate or to the dorms, Kyle chose the dorms.

Thirty seconds later, they pulled into a newly paved lot packed with fancy cars. And through a dense row of privacy evergreens, Freddie could see the dorms. She could see *Theo's* dorm.

She could also see the mausoleum—or at least its domed roof—through another row of pines and firs. And of course, those secret-corner yew hedges.

Suddenly, her heart was beating very fast. She felt dizzy too, and she greatly regretted skipping breakfast (again). She also wished Kyle would turn down the heat.

"Alright," she told Cat and Kyle once they were parked. "You know what to do. Dorms, bathrooms, and if you're still uncaught, call—"

"Cat's cousin," Kyle interrupted with a grin. "He's on bystand right now."

Cat sighed. "He means standby."

"Oh yeah." Kyle laughed. "That too."

And Freddie couldn't help but laugh with him, the precious little airhead. "Alright. When everything is done, call me." She waved Sabrina at them. "And also, if there is any trouble *at all*, call me."

"Aye, aye, Prank Wizard!" Cat saluted, and they all piled

out. While Kyle opened his trunk and handed out supplies, Freddie tugged her new cap low. A duffle and a backpack for Cat, two massive trash bags for Kyle, and a final duffle (in bright leprechaun green) for Freddie. All of the bags were distinctly cubical, thanks to the crates of crickets within, but like the uniforms, the disguises were *just* good enough to hopefully pass muster.

And fortunately, as long as the crickets were being jostled about, they were silent. "See you soon," Freddie whispered, then she waited until Cat and Kyle were out of sight toward the dorms before setting off herself.

She could already see a blond figure lounging like a Gap model against a lamppost near the mausoleum's gardens. Freddie gulped. And gulped again, telling herself those weren't butterflies in her stomach—they were just the residual hum of crickets.

For the first ten steps, the freezing morning air was a relief, but by the time Freddie reached the gardens and hedges, she was numb to her core. These blazers were not good for warmth.

Theo didn't seem to notice Freddie's approach. He was staring at his shoes, hands in his pockets. His face looked marginally better than the day before, in that the swelling had reduced. And against Freddie's greatest desire, she was forced to admit that "beat up" worked unfairly well on Theo Porter. He looked Very Bad Indeed, and with the mausoleum wreathed in morning fog behind him, he might as well have been posing for the opening shot of a new horror film.

All of it was spotless too. Theo and the other students had done a great job cleaning the Prank Squad's mess, and Freddie couldn't decide if she was sad to see her handiwork so easily erased . . . or relieved because she really *was* a Good Girl in the end.

"Nice job cleaning," she called as she strode around a trimmed rosebush and low yew hedge.

Theo jerked off the lamppost, his expression turning mildly aghast as he took in Freddie's uniform. Then he tipped his head sideways and peered beneath her cap's bill. "Gellar? Is that you in there?"

"Barely," she admitted. "This uniform is meant for different proportions, I fear." She flicked at the heavy-duty safety pin.

And Theo's cheeks reddened. He cleared his throat and looked away. "Where did you, uh, even find that getup?"

"A magician never tells her secrets." Freddie hefted the duffle bag higher on her shoulder. "Can I get that key card, please?"

"About that." He sauntered backward, aiming toward the mausoleum with a lazy shrug. "I cannot, in good conscience, allow you to run pell-mell through my library."

"I would *never* run in a library, Mr. Porter."

He smiled—just a flicker. "Be that as it may, you can't get access without me beside you."

Ah. That would not work well for Mission Release Crickets. Freddie hopped after him. "What would it take to change your mind?"

"Nonnegotiable."

"Everyone has a price."

"Not me." He smiled again, but this one did not reach his eyes. "So do you want access or not?" He slowed to a stop before the mausoleum. His hand rested on the marble sign, thumb tapping just over *Le pouvoir réside dans le service.*

(In *The Curse of Allard Fortin*, Edgar Fabre had actually pointed to this quote on the mausoleum as proof that José had cursed his three servants. Because sure, Eddie! Makes total sense.)

"What about first period?" Freddie countered. "You would just skip class?"

"You aren't the only rebel around here."

This argument made no sense, although Freddie couldn't

pinpoint the exact fallacy. "I *told* you, though, Mr. Porter: the library isn't part of our prank. I'm just doing research in there."

"And why should I trust you?" His fingers stilled on the sign. Behind him, one of the busts of José Allard Fortin seemed to be glaring. "I barely know you, Gellar."

Freddie matched the Fortin glare. She and Theo had exchanged saliva two days ago; that ought to count for something. But she also couldn't just stand here in the cold, wasting precious moments of her stolen time. "Fine, Mr. Porter. You win." Freddie thrust out her hand.

"Great." Theo shook it, his grip firm and fingers cold from the marble. "Then away we go. But hey, watch your step; there's a loose brick right there."

The Fortin Prep library looked like every fancy library Freddie had ever seen in photographs. With its gleaming oak shelves and ladders, with its second level of shelves and aisles and polished wood floors, Freddie was both thoroughly in love and also thoroughly intimidated.

In her safety-pinned shirt and hip-hugging khakis, she definitely didn't belong. Which admittedly, she *literally* didn't belong since she wasn't a student. But she at least wanted to look like she could fit in.

After a single swipe at the library entrance with his key card, Theo led Freddie inside. She hurried after him, wondering how much longer she had until these crickets started singing. As long as Theo was with her, she couldn't release them.

What a conundrum. And honestly, it was a wonder Theo hadn't already asked her about her bag. Then again, he seemed preoccupied. That restless energy from Saturday was back, and he kept touching his face. Scrubbing at his hair.

Freddie hardly blamed him. She really wanted to touch his face and scrub his hair too. No human had any right to look that good with a black eye.

A librarian glanced up from a desk at the heart of the room. Theo grinned and waved. "Hey, Mr. Kowalski," he called before strutting by.

Mr. Kowalski nodded back and after sparing a cursory glance for Freddie, he declared, "No hats in the library!"

"Sorry," Freddie replied in what she hoped was a very gruff and very manly voice.

Judging by Theo's smirking side eye, it was not. Fortunately, Mr. Kowalski didn't notice—nor did he watch them cut down an aisle or see how Freddie left her hat exactly where it had been all along. *Nor* did he catch sight of Freddie's oddly shaped bag, which she kept shaking every few steps to ensure the crickets stayed quiet.

Theo led Freddie all the way to the back of the library, to a quiet corner with a low desk as shiny and spotless as every other surface nearby. (Allard Fortin Preparatory School must spend a lot of money on wood polish.)

"Okay," Theo said, slouching onto the edge of the desk and crossing his arms. "Tell me why you're here."

Freddie hesitated. Last night, before bed, she'd worked out an explanation for Theo. Though she didn't like lying, sometimes a detective really had no choice. After all, Theo was the sheriff's nephew and Freddie had now been warned by two separate cops not to look into what was happening at the county park.

Of course, Freddie had also not expected Theo to join her here. Her story from last night wasn't going to cut it as long as he could simply look over her shoulder and see what she was doing.

"Fine," she said with her most dramatic sigh. She yanked off her cap; her hair tumbled out.

Theo tensed against the table.

"I need access to your newspaper collection. Miss Gupta at the Berm Library said that Fortin Prep had original copies of all the local papers."

"We do. Why do you need them?"

"I have a report due," she said, falling back on the same cover story she'd given Mom. Except she improvised: "It's on unsolved murders from the seventies and eighties. The articles I needed weren't at the Berm Library, so here we are."

Theo's eyes narrowed. "Why not get a special research permit, then? Why do you need to *break* in?"

"It's not 'breaking in' if someone is giving you their key card. And I need it now because my paper is due tomorrow."

"Hmmm," Theo replied, and Freddie could tell he didn't believe her. But he also—to her shock—didn't argue. He just straightened and said, "Follow me. And hey," he added over his shoulder, "put your hat back on. You could kill a guy with that hair."

He disappeared down a nearby row, leaving Freddie mildly stunned. He had, yet again, *maybe* given her a compliment? It certainly felt like one in her chest (which had gone all tingly and goopy).

NO, she reminded herself as she hastily stuffed the cap back over her hair. He was a Montague. His compliments were poison; she needed to keep her eye on the prize. *Remember your vow.*

A short walk later, Theo paused before an arched doorway that looked Very Gothic Indeed. He swiped his card over a blocky key reader. A lock clicked, Theo swung the door wide, and after holding it open for Freddie, he descended down a brightly lit stairwell. The stairs doubled back once before opening into a large concrete cellar packed with wooden filing cabinets. Row after row spanned for as long as the library above ran.

It was like a *much* fancier version of Les Archives.

"Wow," Freddie breathed. "That's a lot of newspapers."

"We have one of the best high school journalism programs in the country," Theo murmured, almost like a reflex. Then he cocked his chin forward, hair flopping, and said, "Local papers are that way."

With a surety that spoke of frequent time spent here, Theo led Freddie halfway down the cellar, where he veered right, into a row of more identical cabinets. A desk was wedged between two cabinets, and above it was a recessed window. Morning's first light trickled in.

He waved to the left. "*Berm Sentinel* over there." He pointed toward the window-wall. "The now defunct *Elmore Gazette* over there. And other nearby periodicals are on the right. It's all arranged by date, so . . ." He twirled around to face Freddie—quite graceful. Definitely worthy of the Backstreet Boys.

And, for the first time since Freddie had arrived, some of his restlessness seemed to melt away. Like this cellar was a place that made sense to him. Like *here* he could be at ease.

Freddie understood that. She'd felt the same, sitting in Bowman's car or exploring her way through the tiny police station—or just scouring security footage while hunting for a shoplifter. It was in those moments that Freddie had really felt like *Yeah. This is where I'm supposed to be, finding answers.*

"I'm impressed, Mr. Porter." Freddie set down the bag of crickets at the end of the aisle (giving them a solid kick for good measure). "You know your way around this place."

He bounced a single shoulder. "I was in the journalism program."

"Was?"

A beat passed. Then he amended, "*Am* in the journalism program."

Freddie didn't buy that cover, but she also didn't press him on it. Bad Boys were entitled to their secrets. Plus, she didn't know how much pestering she could get away with before he either revoked her access to this basement or else paid a little too much attention to her duffle bag.

So she opened her arms and declared: "In that case, Mr. Porter, I beg for your journalistic assistance. Please, if you would be so kind, tell me where to find the *Berm Sentinel* from 1975."

A lilt of his lips. A slight nod. "You got it, Gellar. Follow me."

15

Theo led Freddie straight to the cabinets for the *Berm Sentinel*, where tiny labels declared the years and months, and after quickly finding 1975, he flourished his arms and stepped aside.

"The 1975 drawer, my lady."

"Why, thank you, good sir." She bent past him, and there it was: her own sense of calm. That hunger in her belly that told her she was doing what she was meant to do. It felt good—so good she scarcely noticed Theo peeking over her shoulder while she flipped through fat green folders.

Labels winked up at her, organized by month. "October," she mumbled to herself. *Flip, flip, flip.* "October, October . . . here." She grinned and eased the enormous file from the cabinet. Without any concern for Theo, she hurried to the nearest desk.

Inside were all the papers she had combed only yesterday on the microfiche machine. She thumbed through them, untroubled by the black ink left on her fingertips, until finally she reached . . .

October 21.

And then October 23.

She checked again. "Twenty-one." *Flip.* "Twenty-three. What the heck?" She frowned at Theo. Her gut was tickling. "The twenty-second isn't in here. Just like at the library."

Now it was his turn to frown. "That's weird. You're not allowed to take papers out of the collection." He pulled the folder in front of him and counted, just under his breath, through every issue. All the way up to Halloween of 1975.

But there was still no October 22. He shook his head. "Maybe someone left it on the copier?"

"The *exact* date I need?" Freddie's eyebrows lifted incredulously.

"I don't know." He backed away from the desk. "I'll go look. Stay here." In a swirl of detergent-scented air, he spun away.

And for several seconds, Freddie just stood there—completely and totally trapped within a Grave Moral Problem quite worthy of the philosophical greats. For if ever there was a moment for Freddie to release crickets, then now was it. Theo was away, and while *no*, this wasn't where she was supposed to free them, it might be her only chance to do so.

She crept toward the duffle bag. So innocent. Then she bent around the edge of the rows and squinted to the far end of the cellar. Theo had his back to her.

Now was her moment.

Yet for some stupid, *stupid* reason, she wasn't taking it. She was just watching him and chewing her lip. The copier machine banged shut; Theo turned.

And Freddie kicked the duffle. *"Stay quiet,"* she hissed before scampering right back to the desk. She would just have to hope another opportunity came by.

Freddie next turned her attention to the *Elmore Gazette,* not even bothering to remove its October file from the drawer. She searched it right there, and by the time Theo came jogging back (his cheeks deliciously pink) she had already confirmed. "It's missing here too."

"There's nothing on the copier." He came to a stop beside her, head shaking. "Check the *County Weekly,* and I'll look at the *Berm Observer.*"

They each did exactly that, moving on to every local paper or magazine in print during 1975. And for *every single one,* the date of October 22 had been removed.

"Someone took them," Theo declared from his spot beside a floor-level drawer. His thumb toyed with the stitches over his eye. "It's the only possible explanation—except why would someone want them, Gellar? What happened on that day?"

"It's not what happened on the twenty-second," Freddie explained. "It's what happened on the twenty-first." She slid her attention to a green folder before her—November 1975. It would seem several dates from this month were missing, suggesting those issues must *also* have had information referencing the mysterious affair at the county park that got the fête moved.

"So what happened on the twenty-first, then?"

"It's what I told you, Mr. Porter: there was an unsolved murder." That wasn't a *total* lie.

"What kind of murder?" He moved to the desk and leaned against it. A split second later, his arms folded over his chest . . . And a split second after that, his thumb started tapping.

So predictable.

"Why do you care?" Freddie picked through the November issues, counting how many were gone. Six in total.

"I *care* because I'm helping you, and you owe me a full explanation."

Freddie supposed that was fair. "Okay, fine. But don't say I didn't warn you. On October 21, 1975, someone got decapitated in the county park, and as messed up as that was, what makes it *extra* weird is . . . Wait a minute." Freddie frowned Theo's way. "Why did you just cough like that?"

He didn't answer. His whole face had gone white. Even his busted lips had paled, and his black eye looked a sickly green— which was not the reaction Freddie had expected. Mild horror, sure. Disgust, fine. Casual disinterest, maybe. But instead Theo looked like he might vomit. He was even pressing the back of his hand to his lips.

"What . . . makes it extra weird?" he squeezed out.

"There was a hanging shortly before." Freddie spoke these words with total detachment, gaze rooted on Theo. "And then another hanging in 1987. And *another* hanging now—just a few days ago, as you know."

Yeah, he *really* looked like he might vomit. "Hangings?" he said, mouth still covered with his fingers. "Let's look for those." He shoved off the table, a jerky movement. Gone was his earlier grace.

Not his speed, though. In moments, he'd plucked out the 1987 files for the *Berm Sentinel*. He didn't bother closing the drawer before striding back to the desk and tearing it wide. Seconds later, he had found the same article Freddie's dad had cut out only a few weeks before his heart attack.

Freddie watched as Theo's eyes raced over the headline—"Suicide By Hanging in County Park"—and then over the entirety of the article. Somehow, his face went paler.

And Freddie could tell, deep in her gut, that Theo Porter knew something. "What is it?" she asked. "Why do these deaths matter to you?"

He didn't try to deny it. "This." He poked at the headline. "Like you said, a hanging just happened again. And three times is . . . a lot."

"And?" Freddie shook her head. "That's not all that's bothering you. I can tell, Mr. Porter. Is it because of the second body in the forest?"

Theo bit his lip. Then hissed with pain, as if he'd forgotten the gash was just above. "How do you know about that, Gellar? I checked the paper today. There was no beheading mentioned."

Freddie gasped. Her whole body rocked back. "A beheading? How do *you* know it was a beheading?"

Theo's face tightened, like he was remembering something he very much wanted to forget. "My aunt slipped up," he answered eventually. "She mentioned something she shouldn't have, about a body by the beach. No head."

Before Freddie could press Theo with any more questions, he suddenly straightened. And just like that, his pallor was gone; the steady, determined Theo had returned. "You said the same thing happened in 1975? A decapitation on October twenty-first?"

A nod from Freddie.

"But if all the articles are missing, then how do *you* know that?"

"Because," Freddie said, and in quick terms, she described the article she'd found about why the Fête du Bûcheron had been temporarily moved. About a decapitated body and the traumatized drunk guy who'd been with the victim. "That was all the article described, though. No details about *who* those people were or what the police found."

"Okay." Theo drawled out the word as he ran a hand through his hair. "Let's say someone came in here and removed all those articles from 1975. Why not take the ones from 1987 too?"

"I . . . don't know." Freddie *didn't* know. She had come here hoping for answers, and now she only had more questions.

"Let's check the Chicago papers." Theo motioned to an aisle across the room. "If there was something that messed-up happening, then it would have reached the cities." He loped away.

And Freddie scampered after him. Now her gut was really singing. "So you think someone went into the local libraries and removed *all* the articles about October 21, 1975—and no one noticed?"

"What other explanation could there be?" Theo slung into an identical row of cabinets with an identical desk and window. "You know it's not just a coincidence, Gellar."

No. It wasn't. And as much as Freddie appreciated Theo helping her on this . . . She grabbed his arm and tugged him to a stop. "Why do you care?"

He paused mid stride. Then he turned to face her, beat-up and gorgeous. "Why do *you* care?"

"I told you—"

"A paper on unsolved murders? Yeah right." He sniffed. "You're investigating the weird stuff happening at the park exactly like my aunt told you not to."

Freddie gnawed her lip. She couldn't argue with him on that. And she wasn't entirely sure she wanted to. In fact, she was starting to suspect maybe she wasn't the only one with answer-sniffing instincts in her veins.

"I think *you* think something is going on," Theo continued. "Something that connects a suicide to a water bottle . . . and something that got my grandmother put in the hospital."

Freddie's lips parted, her lungs readying to fire out: *Fine. I'll tell you what I know.* But before she could utter a word, a car alarm blasted in the distance. A blaring *wah-wah-wah.*

Freddie's lips clamped shut. This was not good timing, and two whole seconds passed before understanding washed over Theo's face. "Oh my god." He laughed, a bitter sound, and swung his attention to the nearest window. "That's my car, isn't it?"

There was nothing Freddie could do but nod. And cringe.

"*Dammit,* Gellar. What happened to 'the library is for something else'?"

"It *is.*" She pointed to the filing cabinets. "You *know* I'm here for these articles."

"And why should I believe you?" Theo tugged at his hair. "Maybe this is just another prank. Did Davis put you up to this?"

"Who?" Freddie shook her head. "Who's Davis?"

"Did you come in here earlier and steal all the papers from 1975? Just to distract me while your freaking cronies broke into my car?"

"That," Freddie declared, "sounds *ridiculous.* Listen to yourself. How could I have removed those newspapers? I didn't even know you would come down here with me."

Theo blinked. Then deflated, as if realizing this was, in fact, true: Freddie couldn't have possibly known he would insist on joining her.

"And look." Freddie marched toward her duffle bag, hands waving. "Do you see that? Do you wanna know what's inside? It's a crate filled with crickets. I was supposed to release them while I was in the building, but I chose not to, Theo. *Surely* that counts for something."

"Crickets?" Theo stared at the duffle bag. "You and your friends came here to release crickets?"

"Yes."

He ran his tongue over his teeth. "But you're also here to break into my car."

"They aren't *breaking* into your car. Cat's cousin is a perfectly legitimate locksmith."

"That was your idea, though, wasn't it?" He took a step toward Freddie. "No way *they* came up with that."

"No," Freddie admitted. "It was my idea."

"So what if I told you the prank book isn't in there? Your plan completely falls apart."

"Except I wouldn't believe you." Freddie puffed out her chest, refusing to be intimidated by his approach. Theo was only three steps away from her now. "You see, if I were you, Mr. Porter, I would have moved the prank book as soon as I realized the other school knew where it was. The most obvious hiding place would be your car. Because it's locked, of course."

"*Was* locked." He eased another step toward her.

"Fair enough." She shrugged. "It *was* locked."

Another step. "And what's to keep me from running out there and stopping them?"

"Go for it," Freddie dared.

"You mean you wouldn't interfere?"

She rolled her eyes as hard as she could. "I *told* you, Mr. Porter, I'm not here to distract you."

"And what if I said . . ." He paused, jaw muscle fluttering. Tongue flicking over his lips. Then he closed the final step between them. "And what if I said my life was a mess right now? What if I said that all I wanted was to be distracted?"

It took Freddie two heartbeats to understand what he was telling her. Two heartbeats filled with a car alarm and the waking whistle of impatient crickets. Then the reality of his words—of what he was *implying*—careened into her.

Her breath punched out. "I . . . I'm sure there are lots of people who would willingly distract you."

"And maybe I don't want lots of people, Gellar. Remember how I said I'd be impressed if you actually got the log book back? Well, here I am. Impressed."

"Is . . . is this a prank?" Freddie croaked. Theo spoke like a teen movie; people didn't say these sorts of things in Real Life. And they certainly didn't say them to her.

"No." He scratched the back of his neck. "If anyone from Fortin found out I was down here with you, telling you what I just said . . . Well, it would not be great for me."

"So why *did* you tell me? And why are you still here?"

"I don't know," he admitted. "But you're still standing here too, so I figure that has to count for something."

Yes, Freddie was still standing here too—and she supposed he was right: it did count for something.

It also counted that Theo was very close now. Close enough for her to see each of the stitches over his left eye (four of them) and also how bloodshot his black eye really was. And yes, he had been standing close to her all morning, but now it was different.

Now an energy crackled off him that was aching and exposed. That had nothing to lose and didn't care about enemies or prank wars or Montagues at Verona Beach.

This was Theo from the old water mill. This was Theo holding out his iron heart, and suddenly—just like that—Freddie knew what to do.

16

Ever so gently, Freddie reached up and touched Theo's face. Exactly as she'd wanted to at the hospital. Exactly as she'd wanted to all morning. He didn't pull away. He simply watched her, breath held and lips parted.

Outside, the car alarm kept blaring. The crickets hummed and crooned.

Freddie brushed her fingers above his stitches—careful not to caress them directly. Someone had punched him there.

Davis, she thought, recalling what Theo had said only a few minutes ago. *Did Davis put you up to this?* Theo had also said his life was a mess, meaning something must have happened to him since their kiss on Sunday.

Something awful. Something more than just his grandmother in the hospital. Something he thought was worth kissing her for.

Ever so slowly, Freddie moved her fingers away from his eyebrow and down the sides of his jaw. With each inch, Theo sucked in air—just a fraction of a breath, his lungs and ribs expanding each time. His pupils dilating.

Then her fingers reached his lips, and he went completely still.

"I don't want to hurt you," she murmured, running her thumb near the cut over his upper lip. Even broken like it was, the skin was soft.

"You won't." His voice was a warm whisper against her fingertips.

She didn't reply. She wanted to kiss him *so badly* that it hurt. Like a python constricting around her chest. But now that she was standing here, now that she'd caressed his face and he hadn't pulled away—now that she had placed her fingertips to his lips and gotten permission to take this further, she found she couldn't move.

She was still so new to all of this. To boys kissing her and her wanting to kiss them back.

So Freddie simply stared up at Theo, and he simply stared down at her. Blue, blue, intense blue. And somewhere, a million miles away, crickets and car alarms still sang.

Theo was the first to finally move. With barely any shift at all, he twisted his head and kissed the tips of Freddie's fingers.

It was like lighting another sparkler. The feel of his lips against the sensitive skin—it sent Freddie's entire stomach rocketing into her eyeballs.

One kiss became two, Theo's gaze never breaking from hers, and Freddie thought she might faint from that stare alone. Then his own fingers slid up and laced gently around her wrist.

He kissed the inside of her fingers. He kissed her palm. He kissed her pulse point. And if it hurt him to do so, he gave no indication. He just kept staring and kissing and, Freddie supposed, waiting for her to offer some kind of reaction.

But Freddie didn't know what reaction to give. She couldn't breathe. She couldn't think. Everything had gone so blurry around the edges, and all she seemed capable of doing was standing there while her chest wound tighter and tighter.

Until at last, her ribs were so tight that her lungs snapped in two. A soft sigh rustled from her throat.

And *that* seemed to be what Theo had been waiting for. In a fluid, hungry movement, he pulled Freddie to him, knocked off her baseball cap, and kissed her.

But where she'd expected ferocity, she found only gentleness.

It was the softest kiss Freddie had ever received. Softer than she'd even known was possible. Just a slight brushing of Theo's lips, while his eyes—still open—held hers.

Haunting, those eyes were.

For several frozen heartbeats, she held his gaze. It felt so intimate, lip to broken lip and eye to swollen eye. More intimate than their kissing or their touching or their flirting had ever been.

Then it was just too much. The wanting that swelled inside Freddie. The need she felt around Theo—it was just too much, and she couldn't hold back any longer. Her eyes closed and she pressed into him, deepening the kiss. Her tongue flicked out, ever so slightly, and oh, there was that soft sound in his throat, the one she remembered from the old mill. The one he'd made in her dream.

She couldn't help but match it, and without realizing what she did, her fingers curled into his blazer, and she tugged him closer. Closer. Not close enough.

Today, he tasted like spearmint. Like toothpaste and mouthwash and clean, clean boy.

Theo's hands moved to Freddie's hips. To her back. And suddenly they were on her butt . . . *below* her butt and lifting her.

She had never straddled a boy before, and she'd certainly never been lifted by one. But the next thing she knew, Theo was carrying her across the cellar. It was easily the hottest thing she had ever experienced—and also mildly terrifying. She was not a particularly small girl, but suddenly she felt Very Small Indeed.

Then her butt landed on the desk, and Theo was kissing her with all the ferocity of the mill.

Her fingers wove into his hair. She cupped his face. Dug into his back. She couldn't seem to keep her hands in one place, and she couldn't seem to grab enough of him. Especially when he moaned—like he was doing now—and pushed his whole perfect body against hers.

Then Theo was kissing Freddie's neck, and she thought she might actually pass out from all the wanting.

Before she could tell him that, though—before she could tell Theo that he made everything inside her spin out of control—someone cleared their throat.

Someone who *wasn't* Freddie or Theo.

"Alright," the voice said. Decidedly male, decidedly older. "That is quite enough, you two."

Freddie and Theo lurched apart.

It was like they'd suddenly caught fire. They heard that voice; they sprang apart two feet. *Stop, drop, and roll.* Except this fire wasn't going out. Freddie was dizzy like she'd inhaled too much smoke, and it took a solid two seconds for her brain to finally, *finally* process who was standing before her.

It was like being doused in flames all over again—but the bad kind. The *mortified* kind. Her jaw fell open. "Dr. Born?"

"Freddie?" He sounded even more shocked than she was. He also looked mildly appalled.

More heat charged over Freddie's body. She smoothed at her shirt. Glanced at Theo—who was clearly as thrown off course as she was. He also looked *excruciatingly* handsome, with his ruffled hair, busted face, and bright pink lips and cheeks.

Do not look at him, Gellar. Theo was dangerous, dangerous, dangerous. Freddie forced her gaze back to the Unwelcome Counselor. "Why are you here, Dr. Born?"

"Theo was supposed to meet me thirty minutes ago." He shot a stern frown at Theo. "And I was told he had come down here. But what are *you* doing here, Freddie?"

"Um . . . making out?"

Theo choked. Then covered his mouth with his hands, stifling a laugh.

"Yes, I can see that." Dr. Born rubbed his temples. "And honestly, I don't care what the two of you do—*except* when you do it during school hours. Freddie, this isn't even your school. Are you skipping right now?"

"Define 'skipping.'"

"I'll take that as a yes." Dr. Born rubbed his temples twice as hard. Then he glared in the direction of another aisle. "By god, what is that sound?"

Uh-oh, the crickets. New shame swooped through Freddie. The insects were screeching in full force now, and honestly, it was a wonder she hadn't noticed just how loud they were before.

She and Theo were too good at this whole distraction thing.

Of course, now that Freddie was paying attention, she also realized the car alarm had turned off. Oh, crap, crap, *crap*. How long had she and Theo been making out?

Freddie slipped Sabrina from her back pocket. Seven missed calls. Oh boy, she was in trouble. "I should probably go," Freddie murmured, more to Theo than to Dr. Born. "Thanks for your help."

"Wait." Theo glanced briefly at Dr. Born before turning the full wattage of his blue eyes onto Freddie. "When can I see you again?"

Yargh. Freddie's brain inverted, and she desperately wished he hadn't asked that question—and also that the question wasn't making her chest swell like a happy balloon. Not only had she broken her vow to Divya, but now she was going to make plans to do so again. She was a *terrible* best friend.

Despite her utter self-hatred, though, Freddie still couldn't keep her mouth from saying, "Will you be at your aunt's for dinner?"

"Yeah."

"Cool." She smiled shyly. "I could meet you after."

"Okay" was Theo's reply, and he offered a tiny smile of his own. Then, before Freddie could turn to go, he added, "Enemies?"

And Freddie couldn't keep from grinning wide. "In fair Verona." She yanked her cap off the floor, and after scooping up the duffle bag—which instantly silenced the crickets—she scurried past the Unwelcome Counselor Who Had the Worst Timing Ever.

"Bye, Dr. Born," she muttered, firmly avoiding eye contact and hoping he wouldn't say anything.

But *of course* he did. "Don't think I didn't notice you at school yesterday," he called after her. "We still have one more session, you know."

"I know," she trilled, kicking into a jog. "And there is *nothing* I look forward to more!"

Freddie floated euphorically on a euphoric cloud of euphoria.

She was a Criminal Mastermind, dumping crickets into empty bathrooms and making out with Romeos in dark corners. And though she wasn't *happy* that there was a murderer on the loose who had systematically stolen papers from every local archive, it *was* undeniably exhilarating for an inquiring mind like hers.

She felt like she was flying as she ran to meet Kyle and Cat. She reached the mausoleum—now lit by the warmth of full sunrise. She caught sight of the sign where Theo had tapped his glorious fingers. The lamppost he'd leaned against like a teen heartthrob.

So lost was Freddie on her cloud nine that she totally forgot about Theo's earlier warning about a loose brick. Her toes hit it. The paver jiggled. And the next thing she knew, she was flying face-first toward the ground.

Her hands thrust out to catch her, her palms connected with rough stone—and her knees cracked a split second later. *"Owwwwwwww,"* she howled, flopping sideways onto the freezing ground. Her wrists had snapped too hard; the left one in particular was displeased. Also, there was now blood on her palms.

"Awesome, awesome," she gritted out. "Way to stick that landing, Gellar." With her right hand, she pushed to sitting. The stolen uniform was streaked in dirt, and the cap had flown right over the fence and landed on the steps to the mausoleum.

But at least the heavy-duty safety pin had done its job. No single-boob art would be on display today.

"Sorry," she offered the nearest bust of Allard Fortin. "I swear it was an accident."

His glare, unchanged from an hour ago, continued steadily on.

Freddie heaved herself to standing. The duffle bag, now empty, had landed by the sign. She snagged that first, then hopped the low fence and scurried toward the mausoleum. The cap was like a bright red police light. *Criminal!* it cried. *Hoodlum!*

As she tipped down to grab it, her eyes caught on the edge of the step before the mausoleum's door. It was tucked in a shadow, and given that the crypt faced north, that meant it was *always* tucked in shadow. Which was, no doubt, why Freddie hadn't spotted this sooner . . .

There were candles before the door. Three of them. Just squat things made from white wax. Two on the left were melted. One almost all the way to the stone; the other halfway down; meanwhile, the third candle hadn't been lit at all.

Freddie's right fingers eased around the red cap. Her left wrist throbbed. Both of her palms too. But that was a distant, meaningless signal from a body she was no longer quite attached to. Her attention had firmly target-locked onto those candles. Anyone could have put them there. Maybe someone at Fortin Prep was just a little too obsessed with *The Craft*. Or maybe it was part of a Halloween display Freddie didn't know about . . .

But she also couldn't help but think of Edgar Fabre and the unhinged ramblings of his probably-lead-poisoned, certainly-unpaid blacksmith ancestor. Original Fabre had mentioned candles—and how the original settlers of Berme always knew when the Executioners were hunting because three candles would burn near the tolling bell in the Village Square.

Freddie inched forward, her gaze running along the rest of the shadowy door. But there were no other candles, no signs of wax or flame or any marks at all to disrupt the plain stone.

Freddie wet her lips. She really, *really* wished she had Xena here right now, because what if someone hadn't thought Original Fabre was insane? What if someone wasn't just inspired by and copying the alleged methods of execution . . . but was actually convinced it might be real?

Or, pinged another idea in Freddie's brain. *What if someone wants to make it look like it's real? The hunting spirits and blood oath?* It was a very Scooby-Doo theory but still a thousand times more likely than an actual supernatural ritual happening.

She tipped backward until she could see the belfry atop the crypt. The bell that Original Fabre had made had gone missing in 1975—and according to the prank book, that act of vandalism had not been Berm High's doing. Inexplicably, that bell had wound up in the schoolhouse at the Village Historique, and now here it was again, restored to its original home by Freddie's mother, and with a replica clapper hanging inside.

This bell could ring.

But *this* bell hadn't been what Freddie had heard on Wednesday or Friday—or at least, she didn't think it could have been. For one, it was too far for its tolling to have reached her in the forest through all that fog on Wednesday. For two, on Friday night, the sound had come from the west, not the north.

What am I missing? she thought as she inhaled deep and full. (And as her too-small shirt strained against the safety pin.) Something fully logical had to explain a ringing bell in the county park.

Doodle-loo doo, doodle-loo doo, sang Sabrina. *Doodle-loo doo doo!*

Freddie flinched. Dropped her red cap again as she wedged the phone to her ear. "Yeah, yeah, hey, Cat. Sorry. I promise I'm on my way. I just fell and busted my wrist—no, I'm fine. I'm just slow. But I'll be there, okay? Just wait another two minutes, please."

Freddie hung up. Her eyes lingered one last time on the three candles. Then on the original bell with its replica clapper. Her Answer Finder instincts were going to have to wait; now was the time for escape.

And this time as Freddie jogged away, she made sure to avoid the loose paver.

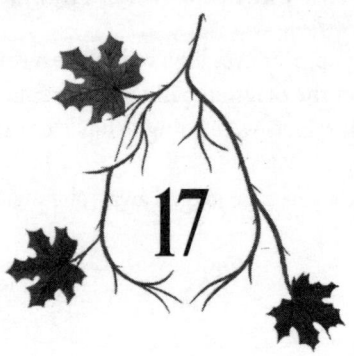

17

When Freddie finally scrambled into Kyle's back seat, Blur's "Song 2" blasted over her at maximum volume. It was a good song, and Freddie of ten minutes ago would have screamed along with it and head-banged just as hard as Kyle was.

Instead, she stared out the window and hugged her aching wrist against her chest. She wondered distantly if Mrs. Iglesias, the school nurse, would let her have some ice.

Right as the song's third playthrough came to an end (because apparently Kyle didn't know how to turn off the CD repeat function), Kyle revved his Jeep into the Berm High parking lot. Cat fluttered a wave for the security guard, who didn't look up from his bodice ripper.

Seconds later, Kyle zoomed into a spot at the back of the lot. It was right as he cut the engine that a cop car pulled in too.

"Balls." Kyle dropped low in his seat. "It's the sheriff."

"Oh, fartknockers," Cat agreed, dropping down with him.

Freddie also ducked low, although she wasn't sure there was much point. Either Bowman was there to deal with skipping students or she wasn't. And judging by the way she was pulling her car to a stop in *front* of the school, Freddie had to guess her business was unrelated to their Ferris Bueller-ing.

Still, just to play it safe, Freddie said: "If we sneak behind the cars, we can get to those dumpsters. Then it's not far to the loading dock that goes into the auditorium. We should be able to get into the school unseen."

"Good call," Cat agreed, and in a flurry of stealthy speed, everyone scuttled out of the car. They convened beside the still-warm engine—and Freddie hunkered close to its clicking, steaming heat.

Which was when Cat seemed to remember Freddie had fallen. "Oh no! Your hand. It's bleeding!"

"It's fine." Freddie shook her head. "I just tripped and landed badly. That's all."

Kyle's puppy eyes drooped. "You shoulda said something. We could have gone by the drugstore and gotten you a wrap."

Freddie smiled—a real smile because Kyle looked genuinely distraught by her pain. "Perhaps you could toss me a Band-Aid?" she quoted. "Or some antibacterial cream!"

This earned her some laughs, and both Cat and Kyle relaxed.

"Also," Freddie went on, "can we please celebrate how we got the crickets delivered *and* retrieved the prank book?"

"That we did!" Kyle cheered, scooting in close to Freddie. He whipped his arm around her and gave her an awkward half-squatting embrace. "All thanks to you, Prank Wizard."

Freddie's smile spread. She really *did* like being called that, and although she wasn't entirely sure she liked having Kyle's arm around her—especially when her left wrist was swelling up—she did appreciate the look of admiration in his eyes.

"Come on," she said. "Follow me." She abandoned the warmth of the exhaust and hurried toward the dumpsters. Cat and Kyle raced behind. Halfway to the dumpsters, though, Freddie made the mistake of glancing toward the front of the school. Just to check where Sheriff Bowman had gone . . .

Bowman was standing at the school's corner and looking *right* at Freddie. As soon as their eyes met, Bowman brought a walkie-talkie to her mouth. Her lips moved. Her legs started stalking Freddie's way.

Oh, crap. It would seem Bowman *was* there for the Ferris Bueller-ing.

"Go," Freddie hissed with a frantic wave at the dumpsters. "Get behind and go to the loading dock. I'll hold off Bowman."

As one, Cat and Kyle spotted the sheriff—and as one, they swore.

"Hurry," Freddie insisted.

"But you gotta come too," Kyle said.

"I can distract her," Freddie insisted with way more confidence than she actually felt. "I've known her a long time."

"But why is she even *looking* for us?" Cat's voice was shrill with panic. "People cut school all the time, and no one cares!"

"I don't know." It was true: Freddie didn't know—though her gut was starting to curdle with a sickening sense that things were about to get really bad, really fast. "Just go, okay? There's not much time."

"Right," Cat exhaled. "Thank you, Freddie. You're a real friend." She shot off toward the nearest dumpster. Kyle, however, didn't move. He simply looked at Freddie. Swallowed once, Adam's apple bobbing, before finally leaning in.

Freddie realized half a second too late that he was going to kiss her—and half a second too late, she realized that she didn't want that at all.

She twisted her head sideways. Kyle's lips connected with her cheek.

"Oof," he mumbled.

"Eep," she replied, and it was like a kettle boiling over. Fiery shame took hold of Freddie's muscles, and in a graceless burst of speed, she sprinted away from Kyle—no goodbyes, no looking back—and ran straight for Sheriff Bowman.

Bowman was halfway across the parking lot when Freddie finally cut into her path. And Freddie realized the instant she caught sight of Bowman's face close up that she had made a huge mistake.

Because Bowman was wearing betrayal in her blue eyes.

Freddie couldn't stop now, though. She had offered to sacrifice herself for Cat and Kyle; she had to follow through. She came to a stumbling stop beside a turquoise Ford Ranger. Two booming heartbeats later, Sheriff Bowman reached her. "Where have you been, Gellar?"

It was not a promising introduction, and one by one, Freddie felt all of her organs squeeze. Oh—and there were her secrets too, just bubbling to the surface and begging for release.

"I get to the high school," Bowman continued, "and what do I learn? You haven't come in today. Does your mother know you were skipping?"

"No, ma'am," Freddie tried, but Bowman was only just getting started.

"I have half a mind to arrest you, you know that?" She sighed, running a hand through her hair in a very Theo way. "Honestly, if this happens one more time, Gellar, I'll have to put you in handcuffs. Do you understand?"

"Not really," Freddie murmured—because she didn't. Since when was skipping school illegal?

Bowman still wasn't finished, though. "I *told* you not to mess around. I *told* you to stay out of trouble. Was I not clear enough on Saturday? No, wait." She shook her head, a disappointed movement. "I know I was clear enough, but you didn't listen. Instead, you went and made trouble again."

Freddie recoiled. There was only one thing Bowman could be talking about, and it did not deserve a reaction like this. "It was just a prank, Sheriff. No one can get hurt from—"

"A *prank*?" Bowman scoffed. "Frederica Gellar, it's called obstruction of justice and worth up to twenty years in prison."

Freddie's jaw went slack. She felt like she'd been slapped. *"Prison?"*

"You lied to me." Bowman waved in the direction of town. "You sent me and my deputies on a wild-goose chase and then you had the *nerve* to give me fake film too, even though you must have known I would catch you! You must have *known* I would walk into that forest and find nothing, and that I would get those photos developed and find them empty—"

"Wait, *what*?"

"—but you still pranked me anyway. Did you think it would be funny, Gellar? Or is this a cry for help?"

Freddie's hands shot up defensively. "Sheriff, I don't know what you're talking about. What do you mean the photos were empty?"

"You know *damned well* what I mean!" Bowman snapped this, her disappointment giving way to anger. "You took photos of an empty forest!"

"But I didn't!" Freddie cried. "I took photos of a water bottle, exactly like I told you—"

"Stop lying to me, Gellar."

"No!" Freddie was practically shouting now. None of this made any sense, and shame welled behind her eyeballs.

Shame, outrage, and something prickly she didn't like.

"Ask Divya! She was with me, Sheriff!"

Bowman sighed again, and in an instant, her anger withered into something more like disgust. "Come *on,* Gellar. Enough of this. Don't throw your best friend under the bus."

"But Divya saw the bottle too! She *did*."

"No, she didn't." Bowman's thumb tapped against her thigh. "I already spoke to her, and unlike you, she told me straight: she did not see a thing."

Freddie's breath cut off. She rocked back, her eyelids screwing shut. This couldn't be happening. Divya wouldn't betray her like that. No, *no*. Freddie dug her knuckles into her eyes and tried to think back to the woods. To what she'd seen and where the bike had been parked and where Divya had been standing . . .

"Oh no," she breathed, horror gathering in her belly. It was 100 percent possible that Divya hadn't seen anything. And Divya couldn't lie—Freddie *knew* that and couldn't blame her for it.

"That's right." Bowman shook her head. "Look, Gellar, you

know how much I care about you—and how much I cared about your father. But I can't keep looking the other way when you make trouble. This time, you've gone too far."

"I haven't done anything," Freddie tried to say, but Bowman wasn't listening.

"The worst is," she went on, thumb tapping harder and harder by the second, "I can't tell if you're really just being a silly kid or if you're actually turning into Frank. Either way, there have to be consequences."

"Sheriff," Freddie begged, hands rising. "I didn't *do* anything. I swear. I didn't prank you and I'm not . . . I'm not my dad. There really was a water bottle in the woods, Sheriff. I swear to you. On my life, on my mom's life—on Divya's! And there really were photos on Xena. And," she added, words spewing out now, "there were photos of Kyle Friedman's basement and our prank at the mausoleum. Did you find any of those? If they weren't on there, then it wasn't my film!"

"Please stop, Gellar."

"But I mean it, Sheriff! I *swear*! Someone must have changed the film!"

Bowman wagged her head, disbelieving and deeply let down. "Sure they did. Someone broke into my police station and switched out the film. Do you even hear yourself? You sound worse than Frank did."

There was that reference to her dad again, and Freddie wanted to scream. Obviously she already knew Frank Carter had been tough to work with and a terrible boss. That he hadn't known when to let things go, and it had ruined his relationships with the people around him. But Freddie felt like there was other critical context she was missing here, all thanks to the *stupid* unspoken rule she suddenly wished she'd never adhered to.

"Get to school," Bowman said. She planted her hands on her hips. "And do not get in the way again, Gellar. We have two feds in town now, and they won't be as lenient as I am. Do you understand?"

Oh, Freddie understood. Loud and clear. She was in deep trouble, and there wasn't a single thing she could do about it.

"Yes, ma'am," Freddie forced out, staring hard at the pavement. *Tamp down thoughts. Tamp down feelings. Focus on the task at hand.* "I understand, Sheriff." Then, without another word, Freddie pushed past Bowman and strode toward the school's front door. As she walked, a fledgling plan unfurled. She didn't need her gut to recognize a murderer behind the scenes, covering up their crimes.

A flesh-and-blood *serial killer,* who had been operating for over two decades. Who was either inspired by *The Curse of Allard Fortin* or trying to re-create it. And since Freddie was the only person around who seemed to realize or care about what was going on, then it fell to her to save the day.

The truth was out there, and she was damned well going to find it.

18

Freddie did not go back to school.

Oh, she walked in so Bowman would see her appearing to follow the rules, but as soon as Freddie was inside, she ducked into a bathroom and counted off a full five minutes before slinking back to the main entrance.

She didn't make it more than ten feet into the autumn cold before a voice called, "Wait!"

Divya.

Freddie skidded around—just in time to be enveloped by Divya's puffer jacket arms. "You must hate me—"

"I would never hate you."

"—but I *had* to be honest with Bowman, Freddie, and I didn't see the bottle." Divya was squeezing Freddie so tightly Freddie couldn't suck in air.

But she also loved the ferocity of this BFF hug, so oxygen could wait a little longer.

"I told her that I believed you, though," Divya continued, voice muffled by hair and sleeves. "I told her you would never lie about something like this."

"I'm sure you did, Divya." Freddie wriggled free from Divya's arms and smiled tiredly. "I appreciate the apology all the same."

For several long seconds, Divya eyed Freddie, a frown cinching across her brow. Until at last: "So what do you think happened?" Her words huffed out in foggy gasps. "I *did* see you take pictures of something."

"Yeah, and that something was a water bottle." Freddie's lips puckered sideways, gauging how much to tell Divya about the Executioners poem and missing articles and possible serial killers inspired by the ravings of a mad blacksmith and his descendant. Everything was still so nebulous in her brain. Just half-formed hunches and clues out of context.

"All I can figure," she said eventually, "is that someone switched out the film. I don't know *how* they did it, but it's the only explanation I have."

"You know why they did it, though." Divya's eyebrows notched up. "I can tell by the way you just said that. You think it was . . ."

"Murder," Freddie finished. "Yeah. Someone is trying to cover their tracks."

"Murder." Divya winced. "I have to be honest that I wasn't convinced that Dr. Fontana was killed, but . . . Well, I believe you now."

"Thanks." Freddie offered a weak smile.

"Okay, then here's what we'll do." Divya looped her arm in Freddie's and twirled them away from the entrance. "We'll stop by your house on the way to grab a coat for you and proper footwear for *me*." Divya frowned down at her clogs as she tried to walk forward.

But Freddie yanked her back to a stop. "On the way where?"

"Where do you think?" Divya pulled again. "You're going to search for that bottle, aren't you?"

"Uh."

"Don't even try to 'uh' me, Freddie Gellar." Divya grinned sideways. "I can see it in your eyes, and as your best friend, it is my sworn duty to aid you. *No one* should go into those spooky woods alone."

"But you have school!" Again, Freddie dug in her heels. "You can't wreck your perfect attendance!"

"Oh, I already took care of that, my Honey Graham Cracker." Divya winked brazenly. "The power of cell phones! All it took was a phone call from the bathroom, and"—she switched to a voice that sounded *very much* like her mother's—"Divya needs to be excused for a dentist appointment for the remainder of the day. We can't ignore cavities for too long!"

Freddie thought she might burst into tears at those words. "I don't deserve you," she said, voice quaking.

"No one does." Divya hip-bumped her. "Except maybe Laina, because she's amazing."

Freddie couldn't argue with that.

"Now, are you coming?" Divya towed one last time at Freddie, and this time, Freddie complied.

"I'm coming." She kicked into a half jog. "And let's hurry, please. I am *freezing*!"

Ten minutes later, the girls raced into Freddie's house. While Divya traded out her Birkenstocks for a pair of Freddie's mom's boots, Freddie pulled a first aid kit from under her bathroom sink. After a few daubs of Neosporin and a wrap spun firmly around her left wrist, she popped two Tylenol, slotted Sabrina into her back pocket, and looped Xena around her neck. Lastly, she slung her winter coat over the ill-fitting uniform. The shirt and pants were already stained from her earlier tumble, so no reason to change now—and no time, either.

With Divya at her side, Freddie wheeled Steve's old bike out of the garage. This time, they also took Freddie's mom's bike. It was even crappier than Steve's, but it functioned and was decidedly more comfortable than riding on handlebars.

However, before Freddie and Divya could actually set off down the driveway, Freddie squared her body toward Divya. As soul twins and BFFs until the day they died, Freddie had to do this.

She had to, she had to, she *had* to.

"Before we go, I, um . . . I need to confess something."

Divya squinted at her warily. "I don't like the sound of that."

"Yeah." Freddie squeezed her bike brakes; they squealed. *Say it, Gellar. SAY IT!* "Erm . . ." Freddie swallowed. Then blurted, "Kyle tried to kiss me."

"*What?*"

Freddie's eyelids fluttered shut. That wasn't what she'd meant to say. Like, at *all*.

"Did you want him to kiss you?" Divya asked.

"No." Freddie opened one eye. Then the other. She was a terrible, *terrible* friend.

"Jeez Louise. No wonder you look like a dejected unicorn, Fred."

"And I feel like one too," Freddie mumbled. Which was true, although not for the reason Divya now believed.

"So what happened?"

"*Ugh.*" Freddie grimaced; her insides grimaced too—both because of the kiss and because this wasn't the story she was supposed to be telling. "Kyle just leaned in, before I could stop him. Then I turned my head at the last second, so he ended up bumping my cheek with his lips."

"Oof. Then what?"

"Then I bolted."

"*Oof* oof." Divya squeaked her brakes for emphasis. "I'm a little confused, though, Freddie. I thought . . . I thought you *liked* Kyle."

"I *did*." With a moan, Freddie doubled over and draped herself across the handlebars. "But now I don't think I do."

Divya leaned over her own bike and peered into Freddie's dangling face. "Does that mean you like Theo Porter?"

"*NO!*" Freddie practically screamed, shooting back upright. "*No*. Theo Porter is the enemy."

"Is he, though?" Divya asked with definite skepticism in her eyes. "I mean, if you like him, then you like him. Will it suck? Sure, because I *really* like Laina, but if you *really* like Theo, then . . . we'll figure it out."

"I don't, though," Freddie insisted, and the grimace in her belly deepened. *Liar, liar, pants on fire! You've already made plans to see him tonight, haven't you?*

"Huh" was all Divya offered in reply.

And Freddie was certain her guilt must have been written plainly across her face. *WORST BEST FRIEND,* it said. *SECRET KEEPER AND VOW BREAKER.* She wanted Divya to get with Laina—she deeply, desperately wanted that. And she didn't want to risk that not happening by fooling around with their sworn enemy.

So it was decided, then: Freddie would cancel on Theo tonight. The kiss from that morning had just been another one-off. End of story.

As Divya flew down the driveway in an air-whizzing roll, Freddie followed.

"So, uh . . . what happened yesterday?" Freddie asked. "When you hung out with Laina—how was it?"

"Ooooh." Divya flashed a wide grin before bursting into a whirlwind description of *every single encounter* she and Laina had shared after school yesterday. And for a few minutes, as the neighborhood blurred past in all its fall glory, Freddie was able to forget her shame and simply revel in all the savory details of her best friend's romantic joy.

"So, are you officially together?"

"I don't think so." Divya frowned, her cheeks flushed from their pedaling. "I guess we're talking? But we haven't, like, defined the relationship or anything."

"But Laina *does* like girls?"

The frown compressed into a squee-like grin. "Definitely. She held my hand this morning before class."

Freddie gasped. "That's huge!"

"It was." Divya gave a happy shiver. "We were at my locker, and she just kind of took my hand into hers." She released one handlebar to display which hand. "And I was trying so hard not to freak out where everyone could see."

Freddie sighed, her insides all flustered and warm. "This is better than any rom-com, I swear. But you better tell me if you do DTR, okay?"

"Uh, duh." Divya gave a playful eye roll. "We tell each other everything, Fred."

Ah, right. Yep, Freddie was officially the worst BFF of all time.

When at last Freddie and Divya pedaled up to the yellow police tape marking the county park trail, both girls were smiling ear to ear about all the gushy Laina details. And they were panting too because, ya know, *exertion.*

Their brakes squealed in earsplitting harmony as they slowed to a stop. They rolled the final steps to the tape. It rattled in the wind, very bright and *very* insistent that people keep out.

Freddie unzipped her jacket (all that cycling had made her hot). Then she pinned Divya with her most serious stare. No more giggling over Laina, no more Kyle or Theo or feelings of shame. What they were doing here was serious, and Freddie couldn't in good conscience let Divya walk in there without knowing all the risks.

"Div, we could get in a lot of trouble if we get caught."

"I know." Divya shifted her weight.

"Like, a *lot* of trouble," Freddie reiterated. "Like get-arrested-and-charged-with-stuff trouble."

"I know," Divya repeated. She drew back her shoulders. "But I can't let you go in those woods alone—and I *know* you'll go alone. Because no matter how terrifying or dangerous things are, Fred, you always jump without looking. I do love that about you, but . . ." Divya gave a little tremble as she scooted her bike closer to the police tape. "These woods are wiggins central."

"Well," Freddie pointed out as she inched her bike after Divya, "the only way to make fear go away is to get to the bottom of it, you know? We have to face it head-on. Like a mosquito bite: the more you scratch it, the faster it heals."

"That is not how a mosquito bite works."

"Sure it is." Another few inches toward the flapping tape. Freddie reached it first. Her sore left hand brushed plastic. Then in a swoop of speed—before she could lose her nerve—she dismounted from her bike, slipped under the tape, and held it high.

Divya followed two seconds later, and after furtive glances all around, the girls set off into the trees.

They were in. Freddie and Divya were now *breaking the law*. And unlike the exhilaration that had sparkled in Freddie's veins whenever she pranked Fortin Prep, she felt only determination now. She was going to make this transgression worth it; she was going to clear her name; she was going to prove that Sheriff Bowman had it all wrong.

"So what's the plan?" Divya's voice was a half whisper, like she was afraid of being overheard. She even rolled her bike with extra caution.

"We're going to find the bottle. Then we're going to take a million photographs of it in the forest. After that, we'll put the water bottle in a Ziploc, I'll develop the photos, and we'll bring it all back to Bowman."

Divya glanced back. "Do you *have* a Ziploc?"

"Always."

"My, my, aren't you quite the Keylime PI."

Freddie barked a laugh—too loud, too false. "That was clever. And hey, this was the spot, wasn't it?" She stopped walking and toed down her kickstand. "Yeah, I'm ninety-nine percent sure this was it." She spun in a circle beside the witch hazel where only three days ago, there *had* been a red water bottle.

"Yeah," Divya agreed, knocking down her own kickstand. "Assuming your bike had been parked here"—she patted her handlebars—"and that I had been dumped on my butt over there . . ." She skipped two steps sideways and squatted. "Yep, that definitely looks the way I remember it."

"Alright." Freddie rubbed her hands together; it was *really* getting cold out. "For argument's sake, let's assume a psycho murderer—"

"Eep."

"—*didn't* steal the water bottle and it simply got knocked by the wind. That means it would go . . ." Freddie squinted at the leaf-covered earth. Then pointed to a spot where the ground turned sharply downward.

Divya's footsteps thudded over to Freddie's side. Her face had settled into a familiar *something does not add up here* scrunch.

"Something does not add up here," she said. "Like, even if the wind knocked the bottle out from under the tree, the ground is still pretty flat. It would have had to roll a full ten feet to even hit that drop-off."

"Well," Freddie declared, tromping ahead, "let's assume that's exactly what happened. If we don't find anything at the bottom of the hill, we'll trek back up here and head in the other direction."

"What about the bikes?"

"Leave 'em. It's not like there's anywhere to hide them anyway." Freddie reached the descent and in a very graceless— and very noisy—stumble forward, she thundered down the hill. Divya crashed a few paces behind.

By the time the ground flattened out again, both girls were red-faced, muddy-booted, and wild-haired. Even Divya's flawless braid had not survived the clawing branches and gnarly underbrush.

"Now," Freddie said, scrambling over fresh detritus, "let's search. Hopefully the red of the plastic will still stand out."

"Against all these fallen leaves that are red, you mean?"

Freddie glared. "Just look, okay?"

For several minutes, the girls scoured the area in silence. They peeked under rocks and inside rotting tree trunks. They kicked up leaves and rustled around in hedges. Freddie was moving in a very meticulous counterclockwise course, letting her eyes move and her gut guide her, until suddenly Divya cleared her throat.

"So, uh, I know you're not going to like what I'm about to say—"

"Uh-oh."

"—but I think it's worth mentioning." Divya plunked to a seat nearby. "Have you considered the possibility that maybe Sheriff Bowman is the one who moved the water bottle?"

Freddie barked a laugh, grinning Divya's way. Then she caught sight of her friend's expression and realized Divya was Very Serious Indeed.

"Are you out of your mind?" Freddie straightened. "You think Sheriff Bowman—*the* Sheriff Bowman who protects this town—moved the water bottle?"

"Think about it." Divya hugged her knees to her chest. "She had access to both the bottle *and* the film. Plus, you called her on Wednesday night. If she was out here murdering someone, then she could have conveniently avoided finding the dead guy when you called, and instead found the drunk party."

Freddie's face wrinkled with a frown. Like, sure, if she cocked her head at *just* the right angle, she could maybe see what Divya was saying . . .

But no. *No.* There was no way her hero, the Blue-Eyed Badass of Berm, was the murderer. Bowman had no motive. Plus, "Explain why Bowman would attack her own mother." Freddie planted her hands on her hips.

"I don't know." Divya shrugged. "But you said yourself the sheriff wasn't at the station when you tried to find help."

Rubbing her eyes, Freddie shuffled toward her best friend. "I refuse to believe Sheriff Bowman is out here hanging people." Her hands fell. "And she's definitely not beheading them."

"Beheading?" Divya squawked. She shot to her feet. "What the heck? When did that happen?"

"Sunday, I think."

"Why didn't you tell me?"

"Because," Freddie began, "I didn't know until this... morning..." The words died on her tongue. Her attention was suddenly snagged by whatever Divya had just been sitting on. "What is that?"

"A trail marker." Divya waved the question aside.

"There aren't any trails out here." Freddie pushed past her best friend and dropped to a crouch before a foot-high stretch of stone. Granite, maybe, and definitely carved by humans. And also *definitely* not a trail marker. There was fresh wax on it, like a candle had recently melted all over the top.

Just like the wax candles Freddie had seen at the Allard Fortin crypt.

"Gravestone," Freddie blurted. Then, louder and excited: "Aha, eureka, and gesundheit, Div! I think you just found a gravestone!"

"Holy crap."

"Look, you can even see the tops of letters here! We need to dig around it and see."

"Um, do we?" Divya recoiled. "I thought we were out here for water bottles. Not *graves*. Also, can we please get back to the beheading?"

"Yeah, yeah," Freddie mumbled, searching for a suitable shovel. "A body was found by the lake without its head. That's all I know."

Now Divya was the one to exclaim, "Oh my god." She clapped a hand to her mouth. "Maybe we should go back to the bikes."

"The lakeshore is nowhere near here." Freddie snatched up a sturdy branch.

"Nowhere near here? It can't be more than half a mile!"

"Yeah." Freddie nodded, because clearly this proved her point. "Nowhere near here. But look, if you help me with this"— she waved to the gravestone—"then we'll get out of here faster."

Divya seemed to realize Freddie wasn't leaving until she'd uncovered the rock, so seconds later, she too was clearing away soil. Soon the letters were fully visible. Worn down, certainly, and with a few letters gone entirely . . .

But still, enough was left behind to read.

Damien, le portier
19 Octobre, 1687

"Who was he?" Divya breathed.

Freddie pursed her lips. *The Curse of Allard Fortin* had said that Ropey, Hacky, and Stabby were originally a footman, a steward, and a carriage driver. And while Freddie might not know much French, *le portier* sure looked like *porter*—which was basically another word for footman.

And, oh god. *Porter* was also the last name of a certain boy she had very much been making out with. Could his family be descended from this guy? It certainly seemed possible, and just because Freddie had established that Original Fabre had been as mad as a hatter over some unpaid bills, that didn't mean the three servants in Allard Fortin's employ hadn't actually existed.

Those servants almost certainly hadn't been *murderous,* but that didn't mean they were never real figures from history.

And now here was one of their graves.

"Aha, eureka, and gesundheit," she said again as she popped off Xena's lens cap. This was a *huge* historical find—and could lead to some really interesting genealogy for the area. Mom was going to flip the freak out in the best possible way. Like, Freddie could practically see dollar signs forming in her mom's eyes already. A gravestone that might link to José Allard Fortin? Bring on that research funding!

Freddie snapped photos of the front of the gravestone, then the back, and lastly the top, where all the wax had collected (and yes, was making all her Answer Finder instincts go wild).

Six pictures later, she fixed Divya with a hard eye and said, "There might be more graves. Look for them."

"On it," Divya chirped. She seemed to have briefly forgotten her horror over the decapitation, and together, she and Freddie scrambled around the clearing.

With forceful kicks, they knocked leaves left and right. Until Freddie's toes kicked stone. *"Ow!"* She crumpled to the earth. "Ow, ow, *ow*."

"Did you find another?" Divya scurried to her side.

"I think so," Freddie groaned. "But don't worry about my health or anything."

"Pshaw. You've already recovered from your wrist—"

"No, I haven't!"

"—so I'm sure you'll bounce right back from this too." Divya punted away the leaves with her toe until a second stretch of stone peered up.

"Well, well, what have we here," Freddie said, and together, she and Divya cleared away the rest of the detritus, a handful of earthworms, and some roly-polies. Soon, the stone was revealed enough to read:

Justin, le charretière
19 Octobre, 1687
Le pouvoir réside dans le service

"Whoa." Divya rubbed her hands together, shedding dirt. "He died the same day as the other guy."

"Yeah, and that's the quote on the Allard Fortin crypt." Freddie's voice was breathy with excitement.

Because here was proof this guy had, in fact, worked for Allard Fortin. Not only did that fully guarantee research grants for Mom, it also proved that at least one piece of *The Curse of Allard Fortin* had held some accuracy.

Freddie took more pictures. A rapid-fire *snap, snap, snap.* Until Divya suddenly cried, "Aha! And to quote you, Fred: 'Eureka and gesundheit!'"

Freddie whirled toward her. Divya had moved a bit outside

of the clearing, toward a cluster of maple saplings. "There's a third grave, Fred!"

Freddie surged over. Like the second gravestone, this one also had no wax on top of it. *Unlike* the other stones, it was almost entirely buried.

"Hey," Divya hissed as Freddie crouched before the third headstone, "do you hear that?"

Freddie tipped her head. *A voice,* she thought. *Coming this way.* It rode the wind that bit off from the lake. And now, a shape was coalescing within the trees.

"Oh god," Divya whispered, tugging Freddie to her feet. "Let's get out of here."

"Wait." Freddie lifted her wrapped hand. Her gut was swelling, but not with a sense of danger or death. This was the keen of someone *else* in trouble. Like when she'd sensed Divya's cat was dying.

The wind butted against Freddie. Leaves clattered, briefly drowning out the voice—briefly hiding the walker behind a curtain of gold and russet.

Then the wind cleared; the leaves fell; and Freddie saw who approached.

"Oh no," she said at the same time Divya cried, "*Laina?* Is that you?"

19

Laina gave no indication that she'd heard Freddie or Divya. Nor that she'd seen them. She strode steadily onward, oblivious to branches or briars or thickets of mud.

And the closer she got, the more Freddie could see. The more Freddie could hear.

In both hands, clasped before her like a prayer, Laina held a flickering candle, and in time to each measured step across the forest, she called: *"Je suis ici. Je suis ici. Commandez-moi."*

"Um," Divya said, eyes flashing to Freddie. "What the hell is going on?" Then she scooted forward, arms outstretched. "Laina? Hey, *Laina.*"

Freddie scrambled after Divya, also shouting. "Laina—hey, *Laina!*" But the class president offered no reaction. She simply walked. She simply chanted.

"Je suis ici. Je suis ici. Commandez-moi."

Wherever Laina Steward was, it was *not* in this clearing. And now Freddie's gut was really on fire.

Divya reached Laina first and skidded to a panicked stop, trying to stop Laina's forward march. But her efforts were useless. Laina simply sidestepped and circled around.

"Je suis ici. Je suis ici. Commandez-moi." The candle dripped wax onto her fingers.

Freddie didn't bother trying to stop her. She just fell into step beside Laina, gaze raking up and down. The other girl was not dressed for this weather—her fishnet-clad legs rippled with chill bumps, and other than a flimsy cardigan, she had no jacket of any kind.

Divya rushed to Laina's other side. Over and over, she said the girl's name—"Laina; hey, Laina!"—but still, Laina continued obliviously on.

So Divya rounded toward Freddie. "What do we do?"

Freddie had no idea. Laina was clearly in some kind of trance, which was way outside the realm of her understanding. Shoplifters she could handle. Even bodies dangling from trees. But unresponsive girls with candles in hand were *X-Files* territory, and Freddie was *not* actually Dana Scully or Fox Mulder.

Laina reached the clearing with the tombstones, while Freddie and Divya trailed behind. To Freddie's shock—though not necessarily her surprise—Laina crossed the clearing and reached the third tombstone.

"*Je suis ici. Je suis ici. Commandez-moi.*" She knelt. "*Je suis ici. Je suis ici. Commandez-moi.*" She held out the candle. Wax fell to the leaves. Then she placed the candle on the tombstone . . .

And it was like a switch going off. One moment, gray daylight bore down. The next, darkness reigned supreme. Clouds that Freddie would have sworn weren't there two seconds ago suddenly swooped across the sky.

Worst of all, though, was the smell. A scent Freddie was beginning to recognize as a harbinger of *messed-up stuff* on the horizon. A smell her gut screeched was wrong, wrong, wrong. Carrion. Rot. *Death.*

"Laina?" Divya asked, cutting in close to the other girl. "Hey, are you—" She brushed Laina's shoulder.

And Laina screamed. Her hands shot to her ears, she crumpled into a ball, and it was like the night with the crows all over again. But worse, because now there was a candle burning and dark clouds and *nothing* scientific or logical that could explain it all away.

Freddie didn't even think. She just lunged, grabbing for Laina. "Help me," she ordered Divya. "We need to get her out of here."

Freddie's fingers connected with Laina's ribs, and as fast as Laina's screams had begun, they broke off. She unfurled in an instant, no time for Freddie to react.

Then she attacked. A blur of trained speed. Freddie's whole world flipped upside down. Her back slammed to the frozen earth, punching the breath from her lungs. Her vision wavered.

Laina straddled her. Her thighs squeezed against Freddie's ribs. Choked off Freddie's lungs. Freddie had just enough time to see Laina's fists swing in before she screwed her eyes shut, and . . .

And nothing. The impact never came.

"What . . . the . . . hell," Laina panted, "is going on?"

"You're awake," Divya cried, and Freddie finally opened her eyes.

Laina's fists had fallen. She gaped down at Freddie. "Oh my god," she mumbled as Divya helped her climb off Freddie. "Oh my god, I'm so sorry. Did I hurt you? Oh my god, I'm so sorry I did this. I don't know what happened."

Freddie didn't know either—just that staying here seemed like a really bad idea. She hauled herself to her feet. "We need to go. *Now.*"

"I agree," Divya said, already peeling off her coat and wrapping it over Laina's shoulders. "She's freezing, and . . ." She didn't finish that statement—she didn't have to. The pinched-lip stare she flung Freddie was more than enough.

"Go to the bikes," Freddie ordered, twisting away. "I'll be right behind."

"Wait, what?" Divya barked at Freddie's back. "Where are you going?"

"I'll be right behind," she insisted, and without another word of explanation, Freddie tugged Xena from her jacket. She seemed no worse for the wear, miraculously, so Freddie crossed to the third tombstone. She cranked Xena, aimed her, and after three snaps, Freddie knelt and started scooping up soil by the handful.

Somehow, despite the raging wind, the candle still burned. White wax had splattered across the stone, leaving marks that were identical to the marks on Damien's headstone.

Scrape, scrape, dig, dig. Time slid past. The wind bit harder, and a growing stink pulsed against Freddie, worse than it had ever been in the archives. Cloying up her nose and filling her sinuses. Dirt was also gathering under her fingernails in soft, sandy grains that she could hardly feel because her fingers were so cold.

Scrape, scrape, dig, dig.

Freddie knew she was going full Agent Mulder here. Pushing things too far in the search for answers, exactly like her dad had supposedly done. But what choice did Freddie have? If she wanted the truth, she couldn't run now.

It made her think of something Mulder had said in season four: *You put such faith in your science, Scully, but from the things I've seen, science provides no place to start.*

Right now, Freddie was inclined to agree. Sorry, Scully, but science wasn't offering anywhere obvious for Freddie to start. Laina had come here, chanting in French, placed a candle on her ancestor's tombstone. Then the sky had darkened, and Laina had fallen to the earth screaming.

Snow began to trickle down. Unseasonably early. Absolutely freezing. Freddie's fingers were completely numb by the time she got as deep as she needed to be—deep enough to make out a first name.

Alexandre, the stone began.

And a few frantic digs after that, the rest of the words appeared. Faded and clogged with dirt, but unmistakable all the same:

ALEXANDRE, LE STEWARD
19 OCTOBRE, 1687
LE POUVOIR RÉSIDE DANS LE SERVICE

"Aha," Freddie whispered. Laina had come with a candle to the exact tomb of someone with a title that matched her last name. That sure couldn't be a coincidence.

Unconcerned with her filthy fingers or Xena's sensitive casing, Freddie snapped two more pictures of the tombstone's face. Then she shoved to her feet and broke into a run. Away from the grave, away from the candle still burning.

Sure, she wanted to clear her name and find the missing water bottle, but the mad ravings of Original Fabre were feeling just a little too possible right now. Freddie knew they weren't—because of *course* they weren't. But her gut wasn't quite connecting with her brain at the moment. It didn't help that the rotten stink was so strong it cloyed against Freddie's skin and slid down her throat with each breath.

She would let herself feel foolish about these irrational fears later—once she was out of these trees and somewhere warm. Also, preferably, somewhere with walls and locks and other people.

Twice, Freddie looked back, half expecting to see a Hangsman or a Headsman with ropes and axes like in her dream . . . But there was nothing. Only falling snow and a smell like dead things lost.

Freddie was drenched in sweat by the time she caught up to Laina and Divya. Her thigh muscles screamed, and the first drips of embarrassment were starting to trickle into her brain. This was *just* a forest; this was *just* a county park; and there were *clearly* no serial killers or dangerous animals in sight.

But that little burst of Scully logic didn't stop Freddie from turning to Laina and asking: "Are you okay to ride a bike?"

"Yeah," the girl said, clearly still foggy—but also determined to push past it and save face.

"Good. You take the orange bike, and Div, hop on my handlebars. 'Cause we're getting the hell out of Dodge."

Freddie sat on the carpet beside Laina. Divya's flowery comforter was wrapped tightly to Laina's shoulders, an afghan draped over her cross-legged knees.

Despite the layers, Laina shivered. Her teeth chattered.

The girls had gone to Freddie's house first so she could grab her stolen copy of *The Curse of Allard Fortin* (and some more Tylenol for her wrist). Then they'd powered onward to Divya's place— empty of parents, and therefore nosy questions, until tonight. After tucking blankets around Laina, Divya had hurried off to make a hot tea. Which had left Freddie alone with President Steward.

The tension in the room was thick. Like need-a-carving-knife thick. Although that was more Laina's doing than Freddie's, since Freddie was too amped up for awkwardness. Her mind was on High Alert with theories and questions and suspicions burning inside her sleuthing stomach.

She kept opening *The Curse of Allard Fortin*. Staring at the poem. Then shutting the book again. All while downstairs, silverware clinked and water boiled.

"I . . . have a sleepwalking disorder," Laina said eventually. These were her first words since Divya had left the room. She gazed helplessly at Freddie. "They're linked to my migraines, we think. And sometimes . . . Well, sometimes this happens. I end up in the middle of the woods."

"How often is sometimes?" Freddie asked.

"Um." Laina shrugged. "Only a few times. It just started last month, but . . . Yeah, I'm seeing an out-of-towner about it." Her eyes dropped to her boots.

And Freddie frowned. Sleepwalkers did weird stuff—sure, she could buy that. But did they walk with lit candles to ancient graves?

"Do you speak French?"

"Huh?" Laina blinked.

"Do you speak French?" Freddie repeated.

"No." Laina wagged her head. "I'm in AP German. Why do you ask?"

Freddie ignored the question. "Do you always go to the county park when you sleepwalk?"

Laina swallowed. "No. I went to Fortin Prep once."

Freddie's eyebrows launched high. "The Allard Fortin crypt?"

"Maybe? I woke up near the parking lot, so yeah. Maybe." She gave a nervous laugh. "I don't remember, and needless to say, that really freaks me out."

"Do you normally carry a candle with you on your . . . trips?"

"I had a *candle*?"

"Leave her alone," Divya ordered, shoving into the room with a teacup and platter of cookies. "She's been through enough today."

"Sorry." Freddie popped up her hands defensively. She wasn't actually sorry, but she could keep her mouth shut. For a few minutes, at least.

Divya knelt beside Laina, and instantly the lines of Laina's face relaxed. She watched Divya set the tea before her, watched as she laid out the cookies, and were this any other situation, Freddie would've been delighted by such a stare and the clear longing in Laina's eyes. The girl was *head over heels* for Divya.

Right now, though, Freddie had other concerns.

"Your family," Freddie said as Laina lifted the tea to her lips. The scent of cinnamon wafted through the room. "Does anyone else sleepwalk?"

Laina winced slightly. "Not that I know of."

"And do you know how long your family has lived in this region?"

"Um." Laina's forehead bunched up. She glanced at Divya. "A long time, I think. Does . . . does it matter?"

"Of course not," Divya murmured. She shot Freddie a glare.

Freddie ignored it. "What's the last thing you remember before you woke up in the woods?"

Laina took another sip and gave another frown. "I was in AP Bio, and then . . ." Laina's hand started trembling. Her eyes squeezed shut. "I don't remember."

"Try." Freddie leaned toward her.

"I think . . . I went to the bathroom, and . . ." She shook her head. "I don't know."

"Please," Freddie pressed.

"Enough," Divya snapped. With shocking strength for someone so small, she grabbed Freddie by the collar and hauled her to her feet. Then Divya dragged Freddie into the hall.

"You need to take a chill pill. What the *hell*, Freddie?"

Freddie's nostrils flared. She knew her best friend was right. She knew she was pushing too hard. *Just like Mulder. Just like your dad.* Laina had been through some serious stuff, and yeah. She needed some relief.

But Laina was also the only person who might be able to fill in some of these gaps in Freddie's brain—and there were a *lot* of gaps. A lot of dots that needed connecting. A lot of truths still out there to be found.

Before Freddie could apologize, though, and explain why she'd pushed Laina so hard, a familiar refrain split the air. Freddie rifled out Sabrina and found a local number lighting up the screen.

"Hello?" she answered while Divya continued glaring.

"Is Theo Porter available?"

"Uh . . ." Freddie's brows drew tight. "May I ask who's calling?"

"This is Joseph. I'm a nurse at the hospital. I was told to call this number when his grandmother woke up."

"Oh." Freddie's brows relaxed. Theo must've given the nurse *her* number, since he no longer had a phone. And wow, that was some serious follow-through on his favor. She really owed him for that.

"Can you pass on the message to Mr. Porter?" Joseph asked.

"Yeah, I'll be sure to let him know."

"Great. Thank you—"

"Wait," Freddie cut in. "Is she allowed to see anyone? Mrs. Ferris, I mean. Can she have visitors?"

"Yes," the nurse answered. Then with a prim goodbye, he hung up.

"Who was that?" Divya asked while Freddie pocketed Sabrina. Her earlier anger was gone, replaced by frowning curiosity.

"It was the hospital." Freddie's mind was already racing ahead. "Mrs. Ferris woke up, and I have a lot of questions for her."

Divya's lips pressed into a line. "Why? What do you think she'll tell you?"

"I don't know. I just think she might know something about . . ." Freddie waved vaguely. "Everything going on. Plus, *I'm* the reason she got hurt—"

"Actually, you're the reason she got rescued."

"—so I want to make sure she's okay."

After ducking into Divya's room to grab Xena and offer Laina a soft "See you later," Freddie met Divya back in the hall. She hooked her arm in Divya's and towed her toward the stairs. "Listen," she whispered. "Don't let Laina out of your sight."

Divya bit her lip. "I mean, she has to leave *sometime*, Fred."

"Does she?" Freddie pulled Divya down the stairs. "Because I don't think she should be alone right now. Like at all. Try to find a way to keep her here. Maybe an impromptu slumber party or something."

Now Divya was really chewing her lip. "Freddie," she said quietly, "tell me straight: Is Laina in danger?"

Freddie's mouth opened. Then clamped back shut. She couldn't lie to her BFF. She felt rotten enough for not confessing to the second kiss with Theo; she refused to keep any more secrets. Like Divya had said, *We tell each other everything*.

So even if Freddie had more questions than answers, she knew what her gut was telling her. "Yeah, Div," she said when they reached the foyer. "I think Laina might be in danger. I don't really know why yet . . . but my gut is telling me we should be afraid. Hey, though," she added at Divya's paling face, "I'll call you soon, okay? If you keep Laina here, then everything will be alright."

20

Freddie found the hospital's waiting area exactly as it had been the day before, minus Theo's restless energy to fill it. Amazing how empty it felt without him there.

No. Freddie's face puckered up as she crossed the beige tiles. *Do not think about him. You're not allowed to think about him. Now or ever again.* She had messed up on the bike ride with Divya; she refused to make that same secret-keeping mistake again.

Fortunately, it took Freddie only twelve footsteps to forget about Theo. Twelve footsteps that carried her right up to Mrs. Ferris's room . . . where her windpipe promptly closed off and her pulse thumped into her eardrums.

An irrational reaction, she knew. This wasn't room 27, and it wasn't Frank Carter waiting on the other side.

Still, it took Freddie three steeling breaths before she finally worked up the courage to touch the silver doorknob of room 34. Then another two breaths before she finally twisted it.

She shoved her way in, half-frantic, half-sluggish, until at last she was inside and the door was clunking shut behind her. Of course, Freddie realized a split second too late that maybe she should've knocked before coming in. Or maybe she should've found a nurse. Or *maybe* brought some flowers or a "Get Well Soon" balloon. Something other than simply barging in.

But it was too late now; Freddie could already hear Mrs. Ferris shifting in her bed behind the blue privacy curtain. The lights were off. The plastic blinds were drawn.

"Rita?" came a feeble voice, at once familiar and at once foreign. Mrs. Ferris had *never* sounded feeble before. "If you've brought me more donuts, I'm going to scream. I told you I wanted beef jerky."

Okay, that sounded more like the Mrs. Ferris Freddie knew. And it gave her the final nudge of courage she needed to march to the curtain and poke her head through.

"Hi, Mrs. Ferris." She tried for a smile. It fell flat.

"Freddie?" Mrs. Ferris blinked, startled. Then she snatched at a pair of glasses looped around her neck. Her blankets rustled.

She looked so frail, her skin makeup-free and her hair unstyled. The hospital gown only made it worse, revealing the sharp lines of her shoulders.

And for a moment, Freddie was completely thrown by it all—by how this vision clashed with her mental image of Mrs. Ferris. Which was why, for several long seconds, all Freddie could do was stare. Gone were the recited words she had prepared on her bike ride. Gone were the planned apologies or desperate pleadings for forgiveness.

This woman was her friend. She was also Sheriff Bowman's mother and Theo's grandmother. What had Freddie *done* to her?

But then, seemingly out of nowhere, Mrs. Ferris transformed. She sat taller. Her eyes flashed behind her thick glasses, and she even snapped her fingers. "Come," she barked. "We don't have much time."

Freddie obeyed, too startled to do otherwise. "Time for what?"

Mrs. Ferris's fingers lashed out. With shocking strength, she yanked Freddie to the bed. Her skin was papery this near. Her blue eyes bloodshot. "How did you know to visit me?"

"Uh," Freddie began eloquently, but Mrs. Ferris wasn't listening. She was already powering on.

"Doesn't matter," she continued. "Rita will be here momentarily, and she must not know about this. Do you understand?"

Freddie didn't understand at all, actually. Sheriff Bowman was Mrs. Ferris's daughter. Why couldn't she know Freddie had come?

As soon as Freddie's lips parted to ask this question, Mrs. Ferris continued: "Just listen to me, Freddie: it's too dangerous. Don't you see? Rita can't . . . resist . . . Just like my Teddy couldn't. So *you* have to figure it all out."

"Figure what out?"

"What I was tracking all these years." The old woman's urgency shifted into something pained. "It started with Rita's brother and a bell no one else could hear."

"I don't understand what you're saying—"

"You know where my house is?" Mrs. Ferris interrupted. "There's a key under the potted basil by the back door. I want you to go inside. Then go upstairs. At the end of the hall is a stairwell into the attic." Each of Mrs. Ferris's words was breathier than the last—although less from exertion and more from urgency. From panic, even. "All the way at the back of my attic, behind an old dollhouse, you'll find a hidden room."

Freddie's eyes widened.

"That's where you'll find the answers you need. More than I can give you right now." Mrs. Ferris flung her gaze to the door. "Lives depend on you, Freddie."

Freddie rocked back. "I don't understand, Mrs. Ferris. What are you *talking* about? You can't just say all this stuff and not explain."

Another blue-eyed blink behind the glasses—but this time it was laced with doubt. She raked her gaze up. Then down. "You're Frank Carter's daughter. I know you can figure this out. I see it in you. No—don't say anything, Freddie. You need to *go*. Rita will be here at any moment."

Freddie didn't want to go. Her mind was reeling, her gut was a block of lead encased in ice, and she had a million questions. A *galaxy* of questions, bright and desperate. But now Mrs. Ferris was shoving at her. Pushing her away from the bed. "Key is under the basil pot. Now, hurry!"

Freddie didn't hurry. Or even move. She just stood there, numbly gawping at the frenzied old lady before her. Because this was seriously more than her brain could work with right now. She had been accused of lying by the sheriff because all of her hard-won evidence had been *stolen*. Then she'd found gravestones in the woods and Laina with a candle.

Now this too? *Now* she was expected to go into Mrs. Ferris's house and find a secret room in the attic?

The room's phone rang. Mrs. Ferris ripped up the receiver by her bed. "Hello, Rita!" she cried, pinning Freddie with a fierce glare. "Oh, you're at the front desk? I'm glad you called up, so I can make myself decent. Yes, I'll see you soon."

She slammed down the phone. *"Go,"* she snarled, and this time, Freddie didn't hesitate. She spun on her heel and bolted from the room. Then down the hall and into the waiting area—where the elevator was already dinging.

No time, no time. The doors slid wide.

Freddie dove behind a potted plant. She was *totally* visible, and her breath came in punctuated gasps. But she couldn't move. Couldn't risk finding a better spot, because there was Sheriff Bowman right there, strutting out of the elevator.

Don't see me, Freddie prayed. *Don't see me, don't see me.*

Sheriff Bowman didn't see her. She was distracted, running her hands through her hair and even muttering to herself as she stalked across the waiting room. Then she was past, and Freddie made her move, quiet as a panther.

She charged for the still-open elevator doors, lurching inside right as they began to close. Pulse plodding in her ears, she waited for the door to finish closing. For the elevator to jerk into a noisy descent.

What the heck had just happened? And what the *heck* was Freddie supposed to do about it all? Mrs. Ferris had acted as if Sheriff Bowman—her own daughter—couldn't be trusted. Like she was dangerous even.

Have you considered the possibility, Divya had said, *that maybe Sheriff Bowman is the one who moved the water bottle?*

Freddie gulped, her throat thick. "It started with Rita's brother," Freddie whispered to herself, repeating what Mrs. Ferris had said. "And a bell no one else could hear." Always, always, everything came back to a bell. A bell that Freddie couldn't find but that she'd heard ringing on two different nights now.

Freddie was shivering by the time she reached the sliding doors outside of the hospital. Not from cold, but from adrenaline. And maybe a little fear too—after all, was she really about to do this? Was she really going to bust into Mrs. Ferris's house and find a secret room hidden in the attic?

It seemed that yes . . . Yes, she was. How Nancy Drew of her. How Fox Mulder too.

By the time Freddie unchained her bike, she was shivering from actual cold. She sorely regretted forgetting her jacket at Divya's, but like mosquito bites and fear, there was nothing to do but scratch at the shivers until they went away.

So after checking that Xena was still secure around her neck, Freddie kicked off into the freezing wind.

Snow still fell.

Mrs. Ferris's house was only a block from Freddie's, so she decided to leave Steve's bike in the garage and trek the final distance on foot. It just seemed wiser for sneaking purposes.

A quick jog carried her across the street, where she cut between the Hansens' and the Chos', then a brief stretch of woods led her to Mrs. Ferris's backyard. Surrounded by a high wooden fence, the yard was mostly just patio and potted plants (that didn't look too good in this weather).

The gate wasn't locked, and although Freddie's teeth were chattering when she slunk inside, she scarcely noticed. Her heart boomed too loudly in her ears, her throat felt like sandpaper, and every nerve in her body was on fire. Sure, Mrs. Ferris might have *told* Freddie to come here, but Mrs. Ferris had also made it clear that if Sheriff Bowman found her, very bad things would ensue.

Things worse than a mere arrest for trespassing.

Freddie found the basil easily enough, and as promised, a rusty key waited beneath. With a furtive glance around, she unlocked the back door and shoved inside.

The first thing she noticed was the warmth (thank god), followed quickly by the smell. Like apples and cinnamon.

Once Freddie's eyes had adjusted to the darkness, she found herself in an old kitchen *crammed* with jars of jam. Like, there must have been at least a hundred of them on every available surface. *Because of course,* Freddie thought. *Mrs. Ferris is getting ready for the fête.* She always had a booth to sell her jams and fruit preserves—and she always sold out.

The next thing Freddie noticed was a letter affixed to the fridge. It had a bright sunburst magnet that stood out in the dark, and after locking the door behind her—then deadbolting it for good measure—Freddie crept over. Under the magnet was a letter with a pink Post-it stuck to the top.

I'll see you soon, Grandma, the Post-it read in a sloping scrawl. *Love, Theo.*

Freddie couldn't help but smile at that. Then she peeled up the Post-it and scanned the paper below. It was an acceptance letter from Allard Fortin Preparatory School, dated April of this year. They were pleased to inform Mr. Theodore Porter that he had been accepted into their prestigious journalism program, and that his financial aid application had been accepted. He would have full room, board, and tuition covered for the 1999–2000 school year.

As Freddie read this, as she ran her finger down the letter, sadness wefted through her muscles. *I was in the journalism program,* Theo had said that very morning, before quickly correcting to, *I am in the journalism program.*

Freddie had to wonder if he'd been kicked out.

Which must have been *her* fault.

She shook her head. She wasn't here for Theo. She was here for answers in the attic.

Freddie traced her way out of the kitchen, giving it one more glance before she left. But other than a yellow raincoat on a hook by the door, nothing caught her eye. So into the living room she wandered. Here, every surface was crowded with knickknacks, framed family photos, and an uncomfortable number of Precious Moments figurines.

It was so stereotypically Old Lady it was almost painful.

A shadowy stairwell waited beyond, so Freddie made her way over. The steps creaked beneath her duck boots, and halfway up, the furnace clicked on—loud enough to send Freddie jumping. Loud enough that she had to stand there mid-step with her hand clutching the banister for a solid ten seconds before her heart finally slowed.

"Nerves of steel, Gellar," she whispered as she resumed her ascent. "Nerves of steel."

She reached the second floor, and there, at the end of the hall as promised, was a door. As Freddie snuck toward it, she passed two open doors. One revealed a tiny bathroom, the faded wallpaper as outdated as the fridge downstairs. The second showed a bedroom with a bunk bed draped in Fraggle Rock sheets.

Freddie approved.

At last, she reached the attic door, and after a brief pause to *listen very hard* over the furnace's blast (and after hearing nothing), she turned the knob and pressed inside. A narrow stairwell met her eyes, lit only by a dim light through a circular window.

At the top of the stairs, Freddie found more issues of *National Geographic* than she had ever known existed. As she twisted around to cross the attic—dusty, spider-y, and with exposed nails in *all* the most dangerous places—she examined the magazines. They went back decades, and the worn creasing in the spines suggested they'd all been read cover to cover. Several times.

Next came old toys. Heaps and *heaps* of them—and ahead in the weak light, Freddie could see the dollhouse Mrs. Ferris had told her about. It was as tall as Freddie's waist, with as many steeples and gables and what-have-yous as Allard Fortin's estate.

Freddie's boots thumped over the attic. Floorboards groaned. She reached the dollhouse and peeked behind. Her lungs tightened. A small door waited. The kind that led into crawl spaces and murder dungeons. It wasn't well hidden, though, and now that Freddie was looking, she realized no cobwebs clustered here. Nor did dust. In fact, a streak of clean wood suggested the dollhouse had been moved.

Recently.

Freddie inhaled deeply, senses sharpening and logic waking up. Mrs. Ferris had been in the hospital for two days. This could *feasibly* have been her doing. But cobwebs formed fast. Freddie knew that from her days of cleaning at City-on-the-Berme, yet there wasn't a single web between here and the doorway.

Maybe Mrs. Ferris had told someone else about this secret area?

Ducking down, Freddie gently turned the knob. It squeaked. The door pulled wide, revealing a tiny room tucked beneath the roof's support beams. A string dangled down, and when Freddie yanked it, a lone bulb flashed on.

She winced. So bright. So obvious. She hastily shut the door behind her.

Unlike the rest of the attic, everything here was meticulously organized in boxes. *Tools,* read the closest. *Documents,* read the next. And a third, unlabeled, sat in the farthest corner.

It was the massive corkboard leaning against the sloped beams that captured Freddie's gaze. She scooted in close. On one half was a topographical map of the county park. Someone had drawn in all the trails with a red marker. They'd marked the Village Historique too, and the parking lot and the archives, and...

The gravestones.

Or that was what Freddie assumed the three red Xs labeled *burial site* meant. She set down her flashlight and snapped a picture of the Xs. Then she moved to the second half of the corkboard.

Her eyes widened as she beamed her flashlight over it. "Holy smokes." This was even better than the map. The page was shorter and the edges had been folded inward, but there was no mistaking what she was looking at: three family trees, tracing all the way back to 1679. It began with a Portier, a Steward, and a Charretière—the same titles inscribed on the three gravestones.

And the same roles referenced in *The Curse of Allard Fortin*: a footman, a steward, and a carriage driver.

Freddie quickly snapped a photo, then kept on snapping all the way through to the present day, unfolding the enormous page as she went. Tens of names unfurled before her. Generation upon generation of descendants of the three men who *must* have worked for Allard Fortin.

Ropey, Hacky, and Stabby. A footman, a steward, and a carriage driver. They'd each had children here, and those children had continued to live here for generations.

It was when Freddie reached the 1950s, though, that the family tree changed. The names were still there, but now they'd been scratched out. And not just casual strikethroughs, but scrubbed away so hard that the black pen had torn the paper.

It was as if someone hadn't simply tried to erase these people from the family trees but had tried to erase them from life entirely.

Freddie gulped and snapped one more picture before turning her attention to the boxes. With her flashlight back in hand, she opened the one labeled *Tools*—only to instantly rear back. She had no idea what she'd expected to find inside, but it definitely hadn't been what glittered up at her.

Handcuffs. A rope. Duct tape. And zip ties.

Okay, sure. Those were tools, alright. For *murder*. And not supernatural murder either, but, like, *legit* murder by a very human hand.

Stomach roiling, Freddie took a picture of the contents. Then plunked the lid back on and shoved the box aside. Her skin crawled. She didn't think Mrs. Ferris was a killer, so what were these things doing in her attic?

With shaky hands, she next opened the box labeled *Documents*. It was almost entirely empty save for three handwritten copies of "The Executioners Three." The topmost page was clean white printer paper with 1999 scribbled in the corner. Beside the poem's second and third refrains were the dates October 13 and October 15.

Freddie's breath hissed out. Those were the dates of the hanging and the decapitation—and they matched up with the verses for the Hangsman and the Headsman. Meanwhile, next to the line *The Oathmaster is waiting* were the words *He's back*.

Well, clearly the *he* in question was the serial killer, and presumably this meant Mrs. Ferris had been trying to track him. The question was *why*, and what did it have to do with her children and the bell?

The next copy of the poem, handwritten on faded notebook paper, was dated 1987. Another date had been scrawled beside the Hangsman's verse: October 16. That, of course, matched with the newspaper articles Freddie had found in her dad's box and at Fortin Prep.

On the back, there was another note: *The fog and crows rise again, but no one is here. Rita is traveling, and Teddy and Justine live in Chicago now.*

Then, added in thick red marker below that was: *I am so sorry, Frank.*

Freddie swallowed, her throat suddenly shut tight. She'd already known that her dad had gone looking for answers about this. She couldn't let a fresh monsoon get the better of her simply because that was her dad's name right there.

Tamp it down. Focus on the task at hand.

Freddie forced her gaze back up to the other notes. Rita was obviously Sheriff Bowman. And Teddy must be Theo's dad, who'd moved to Chicago. Justine, therefore, must be Theo's mom.

For some reason, Freddie's gut gave a hard *clench* at that thought. As if to say: *This name is important. Don't forget Justine.*

Hadn't one of the Executioners been named *Justin*? Could Theo's mother be descended from the Charretière line? That would make him a *double* descendant . . .

Freddie turned to the final copy of the poem, on an even rattier piece of lined paper, dated 1975. It was the same handwriting as before, but swoopier, as if Mrs. Ferris—assuming that was who had kept these notes—had been younger. More dates filled the margin, and beside the Headsman's stanza, it also read: *Poor Edgar. Teddy blames himself. He tells me he hears a bell and can't resist it. I have found him sleepwalking twice now in the forest with no memory of how he got there.*

Freddie bit her lip. There was so much to take in right here.

Poor Edgar had to refer to Edgar Fabre—although why? What had happened to him in 1975 that Teddy would blame himself for? Edgar would have been pretty old by then, and hadn't he been run out of town?

As for the bell that Teddy claimed he'd heard—which *had* to be the same bell that Freddie kept hearing—what did it mean that he couldn't resist it? Mrs. Ferris had said Sheriff Bowman was the same. Plus, he'd been found sleepwalking just like Laina had.

So maybe someone was hypnotizing them all. Hypnosis

had triggers, right? So the bell could be the mechanism that controlled them to . . . do what?

Freddie would have to research that hypnosis tomorrow at the library. And she could do a cursory search tonight with Ask Jeeves once she got home.

She rubbed at her eyes. This was a lot to take in. A lot of lines drawn on a murder board that currently existed only inside her brain. She needed to sit down and try to map it all out in an organized fashion.

After returning the three poems to their box, Freddie finally turned her attention to the last box. The one without a label, lurking in the shadows. While the others were all brown filing boxes, this one was white. Newer. Cleaner.

Later, Freddie would *swear* she'd known what she was going to find before she'd even pulled off the lid. She would *swear* her gut had already sensed the box's contents, her mind had already decided.

She pulled off the top, and there it was: a red water bottle with *Wed. run, lap 2* on the side.

Beside it was a roll of 35mm film.

And under it was a sheaf of stolen newspapers.

"Aha," Freddie whispered shakily, "eureka, and gesundheit." Here was all of her serial killer evidence. Just staring up at her in a secret attic room that no one was supposed to know about except for Mrs. Ferris. A woman who was supposedly attacked by a wild animal. A woman who was afraid of her own daughter and could only turn to Freddie for help.

Heart thundering, Freddie wrapped her right hand in her sleeve and withdrew the topmost newspaper. In huge letters, it declared, "Headless Body Found in City-on-the-Berme." Below was a picture of two young men, arm in arm and grinning before Elmore High School. *Teddy Porter,* the caption said, *who found the body of his friend, Edgar Fabre Jr.*

Freddie's lungs deflated. Air whistled through her teeth. Because holy moly, this was a clue. It wasn't Edgar Fabre *Senior* that her dad had believed was still alive—it was the son. *Junior* was the one who maybe hadn't died.

Except, how could one even fake a decapitated body? And for what purpose? Sure, Freddie could see why he might have had a motive to kill if he'd wanted to prove his dad's book was real. And if he'd wanted to show everyone in Berm that Original Fabre hadn't just been a disgruntled blacksmith with outstanding money owed.

But the amount of work that would have to go into a scheme like this—from faking his own death to multiple killings over twenty-four years...

Freddie's face folded into one of Divya's *something does not add up here* expressions. And in a numb, hazy movement, she clicked Xena's film advancer and pressed the viewfinder to her eye.

Snap! Light flared. The face of Teddy Porter was captured on film, the resemblance between Theo and his dad unmistakable. Then, with her fingers again wrapped in her sleeve, Freddie withdrew more newspapers. The stack included all the 1975 editions missing from the Fortin Prep collection, as well as envelopes of microfiche from the library. There were also extra copies of the same newspapers, as if the killer—*Edgar Junior*—had gone to neighboring libraries and relieved them of their editions too.

Freddie cranked Xena again, ready to grab a picture of the whole article cache... except Xena wouldn't move. "Crap," she snarled. She had taken all the pictures she could. Frantically, she patted her jeans pockets. Front, back, front again. But there was no spare film. *What a rookie move, Gellar!* Mulder and Scully would *never*.

But okay, okay. This would be fine. All Freddie had to do was come back later. She knew where the key was, and surely if she came during the middle of the night, there'd be no risk of getting caught by a murderer.

Freddie was just picking up the newspaper to return it to

the box when the house shook. A sudden slam that rattled everything.

Freddie froze. *The furnace,* she thought. *It's probably just the furnace.* It wasn't the furnace, though. Someone was in the house, and now their stomping feet were coming this way.

21

Freddie didn't think. She just acted. First, she shoved the film canister into her pocket. Then she flung everything back into the box and thrust it into the corner. Last, she bolted for the tiny attic door.

She tried to tiptoe, but she could only move so fast and stay quiet.

Footsteps thumped on the creaking stairs between the first and second floors. Then those footsteps crossed down the hall... And then they reached the end.

It was right as the attic door squealed wide that Freddie reached the dollhouse and switched off her flashlight. She was still exposed, though—no time, no *time*.

Freddie lurched sideways behind a refrigerator box labeled *Rita's toys*. Beside it were more heaps of *National Geographic*. Enough to block her if she cowered low.

It wasn't until the person reached the top of the attic stairs and shuffled into the main space that Freddie realized she'd left the door to the secret room open.

CRAP, she screamed inwardly. *CRAAAAAP*. But there was nothing she could do now. Nothing except curl as small as possible and cover her mouth to muffle her rough exhales.

The person shambled toward her... then past. Heavy footsteps. Oblivious and unhurried. Until they reached the dollhouse.

There they froze, and the room seemed to shrink inward. Freddie stopped breathing. She just listened, listened. Exactly as she knew the other person was doing too.

Listening, listening.

Her heart was a timpani. Her blood roared in her ears, and in quick, skittering thoughts, she tried to map out an escape route. From this angle, she could run for the stairs, staying behind the magazines the whole way.

But the person would be faster. They would reach the stairs before she could.

CRAP.

After an eternity of frozen time, of listening and screaming in her brain, a new sound scraped out. The person was moving again. Ducking into the hidden room in a whisper of fabric against the doorframe.

The door clicked shut.

And Freddie thought she might pass out from relief. She wheezed in a shallow breath. Let her hand fall from her mouth. And for several long seconds—or maybe minutes—she stayed that way. Still listening, still bracing for the person to realize they were not alone.

But nothing happened. Noises like boxes being moved and papers being shuffled filled the space, but that was it.

Which left Freddie with two choices. She could either wait the person out, leave after they were gone . . . or she could make a run for it now. The latter option would be loud. There was no way to get around those creaking stairs or the squealing hinges on the attic door.

So Freddie decided she would wait. Even though every second here was agony, it was her safest bet. Plus, if she could angle herself just right, she might be able to glimpse who had come in. Was it Sheriff Bowman or was it someone else like Edgar Fabre Jr., perhaps?

Yes. That was what Freddie had to do.

After carefully checking Xena wouldn't knock into anything,

Freddie unfurled and eased onto her hands and knees. Her left wrist howled anew. Her palms burned. But she ignored the pain and crawled toward the stairs. If she waited at the edge of the magazines, then when the person descended, she could peek around and see them from behind.

Every inch Freddie moved, she paused. She listened. But the person in the secret room remained unaware; she was still safe. For now.

She reached the last stack of *National Geographic*. She tucked in her legs, ready to resume her earlier pose . . .

And that was when it happened.

Doodle-loo doo, doodle-loo doo, doodle-loo doo, doo!

Freddie's Nokia started ringing. So loud. So unmistakable.

She ripped it from her back pocket, but it was too late. A second round was already blasting out.

Doodle-loo doo, doodle-loo doo—

Freddie slammed down the Power button. Her mind had wiped clean, a state of pure terror broken only be the gunfire of her heartbeat.

She had no choice now. She had to make a run for it.

In a bolt of speed, her muscles taking over—flight *dominating* over fight—Freddie pushed to her feet. She ran for the stairs, reaching them right as the door to the secret room swung wide. But Freddie didn't look up, didn't slow as she barreled down.

She had *maybe* a three-second head start on whoever was back there, and she had to use those precious seconds well.

She yanked open the attic door and slammed it shut behind her. Four bounding steps and she reached the stairs. She flew down, two at a time, before reaching the landing.

The attic door slammed a second time. The house rattled.

No time, *no time.*

Freddie leaped across the living room, grabbing the edges of the couch, of an armchair, and using them to fling herself faster.

She hit the kitchen. And again, she grabbed the edges of furniture—but this time, to slow down her pursuer. One chair.

Two. She knocked them over. They crashed sideways, *maybe* buying her one extra second.

She heard glass shatter. She didn't look back to see if it was jam or something else.

Then she reached the back door, and thank god it wasn't locked. She turned the knob—its cold brass scratched and worn—and her eyes caught on the yellow raincoat beside the door.

Freddie grabbed it, wrenched the door wide, and burst out into the frozen afternoon. Again, she yanked the door shut behind her. Then she ran, pulling on the raincoat.

Freddie didn't *think* her pursuer had gotten a good view of her. She didn't *think* she'd been in their line of sight, and as long as she didn't look back, then maybe this person would never see who she was.

She towed the hood in place and sped for the patio. Xena banged against her chest. Snow dusted everything now, lightening the amber and yellow trees—and meaning no matter which way Freddie ran, she left tracks.

She flung the gate wide and raced into the woods. She didn't take the route she'd taken before, but instead cut right and crouched low enough that the fence blocked her from view.

Until the fence ended.

And behind her, she heard the door to Mrs. Ferris's house crash shut. Her pursuer was on their way.

Freddie straightened and flat-out ran. Faster than she'd ever known she could run. Her camera thumped new bruises. Her breath came in panicked gasps.

She didn't look back, even though she wanted to. Even though she was *desperate* to know who had been in that attic with her. Three houses streaked past. Two more fences. Then Freddie reached a street. If she cut right, she could loop down onto her own street, but that was too obvious. Right now, she just had to keep moving *away* and get to someplace no one would look for her.

Freddie crossed the street. Hopped the curb. Cut over someone's lawn and into a small strip of woods that would lead to downtown Berm.

When at last Freddie was tucked inside the trees, she risked a glance back. No one was there.

Freddie wasn't stupid enough to slow, though. Her pursuer might simply be in a car now, preparing to cut her off ahead. Or maybe they'd taken a different route and would pop out from the other side of these houses.

She couldn't stop. She couldn't slow.

It wasn't until Freddie reached the edge of downtown Berm, where a line of "antique" shops (aka junk shops) marked this corner of blocks, that she finally eased her pace. She could barely breathe. Her legs had turned to Jell-O.

With a whispered apology to Mrs. Ferris, Freddie ducked inside the first junk shop she found—All's Sell That Ends Sell—and tore off the yellow raincoat. She hung it on a coat rack by the door, then dipped back into the evening.

The sun was almost gone behind the horizon now, and snow clotted thicker as Freddie hurried through downtown. She was careful to keep her pace casual, her hands dug into her pockets like she was cold but not *too* cold. Like she always walked around Berm at sunset with a camera around her neck.

Jack-o'-lanterns leered at her. The fairy lights seemed to laugh.

By the time she reached the central block—where Mr. Binder's shops all stood—the sun was setting. Freddie was shivering, but it was a vague, unimportant problem. One her mind hardly registered because it was clotted too thick with memories and theories and a constant play-by-play of what had just happened.

At a slender alley, Freddie cut left to circle behind the stores. A small parking lot served the city of Berm when the limited street parking could not. It was also where the back door to the Frame & Foto waited—and where Greg kept a spare key in a lockbox.

The lot was almost completely empty; stores closed early downtown, and Greg's Chevy was nowhere in sight. Upon reaching the three steps leading up to the Frame & Foto, Freddie gave her reflection a cursory glance in the glass back door. Her nose and cheeks were pink. Snow dusted her hair. Other than her bandaged wrist, though, she looked like her normal self.

The lights were out in the back hall. She knocked anyway. Then knocked again, but when Greg didn't appear in the hall after thirty freezing seconds, Freddie gave up and twisted to the lockbox.

Fingers clumsy with cold, she punched in the key code: *0-4-5-1*. A click sounded; the lockbox swung wide.

Freddie snatched out the key, and relief surged through her as she fumbled open the lock and shoved inside. Heat gusted against her, along with the pungent odor of darkroom chemicals. Before she could push all the way inside, though, a voice called her name. A voice from behind, in the parking lot.

"Gellar?"

Freddie's throat closed off. Fear pummeled in. She half leaped around.

But it wasn't Sheriff Bowman or an axe-wielding murderer striding across the parking lot. It was Theo Porter. He stood beside his Civic, a plastic shopping bag dangling from his left hand.

And now he smiled. Now he waved.

22

For several seconds, Freddie had no idea what to do. Theo Porter was Sheriff Bowman's nephew. He knew where Freddie was now, which meant he could tell his aunt. Maybe he'd *already* told his aunt.

But no, no. That didn't make sense. Freddie had only just arrived here, and Theo seemed as surprised to see her as she was to see him.

She forced a smile from her spot, half squeezed through the open door. "Just a sec!" she shouted, then she slipped inside and let the door swing shut behind her.

She would have to go back out there. She would have to talk to Theo, even if she didn't know what to say. *Hey, your family has some scary stuff happening. Any idea why your grandma has a secret murder room? Also, is your aunt possibly working with or hypnotized by a serial killer?*

Plus, the truth was, if not for whatever had just happened at his grandmother's house, then Freddie would have wanted to go see him. She would have been giddy and buoyant and flushing all the way to her core that Theo was *right over there* and smiling at her.

Freddie's hands trembled slightly as she removed Xena from her neck and hung the camera on a coat rack by the door. Snow melted off her boots and onto the linoleum. Next, she withdrew the film canister and Sabrina from her pockets, then placed both items on the flat top of the coat rack. The power on her phone was still off, but she was afraid to change that. As if, even now, the ringing might alert the person from the attic of her whereabouts.

She exhaled thickly, smoothed at her too-tight uniform and her hair, then finally Freddie thrust back into the dregs of a gray sunset. The parking lot swept against her in a slurry of cold and snow and drifting white. Yet standing stark against it was Theo. He still waited by his car, the driver's door open and the plastic bag no longer in hand.

"What are you doing here?" he called as Freddie hurried toward him. His blue eyes were bright, even the swollen one, and his lips were quirked handsomely to one side. Despite the fading bruises, he looked polished, he looked poised, and he looked . . .

Happy.

It was strange, actually. So completely at odds with the Theo that Freddie had kissed only that morning. The one who had needed distraction because his life was a mess right now.

"Why are *you* here?" Freddie countered, hoping he wouldn't catch her blatant deflection. She was just her Usual Self: Frederica Gellar, obsessed with Lance Bass, *The X-Files,* and any mystery that might need solving. *This* Freddie had not just found a secret room in Theo's grandmother's house, and *this* Freddie had not just fled someone who was probably a serial killer or controlled by one.

Freddie came to a stop several paces from him. He still wore his Fortin Prep uniform, but no tie now. And he'd loosened his shirt collar, which looked good. Like, really good, with just that glimpse of a collarbone and pale skin.

"Beef jerky," he said simply.

Freddie kicked up an eyebrow. "Huh?"

"Beef jerky," he repeated, and this time he nodded toward the open car. "My grandmother's awake, and she has a hankering for it. So I just stopped in the drugstore before it closed."

For half a breath, Freddie didn't react to this statement—because how *should* she react? "You, um . . . you must be so happy," she said eventually. Not an admission of having met Mrs. Ferris, but also not a denial.

"I am indeed." Theo's head tipped sideways. "But didn't the hospital call you? I gave them your number."

Oh. Right. He knew about that part because he'd set it up.

Freddie's lips compressed. Then parted. Then compressed again because the reality was that she sucked at this. She wasn't good at gauging whether a lie would make things better or worse. And she was also stretched so thin by adrenaline she didn't think she could manage a lie anyway.

So Freddie did the only thing she could think of to sidetrack Theo: she marched up to Theo, grabbed his blazer collar, and kissed him.

It was a simple kiss. Freddie's lips against Theo's, and nothing more. Or that was the plan, at least—the haphazard, slapped-together plan of a terror-crazed mind. She would kiss Theo Porter; then she would flee back into the Frame & Foto.

Unfortunately for Freddie, this plan was dashed to pieces as soon as it began. Because Theo tasted like honey. Like honey and boy and breathless moments by a historical water mill.

So instead of pulling away, Freddie just stood there, her fingers wound into Theo's jacket. Her lips resting against his.

She actually would have stayed like that forever if a car hadn't rumbled past and distracted her. Distracted him too, and forced them both apart.

Blinking, Freddie watched the SUV putter by. It had been the last vehicle in the parking lot, save for Theo's.

"What," Theo began roughly, "was that for?"

Freddie glanced back at him, dazed. Her brain, which had hardly been organized before, was a fun house of chaos, noise, and distorted mirrors everywhere she turned.

She slowly released his blazer. Then she brought her cold finger to her lips. *Honey.*

Freddie swallowed, knowing she needed to say something. Theo was staring at her, and each second that slid past sent his brow slanting farther down.

Find words, Gellar. Any words. "I like you," she said. *Not those words, though.*

She rocked back a step. Then two, and oh god, what had she just done? She pressed her fingers harder against her lips, as if this could somehow suck her confession back in.

Theo's face—his handsome, broken face—went very, very still. "Oh," he said. More exhale than actual word.

And Freddie's heart sank low.

Low, low, *low*. All the way down to her toes and into the asphalt—because oh *god,* what had she just done? She must look like a royal fool, soaked through with snow and confessing feelings that appeared to be one-sided.

Of *course* Theo didn't like her back. *Obviously.* They were enemies of Verona Beach, and Freddie had just let her fear-addled mind erase all sense.

"I know we don't know each other well, but I feel like . . . like if we *got* to know each other, then maybe we would . . ."

No, no. This was making it worse. Freddie could see Theo retreating. She could see him flinging up walls, and at any moment, he would scrub a hand over his hair and then stuff both fists into his pockets.

"I mean," she blurted, voice lifting. Words coming faster. "I . . . I feel like we're a lot alike. We both like finding answers, you know? And we both like plotting pranks . . . And you like boy bands, and I like boy bands. And sure, there *is* the issue of Backstreet Boys versus NSYNC, but I don't think that's a dealbreaker, do you?" *Oh my GOD, Gellar, STOP.*

Freddie couldn't stop. Her ears were ringing, and her blood was positively boiling—both with the adrenaline from earlier and now new surges to muddy the water. Meanwhile the mirrors in her brain were warping her in every possible direction, so she couldn't keep track of a single coherent thought.

The only thing that made sense or stood out right now was the truth. And the only truth that she was actually *allowed* to talk about was the one that was currently tumbling from her mouth.

The truth about how much she liked Theo.

The truth about how much she wanted to see him when he wasn't around and how kissing him made everything in the world fall away. About how he made her laugh, even if he was the enemy, and how his lips tasted like honey.

"Which *why*," she demanded, "*why* do you taste like honey? That doesn't make any sense, Mr. Porter, and that was *not* mentioned in the PG-13s. Neither was the fact that hormones would make me completely silly.

"But then that makes me wonder if these *are* just hormones—or if maybe they're something else. I don't know. I've been so fixated on fulfilling my sacred vow to Divya because I don't want to mess up her shot with Laina that I haven't really considered all the angles. All these . . . these feelings." Freddie clutched at her stomach; it was on fire in a Very Bad Way Indeed. "And look, I don't care if you don't feel the same way about me."

"Freddie," Theo said. Cold sunset swept over his face.

"Actually, that's not true," she amended. "I *do* care if you don't feel the same. But no matter what happens, I need to tell Divya the truth. Because best friends aren't supposed to lie to each other, you know? And I did. I lied by omission."

"Freddie."

"God, I bet this is what Y2K feels like." She shook her head.

"Freddie," Theo repeated again. Now he looked slightly annoyed.

"Don't say anything. Please." She lifted her hands, half-beseeching, half-defensive. "In fact, can we just pretend this conversation never happened? I'll go my way and you can go yours. And . . . I'm sorry," she finished. "Really, I am."

Freddie shifted, ready to bolt. Theo's voice cut out, *"Wait."* He had also removed his blazer and was holding it out to her. "Here," he said curtly.

"Um." She frowned. "What should I do with it?"

"You should put it on." He shook it at her. "You're freezing."

"Oh." She swallowed. Then shrugged. "It's fine. I'm going inside now, so I don't need it."

"You *do* need it," he insisted.

"Why?"

"Can you please stop asking questions and just put on the jacket?"

"Absolutely not." She'd just plumbed the depths of her soul for him, and now he had the nerve to look annoyed? "That's how people get murdered, Mr. Porter."

"By *school uniforms*?"

"By doing what strangers tell them to do!"

"I'm not a stranger." He scowled. "You just told me how much you liked me."

"And you didn't respond!"

"Um, I tried to respond, but you were like a freaking freight train going over a cliff. Now *please* put on the jacket."

"*Why?*"

"Oh my god!" He flung up his hands—and the blazer. "I want you to put it on because I'm going to kiss you for a very long time, and I don't want you to be cold."

Freddie's eyes widened. Her mouth fell open. Because this was definitely not what she'd expected Theo to say—although it was definitely something she'd hoped he would say.

"I had all these plans to be super smooth," Theo continued, stepping in close. "You were going to put on the jacket and I was going to tell you that I finally understood that stupid NSYNC song."

"You mean . . . 'Tearin' Up My Heart'?"

"Obviously." He opened the blazer and swooped it around Freddie's shoulders. It smelled like newspapers and detergent.

And it was warm.

She slid her arms into the loose sleeves.

"But of course," Theo went on, "you refused my jacket because you're stubborn—"

"Because you didn't ask *nicely*."

"—and now the moment for my smooth words has passed."

"Oh." Freddie blushed.

"Yeah. *Oh*." He eyed her for several seconds, tongue running over his teeth and hands still holding the blazer collar. He was close enough for Freddie to kiss him. For her to rise onto her toes and resume what she'd begun.

"Theo," she said softly.

"Freddie," he replied, moving closer by a single inch. Close enough that Freddie had to tip her head back to hold his gaze. And close enough that she could feel the heat off his body and see how large his pupils had become.

Then that was it. The point at which the air between them shifted, and suddenly they were kissing again.

23

Here was one thing Freddie knew about kissing Theo Porter: the world made a lot more sense this way. She felt safe. She felt grounded. No fun house mazes to scuttle her brain. It was just Freddie and Theo. And this time, when Theo bent slightly to cup his hands beneath her butt, she was ready for it. *This* time, when he hefted her up, her legs instinctively slung around his waist and her arms clung to his neck.

Theo carried her around the car door, still kissing her. Like he could never stop. He kicked the door shut as they passed—which was a *stupid* sexy move, and Freddie found herself kissing him all the harder for it.

Then he pressed Freddie onto the car's hood and pressed himself against Freddie. The car was warm beneath her. Damp with melted snow too, but the blazer protected her.

His blazer that he had given her to keep her warm.

Her legs squeezed more tightly around him, and she slid up her hands to rest on Theo's chest. He had such a nice chest, and Freddie especially liked the way his heart thumped against her palm.

Distantly, she realized Theo's shirt was now wet with snow. And distantly, she realized he must be freezing without his blazer on. But that was a cursory, unimportant problem.

All that mattered right now was kissing Theo.

"Just . . . to clarify," Freddie murmured between kisses, "this *does* mean you like me too, right?"

"Yes," Theo said raggedly. "Wasn't that obvious?" He dragged kisses over her jaw. Onto her neck. "I told you, it's tearing up my heart when I'm with you, and when we are apart, I feel it too."

"Ah," Freddie replied, and she couldn't help it: she laughed. An irrepressible sound that fizzed up from her lungs.

Because really—no boy should be allowed to quote NSYNC *and* kiss her neck at the same time. It was like having every fantasy come true at once. All that was missing was Lance Bass, and honestly, she wasn't sure she wanted him anymore.

Theo Porter was more than enough.

Theo stopped kissing Freddie's neck and looked at her. "You're laughing at me."

"No." She tugged him back to her. "I'm laughing *with* you."

"But I'm not laughing."

"You should be, though. I mean, look at us: a few days ago, you hated me."

"No, I didn't." Theo rested his forehead against hers. "I never hated you, Freddie. At least not after meeting you at the Quick-Bis."

"Oh?" This was news to Freddie. Good news that she liked very much. "Why is that?"

"Because you made me laugh. Not many people can do that. Also"—Theo offered a cocky grin—"I have a thing for girls in glasses."

Now this was *really* news to Freddie. Her eyebrows shot high. "You could have told me that sooner, you know. Then I would have worn them every day."

"And then you would have killed me." He bit his lip—swollen and red. "I mean, glasses *and* this hair? Do you have any idea what power you wield, Freddie Gellar?"

"You . . . like my hair?"

"Do I like your hair?" Now he was the one to laugh while he brushed a stray curl from Freddie's face. He tucked it behind her ear, and for half a frozen moment, Theo stared at her. Lips parted, gaze hungry, and . . .

And there was something more, Freddie realized—a look on his face that she had never seen anyone direct at her before. That she'd never known she *wanted* to see.

As if Theo couldn't believe his luck, like he was afraid that if he moved, it would all come crashing down.

And there was that vulnerability too—the tortured Theo from that morning. The one that, Freddie supposed, always lived beneath his smooth words and smiles.

She had no idea who moved first after that. All she knew was that one moment, she and Theo were a few inches apart. The next, their lips were crushed together.

Fast, vicious kisses with his fingers tangling in her hair— hair she now knew he loved. Freddie clutched at his busted, beautiful face while they pushed harder against each other. No cold, no rising night, no empty parking lot to encircle them.

She could feel Theo's desperation. He wanted distraction, salvation, and relief from whatever it was that tormented his blue eyes. His need filled each kiss, and *god,* she liked it.

Except no, this was more than just liking. She *needed* it. As badly as he did, she needed distraction and salvation and relief. But until right now, she hadn't realized how much she hungered for them.

Because Freddie's world was also a mess. There were murders and secrets and poems about executioners tangled so thick she didn't know where one knot ended and the next began. Yet right now, none of that mattered. Not while Theo Porter was kissing her.

Theo slid a hand into the blazer, moving toward Freddie's back. Her shirt had ridden up; his cold fingers brushed bare skin.

She stiffened with surprise.

Theo stiffened too. "I'm sorry." He yanked his hand back. "I didn't mean to—"

"Wait." Freddie caught his wrist. Then ever so slowly, she returned his fingers to her skin.

"I like it," she told him.

"Oh," he replied.

"Now kiss me," she commanded.

And Theo did. A sweet kiss this time—slow and thoughtful while his fingers traced gently across her hips. Up her spine.

Freddie had never been touched there before. She had always been too shy with Carl. Perhaps ashamed even. After all, none of the girls in *Seventeen* magazine had the same softness or curves that she had.

But with Theo, she found she didn't care. He enjoyed the shape of her, and that knowledge was... well, *intoxicating*. Freddie's heart thudded in her abdomen. In her skull. Then a moan left her throat, the softest of sounds.

And it was like a fuse going off. Suddenly the kisses were no longer sweet. Suddenly she and Theo were clinging to each other with another level of desperation and hunger.

They would have gone on forever like that too, if headlights hadn't beamed over them. If an engine hadn't abruptly filled the air. Freddie and Theo pulled apart, startled, as headlights blazed through the snow.

A Jeep, Freddie realized as it skidded to a stop.

The driver's door flung wide. "What the *hell* are you doing?" a voice bellowed. Then Kyle Friedman materialized through the snow. He was charging their way. "Get off her!"

Before Freddie or Theo could fully react, Kyle reached them. He slammed into Theo, and they crashed to slick pavement.

Freddie almost crashed too, but somehow she managed to scrabble backward just in time. "Stop it!" she shrieked, and she vaulted after them. *"Stop it!"* She grabbed at Kyle's shirt and pulled with all her strength. But it wasn't enough. Not even close.

Kyle was flailing and Theo was flailing and punches were flying everywhere.

More Jeep doors opened. Then voices zoomed in—and people came with them. First was Luis, grabbing for Kyle along with Freddie. Cat followed next, shouting at Kyle to *calm the hell down!*

And last was Divya, shouting at Freddie, *This was why you didn't answer your phone?*

Freddie didn't respond to her best friend. She couldn't. Not through all the chaos, not with everyone yelling and Kyle still whaling on Theo and Theo still whaling on Kyle, and both of them tumbling over snow-sodden asphalt. They were a tangle of shadows spotlit by headlights.

Only with Luis's help and three more grunting tugs did Freddie finally wrench Kyle off of Theo. Then while Luis towed Kyle away, Freddie dropped to the ground beside Theo. His white uniform shirt was soaked through and streaked with parking lot filth. And his eyes . . .

Oh, his blue eyes were wild with rage.

Freddie offered him a hand. He didn't take it. Instead he shoved to his feet unaided and barked, "What the fuck, Friedman? What the *fuck*?"

"What the *fuck* to you!" Kyle roared, trying to break free from Luis. But Cat lunged in and grabbed him too. "What were you doing to her, Porter?"

"*Doing* to her?" Theo huffed a laugh. "It's called making out, Friedman. See, when a guy and a girl like each other very much—"

"Freddie doesn't like you," Kyle interrupted. "Right?" He swung his gaze to Freddie. "Tell him that you don't like him and that you . . ." Kyle trailed off. Then abruptly stopped struggling against Cat and Luis.

And for the first time since his arrival, he looked at Freddie. Like *looked* at her. "You're wearing his jacket," he said slowly.

Freddie gulped. Then nodded.

"So you wanted . . ."

Another nod. "Yeah, Kyle. I did."

"But I thought . . . I thought we were . . ." He motioned between them. "I mean, you wore my jacket on Friday, Freddie."

"I'm sorry," she replied, even though she *actually* wanted to scream: *THAT DOES NOT MEAN WE ARE DATING.*

And yes, she might've had a crush on him last Friday, but as far as she could tell, she had done nothing whatsoever to lead him into expecting more. Not to mention, they had spent all of high school in the same homeroom and Kyle had never ever noticed her before. Now suddenly he liked her and was jealous?

But that was a problem to be dealt with later. Right now, Freddie had five people gaping at her—and all of them waiting for her to do something.

Divya was the one that Freddie turned to first. She hated the confusion knitting over Divya's brow. She *hated* the disappointment sloping across her lips.

"I'm sorry," Freddie said again, and unlike with Kyle, she meant it this time. "I was going to tell you."

"Going to tell her?" Cat demanded. "Tell her what? That you're consorting with the enemy?"

"I have a name," Theo muttered.

"Yeah," Kyle snarled. "Douchebag."

"Eat it." Theo puffed out his chest—which prompted both Kyle and Luis to puff out theirs.

And suddenly she'd had enough. The posturing. The pointless hatred between two sides. Montagues and Capulets that could only resolve their differences through *murder*. It was stupid, stupid, stupid. But before Freddie could bark *STOP THIS!* at all of them, Divya stepped in and beat her to it.

"Stop!" she screeched, rounding first on Kyle and Luis. Then on Theo. "Just *stop*, all of you." Lastly she turned to Freddie. Her cheeks were flushed with cold—and with emotion too. "Laina is missing, Fred. That's why we're here. I went down to my kitchen and when I came back up, she was gone."

No. Freddie's lungs inverted. Her gut swept down to her toes.

"I tried calling you," Divya went on. She walked toward Freddie. Snow flickered across her black hair. "But your phone was off, and your mom didn't know where you were. Since the library was closed, I figured you had to be here."

Good detective work, Freddie thought, and if the moment had been anything but *this* one, she would've said so. Instead, she asked: "And you tried Laina's house?"

"Of course, but her mom hasn't seen her, and she's not answering her phone. So I called them." Divya waved to Cat, Luis, and Kyle. "I didn't know who else could help me."

"Right." Shame spiderwebbed through Freddie's belly. Her friend had needed her, and she hadn't been there. "And . . . and did you explain to them what's going on with Laina?"

"You mean that Laina sleepwalks?" Cat folded her arms over her chest. "She did."

Okay. Okay. Freddie could figure this out. She *had* to figure this out. Although first she turned to Theo. He had been watching this whole exchange, locked up and closed off. Freddie approached him, and though she didn't want to, she removed his blazer. Cold rushed in. "You should go, Theo."

He wet his lips. "So you're choosing them?"

"I'm not *choosing* anyone." Freddie offered him the jacket. He didn't take it. "But I have to deal with this, and you have to see your grandmother."

He winced, a tiny movement around his eyes. As if, in all this madness, he had forgotten Mrs. Ferris and the beef jerky. Freddie almost had.

"Okay," he said softly. Then before Freddie could stop him, he leaned in and kissed her on the forehead.

It was a curt movement, like he didn't want to do it in front of everyone but rather *had* to. Like it was Very Important that Freddie see he wasn't upset with her. "Keep the jacket," he said, "and I'll call you later."

Theo stalked away.

"Piss off, Porter!" Kyle shouted at Theo's back.

And Theo answered with an expertly flicked middle finger before slinging into his Civic. A heartbeat later, the car revved to life. Two heartbeats after that, and it was pulling away.

"Alright," Freddie said, once Theo was out of the parking lot, "the first place we should look is at Fortin Prep."

"Um." Luis barked a laugh. "You're not going anywhere with us."

Freddie blinked. "What? Of course I am."

"Definitely not," Cat chimed. She planted her hands on her hips. "We don't need your help, Freddie, and we don't want it."

"Are you serious right now? I *sacrificed* myself to the sheriff earlier so you and Kyle could get away, and this is how you treat me?"

Cat cringed, but before she could answer, Kyle declared, "That was before we caught you hooking up with the enemy." His lips curled back and Freddie wondered how she had ever found him cute. "Now we've seen your true colors."

"Fortin Prep colors," Luis added.

To which Freddie could do nothing but gape—because *how* could this be happening right now? "Laina is missing," she sputtered at them, "and you guys are worried about some stupid rivalry?"

"Stupid?" Cat repeated. "You're part of it, remember? You were the Prank Wizard!"

"Of course I remember!" Freddie opened her arms. "But none of that matters right now. Divya, tell them that I can help you find Laina." She whirled toward her best friend.

But as soon as she caught sight of Divya, she knew her best friend couldn't help her. It was clear from the slant of Divya's brow that she *wanted* to . . . but she was also thrust into a terrible choice. Freddie had the knowledge; Kyle had the transportation; and right now, speed mattered most.

Freddie understood this. "Fortin Prep," she said softly. "Start there, Divya. At the crypt. It's easier to search, and Laina said she's gone there before. After that, check the gravestones from earlier. But be careful. I mean, really careful. Those woods are not safe."

Divya gave her a sad smile. "Thanks." She turned to go.

"Wait."

Divya glanced back. "Yeah?"

"I'm sorry."

"I know." Divya shook her head. "And I'm sorry you were too afraid to tell me about Theo."

"Call me if Laina's not at Fortin Prep, okay?"

"Yeah." Divya wet her lips. "I'll call you when we find her."

Freddie didn't watch the Jeep leave. She didn't watch her best friend walk away or her ex-squad vanish into the snow. For one, she was freezing and just wanted to get inside. Even slipping back into Theo's blazer hadn't been enough to fight the cold.

For two, there was just *so much* she had to do now. Film to be developed, theories to be spun, and evidence to be catalogued. Plus, if Laina wasn't at the mausoleum or at the gravestones in the county park, then Freddie needed to figure out where else to send the Prank Squad.

She pushed into the Frame & Foto, briefly reveling in the heat that blasted against her. After grabbing Xena and the film roll, she headed for the darkroom. Never had she been so grateful for the silence of the store as she was right now—nor for the pungent odor of the darkroom's chemicals, its familiar canisters and sinks and clothespins. She was safe here; she was alone; she had work to do.

Because for all that she had briefly related to what Mulder had said about science providing no place to start, it was Scully's response that Freddie always relied on: *Nothing happens in contradiction to nature, only in contradiction to what we know of it. And that's a place to start.*

Nothing might make sense right now, but Freddie had heaps

more information to work with than she'd had a few hours ago. And that was absolutely a place to start.

Freddie yanked a piece of paper from the laser printer in the corner. Then she plopped onto a stool beside the nearest stretch of counter and plucked up a pencil.

"You want people who keep journals," Bowman had told Freddie the summer before. "They're always the best for accuracy because they're used to writing down the memories of their day. They're used to taking notice and turning it into words. So, if there's ever something that you want to remember, Gellar, write it down."

Freddie did exactly that, starting as early in the day as she could. With Sheriff Bowman showing up at the school. Then the woods. Then Laina and the candle and the words she'd been saying (Freddie had *no* idea how to spell French, so she just wrote it down phonetically). *Juh sweez eessee.* Next, she wrote down everything that Laina had said in Divya's bedroom, about sleepwalking. About seeing a counselor from out of town.

Then came Mrs. Ferris. Then came her attic and all the weird stuff in the secret room. *Everything* Freddie could remember, she scrawled down. Sometimes, she'd jump back up to an earlier moment and write in an extra detail—the direction of the wind, the depth of the gravestones in the earth. Sometimes she'd shoot ahead, afraid to lose a memory if she didn't scrawl it down right away.

Once all of today was recorded, she moved backward in time: every single moment from the past week she scribbled onto printer paper, from newspaper articles to *The Curse of Allard Fortin* to even that dead smell that had filled up the archives. When she'd finished recording all her memories, she grabbed scissors and cut everything into individual sections.

Here was the information on the Executioners. Here was what had happened in the attic and what she'd found. Here was what she and Divya had seen on the tombstones. On and on, until she had several stacks and a lot of clues to work with.

Finally, Freddie grabbed tape and set to building herself a murder board on a stretch of blank wall. She lost all track of time. She was in the zone. She was doing the thing she'd been born to do—the thing that her dad had apparently been born to do too. He might have been a bad father, a bad boss, and a bad husband, but he'd been a *great* detective. And right now, what Berm needed was a detective.

Tamp down thoughts. Tamp down feelings. Focus on the task at hand.

When all the papers had been fastened to the wall, she stepped back and admired her handiwork. It was absolutely worthy of Fox Mulder's messy office—and it was much easier to study and find connections this way.

And what a lot of connections.

But also, what a lot of holes.

Sometimes people died; sometimes a bell tolled from nowhere; and sometimes descendants like Laina and Bowman and Teddy went off sleepwalking when they heard the bell.

At that thought, a new idea sizzled into Freddie's brain. She snatched up a final sheet of paper, and in frantic, sloppy scrawl, she wrote down the entire Executioners poem. She'd read it so many times in the last few days the whole thing was firmly planted in there. Especially the last line of the last stanza:

The Oathmaster is waiting.

That was the *person* to tie all these parts together. *That* was the serial killer behind all these deaths. And all signs currently pointed to Edgar Fabre Jr.—assuming he really hadn't died in 1975. Sure, Teddy Porter had believed the body he'd found had been his friend's, but there'd been no head attached to prove it . . .

"Aha," Freddie sighed. "Eureka and gesundheit." There had been a missing person in October of 1975 from Elmore. Freddie had seen that on the microfiche at the library, but she'd dismissed it at the time. Could that person have been the actual body that Teddy had found?

There was only one way to find out, and that was to track

down Edgar Fabre Jr. His family had been run out of Berm, but the photo of Teddy and Edgar had shown the young men in front of Elmore High.

So maybe when Edgar Sr. had fled the area, he'd only actually moved twenty miles north of here?

Alright, Freddie knew who she had to track down, and she had a solid foundation for where to start. Now she just needed to develop all her photos from Xena and then maybe pass those images off to the two visiting federal agents. Because Freddie wouldn't be foolish enough to go to Bowman again.

And honestly, props to Divya for actually being at least partially right back in the forest when she'd speculated Bowman might have been the one who'd moved the water bottle. She probably *had* been the one, but only because she'd been hypnotized by Edgar Jr.

God, Freddie hoped Edgar didn't try to take control of anyone else. Bowman, Laina, Mrs. Ferris . . .

Would he go for Theo next?

At that thought, a new idea lightninged across Freddie's brain. "Justin," Freddie hissed to herself, gazing again at her murder board. "Justin, Justin, Justine . . . *Justine.*" She found the paper where she'd written Mrs. Ferris's words: *Teddy and Justine live in Chicago now.*

She stared at them.

Teddy and Justine live in Chicago.

Freddie had already wondered if maybe Justine was a descendant from Justin Charretière. And she'd already wondered what it might mean if Theo was descended from not one Executioner, but two . . .

She hadn't, however, thought what that might actually mean for Theo.

"Holy crap," Freddie breathed. She gawped at the murder board for a full two seconds. *One Lance Bass. Two Lance Bass.* Then she burst into action, grabbing for paper and pencil. In a fraction of a second, she wrote down:

Two candles now lit on the graves. One for Bowman's ancestor: Portier, aka Ropey, aka the Hangman. One for Laina's ancestor: Steward, aka Hacky, aka the Headsman.

One candle was still missing, though. Presumably one that would also end up lit at Allard Fortin's mausoleum.

One for Theo's ancestor: Charretière, aka Stabby, aka the Disemboweler.

Freddie needed to get to Theo.

HUNTING

Theo hadn't known death could happen so fast. It had been slow with his mom. Lots of trips to the hospital. Lots of pinched-faced doctors and sympathetic nurses and the never-ending red that rimmed his dad's eyes.

This time, though, death had come without warning.

One minute, Theo was on top of the world: Dr. Born was going to vouch for him with the Fortin Prep disciplinary board, Freddie Gellar had said she liked him, *and* his grandmother had finally woken up.

Sure, the Berm High kids were a bunch of pricks, but their onslaught in the parking lot hadn't ruined his evening. They were nothing more than an annoyance. Kyle Friedman couldn't destroy all the good that had just come Theo's way.

She's awake, Aunt Rita had said over the phone only one hour before. *And she wants to see you.* Except that Grandma didn't want to see Theo anymore. Because now, Grandma was dead.

"I'm so sorry," the tall, willowy doctor told Theo while he stood in the hospital hall holding the beef jerky she'd requested. Fluorescent lights buzzed. "We did everything we could for her."

"Sure," Theo replied—because what else was there to say? They'd done everything for his mom too. But that hadn't made a difference in the end. "Can I . . . see her?" He waved to the closed door.

Room 34, where somehow, in the hour since Aunt Rita had called, everything had gone horribly wrong.

"I'm afraid not." The doctor wagged her head. "I'm sorry, but we had to move her body to the morgue already."

Theo swallowed, searching for the right words to respond with. The doctor's expression was so sympathetic it was starting to piss him off. It was like this woman expected him to cry—like she wanted him to be upset and howling and reacting more strongly than he was. But how could he freak out right now? None of this felt real. Not the plastic bag with beef jerky clutched in his left hand, nor the freshly busted knuckles on his right.

His grandmother might be a corpse cooling in the morgue, but all Theo had to go on right now were memories—and in those memories, she was very much alive.

So instead of a meltdown, Theo opted for a question: "Do you know where my aunt went?" There was no sign of Aunt Rita here, and he hadn't seen her squad car in the parking lot.

"I'm afraid I don't," the doctor answered, her overdone sympathy giving way to overdone thoughtfulness. Squinting, she turned to the nearest nurse, a man focused on his clipboard. "Joseph, do you know where the sheriff went?"

"I haven't seen her since we told her about her mother." That was all Joseph said. No *sorry for your loss* or *I wish I could help you*. He didn't even look up from his clipboard.

Yet Theo found he preferred that blunt honesty to the doctor's squinching pseudo-sympathy.

After gruff *thank-you*s for both the doctor and nurse, he left room 34 behind. The plastic bag rustled with each step. An awful sound. Overloud in Theo's skull as he crossed the waiting room. As he boarded an elevator, thumb bouncing against his thigh. Then as he left the hospital entirely.

Maybe if you'd driven faster, he thought. *Maybe if you hadn't made out with Freddie Gellar or fought with those Berm High shits, then you could have reached her before she died.*

All the way across the parking lot, the inner accusations spun. On the drive through downtown, past the lakeshore, and finally onto the Fortin Prep campus.

You were too slow, Theo. Too slow, too shitty, too behind.

He picked the farthest parking spot from the dorms. No lights. Only forest and shadows and untouched snow.

You were too slow. He parked the car. *Too slow, too shitty, too behind. And now Grandma's gone, and you'll never get to say goodbye.*

"Dammit," he whispered, turning off the car. Silence thundered in.

You did this, Theo. Because everything you touch turns to shit. You did this, and now you get to live with it.

"Dammit," he repeated, louder now. Then he snatched the plastic bag off the passenger seat and kicked outside. Cold poured over him. The snow had stopped falling, but there was enough sprinkled down to brighten the night to an eerie glow.

Theo stalked toward the nearest trees and launched the bag of beef jerky. Without waiting to hear if it landed, he stalked away. Past his Silver Sweetheart, as busted as it was, and toward the nearest path. He would go to the library. Not because he needed to but because it was better than sitting in his dorm room with the empty walls and people like Davis lurking next door.

Theo's footsteps crunched across the snow. It was slick, but he didn't let that slow him. He walked faster. Faster. Until soon, he was flat-out running into the mausoleum gardens. Past snow-dusted roses and the lamppost where he'd met Freddie Gellar a lifetime ago.

The loose brick got him. The one he'd warned Freddie about. It seemed to leap up and knock him down.

His footing failed. He flew toward the sign. His palms hit the marble. His chin too. And just like that, he was on all fours, his face right against the words *Le pouvoir réside dans le service.*

"Dammit," he wheezed between breaths. Snowmelt wet his fingers. His chin throbbed, and he wanted to scream that none of this should be happening.

Why him? Why now?

Theo shoved roughly to standing. He wiped his wet hands

on his pants. Then dragged a sleeve over his face. He wouldn't cry here. He wouldn't feel. He'd just get to the library and lose himself in the cellar where everything made sense.

Yet as he limped away from the sign, he spotted the brick that had tripped him.

It had torn free from the path and now rested a few feet away. Frowning, Theo's gaze shot to where the paver had been, to the dark hole now gaping upward.

Something glittered inside. It made Theo swallow, and, for a brief flicker of time, he forgot all about the ringing ache in his palms or the snow that had soaked into his pants.

In fact, as Theo approached the hole, a new feeling swelled in. A piercing sense that there was something he ought to be doing right now. Something important that he'd forgotten about. Like maybe he'd hidden this thing here a long, long time ago in hopes that he would one day be able to use it.

He slid his hand into the gap in the bricks. His fingers touched cold iron. Then he curled his grip around it and pulled the fist-sized item free. Moonlight glittered over it. Dirt too, since it had been hidden beneath a brick for who knew how many decades. Perhaps it had once had a shape—one that was distinct and recognizable—but now it was just a worn-down lump of freezing iron.

Theo sucked in a long breath. The pain in his chin and palms was rippling away. So were thoughts of his grandmother, until all that remained were Theo and this iron heart.

Come, said a voice, deep, *deep* in the back of Theo's brain. *We have work to do.*

"Yes," Theo replied. Work sounded good to him right now. He tucked the iron heart into his pocket. Then he pushed to his feet and set off for the trees. Ahead was the one who was calling him. The one he'd already met once, beside a lakeshore last week. The one who was hazy, hungry, and reeked of forgotten death.

Yes, yes.

They had work to do.

24

There were some truths that were just too big to contain in a single person's mind. Like, for all that Mulder made it seem so easy to believe in conspiracies and aliens, that was only TV. Fox Mulder was fun to watch, but everyone knew that wasn't real life. *Freddie* knew it wasn't real life.

People didn't really hypnotize others or try to re-create old, forgotten ghost tales to clear their family name. Except . . . it sure looked like someone had right about now.

And Freddie's dad must have come to the same conclusion, as proven by the box in the basement. Maybe if Frank hadn't died right in the middle of his investigation, then the murderer would have been caught twelve years ago . . .

Oh Jesus. Freddie wasn't sure she wanted to finish this thought. But it was too late, of course. Her eyes had already latched onto her ghost-filled murder board. Her brain had already finished doing the math.

It wasn't a heart attack that killed him.

They'd said the body was too awful for a child to see. They'd said a five-year-old shouldn't witness it. And there had been all those doctors and nurses covered in blood, rushing in and out of his room.

But that was not how people died when they had heart attacks. That was how they died when a serial killer decided they'd had enough of someone on their trail.

Maybe this is why the unspoken rule exists, she thought numbly. *Maybe Mom and Steve and Bowman all knew Dad died in a horrible way.* They might not have known it was *murder,* but they had to have known it wasn't cholesterol.

Freddie stumbled out of the room. She needed to keep her thoughts and feelings tamped down so she could call Divya. Maybe the Prank Squad had found Laina—maybe Freddie had gotten all of this wrong, and it would turn out to be a really epic prank. No serial killer or hypnotic sleepwalking, no attempt to re-create a story about spirits and blood oaths and murder . . .

She reached the coat rack. Her hands lifted to the flat shelf. Her palms patted. And patted.

And patted.

But there was nothing there. No phone, no device to power on and use. Which meant someone had moved Sabrina. And that meant someone had *been* here.

Reality hurtled into Freddie. *Maybe it's Greg,* she thought wildly, spinning toward the hallway—only to find no light shining through the cracks of his office. And no light from the main store either, at the end of the hall.

Freddie's heart kicked to max tempo. Her adrenal glands spurted to *on,* and once again, her gut was *screaming* at her to move. Immediately, while she still had a chance.

She obeyed, twisting for the back door. But she only made it two steps before a figure stepped into view outside. Hulking and vague through the glass, their arm was reaching for the handle.

Not Greg, her mind processed. *Too short to be Greg. Run, Freddie. Go.*

Freddie did exactly that. She hurtled away from the door. Straight for the main shop. She heard the door open behind her. She heard footsteps squeak inside. Definitely not Greg, or he would have called her name.

She reached the archway and veered left to circle around the main counter. Everything was dark. Just shapes and shadows in her way. But Freddie knew this store well. She had spent countless hours at the Frame & Foto, learning how to use the fancy darkroom and watching Greg develop his photos.

Which was why she knew that on the walls, meticulously hung, were Greg's most popular photographs. And it was why she knew that to her right was the Nikon display (where she'd gotten Xena), while straight ahead was the Canon display.

Freddie glanced behind her as she cut around the Nikons, certain she'd find her pursuer at the archway. Except no one was there. She slowed, feet skittering with confusion. Her pulse cannoned in her eardrums. *Where could they be? Where could they be?* Had she just imagined everything?

No, her gut told her. *Keep running.* She launched back into her sprint around the Nikons. And that was when it happened— *that* was when the person stepped in front of her. A human shape who just melted out of the tripods.

Freddie toppled into them. Her fingers touched a sleeve, but before she could look up to see who was attacking, a cloth slammed against her nose. Sweet fumes barreled in. Darkness rippled across her vision. Her entire body went limp.

It was as she tumbled to the floor that Freddie had just enough awareness to spot two things.

First: a gleaming sheriff's badge.

And second: another figure moving into Freddie's vision. Someone taller, broader, and draped entirely in shade.

Edgar, she thought hazily as she hit the floor. *Are you Edgar?*

The world went black.

It was the bells that roused Freddie. Three sharp peals that reverberated through her brain. Shredded at her skin.

Thrice rings the bell, she thought groggily, as her eyes opened. As white snow and bitter cold swept in. *No chance to atone.*

The world hung sideways, dark forest and frozen shadows. Freddie knew, without words actually forming in her brain, that she must be in the county park. How she had gotten there, though . . .

That was a mystery. One neither her brain nor her gut could unravel. Her head pounded. Her left wrist was a burning throb. And her stomach roiled like vomit was on the way.

She blinked away snowflakes on her lashes. Nothing looked familiar from her spot upon the snow. It was just an army of skeletal pine trees. Row upon row, awaiting their marching orders.

If Freddie were smart, she would stand up and figure out where she was. If she were smart, she would get up and try to run. But that feat seemed impossible. Too high, too far, too challenging.

You're delirious, she chided. *You need to get up, Gellar. Now. You will freeze to death if you don't.*

She didn't get up. Instead, she thought back to the Frame & Foto. To the glass front door, that she'd almost reached. Then she thought back to the white cloth that had been shoved into her face. And to the gleaming sheriff's badge.

At that thought—at that memory—a gag reflex scorched up Freddie's gullet. Hot and heavy and surging in too fast. She tried to rise. Tried to haul herself onto her knees before the bile surfaced. But as soon as she drew her hands beneath her, she found her body didn't want to comply.

It *couldn't* comply.

She was bound.

Freddie vomited then. It burned out of her mouth and down her face. There was no time to worry about that nor time to clean up or brace for the next gag, rising fast.

Freddie was tied up, lying on the snow. And she was all alone in a dark, dangerous forest.

She blinked down at her arms, fighting the next round of nausea. Her wrists were bound with a zip tie. *Just like you saw in Mrs. Ferris's attic.* Attached to the zip tie were a pair of handcuffs—also familiar—and those in turn were fastened to another zip tie around Freddie's ankles. She couldn't even unfurl her body if she wanted to.

She was well and truly trapped, stuck in a crooked fetal position while frostbite and hypothermia shivered in.

Okay, Gellar, she told herself, swallowing back more bile. *You can do this. Tamp down thoughts. Tamp down feelings. Focus only on the task at hand.*

With a grunt, a shove, and great *clenching* of her abdominal muscles, Freddie rolled upright. The forest dipped as blood rushed from her head. She blinked. Then blinked again until the trees righted themselves.

No familiar markers stood out in the darkness. No archives hut nor gravestones with candles. However, if Freddie listened . . . Yes. Great cracks split the night every few seconds—and she knew that sound.

Ice.

Freddie must be somewhere near the lakeshore, and the lake must have already frozen over. It was months too early, but she couldn't say she was surprised. After all, third came the ice, wreckt upon the stones. Then thrice rang the bell, no chance to atone.

Freddie had heard the bells. Now she heard the ice.

And that meant, at least according to the poem, the Disemboweler would be hunting. *Theo,* she thought. He'd been on his way to the hospital after the Frame & Foto. Surely Edgar Jr. couldn't have gotten control of him there. Assuming Edgar really was using something like hypnosis to control the descendants of the first Executioners, wouldn't that require privacy and solitude?

Something about that tickled at Freddie's brain. Although it vanished as quickly as it appeared. She was too cold to think clearly. She needed to get out of this snow, out of this forest— and to do that, she would need to get out of these zip ties.

Thanks to a bored afternoon with Ibrahim during her last internship, Freddie actually knew how to get out of zip ties: if you use something small and sharp to release the fastening mechanism, you can slide them right off. The problem was, where was she going to find something small and sharp in the middle of a snowy forest? Paper clips like she'd used that day were, unfortunately, not in abundance here.

But you have something even better.

Freddie laughed. A shuddering, frostbitten laugh because this Fortin Prep uniform was turning out to be more useful than she ever could have predicted.

It took her numb fingers two attempts to release the safety pin holding her shirt together. And once the pin sprang open, a fist-size gap suddenly opened on her chest. But she scarcely noticed the fresh cold and wet against her skin; all her attention was on maneuvering the safety pin into a zip tie's fastener.

On that day at the station with Ibrahim, Freddie had been embarrassed that his handsomeness had made her a silly, trembly fool who kept missing the mechanism. Now she was grateful that *nearness of a dreamboat* had had the same effect on her muscles as *brutally frozen cold*.

With handcuffs clinking, Freddie started with the zip tie around her ankles, losing track of time as she tried to shove the pin into the tiny plastic lock. As she prodded and wriggled and tried to hit the right spot that would release the mechanism. Then she felt it connect, and with a yank of her ankles, she tore the zip tie wide.

She was full-on shivering now, and her fingers had gone from bright red to pale, bloodless blue. The scrapes on her palms were dark lines she couldn't feel.

The swollen wrist, though—she felt that.

A killer is coming for you, her gut reminded. *You need to move.*

Without bothering to unbind her wrists or remove the dangling handcuffs, Freddie pushed to her feet. Everything looked different at this hour—and with a fresh dusting of snow. Although that groove on that hill over there . . .

She'd just been here, hadn't she?

Are you sure this path is a shortcut? Divya had asked.

Of course it's a shortcut, Freddie had replied. Now here was the same "path," the same ephemeral stream filled not with mosquitos, but with snow. This was the end of the stream, where it would gather in a completely mosquito-infested pond. If Freddie followed this uphill, she'd reach the archives.

And in the archives, there was a telephone.

Freddie set off.

25

If Divya had thought the archives were wiggins central during the day, Freddie thought as she galloped toward the woodsman cottage, *she really should see it at night.* No Keebler elves would be toppling out of there now.

Serial killers, though? Definitely.

Freddie ran right up to the archives door. The red of the window frame beside it looked like blood. A nail was sticking out too; she should probably tell Mom about that.

Or maybe you should just get out of these woods alive!

She tried the door handle, but it didn't budge. Breaking and entering it would have to be. She spun around, searching and searching until she spotted a hefty oak branch ten steps away.

Freddie didn't have much in the way of upper body strength. Plus, her wrists were still bound, handcuffs dangling down, and her left wrist was swelling more and more by the second. But didn't adrenaline turn people into Super Strong Muscle Machines? Who could lift a car off of a baby or something?

The answer, Freddie soon learned, was *no*. At least not when you were Freddie Gellar. Her first swing at the window bounced back right at her face. She barely bit back a yelp before it bonked her forehead.

She swung again, aiming lower. Again, again. But of course the window was freaking *weatherproof,* to protect Mom's precious historical documents. By the fourth swing, Freddie had to accept this wasn't going to work. That she would be better served running the half mile to the Village Historique and trying to use the phone there.

Freddie dropped the stick. Her breaths sawed in, sawed out. She swiveled to aim for the Village . . .

And that was when she saw it: the figure in the snowy autumn trees. Fuzzy and cloaked in the rotten stench of impending death. It moved toward Freddie with a slow, methodical stamp.

Then a different body slammed into Freddie. So sudden she hadn't heard it coming. So fast she had no time to react before she was smashed to the earth. Her skull slammed down. Stars and darkness splattered in.

Fingers closed around Freddie's neck and thighs squeezed around her rib cage.

Freddie struggled and squirmed. Clawed her zip-tied hands at some unseen face and unseen body. The handcuffs were still attached to her zip-tied hands, doing more damage to Freddie than her attacker. And no matter how hard Freddie fought—no matter how hard she strained to see—all she got were shadows. It was like a black fog had swept in, and somewhere inside there was a figure she could not seem to grab hold of.

And flames. There were flames in there too, flickers that danced off a hidden skull.

The fingers at Freddie's neck squeezed tighter. She choked. She wheezed. She fishtailed and writhed. And it was like two tracks were playing in her brain. On top was a track screaming, *Stay alive!* The track below that was saying, *This has to be a hallucination, and any moment now, you'll snap out of it.*

She *had* to snap out of it because right now, no breath was entering her lungs. No oxygen was reaching her brain. But no matter how hard she fought, she couldn't stop the hand at her throat.

She couldn't avoid the face now leaning in. *"Libérez-nous,"* they whispered.

And Freddie realized she knew that voice. She knew that shadowed face, even if the eyes were now filled with flame. Laina hissed, teeth flashing, and Freddie could have sworn she saw smoke coiling off the girl's tongue.

"*Libérez-nous.*"

Tighter, tighter. Laina's fingers squeezed *tighter.*

Libérez-nous. The words scraped inside Freddie's skull. Meaningless, yet inescapable. And also undeniably pleading. There was a desperation in that voice and an ancient sadness in the fathomless, flame-fueled eyes. *Libérez-nous.*

Suddenly, the pressure at Freddie's windpipe released. An abrupt influx of air, air, *air.* A heartbeat after that, the weight on Freddie's chest leaped free.

Laina was gone. The shadow was gone.

Divya's face swam into view. She was there—*right there*—and trying to help Freddie rise. *And Cat too,* Freddie thought, as a second face materialized from the darkness.

"Get up," Divya and Cat were saying in voices that sounded too far away. Like Freddie was in a swimming pool and they were shouting from the opposite end. "Get up, Freddie—you *have* to get up."

So Freddie got up. Somehow, with limbs made of ice and a brain made of fog—and with hands still bound by zip ties and a dangling set of handcuffs—she got up. Only to find Kyle and Luis by the archives.

Luis held a baseball bat and he was yanking at it while Laina clutched the other end in her hand. It was as if he'd swung it at her, and she'd stopped it midair. Effortless. A Super Strong Muscle Machine that Luis could never win against.

Flames licked off the bat's edge, but that wasn't what made Freddie gasp. *That* was Kyle, dangling from Laina's other hand as easily as a doll. She held him around the throat, and already, his movements grew weak.

"No," Freddie tried to yell. Except that the word came out as garbled as the night—painful too, her throat having just been shredded by hands that had been way too strong. *Supernaturally strong?* her brain tried to ask, but she elbowed that thought aside in favor of surviving this moment.

"Let him go, Laina!" She stumbled forward. Laina's back was to her; Freddie would attack if she had to. *"Let him go!"*

Clang. A bell tolled. Piercing, distant, yet also thrumming straight down into Freddie's gut.

Laina's head snapped toward it. *Clang.* She released Kyle. He crumpled to the snowy ground, coughing and sputtering. *Clang.* She released the baseball bat and bolted. A streak of fire-tipped shadows. Of unnatural speed and the stench of putrid flesh.

Then the last echoes of the bell ended, and Laina was gone.

For several seconds, no one moved. Not even Kyle, crouched and clutching at his throat. It was like everyone was afraid to breathe. Afraid to even think about what had just happened.

Until Kyle started coughing, and suddenly everyone was moving. Luis and Cat reached for Kyle. Divya grabbed for Freddie's bound hands.

"Oh my god," Divya said. "What happened to you?"

"No time." Freddie's vocal cords were shredded. "We need . . . to get in there. In the archives." She didn't know why the bell had rung again, and she also still didn't know *from where*. But three tolls meant the Disemboweler was hunting—human or maybe otherwise—and Freddie didn't want any of her friends to be outside a moment longer.

"You're tied up." Divya held fast to Freddie's shoulders. "How did you get here? What happened?"

"I'll explain inside, Div. There's a phone in there. Luis? The window—break it."

"Yep," he said as he tugged Kyle to his feet. And seconds later, with Cat to prop up Kyle and Divya still holding Freddie, Luis had his bat ready. "Hey, batter, batter," he murmured.

The window didn't stand a chance. Glass shattered in a sound that was both *magnificent* and *way too loud.* Heat rolled outward.

Luis swung again. Again. Until enough of the glass had fallen out for him to reach through and unbolt the door.

Freddie was the first to shove inside. "Come on, guys," she called, hugging her left wrist to her chest. "And lock the door behind you."

The handcuffs attached to Freddie's zip-tied wrists clanked as she climbed down the ladder into darkness. Every movement sent pain through new bruises, new scratches, and above all, her left wrist.

She tumbled off the ladder and grabbed at the light switch. It was a risk, turning on the light. But then, it wasn't as if being in the dark had kept them safe. At least now, there were walls.

Flip. Light bathed outward, fluorescent and searing. Freddie squinted into the bunker-like space stretching ahead. Grunts behind signaled Divya had arrived too. "It's so warm. Thank god."

"Phone" was all Freddie replied, and she launched toward the central support beam with its legally required emergency gear. (Although she would bet *murderers* weren't the emergency anyone had ever planned for.)

Freddie laughed. A weak, hysterical laugh as she aimed for the central pole. She yanked down the first aid kit. "Scissors," she told Divya, shoving it toward her. "I need to cut these zip ties."

"On it." Divya tore open the metal box, and moments later, Freddie's wrists were free. The handcuffs fell to the floor, landing on Freddie's frozen feet. *Now* she was able to grab for the phone.

Savoring the full freedom of her arms and hands, she dialed the police station. Bowman obviously—and frankly, *thankfully*—wasn't there, but maybe the deputies were. And maybe the feds were with them, since boy did this feel like a job for federal agents with federal agent weapons and skills.

Three rings sounded before Ibrahim's voice came through. "Berm Sheriff's Department—"

"*Ibrahim!*" Freddie half shrieked. "The murderer is here.

At the county park. Me and a bunch of other students, we're stuck with a serial killer. Please, Ibrahim—send help."

"Uh, who's calling?"

"Freddie Gellar." She cursed herself. She was smarter than this. Cooler under pressure. *Give him the facts. Channel Bowman . . . no, scratch that. Channel Bowman when she isn't under a murderer's control.* "We're at the Village archives, and it's dangerous. Like, really dangerous. There are several murderous, erm . . . *individuals* hunting us. So please, send a lot of people. Especially those feds that you mentioned are in town."

"And send guns," Kyle inserted. He and the others had now reached Freddie. They clustered around her like the worst kind of peanut gallery. "'Cause there's, like, fucking demons here."

"And an ambulance," Cat suggested. "For Laina."

Freddie waved them quiet. Ibrahim was talking at the same time, and she couldn't listen to them all. "Listen, Freddie," Ibrahim said in a tone she didn't like. "Bowman warned me you might call about something like this. But she said you're just pulling pranks, and so I can't—"

"NO." Freddie screamed into the phone. "We are literally going to *die* if you don't send help right now, Ibrahim. To the archives. You have to believe me—"

Divya snatched the phone away from Freddie. "Hi, Deputy, this is Divya Srivastava. My mom cuts your hair. And I can confirm everything Fred is saying right now. I'm here with three other students who can all back her up. This isn't a prank. We are in *serious* danger, and we need help . . ."

She trailed off. Her eyes grew huge. "It went dead. Oh my god, Freddie. The line just went dead."

"No, no, no," Luis said. "This can't get any worse."

Yes it can, Freddie thought. And sure enough, the lights snapped off.

Cat screamed. Kyle swore. And Divya clutched at Freddie in this new, total darkness. It had been bad enough on Saturday when the lights had turned off, but at least it had been daytime.

Now there was absolutely nothing to see by. And oh yeah, a serial killer was somewhere in the dark.

A serial killer who was now calling out: "I know you and your friends are in here, Freddie. And there's only one exit, so you might as well come forward nicely with your hands up."

Freddie felt as if all of her insides constricted at once. Like she was a plastic bag and a vacuum had just sucked out all the air. Because she knew that voice. Oh god, she knew that voice.

"Dr. Born," Divya hissed at Freddie. "That's *Doctor Freaking Born*."

"I have a gun," he went on. "In case you're wondering why you should listen to me."

Of *course* it would be Dr. Born. Of *course*. Freddie was downright furious with herself for not figuring that out sooner.

Dr. Born hadn't only been counseling Freddie and Divya—he'd been helping Theo too. And Freddie would bet he was also Laina's out-of-town counselor.

That would have given him perfect access for hypnotizing the descendants of the Executioners.

Except you know it's not just hypnosis, Freddie.

She punted that thought aside. She could dwell on science versus supernatural later. For now, she needed to get herself and her friends the *hell* out of these archives. "Window," she whispered at Divya. "At the back, remember? Go." She nudged at her best friend in the darkness. "Use the shelves to feel your way there."

Divya didn't move. "What about you?"

"I'll be right behind."

"Fred, *no*."

"I promise." She pushed again, and this time, Divya obeyed, grabbing at everyone else with a quiet *Follow me*.

They tiptoed away.

They were too loud, though. Every footstep, every rustle of fabric was an explosion in Freddie's ears. But then . . . maybe as long as Dr. Born believed there was only one way out of here, noise was okay. Especially if Freddie gave them cover.

She cupped her hands to her mouth. "Hey, Dr. Born! I was wondering when we'd get that last counseling session. I'm ready to talk, just so you know. Because oh *boy* do I have a lot of feelings right now. Am I correct in thinking you killed my dad?"

A soft laugh slithered out. Impossible to pinpoint in location, although she thought it might've come from the ladder's hatch.

"Let me see if I've got the rest right too," Freddie continued. "Your real name is Edgar Fabre Jr., and you never died. It was someone else who had their head cut off, wasn't it? A missing person from Elmore is my guess."

Freddie clutched at the support beam, cold at her touch. "Was his name Born by chance? Or is there some other guy you're pretending to be? I hope you realize that identity theft is a federal crime, punishable by up to thirty years in prison."

"That," Dr. Born murmured, "is the least of my sins."

Crap. Freddie's heart slammed into her skull. His words had pinged as if from only a few rows away. She'd have to sprint if she wanted to reach the back window with her friends now. Or . . .

Freddie grinned as a new idea formed.

"Well, no wonder I didn't like you when I met you, Dr. Born! Or should I call you 'Junior'?" Freddie patted and patted until she found the fire extinguisher. "I don't know if you know this about me, but I'm kind of famous for my gut. And I could just *tell* there was something off about you. How else to explain why I was so opposed to our counseling session? It's like my instincts just picked up right away that you were trouble."

She grabbed at the fire extinguisher, fumbling it off its holder. There was supposed to be a pin on it. Something to release the foam . . .

Freddie found it. She yanked it free. Then scooted full speed into the nearest row of shelves.

"I mean how many people have you killed over the last twenty-four years, Dr. Born? You're trying to reenact the poem from your blacksmith ancestor, right? By murdering people in the way the poem describes? I'll admit, though, I'm still kind of hazy on a motive. Care to share with the class?"

No answer, but that was fine. Freddie was on a roll.

"Alright, I'll hazard a guess. You wanted to trick the people of Berm into thinking everything from *The Curse of Allard Fortin* was real. I mean, the whole town rejected you and your family. They laughed your dad right out of town after the Allard Fortins sued him into oblivion. I'm not the counselor here—and, I guess, neither are you—but I'm going to assume all that rejection made you pretty mad.

"But to respond with *murder*, Dr. Born? That feels like overkill. Pun totally intended."

Still no answer, but as Freddie dipped out of the row to slink along the left wall after her friends, she glimpsed a flicker in the darkness.

It was candlelight guttering, and Freddie's breath hissed out. Dr. Born was farther away than she'd feared. Excellent.

She picked up her speed.

"It must really upset you that every time you killed people, the locals just chalked it up to suicide or an accident. What a bunch of oblivious fools, am I right—"

A flashlight beamed into Freddie's eyes. She screamed and squeezed the extinguisher.

Foam sprayed out, a spew of white to fill the air. Dr. Born barked with shock, with rage. And Freddie charged him, spraying, spraying, *knocking* past. Then finally sprinting sideways down the center aisle of the archives again.

She ran, not for the window, but for the ladder—just in case her friends needed more time to escape.

And as she ran, she aimed the fire extinguisher behind her. It was loud, violent, and absolutely ruining Mom's documents . . . But Freddie was pretty sure Mom would choose her daughter over a bunch of books.

Maybe.

Probably.

On a shelf near the ladder, Freddie passed the candle. A clever ruse . . . and too much light. So she blasted foam. Darkness once more took hold. And Freddie, with one hand in front and the extinguisher still spewing out behind, found the first rung on the ladder.

She dropped the extinguisher and climbed.

26

Snow-crusted leaves crunched beneath Freddie's feet. Frozen leaves too, while branches snapped and cracked and tore. Each breath was a harsh boom in her skull, a harsh burn inside her lungs.

There was no one outside the archives hut—one small win, Freddie supposed. Divya and the Prank Squad must have gotten away, and maybe by now they were at the Village placing another phone call.

Luis was the fastest on the cross-country team, right?

Since Freddie's hands were free and her body warmer, it made ascending the streambed toward the Village easier. Although hardly *easy*. Nothing looked quite right at this hour. The snow hid dips and rises, and she was pretty sure she'd lost one of her contact lenses.

Or maybe she had a concussion.

Or maybe this was just what happened when the body got slugged with hit after hit of adrenaline. Either way, the left half of the world was blurry and Freddie deeply regretted ever returning Lance Bass to Divya. *None* of this would have happened if she'd only kept that freaking keychain a few days longer.

Four times, she almost tripped. And once, she did trip, landing on her shoulder with a *woof* of bright pain and slash of frozen cold.

Then Freddie got back up again and continued on. She *had*

to. She couldn't stop. She couldn't slow. All she could do was pretend she *didn't* notice the stink gathering in the air. That she didn't see flames in her periphery...

Her footsteps faltered. That was Sheriff Bowman on the left. Freddie didn't need both contacts to recognize the shape of her hero. Nor to see a rope of fire dragging behind as Bowman took incomprehensibly large steps.

At the exact same distance on Freddie's right was Laina, a burning axe in hand. Because why not? That was totally normal stuff. Definitely *not* supernatural.

Seriously? said a small Fox Mulder on Freddie's left shoulder. *How much proof do you need, Gellar? We have left the confines of science!*

No, no, no, insisted a miniature Dana Scully. *There's always a reason rooted in nature. You just haven't found the reason yet.*

Or, came the lizard part of Freddie's brain, *maybe it doesn't matter what's actually happening and you just should really focus on staying alive?*

Heat radiated through the forest in waves—and with it was the rotting air. It grated against Freddie's neck like a tightening rope. It shoved down her throat like blades. And it gave Freddie no choice but to keep on running.

She reached the path into the Village. The same path Luis had jogged down only five days ago before giving Freddie an unexpected greeting. There was the blacksmith's hut ahead, modeled after Original Fabre's smithy.

Which *wow*, Freddie had never hated the old blacksmith more—and honestly, she was glad there was still bird poop on his sign. After all, it was his stupid diary that had gotten Edgar Senior all riled up enough to publish "the truth," and that failure had in turn gotten Junior all riled up.

She thundered past. Here was the old schoolhouse, no fairy lights twinkling in the cupola. Only the broken replica bell to creak, creak, creak on the wind.

Freddie lost sight of Laina. Only Bowman remained in view, stalking through with ghostly, intangible flames that melted nothing and sparked no trees.

Bowman was speaking now too, her voice as loud and clear as if she stood right next to Freddie. She murmured: *Libérez-nous. Libérez-nous.*

That was when Freddie noticed light shining ahead. A stage light, as if the Lumberjack Pageant were about to begin, and soon a bunch of teens in 1600s garb would start talking about Allard Fortin and his generosity.

Freddie rounded the school into the Village Square—where yes, a stage light was indeed turned on. And fixed right onto Theo.

Because of course it was Theo. It really *was* just like Freddie's dreams.

Dreams came again, she thought, remembering what her dad had written. *Always the same. The Village Historique. Ghosts hunting.*

Why had Dad had those dreams? Why had Freddie? Was it their instincts interpreting data faster than their logical minds could keep up? Or was there truly a supernatural force at work here?

WHO CARES? Freddie's lizard brain screamed. *STOP TRYING TO LOGIC THIS OUT, GELLAR! GET TO THE PHONE.*

Freddie did not get to the phone. Instead, she pumped her legs faster and aimed right for the stage. Right for Theo. Her feet felt like wheels beneath her. Like she wasn't attached to them at all and they were just rolling her ever onward. The steps onto the stage were so close. The same steps she and Theo had skipped up while Fortin students had teased. While Mr. Binder had barked orders about where to stand and what to say . . .

Freddie wished she had a script now. She wished she weren't relying on some *completely* insane dream in total contradiction to nature, filled with starlight and flames and Theo.

The stage light flickered the closer she got. Then tore off in a brutal *whoomp* right as Freddie hit the first step. Freddie didn't stop her approach. Not when the stink of rotten organs was thick enough to crawl down into her belly. Nor when she saw Laina and Bowman swerving closer on either side.

She just hauled up the steps. "Theo," she rasped. "Theo, look at me."

He didn't look at her. He stood there, completely still and cast in shadow. The sets around him made dark shapes—a tree, a hut, that stupid pole for "chopping down." *Or*, Freddie realized, *for disemboweling.*

Wind slid over Theo, pulling at the hair Freddie had run her fingers through only hours ago. He looked the same—unhurt, thank god. But empty. There was no consciousness in his eyes. No reaction when she slung to a stop and clutched at his arms.

He was colder than Freddie. Colder than the snow.

"Theo," she said again, her words coiling with steam. "Please, answer me." She reached for his face, still broken. Still beautiful.

But he offered no response. This was not the Theo Porter of her dreams. He didn't acknowledge her or say, *Take it. Only you know how to break it.*

Instead, Laina and Bowman were stalking in closer. Closer. To the stage now. *On* the stage. *Libérez-nous. Libérez-nous.* Their voices rushed out, layered like a hundred souls whispering at once. Bouncing and sliding around Freddie, probing beneath her skin and into her spine.

"Theo," Freddie said once more, and this time, she rose onto her toes and kissed him. Exactly like the dream. Exactly like their pageant practice when everything had changed between them.

But Theo didn't lean in; he didn't make a small sigh.

A screech split the night: "You give counselors a bad name!"

Freddie whipped around, adrenaline surging into her bloodstream all over again . . . only to immediately run dry. Because there was Dr. Born, and walking before him with her hands held high was Divya. Her eyes were huge and white in the shadows. She didn't look scared, so much as *pissed*.

"I hope my dad didn't pay you much," she seethed as Born pushed her toward the stage. "And I definitely expect you to give him a refund."

Dr. Born looked just as pissed as Divya with foam all over his puffer jacket and face. It blended his beard into his skin into his hair. Only his eyes were clear, that dark, piercing brown that Freddie had first noticed in the principal's office.

He didn't look like Ross from *Friends* anymore.

"Let her go." Freddie lurched for the end of the stage. "You don't need her, Dr. Born."

"No," Dr. Born agreed with a glimmer of a smile. "I don't."

"What do you want from her, then?"

Divya was at the stage steps. Up, up, up. Now she was on the stage and tottering toward Freddie. "I'm sorry." Her fury was giving way to horror. "I stayed back to help you, but I've only made it worse."

"Let her go," Freddie repeated as she tugged Divya behind her—and forced Dr. Born to train his weapon on Freddie instead.

Which she could see now, very clearly, was a handgun. A familiar one, actually, that she was almost certain had come from Sheriff Bowman's holster.

Freddie suspected Dr. Born wouldn't appreciate being told he needed a license for that.

"Please, let Divya go, Dr. Born. You can have *me*. Just like you originally planned."

"No, no." Dr. Born ambled closer, his own fury settling into something more like amusement. Freddie could see every streak from the fire extinguisher's foam. Every blister, where the chemical had wrecked his skin. His eyes were bloodshot too, as if spiderwebs spindled across the sockets.

"I've gotten really skilled at making deaths look like accidents, so no, Freddie. I won't let Divya go, because I don't need to."

"Accidents?" Freddie blinked. "You mean . . . you didn't want people to notice the murders?" There went Freddie's entire theory, then.

"I didn't." Dr. Born gave a crooked, almost rueful smile. "At least, not right away. Do you have any idea how hard it is to get a hanging, a beheading, *and* a disemboweling all lined up in a row without getting arrested? You have to find the perfect victims that no one will miss. You have to kill them here, where the original Executioners were buried. And then it all has to happen in the right order within a matter of days; otherwise, you have to start all over again.

"I learned that the hard way many years ago. Trial and error." He laughed now, a bright, happy sound. "I couldn't let a pesky little police investigation disrupt my plans. But now, here I am. So close to finally finishing."

"Finishing what?" *Think, Gellar. Think. Stall for time.* Maybe if she could get Divya to move all the way to the back edge of the stage, then Divya could duck behind the curtain and run.

It was at least worth trying.

"You only need one more victim, right?" Freddie continued. "So take me and let Divya go. Then let Theo go too. Please." As Freddie made this plea yet again, she nudged at her best friend, shoving her in the general direction of *backward* and *away*.

"Freddie, Freddie, Freddie." Dr. Born shook his head with disappointment. As if Freddie were a student he'd been so sure would ace his test but now was failing it. "You *did* read the poem, right? I know you were in Mrs. Ferris's attic earlier."

Freddie swallowed.

"So that was you in the attic?" Freddie asked, pushing once more at Divya. They were both creeping ever so slowly backward.

"Of course it was me. Because anything the descendants know, I know too." He motioned to Bowman, still hovering nearby with flames beginning to curl off her. "That includes Theo and Laina here. They can't help it. Not once the bell and the curse take control of them. And poor old Mrs. Ferris—she was trying so hard to understand what was happening to her children. She got close, but she didn't quite figure it out."

"So you were the one who attacked her?" Freddie asked. *Step, nudge, step, nudge.* Freddie and Divya were almost to Theo now, meaning almost halfway across the stage. And although Dr. Born was also tracing this way too, he moved with a languid, unsuspecting ease.

He was *enjoying* this teachable moment. He was *enjoying* getting to talk about all the secrets he'd kept for so long.

"I didn't attack Mrs. Ferris," he said. "I didn't need to. By then, I had control of her daughter. And just as I know whatever the descendants know ... well, they'll also do whatever I tell them to do."

Dr. Born snapped his wrist.

And in a movement too quick to see, too strong to resist, Theo grabbed onto Divya.

She screamed as his arms latched around her upper body. Freddie screamed too. "Theo, *no!* Don't do this!"

"Let me go!" Divya wrestled and kicked. "Let me *go!*"

He didn't let her go. He didn't seem to see or feel Divya fighting him at all—and he didn't see or feel Freddie grasping at his arms and begging him: "Please, Theo. Stop this! *Please!*"

No matter how hard Divya writhed or how much Freddie pushed against him, he was as impossibly strong as Laina had been.

So Freddie whirled around to face Born head-on. The man was chuckling, a raspy sound as chilling as the wind—and not because it was a diabolical laugh, but rather because it wasn't. This was just a regular old laugh from a regular old guy who'd heard a regular old joke with a solid punch line.

"Stop this, Dr. Born. Edgar. *Whoever* you are. Stop it, please."

"Or what, Freddie?" He grinned. "What exactly do you think you can do here?"

"This," she said, and she leaped at him. Her hands were claws reaching for his face. Her teeth were bared, and she *roared* an echoing battle cry.

It was a valiant effort. Truly. But it was guided less by her brilliant gut and more by sheer desperation. So her attack, of course, did not succeed.

All she did was get the gun's barrel thrust directly into her face.

Behind her, Divya shrieked. Freddie heard her friend kicking harder at Theo. But she could do nothing except go very still and raise both her hands.

She'd never been this close to a gun before. She'd never realized how a cold barrel would feel on her cheek or how death so close would make everything inside her slow down. Each and every one of her muscles felt turned to stone. Even her throat as she said: "I know you plan to disembowel me, but I won't do it." She swallowed. "I . . . I won't walk myself and my own intestine around that pole."

"Freddie." Dr. Born was so close Freddie could see every line caked with the emergency foam. Every swollen, throbbing vessel in his dark eyes. "My fight isn't with you, don't you see that? You're just another victim—we *all* are—of the Allard Fortin curse."

"Then let Divya go. Let me and Theo and Laina and the sheriff all go. You don't need us."

"Oh, but I do, Freddie." He pressed the gun harder into her cheek. His hands had the same blisters as his face, pocking across his knuckles.

He pushed, giving Freddie no choice but to stumble backward. Three steps. Four. She was almost to the fake tree. She was certainly within reach of Theo again.

Meanwhile Dr. Born was sliding his empty hand into his jacket. Then with aching slowness, he withdrew a long knife. The sort Steve would use to cut a roast.

Or that a disemboweler would use to cut an abdomen.

Stabby, Freddie thought uselessly. *I am going to die by Stabby, and the dreams about this moment were all wrong.*

She shuffled backward another three steps. She was right next to Divya now.

"Please," Freddie said, afraid to blink. Afraid to look away from Dr. Born's fingers. "Please, Dr. Born—I mean, Edgar. I'll tell the whole world that your dad was right. That's what you want, isn't it? You want them to know there really *was* a curse and the Allard Fortins didn't deserve any of their riches. Well, I believe you now! So we can . . . we can republish the book and finally get some justice! Please, just don't kill me, okay? Just let me go. Let all of us go."

Dr. Born sighed, head shaking with true disappointment now. "You really missed everything, Freddie. This isn't just for my father. This isn't just for redemption of my family or our ancestor from three centuries ago. This is about the Allard Fortins.

"None of this madness would have happened if not for our *beloved* local founder. He was a stingy, violent monster—and his descendants were no better."

"They knew of the curse?"

"They didn't have to. They already had all the wealth and power they needed—and that alone does more than enough damage."

Okay, sure, Freddie supposed she could tip her head at *just* the right angle and follow this argument. Wealth and power could be used to control just as much as a curse could, and maybe the Allard Fortins weren't worth all the adoration they'd always received.

But that sure as hell didn't justify *any* of the monstrosities Born had committed.

"The Allard Fortins didn't care about my father," Dr. Born went on, upper lip twitching. "They didn't care about me or my mother or how they'd ruined our lives just to protect their name and legacy. We had no friends, no money, and the stress of it—the shame—it killed my father."

Again, Freddie found herself understanding, a twist of sympathy that spiked through her for the lonely, hurt boy Dr. Born might have been.

Except no! Don't let him get in your head, Freddie! Keep stalling, keep thinking. You can get out of this!

"I'm sorry it was so hard for you." Freddie was careful to keep her eyes locked on Dr. Born's face. Careful to keep her hands up and *not* look at how close the knife was to her abdomen. "But you did have one friend, right? Theo's dad. I saw the picture of you two, and he was devastated when he thought you'd died."

It was the wrong thing to say. Freddie saw that as soon as the words left her tongue. But it was also too late to suck them back in. To hit CTRL+Z and undo them.

"You think Teddy Porter was my friend?" Dr. Born slowly, slowly pulled his knife away from Freddie. "The man who fell in love with an Allard Fortin, even when he *knew* what their family had done to mine? Oh, Freddie, Theodore Porter was not my friend, and the day that he abandoned me for Justine was the day I knew what I had to do."

Oh crap. Freddie felt as her whole world flipped. As her organs and her brain and her eyeballs did a great heave-ho with this fresh monsoon of knowledge. *Justine was Theo's mother. Justine was an Allard Fortin, not a Charretière.*

"I can see you've sorted it out now." Dr. Born smiled, and his knife changed directions like a compass swerving north. "Theo here is the last of the Allard Fortin bloodline. And so *Theo* here is the one who must pay for all their crimes."

27

What happened next was a blur of so many things that it was an actual sensory miracle Freddie's brain could keep up—and with only one contact lens too!

First, Theo released Divya in a hard shove that sent her toppling forward into Freddie. But where Freddie expected to land on Dr. Born and his gun, she instead hit only empty air and fell completely off the stage.

Her left wrist didn't appreciate the landing.

By the time she was upright again, she saw that Dr. Born had stalked in close to Theo, and that Theo had opened his arms wide.

Dr. Born stabbed.

The knife slid into Theo's abdomen. No resistance. No reaction.

Blood burst forth.

"No!" Freddie screamed at the same time Divya wrenched Freddie violently away from the stage.

"Freddie, leave him! We'll get help!"

Freddie didn't want to leave or get help. In fact, she wanted to attack Dr. Born with all her strength. The man was literally *slicing* into the guy she was falling for, and he would soon find the intestine. He would soon dig it out and make Theo walk his own bowels around the pole.

Yet before Freddie could push past Divya or shout at Dr. Born or attack, heat pummeled in.

This was no gradual dip out of snow and frozen autumn. This was a sudden wave of summer roast that barreled straight across Freddie.

One pulse, and it felt like searing flames had engulfed her body.

A second pulse, and the flames reached her skull.

And lastly, a third pulse with a voice attached to it. *Come,* it seemed to say. *We have work to do. Our oath is summoning.*

Oh no. Freddie pitched sideways. So hot. So lost. There was someone inside her head, and they were talking to her as if they'd always been there. *I really did have this all wrong. Theo was the last Allard Fortin.*

And I'm the Charretière descendant.

I'm Stabby.

I'm the Disemboweler.

Yet for Born to actually gain control of her body and fully awaken the ghost of her ancestor inside her, he had to first kill someone the correct way . . . just as he'd had to hang someone to gain control of Bowman. And he'd had to decapitate someone to gain control of Laina.

Now, he had to disembowel Theo.

It was the only way to finish what he'd set out to do.

"Freddie!" Divya's voice was a million miles away. Another universe. Another lifetime. "Freddie, what's *happening* to you?"

A fair question, and one Freddie really couldn't have answered even if she'd had control of her own body. She could feel Theo's life draining into her. She didn't want it—she didn't *want* to feel his soul feeding these flames, with those gentle blue eyes and his constant, restless need. But she also couldn't stop the curse.

Yes, said the voice inside her skull. *We are bound to the bell. Bound to the Oathmaster that rings it.*

"Oh my god, where are they?" Divya was shouting into Freddie's ear. "What the hell is taking them so long—" Her words snapped off as a new sound carved in. Sharp as the knife now stealing Theo's life from him.

An engine.

Freddie slogged her head up, and through flames of an old curse that definitely proved miniature Fox Mulder had been right, she saw a black Jeep revving this way.

Kyle and his reckless driving.

Kyle finally getting to embrace his one talent for running things over.

Freddie would have laughed if she'd had any control over her own body. Instead, she simply watched—as lost in herself as Theo had been. As lost as Bowman and Laina too. The Jeep launched right through the Village Historique. It charged into hay bales and smashed over jack-o'-lanterns. Then it rammed across the schoolhouse benches like a monster truck, only missing Freddie because Divya dragged her out of the way.

The Jeep careened into the stage, a noise so loud it briefly dominated all other sounds. Even the ones inside of Freddie's brain.

And with that noise came a burst of clarity. The ritual to kill Theo had paused; the Disemboweler's oath was briefly held at bay; and for a fraction of a heartbeat, she was Freddie Gellar and *only* Freddie Gellar.

No Stabby. No flames. No commands from an Oathmaster with a bell.

Freddie cranked up her spine. *The bell.* That was what it had always come back to, in all her investigations. In all her clues and discoveries.

The bell.

"The schoolhouse," she croaked at Divya in a voice that was all her own—for now. "We need to get into the schoolhouse."

"No, Freddie." Divya gawped at her. "We need to go!"

Freddie didn't listen. Instead, she tore from her best friend's grip and bounded away from the stage, away from the Jeep wrecked against it and spewing steam into the night.

Away too from Luis bursting out a passenger door with an axe and Cat right behind with the baseball bat. Away from

Kyle bellowing for Divya and Freddie to *Come on! Get in the Jeep!*

Above all, Freddie bounded away from Dr. Born while the ritual was paused and he was distracted.

"Freddie, what are you *doing*?" Divya chased hot on Freddie's heels. "What's in the schoolhouse?"

"The . . . bell," Freddie panted, rounding past splintered and toppled benches. "We have to break the bell, Div. Don't you see? If we break it, the curse ends."

It was clear Divya did not see, but that was fine. Freddie didn't need her best friend to understand. Hell, Freddie herself was still blundering her way toward clarity. All she really had right now was her gut telling her what to do.

And the dreams—they had always ended in the schoolhouse with Theo saying: *On n'est jamais si bien servi que par soi-même.*

One is never better served than by oneself.

So if Freddie wanted this done right, she had to do it—and the *it* in question was breaking the bell. *That* was what dream-Theo had wanted from her—and *that* was what only Freddie could do.

Because it had never been a replica inside the cupola. All this time, it had been *the* bell that Original Fabre had made. Freddie had no idea when Dr. Born might have switched it out since Mom had gotten the replica made . . . but he absolutely *had* done so. Which was why Freddie had noticed just last week how beaten and weathered the bell was looking.

She'd also noticed how the lights kept getting knocked down—not from the wind, but from Dr. Born right over there on the stage.

And she'd also noticed the bell ringing from the west, where this was the only bell she knew of. Yet it still had never occurred to her that someone might be climbing up there at night, shoving a clapper into the bell, and ringing that tin and copper for all it was worth.

Libérez-nous, Freddie thought.

She sprinted past smashed pumpkins and fallen heaters. Over hay bales and extension cords and puddles of melting snow. Divya was right beside her the whole way.

Red clapboard siding swam into Freddie's vision. Wet leaves slapped beneath her and Divya's feet. No wind, nor even the stink of dead things here. Each breath was a harsh boom in Freddie's skull. A harsh burn inside her lungs.

She and Divya swung around the old schoolhouse, and it was almost like Thursday afternoon all over again. They were here to clean up a mess. They were here to get a special bell ready for a special day.

They punched through the door where Divya had slouched and played Snake. They thwacked over the floorboards where Freddie had swept, but now with no benches to get in their way. Just the ladder ahead.

Libérez-nous.

Freddie reached the ladder first. As she expected, the fairy lights had once more been knocked down. Before she could start to climb, though, Divya barked, "Wait!"

"No time," Freddie started to say, but then Divya was yanking something out of her pocket.

Something so familiar Freddie actually choked.

It was the heart of iron from her dreams—except now she could see it wasn't a heart at all. It was a bell clapper.

"Theo gave it to me," Divya said on rasping breaths. "When he was holding me, he pushed this into my pocket. It must be for you."

"It is," Freddie said, and she yanked it from Divya's palm. "And I hereby take back *any* mean comments I made last week about your helpfulness. You are officially the most helpful best friend of all time and I love you forever."

"Duh!" Divya called as Freddie leaped onto the ladder and scrabbled up as fast as her limbs would carry her.

The bell above *creak-creak-creaked*, not from wind, but from Freddie's movements in the cupola. There was definitely a clapper inside the bell now—and presumably a clapper that Dr. Born had kept after he first stole the bell in 1975.

Freddie reached the final rung. There was the Village Historique spread before her, now ripped apart like Looney Tunes' Taz had swept through. (Which, note to self: Taz was a good nickname for Kyle.)

There was Theo, bleeding and statuesque upon the stage. There was Dr. Born, his gun aimed at Kyle while he roared at the Prank Squad to "Stay back!"

A shot cracked into the night. Freddie thought she saw Kyle fall. She definitely saw Bowman and Laina—still wreathed in unmoving flames—burn brighter. Blindingly so. But she couldn't worry about any of them right now. She knew what she had to do; she knew *how* she had to save them.

Freddie turned to the old bell, made by Original Fabre three hundred years ago to replace one that had broken in the cold . . .

From a clapper that was too big for it.

"The ratio of tin to copper," Freddie whispered, quoting Mom from the night before, "changes the color of the verdigris and the strength of the bell."

She unhooked the clapper currently inside. It was heavy but noticeably smaller and lighter than the one Theo had somehow gotten ahold of.

Freddie tossed the newer clapper out the cupola window. It struck shingle and slid downward, a sound lost to the growing sense that Freddie was about to lose control of herself. Again.

Because Stabby was starting to wake up once more.

Libérez-nous.

Freddie found the end of the bigger clapper. The heart of iron that wasn't a heart at all. And with only a little clumsiness, she slotted it into the weathered bell. Now she just had to pray it was big enough and the bell old enough, weak enough to break from her swinging.

She leaned backward and shoved the bell. The clapper hit as it was meant to do.

Clang!

The sound was so loud it vibrated into Freddie's skull. Into her teeth and brain cells. A thousand little legs to dig, *dig* into her Charretière DNA, just like the daddy longlegs she'd been so afraid of getting in her hair.

She watched as Bowman, still wreathed in flames beside the stage, suddenly turned to face Freddie.

The bell swung back Freddie's way, but she caught it before it could hit her face. She shoved it again. Full force. *Clang!*

Now Laina turned to face Freddie too.

Another shove. Another bone-rattling *clang!* and now Freddie felt the Disemboweler inside her perk up. The spirit wasn't awaiting commands, though, because Freddie wasn't the one to whom his soul was bound.

Instead, he was awaiting the final step. The final moment that would end the curse he'd been bound to for so long.

Libérez-nous. Only you can break it.

Freddie swung the bell one last time, and the clang that ripped out was briefly deafening. The bell heaved away, then back toward her. Too strong to stop. An onslaught of tin and copper that slammed into her face and knocked her off the ladder.

But as gravity took hold and carried her body toward the schoolhouse floor, Freddie felt the bell crack.

And she *felt* as the Disemboweler's spirit crawled out of her body and shot toward Dr. Born in a streak of vengeful flame. *Libérez-nous,* the ghosts screamed in voices that were impossibly loud. *Libérez-nous.*

Free us, Freddie finally interpreted, even though she'd never cracked open a French-English dictionary in her life. That's what they were saying: *Free us.*

Justin Charretière had lived here in City-on-the-Berme. So had Damien Portier and Alexandre Steward. Ropey, Hacky, and Stabby—three spirits who'd just wanted to be set free for such a very long time.

And three spirits who knew that one was only ever truly served by oneself.

Freddie hit the schoolhouse floor.

The ghosts fell silent.

Freddie's ankle was not happy with her. Her wrist, meanwhile, was definitely headed toward *needs medical attention*. But at least that was the only damage on her person, and once she and Divya limped outside of the schoolhouse, Freddie saw just how badly it could have gone for her and her friends.

And not just for them, but for all of Berm if Dr. Born had actually finished killing Theo and set the Executioners on a killing spree.

Because Dr. Born was dead now and in the most horrific way possible.

His headless body hung by his own intestines wrapped around and around the stage pole, glistening like bloodied fairy lights in the night. His head, meanwhile, was a full twenty feet away, plopped onto a pile of jack-o'-lanterns. The fire extinguisher foam had turned it to a garish, bug-eyed white in a mound of orange.

By the time Freddie actually reached the stage, sirens were audible in the distance. Thank god, because neither Theo nor Kyle looked good—although at least Kyle appeared to only have had his shoulder grazed by Dr. Born's attack.

Theo's abdomen, however, was most definitely impaled. "I told you . . . you were dangerous," he murmured as Freddie dropped to his side. Cat had pressed her sweater against him, and now Freddie took over holding it against the wound.

"Stop talking," Freddie ordered. "EMTs are on the way."

Theo grunted. He was so, *so* pale. Way past *Interview with the Vampire* and heading toward full-on corpse territory.

"I'm sorry this happened." Freddie gripped his jaw, forcing him to keep his eyes open and locked on hers. "I'm sorry I couldn't stop him. Look at me, Theo. Stay awake."

"Right . . . so what . . . did happen, Gellar? I'm . . . hazy on the details."

Before Freddie could respond—or apologize all over again—two ambulances arrived. Thanks to Kyle, there was no need for any of them to stop in the parking lot. They were able to speed right up into the Village Square.

One pair of EMTs went to Kyle, and a second pair shoved Freddie aside to access Theo. They had a stretcher, and with the practiced ease of experts, they took charge of him and his injuries.

He groaned as they lifted him, but once he was strapped on, he spared a final half-conscious smile for Freddie. "So dangerous," he murmured.

Then the EMTs hurried him away.

Freddie tried to follow, but they wouldn't let her. And it was only as she watched them slide him onto the ambulance that she realized Dr. Born's head was right there on top of the jack-o'-lanterns. But the two EMTs didn't notice. Nor the other pair as they rushed Kyle away.

More sirens came. More lights. Then emergency blankets over Freddie, over Divya—over every member of the Prank Squad as they tried to explain to the newly arrived Ibrahim and Deputy Knowles what the *hell* had just happened.

Yet as Freddie listened to her friends ramble and shout, she realized the Prank Squad actually had no clue what had gone down. Instead, it was like they were all forgetting in real time what they'd just seen, and Freddie watched as one by one—Luis, Cat, and even Divya—rationalized it into a murderous therapist with a gun.

Somehow they just erased the parts where Laina almost broke them in half and flames had come off her body.

Freddie soon learned that Bowman and Laina were no better when she was guided with them toward the water mill by a woman and man who could not have been more obviously federal agents than if they'd worn neon signs on their foreheads.

In their matching bulletproof vests and dark jackets, the duo could have literally just walked off the set of *The X-Files*.

"I'm Agent Harris." The woman flipped out a badge. She had dark skin, and her dark curls were tucked under a navy-blue cap. "And my partner is Agent Li."

She notched her head toward the pale man at her side, who was currently frowning toward the stage. *He* at least seemed to see what had happened to Dr. Born, even as literally no one else did. The three firemen clearing out debris passed by Dr. Born's head without a second glance—repeatedly. And Ibrahim, Knowles, and the Prank Squad never once looked at the stage.

"We understand," Harris continued, "you've been through a lot tonight, so we won't keep you long. But we do need to get statements from you—and we also want to make sure you understand that what happened here tonight isn't unusual. In fact, it's more common than you'd think, and we have special resources to help people like you."

Bowman shook her head, frowning. "I . . . have to be honest, Agents, I don't know what you're talking about right now. Why are we here?" She glanced at Laina. Then Freddie. "And what happened to us?"

Laina shivered so hard her emergency blanket crinkled. "Yeah, I don't understand either. Was I sleepwalking again?" She too looked at Freddie.

But Freddie didn't answer. After all, what could she say? It was probably better for the both of them if they never remembered what the heck they'd gone through—or what the heck they'd almost turned into.

The two agents seemed to agree. "Memory lapses aren't unusual." Li pulled a card from his jacket. "But if either of you need help—or if you find you simply want some answers, then here's how you can contact us."

"We've got stations all over the country," Harris added. "And we have agents always manning the phones."

Laina didn't take the card; Bowman did. Her head kept wagging, though, and her brow stayed pinched as she examined it. "My nephew," she said eventually. "Can I go to him now?"

"Good idea." Harris nodded. "And when he wakes up, let him know we're here for him too, if he needs us."

An absent nod from Bowman as she palmed the card into her pocket. Then she laid one hand on Laina's forearm and her other on Freddie's shoulder. "Let me get you two home."

"Um," Freddie said. "If it's okay, I'd rather leave with Divya."

"Right, sure." Bowman's grip briefly tightened on Freddie's shoulder while her eyes searched Freddie's, as if confirming that Freddie really was as calm and unfazed as she seemed.

A wind whispered over them. A natural one that smelled like October and car fumes and broken pumpkins.

And eventually Bowman seemed to decide Freddie *was* okay enough to be left behind, since she nodded once for Freddie. Then once for Laina. "Come on, Laina. Let's get you out of here." Together, emergency blankets crackling, they shuffled away.

Which meant Freddie could finally turn her full attention onto Agents Harris and Li—neither of whom looked surprised by Freddie's choice to hang back.

"You," said Harris once Laina and Bowman were out of earshot, "have the look of someone who remembers everything that happened here. So we're going to need to rely on you for a full statement. Think you can manage that?"

"Yeah," Freddie said. "I can manage." Her voice was tired but surprisingly strong given all she'd just gone through. "Although . . ." Freddie glanced toward Dr. Born. There was still no one going near him. "Can no one see him hanging there?"

"They can." Li's expression folded into something thoughtful. "They just choose not to. It's a common defense mechanism in situations like this. We see it all the time. The brain just shuts out anything it can't explain."

"Situations like this?" Freddie repeated.

"Unexplained phenomena," Harris inserted. "That's the official term for them."

"So you're telling me this was all real tonight? Blood oaths and murderous spirits and . . . and *magic* bells?" Freddie wet her lips. To her surprise, she tasted blood and felt the heat of a fresh cut.

"Definitely looks to be real." Harris gave an almost flippant shrug. "Most of the time, when we go to sites like this, nah. They aren't real at all. But sometimes? Well, you've seen for yourself."

Nothing happens in contradiction to nature, Freddie thought. *Only in contradiction to what we know of it.*

Freddie shivered, hugging her emergency blanket to her. Across the square, she could see the Prank Squad had finished giving their statements. Now they were being pushed into Ibrahim's and Deputy Knowles's squad cars, presumably to be taken home.

All except Divya, who kept flinging her hands in Freddie's direction, as if she wouldn't leave without her bestie, and how *dare* Ibrahim suggest otherwise! Did he know that her mom cut his *hair*?

Freddie huffed a laugh—a sound filled partly with amusement for her friend, but mostly just frustration at these two agents standing beside her. "If you both know that sometimes these situations are real, why didn't you intervene sooner? Like, I don't know if you've noticed." Freddie waved to the destroyed Village. "But things got pretty deadly, and we could have *really* used some help here sooner."

Agent Li grimaced. "Yeah, that's on us. We only just got a full idea of the case two hours ago, after a warrant finally came through that let us search Anne Ferris's house. We were just starting to explore her attic when we got a call from Deputy Abadi."

"Right." Freddie hugged at the blanket again. She was suddenly feeling the weight of everything that had happened.

The *gut punch* of how this night could have gone if Ibrahim hadn't actually summoned backup.

How long would Theo and Kyle have been waiting for emergency assistance? Would they have died like Dr. Born had?

"Look," she said wearily. "I know you guys want this statement from me, but can it actually wait? My adrenaline is all spent up, and my insides feel like someone scooped them out of a jack-o'-lantern. So . . . so I'd really just like to go home now, with my friends. If that's alright." She pointed toward Divya, who was waving both hands over her head.

"Right." Harris nodded. "We understand." She exchanged a glance with Li, who sighed but also tipped his head in agreement.

"No problem. If you can just give us your name and address, we can stop by your home tomorrow. And here, have one of these." Li fished a card from his pocket and handed it to Freddie.

Who huffed another laugh—this one mostly just amused. Because the card read: *Federal Bureau of Investigation. Department of Unexplained Phenomena*. "So there is an entire department just for this kind of stuff. Like on *The X-Files*."

Li scowled. Harris rolled her eyes. "No," they said in unison. "It's not like *The X-Files*."

Which only made Freddie laugh again, since she didn't believe them *at all*. "Thanks," she told them as she pushed the card into her pocket. "And I'll see you both tomorrow." With a turn, she hobbled back toward the Village Square.

Dr. Born's head still steamed into the night, untouched. His corpse still swung side to side from his own intestines, and each gust of wind made him spin.

Yet somehow, *still*, no one noticed him.

Certainly not Divya, who immediately enveloped Freddie in the Greatest Best Friend Hug of All Time.

"You have a daddy longlegs in your hair," she said as she squeezed and squeezed and squeezed.

And Freddie laughed one last time. A bright, bubbling sound that hovered on the verge of hysteria and was so at odds with the destruction all around. But hey—she was just so happy to be alive.

"Let's go, Div." She took her bestie's hand into her own and climbed into Ibrahim's squad car.

The last thing Freddie saw before they left City-on-the-Berme was the bell inside its cupola. Fully broken now, and Freddie hoped broken forever.

No bells are rung, she thought as they left it behind, *when the Three leave the gate. Libérez-nous. Free us.*

28

The funeral for Mrs. Ferris was on an unseasonably warm day. No wind blew, and the sun baked down through barren branches. Sheriff Bowman had waited to have the funeral until after Theo had been released from the hospital, so it was now five days since everything had gone down at City-on-the-Berme.

As funerals often were in Berm—where everyone knew everyone—the cemetery was crowded. Mrs. Ferris had been especially beloved, always at the heart of the small town and its talky people.

Freddie cried. Mom cried. Steve cried. Not Sheriff Bowman, though, or Theo. Nor Teddy Porter, who'd come from Chicago. The trio stayed tucked off to one side, Teddy with his arm around his son, helping Theo stand.

The official story was that Mrs. Ferris had died from the wounds of an animal. The story that Harris and Li had told Freddie privately was that Edgar Fabre Jr. had actually killed her in the hospital once he'd realized his first attack had failed.

It was awful, and the fact that Edgar had faced a gruesome sort of justice didn't make it any *less* awful. So Freddie let herself cry as hard as she wanted. For Mrs. Ferris, for Dr. Fontana, and for everyone else who'd died by Edgar's hands.

And maybe most of all, Freddie cried for her dad.

Which was why, after the service, Freddie made her way to his grave beside a towering willow. The granite gravestone had simple, hard lines and read, *Frank Carter, 1951–1987. Protector of the people.* Next to it was a stone bench that had been donated by the town. *In honor of Frank's service to the city he loved.*

"Hey, Dad," Freddie murmured as she sat. "I know I don't come often, but I was thinking maybe it's time to change that. Plus, Mom actually talked about you last week. Wild, I know, but maybe that means it's time for a new house rule: *Thou shalt discuss Frank Carter.* Especially since it seems . . . Well, I guess I'm a lot like you.

"I know you weren't keen on being a dad—but you *were* keen on being a sheriff. And I get that. I don't hold it against you or anything. Plus, I'd like to think if . . ." Here, Freddie's voice cracked.

She scrubbed at her nose and tried again. "I'd like to think if maybe you hadn't died, we'd have eventually gotten to know each other. Especially once you saw that I was an Answer Finder just like you.

"Although, I'm sorry you never got all the answers you were looking for. You were right, though: Edgar didn't die. And I never would have figured that out if not for the clues you left behind. So thank you. You saved a lot of people in the end.

"And as for your dreams, well . . . they were real. I guess we're descended from a carriage driver who was forced to come here three hundred years ago and—get this, Dad—disembowel people for José Allard Fortin. Crazy, right?"

Freddie paused, chewing at her lip. There was still so much to say, yet all her words felt too small. Too easy. How could she even begin to articulate everything she'd tamped down for the last twelve years?

Then again, she supposed she didn't have to say everything in one go. This was hopefully only the first of many more grave visits to come. And heck, for all she knew, her dad was actually nearby and listening to her one-sided conversation.

After all, if spirits could haunt the forest and blood oaths could control people, why couldn't her dad also be hovering somewhere just out of sight?

"Hey, Gellar."

Freddie spun around to find Theo scuffing her way. He wore a suit under a black wool overcoat, and at first glance, he looked fine. But closer examination revealed a hunch, as well as a slight bulge around his abdomen where bandages kept his stitches protected.

Freddie leaped for him, careful to only touch his back when she reached him. "What are you doing, Theo? You're not supposed to walk this far."

"I wanted to see you," he admitted. "Is this your dad?"

Freddie nodded. "You should sit." She motioned to the bench, still warmed by the sun.

Theo didn't answer. Nor did he move. Instead, he murmured: "I . . . I had a dream last night, Gellar. That I went to the Allard Fortin crypt and found something only I could find."

"Ah."

"And then I gave it to you." He turned his blue eyes onto Freddie. With the sun in them, the pupils were small. The blue an icy crystalline. "But I don't think it was a dream, was it? I think it really happened. And . . ." He shook his head, lifting one hand to rub at his temple.

Until this made the muscles in his abdomen contract, which in turn caused him pain. Silly boy.

Freddie glared. "Sit," she commanded, and she forcibly lowered him onto the bench. Then she took sentry in front of him, her legs touching his knees so he couldn't try to stand again.

"Yes," she told him. "It all really happened, and I remember it too. I can explain everything, if you want, but . . . well, I'll warn you now: it's kind of hard to believe."

"Harder to believe than the fact that my mom was apparently an Allard Fortin and I get an inheritance when I turn eighteen?"

Freddie laughed, a pitchy sound because it wasn't actually funny—but she could also sense that Theo wanted this moment to be light. That sometimes making jokes was easier than digging into the darkness.

"I'm surprised you remember anything," Freddie said truthfully. "No one else in town does."

"I mean, I can't say I *want* to remember, and it feels like my brain is trying to stop me from it. But . . ." A shrug. Then a wince from the subsequent pain. "I don't like not knowing."

No. He didn't. Freddie had already learned that about him back in the Fortin library. Because he really *was* just like her in this regard. He needed answers, and he'd rather have them, even if the cost was high.

"Well," Freddie said, "it's a long story, and it's cold out here." She shivered. "Plus, there's a reception we need to go to."

"Not yet, please. And here." Theo shifted as if he was going to peel off his coat, but Freddie grabbed his wrists.

"Don't be stupid. That will hurt."

"Not if you help me." He smiled crookedly, head tipped higher to hold her gaze. She was very close now.

"I'm not going to undress you at a cemetery. By my *dad's* grave."

"Undress me?" His blond eyebrows shot high. The smile twitched wider. "Gellar, your mind went to a very different gutter than mine did."

Suddenly Freddie was not cold at all. Heat fanned through her chest, her shoulders, all the way up her neck and across her face. "I didn't mean it like that, Mr. Porter. I just . . . I think the optics . . . at a funeral . . . *ugh*, stop looking at me like that."

"Like what?"

"Like you're laughing at me."

"I'm not laughing at you." He *totally* was. "This is my impressed face, Gellar. And my thank-you face." He tugged his wrists free from Freddie, but rather than draw away from her, he slid his arms around her and pulled her close.

His head was against her stomach, and he looked very vulnerable. Very handsome too. (And also still quite tortured.)

"Thank you, Freddie Gellar. I might not remember everything that happened last week, but I do know I'm glad you were there for it all. And I'm glad you're here with me now."

"Yeah." It was all Freddie could think to say. He was hugging her and it was kind of the best feeling ever. She'd visited him every single day in the hospital, but this was their first *real* conversation without nurses or doctors or family nearby.

And it was definitely their first embrace.

Which made Freddie's heart do unexpected thumpy things inside her rib cage—a drumbeat he could probably hear with his head pressed against her like it was.

It also made her throat ache. Like she wanted to cry—for him, for herself, for Mrs. Ferris and for Dad—but she'd already drained her entire Emotional Quota for the year and there were no tears left to shed.

So she hugged Theo back, and together, they enjoyed a shining sun while the wind held back its fangs.

Autumn had swung back to its expected frost by the time Freddie met with Harris and Li to say goodbye. The partners sat on a bench at Fortin Park downtown, where the maple trees had lost the last of their leaves in the night. A crunchy covering that brightened an otherwise gray morning.

They both wore sunglasses and nondescript black coats, and it was just a little *too* obvious that they were Out-of-Towners Up to Something.

Freddie had to bite back the urge to sing, *Here come the Men in Black! They won't let you remember!*

To be fair, it was actually a stunningly accurate song lyric. Except it wasn't so much that the Department of Unexplained Phenomena wouldn't let anyone in Berm remember, so much as—just as Li had told Freddie a week ago—people seemed *really good* at not noticing what their brains couldn't explain.

Which meant, as far as Freddie could tell, she was the only person in all of Berm other than Theo who actually knew what had happened last Wednesday night. Laina, Bowman, the Prank Squad—they were still firmly locked on the *It Can All Be Rationalized* train.

It was most certainly for the best, since it was way easier for them than being on Freddie's *The X-Files Are Real* train. Because the thing about learning that nature was actually way more deranged than she'd ever imagined meant she had an endless supply of questions brewing in her brain.

It was honestly overwhelming for an Answer Finder such as herself.

Although, it was also quite *exhilarating*.

"You're really quite unusual," Harris had told Freddie during their first debriefing last Wednesday morning. "Few people can keep it all in their heads, so it's helpful when we find someone able to fill in so many gaps."

Sure enough, with Freddie's assistance, Harris and Li had been able to paint a detailed picture of the Executioners and the original José Allard Fortin curse. Of the bell that had controlled their spirits and the Original Fabre who'd made that bell.

In turn, the agents had painted a clearer picture for Freddie. They told her no one had even known there was a curse, much less that the spirits could be reawakened. Not until Edgar Fabre Sr. had found the old diary —that was the first time anyone had even conceived of such a possibility. And while Edgar hadn't been foolish enough to try to summon the spirits by killing someone in the manner the poem had described, his son had clearly had no such qualms.

Throughout all of their debriefing sessions, Freddie had tried to also uncover as much as she could about Harris, Li, and the Department of Unexplained Phenomena. Unfortunately, all she'd come away with so far was that they called it the DUP for short (pronounced *dupp*) and most questions were countered with *We aren't at liberty to answer that.*

Including the one Freddie asked right now as she rolled her bike to a stop before their bench. "What about extraterrestrial ice parasites?" Freddie toed down her kickstand. "Those were in season one of *The X-Files,* and they sent the host into a murderous rage. Seems plausible to me."

"We're not at liberty to answer that," Harris said right on cue. Of the two agents, she was the More Chill One, and right now, she was pulling a tin of Altoids from her pocket. She offered one to Freddie, who took it happily.

She offered one to Li, who did not. And to be fair, he had a Diet Coke in his hand—because he always had a Diet Coke in his hand. Freddie had learned over the last week that these were their respective schticks: Harris chomped Altoids, while Li pounded Diet Coke. And it had prompted Freddie to do some serious soul searching for her own schtick. Having Xena around her neck wasn't enough. Carrying Tic Tacs or gum felt too similar to Harris. A thermos of coffee wasn't interesting, and she had no desire to take up something gross like smoking.

But that was fine. She also had plenty of months before she needed to find her schtick and blend in with the other DUP agents . . .

Li stood now, more than doubling his height. "Don't forget to, uh . . ." *Yawn.* "Call us if you need any help dealing with all of this stuff. Your historical village should be fully scraped—"

Scraped, Freddie had learned, was what they called *cleaning up all the supernatural evidence and restoring a site to its original state.*

"—and things seem to be back to normal in your town. But you'll be a better judge of that than us. So if anything comes up, you know how to reach us."

Indeed, Freddie did. But she also agreed with Li that everything in Berm had pretty much gone back to normal. Even the official story of a "murderer loose in the forest" had already faded into the background. People were more invested in the Fête du Bûcheron that was five days away—and in ensuring no funny business unfolded during the jack-o'-lantern contest—than they were in the drama of last week.

Seriously: Harris and Li literally did not *need* a Men-in-Black mind-eraser thingie. People just did it naturally.

"Any final questions before we leave town?" Harris asked. She also stood now, crunching into her Altoid.

"Yes!" Freddie leaped at this opening. "I have two questions, actually. First, are vampires real? In season two of *The X-Files*, they are and they steal blood from blood banks. I feel like, if this were accurate, we'd hear more often about blood bank theft. But then . . ." Freddie bounced her shoulders. "I've also seen firsthand how you guys *scrape* after a crime scene. So, are they real or not?"

Harris cleared her throat, noticeably not answering the question, while Li opened his Diet Coke in a *pfffft* of released carbonation.

"We're not at liberty to answer that," he said eventually.

And Freddie beamed. That, she felt, was probably the closest she'd ever gotten to a confirmation so far. "Good to know. Be on the lookout for vampires."

"And your second question?" Li prompted, lifting the bottle to his lips.

"Will you hire me after I graduate in June?"

He choked, half spitting his soda out, while Harris's eyebrows shot so high they pulled two curls loose from her bun. "Um, you're a little young, Ms. Gellar."

Freddie lifted a palm. "I turn eighteen in April, which is old enough for a summer internship. I asked Jeeves what the federal standard is."

"Yeah, but we're also not like other federal departments." Li wiped his mouth.

"True," Freddie forged on. "But you told me yourself that I'm unique because I not only *remembered* what happened here, but I also *accepted* it so easily. Surely you would want such a skillset in your internship pool—"

"We don't have interns."

"—and I will also add," Freddie launched her voice a bit louder, "that I am locally known as the Answer Finder. Because I'm very good at sniffing out answers, obviously, and I helped the sheriff catch a shoplifter last year." She flipped her hair. "I'm also known as the Prank Wizard, although I suspect that's less relevant to your needs.

"Still, you won't find a better intern for your branch in Chicago, so you can expect to hear from me in six months."

"Except we still don't do internships," Li said.

"Oh, but you *will*." Freddie bared her most charming grin. "Look—your partner has already accepted this fact. Tell him, Agent Harris."

The woman laughed. "I didn't say anything!"

"Yes, but I can tell by that twinkle in your eye that you already know I'll be at your side soon enough, helping you track down vampires."

Harris shrugged at Li. "She's persuasive. You gotta give her that."

Li only scowled. "Look." He screwed the top onto his soda. "Just stay out of trouble, okay, Ms. Gellar? Yes, you have a . . . *talent* most people lack, but don't be stupid about it."

"Absolutely." Freddie smiled sweetly.

"No, but *really,* Ms. Gellar." This was Agent Harris. "Please don't go looking for unexplained phenomena. It's dangerous."

Freddie nodded solemnly. "The truth is out there." She turned to leave, bike wheels squeaking.

And Harris—after a surprised snort—called: "Okay, we heard that, you know."

"Heard what?"

"That you just quoted *The X-Files* instead of agreeing."

"Oopsies!" Freddie swung her leg over the bike seat and flung a final, innocent grin at the agents. "See you in six months, partners! And don't you worry, because I'll definitely have a schtick by then."

She pushed into the pedals. The bike squeaked anew, and if Harris or Li shouted anything after her, Freddie didn't hear.

The October wind bit across her. Fallen leaves smeared by.

29

Thanks to the incredible scraping skills of Agents Harris and Li—and thanks to the terrible memory skills of the entirety of Berm—the Fête du Bûcheron unfolded on Halloween without a hitch.

Sure, some of the schoolhouse benches had been replaced by a hodgepodge of lawn chairs from different yards across Berm. And yeah, the stage was crooked and missing the tree that would normally get sawed in half. And okay, the absence of Mrs. Ferris's jams made everybody cry at least once.

But there was enough hot cider—most of it spiked—and enough Halloween cheer to keep the fête running smoothly. Even the jack-o'-lantern contest went by with only three accusations of bribery and one accusation of sabotage.

Perhaps most important of all, there was so much money flowing from wallets into the Village Historique coffers that Mom was borderline euphoric all day—which in turn made Freddie borderline euphoric as well. Until right now at least, at the final event of the day: the Lumberjack Pageant.

"Call him again," Mom said, her knuckles pressed against her cheekbones. "He's *your* boyfriend."

But he wasn't. That was part of the problem here. Theo and Freddie hadn't *defined their relationship*, and for all she knew, he might never answer another phone call from her again.

"I have tried six times now." Freddie glared at her mom, narrowly missing Mr. Binder as the two of them performed a complex line dance of anxiety behind the Lumberjack Pageant stage. Freddie's gown swished around her anachronistic duck boots with each step. "Theo knows what time they're supposed to be here."

"And we are now past that time." Mr. Binder hugged his script to his chest. Like Freddie, he was dressed in the pseudo-1600s lumberjack gear (he would be playing Lumberjack Number Three tonight). Unlike Freddie, he had wisely added a puffer jacket over his costume.

"Was it all a prank?" Mom asked, her face sagging with despair. "Was it all a part of your wretched *war* with Fortin Prep?"

That thought had most definitely crossed Freddie's mind. How else to explain why none of the Fortin students had shown up tonight? They'd come diligently to the rehearsals (except Theo, who'd been in the hospital). They'd accepted their costumes, *and* they'd all definitely said they'd be here by seven o'clock on Halloween night.

But nope. Not a one was here, not even Theo.

The sounds of the audience billowed against the curtain. They were impatient for the pageant to begin (and, in turn, for the Most Outrageous French Accent Contest to begin).

"Freddie!" Divya zipped around the stage, her eyes huge. She was dressed like a super-sexy (and definitely *cold*) skeleton. Right behind her was a nunchaku-toting skeleton who, like Mr. Binder, had wisely chosen to wear a jacket atop her costume.

"What is the holdup?" Divya asked, forcing Freddie to stop pacing. "People are getting impatient, and Kyle actually suggested driving his Jeep into the stage again." Divya glanced at Laina. "I don't *think* he was serious?"

Laina shrugged. "With him, it's hard to tell."

"Divya, it causes me great pain to say this, but . . ." Freddie screwed her eyes shut. "I fear that it was indeed a prank all along, and now the Fortin students will not be showing up for the pageant. But before we all freak out!" she added, snapping her eyes wide again. "The show will go on! Frederica Gellar in three acts is still an option. Just give me that script, Mr. Binder."

She thrust out a hand.

But Mr. Binder did *not* give her the script. "There are two of us, Freddie. We know the story well enough that I'm sure we can ad lib a show."

"We can help too!" Divya cried. "I mean, we're dressed like skeletons—"

"Sexy ones." Laina grinned at her girlfriend. (Yes, *girlfriend,* since *they* had actually defined their relationship.)

"—but that doesn't mean we can't help. And I know Cat and Luis'll help too. And Kyle . . . well, I'm not sure I'd trust him near the stage."

"Yeah, no." Laina made a pained expression. "But definitely the rest of us can help."

Mom sighed, a sound that was likely the Most Dejected Sound in the history of Dejected Sounds. "I suppose *a* show is better than *no* show. And maybe I can put a fifteen percent discount on the cider, so Elliot Harper won't get cranky and write a mean editorial in the paper like two years ago."

"Don't worry, Mom." Freddie clapped her hands onto her mom's shoulders. She was in Prank Wizard mode, on the prowl for the easiest solution with the broadest impact. "We'll make you proud. I'll get this show started as Traveler Number One—all alone and weary of the world. Laina, you'll get the rest of our cast assembled. And Divya, you get your French accent ready because you're up next as Berme Resident Number Two."

As Laina shot off and Divya bent over the script with Mr. Binder, Freddie gave her mom an overly cheerful thumbs-up. Then she rolled her shoulders and stomped up the steps onto stage.

The instant she pushed through the curtain, though—upon which was the painted scene of a snowy logging settlement—the whole crowd went silent. It didn't matter that the stage light wasn't on; Freddie was hardly invisible.

And *wow,* there were a lot of people out there. The entire

town, of course, with Bermians clustered into any space beside the heaters that they could fit. In fact, this might be the most crowded the fête had ever been.

Which was great for Mom's annual budget. Not so great for Freddie's sudden onset of stage fright—a sensation she'd never felt before. Then again, she'd also never been called to perform on the stage where she'd nearly died and watched her not-a-boyfriend nearly die too.

It was kind of a lot. Even if no one else here remembered what had happened, Freddie sure did.

Someone coughed. Freddie's eyes shot to Steve, dressed as a ghost with white strips of cloth all over his body that made him look more like an unraveling mummy than a proper haunting. He was mouthing something Freddie couldn't decipher.

Then a phone rang. A *doodle-loo doo, doodle-loo doo* that transported Freddie back into Mrs. Ferris's attic before her whole life had unraveled.

Then someone in the crowd dropped an f-bomb in a way that suggested they'd just spilled hot cider all over their pants.

Then, Freddie realized what Steve was trying to tell her. *HE IS ALMOST HERE!* That's what her stepdad was mouthing—and also why he was now pointing toward the Village Historique's distant entrance.

Where sure enough, if Freddie squinted past La Taverne, she could just make out a stampede (or was it a *herd*?) of lumberjacks thundering this way. At the front, jogging in a way he absolutely was *not* supposed to be jogging, was Theo.

In seconds that felt like lifetimes, Theo and the other Fortin students pushed right through the audience to reach the stage. Meanwhile, Freddie could hear Mom and Mr. Binder and Divya all cheering from behind the curtain.

The audience was actually cheering too, as if they thought this was all part of the show. And Freddie supposed it could be. Didn't pro wrestlers go storming through the crowd before a match? Maybe lumberjacks should do the same.

With only a slight limp to betray his pain—and a flush on his cheeks that wasn't from the cold—Theo climbed the steps onto stage. He looked entirely too gorgeous in his costume, and Freddie found herself annoyed by this fact. She looked *ridiculous* in her gown. Meanwhile, he pulled off a French bûcheron as easily as he pulled off a Fortin Prep uniform or a pair of khakis and his Vans.

Even in the hospital, he'd looked good in a papery hospital gown. It was *deeply* unfair.

"I know," Theo said as he came to a stop before her. Teenage lumberjacks streamed by, aiming for the curtain. "I am so sorry."

Freddie's face scrunched up. "You're sorry for looking hot?"

Now his face scrunched up too. "Um, no. For being late."

Right. Duh.

"Although," Theo continued with a sly smile, "I'm glad you think I'm hot."

"Pshaw." Freddie swatted the air. "Don't let it go to your head, Mr. Porter. But why *are* you late?"

The stage rattled as more members of the cast rushed by. And Theo sighed. "My fellow students thought it would be funny to skip as a prank. So I opted to divulge my lineage as an Allard Fortin to them and then threaten them all with expulsion."

"Can you do that?"

"Of course not." Theo grinned. "But what good is a fancy name if I can't use it?"

"Well, my mother and I thank you. Even if it does confirm my suspicions about you."

His eyebrows lifted. "And what suspicions are those?"

Freddie slid her hand into his, so she could tow him toward their starting spots on the stage. "That you're actually a Very Good Human Indeed. And in case you can't tell, I am saying that phrase as a proper noun, so you know it's serious."

Theo laughed as they came to a stop over two taped Xs. "Then I should warn you, Gellar, that you might reconsider your opinion of me once you see how thoroughly I plan to kiss you."

Freddie flushed. A delighted flush that made her stomach flip not once, not twice, but *thrice*. "Well, in that case, I guess we're both Very Bad Humans Indeed, since I plan to do the same."

Before Theo could respond to this, the stage light flashed on. The audience cheered, and finally—finally—the pageant began in earnest.

As did the accompanying contest, which Freddie was absolutely determined to win this year. Starting right now.

"LET US BEEGIN!" she cried, flinging her arms wide while the people of her town hooted and hollered and clapped like the wild bûcherons they were. "WELCUMMMM TO ZEE VILLAJJJ EE-STORRRR-EEECK! WE 'OPE YOU ENJOY ZEE SHOW!"

The Lumberjack Pageant, 1999
by Jim Binder

Act 1
Scene 1

Outside Berme logging settlement, 1677

TRAVELER NUMBER ONE and TRAVELER NUMBER TWO hurry onto stage, looking cold and weary.

TRAVELER NUMBER ONE

    Thank goodness we have finally arrived, for 'tis cold here in autumn.

TRAVELER NUMBER TWO

    It's all right. I am here to keep you warm, my love.

TRAVELER NUMBER ONE

pointing

    Look, my love, through yonder trees. Maybe 'tis a logging camp. I have heard of a generous man named Allard Fortin here. Perhaps 'tis he?

TRAVELER NUMBER TWO

    I think you are right, my love. Let us approach and see.

TRAVELER NUMBER ONE and TRAVELER NUMBER TWO kiss affectionately and exit upstage left.

No really, exit upstage left, Freddie.

Oh my god, I'm serious, Freddie Gellar. You and your boyfriend get off this stage right this moment.

LUMBERJACK NUMBER THREE

rushing onto stage

    Oh look! Two new travelers! Time to go!

pushing at TRAVELER NUMBER ONE and TRAVELER NUMBER TWO

    No, but really. Berme is *that* way. So come on, you two.

pushing even more forcefully at TRAVELER NUMBER ONE and TRAVELER NUMBER TWO

    Move *this instant* or you're going to get an F in chorus, Freddie! And if you think that abdominal wound hurts right now, Mr. Porter, just wait until I'm finished with you. And all of you out there in the audience, stop cheering! They're *teenagers*, for goodness' sake.

ENDING

Things were looking up for Theo Porter. Sure, he had a hole in his stomach that hurt like hell and someone had spilled hot cider on his boots. But it was so easy to forget that when he was kissing Freddie Gellar.

She made everything easy, from understanding what had happened to him to actually imagining a future.

Above all, kissing her was easy. Just the most natural thing in the world. Theo forgot he even had stitches across his abdomen because her lips and her sighs and her fingers were the most potent painkillers.

So it was inevitable that they would—once more—lose themselves in each other on stage, audience be damned. Just as it was inevitable that, after being forced off by a frantic chorus teacher, they'd aim for the shadows behind the water mill.

It was a place Theo had started to think of as *their* spot, ever since that first pageant rehearsal that had changed everything between them.

They half ran, even if it really *was* against the doctor's orders, and the almost boisterous noise of the pageant faded, softened, muffled completely as Freddie pulled Theo around to the other side of the mill.

In moments, the only sounds were voices echoing into the night and the soft burble of wintery water.

"Gellar," Theo said softly as his hands slid around her waist and he pulled her close. He'd never known he could find 1600s garb this sexy, but he was really into it on Freddie. With her wild hair and sharp eyes, with her curves and her wit . . .

"Yes, Mr. Porter?"

"I would like for you to know that you are just as good at distracting me now as you were two weeks ago. I mean, technically I have an abdominal wound that's four inches long, but I don't feel a thing when you kiss me."

"Well, I do have that effect on everyone." Freddie preened, flipping her dark curls over one shoulder—and revealing the pale line of her neck.

Theo had to forcibly restrain himself from immediately kissing her there. He wanted to have this conversation first. It was important. So much of his life really *was* looking up—he had a guaranteed spot at Allard Fortin, as well as more than enough money to fix his Silver Sweetheart, pay for college, *and* get his dad a better apartment.

But Theo wasn't sure he could really enjoy any of it until he said exactly what he needed to.

And in turn, heard what he really wanted to hear.

"I hope you don't actually have that effect on everyone," he told her, half in jest. Half serious. "Because . . ." He swallowed. "I'd prefer it if you only had that effect on me."

Freddie sniffed primly. "In that case, I regret to inform you that it isn't something I can turn off and on again. It's a constant state of being."

"I believe it, Gellar. But . . . Well, do you think you could grant me exclusive rights?"

"You want exclusive rights to my charm and cleverness?"

"Yes. And to, ah, your distraction techniques." Theo's gaze raked over her face, then her neck. "Assuming those rights are still available."

She smiled now. That bright, delighted smile that she was never too shy to share with the world. "I might consider such exclusivity, Mr. Porter, depending on what you offer in return."

"How about instead of considering what you'd get from me, you instead consider what you *wouldn't* get. Because you see, you are my fire."

She gasped, recoiling far enough that she hit the water mill. "You wouldn't dare."

Theo grinned. "The one desire."

"No, no, no. If you continue to quote the Backstreet Boys at me, then I cannot be held accountable for my actions."

"But Gellar, you have to believe me when I say, I want it—"

Freddie kissed him. A hard, hungry kiss on the lips that made Theo move just as hard and hungrily against her. Perhaps too hard and hungrily, given his stitches . . . But it was so easy, so natural.

When at last they pulled apart, both fully breathless, Theo murmured: "You really are dangerous, Freddie Gellar. But I guess . . ." He smiled. "I want it that way."

"How dare you!" Freddie smacked him lightly on the arm . . . and then kissed him on the lips all over again.

And together, Theo and Freddie practiced their very best distraction techniques while the autumn wind whispered, a cold stream trilled, and a positively effervescent Fête du Bûcheron rallied late into the night.

ABOUT THE AUTHOR

Susan Dennard is the award-winning, *New York Times* and *USA Today* bestselling author of the Luminaries trilogy, the Witchlands series, and many more books and tales beyond. Her stories have been translated into tens of languages all over the world. Before becoming an author, she got to travel globally with her MSc in marine biology. She also runs the popular newsletter for writers *Misfits & Daydreamers*. When not writing or teaching writing, she can be found playing dress-up with her daughter or mashing buttons on one of her way too many consoles.

susandennard.com
luminerds.substack.com
Instagram: @stdennard

THE LUMINARIES

By Susan Dennard

A *New York Times* bestselling high-octane contemporary YA fantasy of deadly Luminary hunter trials in a monster-filled forest, perfect for fans of *The Chilling Adventures of Sabrina*.

Hemlock Falls isn't like other towns. You won't find it on a map, your phone won't work here, and the forest outside town might just kill you…

Winnie Wednesday wants nothing more than to join the Luminaries, the ancient order that protects Winnie's town—and the rest of humanity—from the monsters and nightmares that rise in the forest of Hemlock Falls every night. Ever since her father was exposed as a witch and a traitor, Winnie and her family have been shunned. But on her sixteenth birthday, she can take the deadly Luminary hunter trials and prove herself true and loyal—and restore her family's good name. Or die trying.

But in order to survive, Winnie must enlist the help of the one person who can help her train: Jay Friday, resident bad boy and Winnie's ex-best friend. While Jay might be the most promising new hunter in Hemlock Falls, he also seems to know more about the nightmares of the forest than he should. Together, he and Winnie will discover a danger lurking in the forest no one in Hemlock Falls is prepared for.

Not all monsters can be slain, and not all nightmares are confined to the dark.

▶ Daphne Press